MAGEBLOOD

Book One of the
MEPHISTO'S MAGIC ONLINE Series
Written by CHRISTOPHER JOHNS

D1602254

This is a work of fiction. Names, characters, places, and incidents either are the products of the author's imagination or are used fictitiously. Any resemblance to actual persons, living or dead, businesses, companies, events, or locales is entirely coincidental.

MOUNTAINDALE
PRESS

TABLE OF CONTENTS

DEDICATION

This book is dedicated to my friends and family, my lovely fiancée and everyone out there who supported me as I tried to find myself in this wonderful, mysterious, and fulfilling craft.

Thank you.

CHAPTER ONE

There's a lot to be said for those who can create something from a simple idea. Something like a ground-breaking game with all kinds of new features to wow people in a technologically advanced game saturated society. That's saying a lot. And it's a great deal of work, blood, sweat, and tears to accomplish even a modicum of what most construe as success.

Almost enough that one would contemplate selling his soul to the devil in order to make his dream come true. What's one infinitesimal, abstract idea of being when compared to seeing the look of joy in your daughter's eyes when she sees the characters she helped make up in three dimensions? Her best friend's grin when he talks about sorcery and magic as if it's more real to him than the ground beneath his feet?

Would you do it? Sell your soul to some cosmic force to create your wildest fantasy? Wouldn't you?

Sounds like a decent deal to some, of course, no one ever really reads the fine print. Always read the fine print.

I implore you to always doubt the honeyed words thrown your way.

Because the devil is in the details, kids.

***

I logged out of the game that my friends and I had been streaming, smiling because the night was still young and my best friend was coming over for movie night. I had the nicer stuff and the most space, so she usually came here. My streaming equipment glimmered in the dim moonlight, shiny despite my attempts to wear it down slightly. Streaming could be lucrative at times, but it was money from the family that had helped finance this home and all the accouterments inside.

Some smart investing on my dad's part when I was a baby had seen the family become wealthy. Astronomically so. Dad still worked, mom did too—because they were workaholics and needed something to do to "help the world." So, off on their mysterious adventures to far off lands 'round the globe they went. I helped them where I could, but that was about it. This was a way for me to do something I loved and give back. Everything I made through streaming, I either donated or put into savings.

I walked into the bathroom for a shower, the black and white tile in the room lending it a more serious tone than my normal tastes.

Ma had been insistent that a colorful bathroom looked tacky, and with all the modern amenities in it, it looked slick. The toilet was the latest model, and it had a heated gel seat, so it was a throne. The shower blasted water from all angles, so a shower was an interesting time. The waterproof monitor in the thing was pretty expensive as well, but with some of the settings it had, you needed to be able to see them at all times to correct them to your pleasure. Or that was what the salesperson had said, at least. I mainly used it to check security at the door and to watch the news.

The lights in the bathroom dimmed and brightened via a dial on the counter display screen. The sink was black granite; cold, but a very classy touch. Made me miss having my folks around after I had remodeled, but their work was important, and I couldn't begrudge them their right to follow their hearts.

I tossed my sweaty, shoulder-length hair from my face. It was hot work, gaming. As I looked into the mirror, I wasn't surprised to see my hair, exactly like my dad's telltale dark hair.

Except that I had portions of it striped and dyed crazy colors. Not to be rebellious–I just liked colorful things. There were purples, reds, pinks, grays, blues, and my favorite neon green.

Beneath the unruly mop of color was my face. I had green eyes that people liked. Dark eyebrows and angular cheeks with five o'clock shadow. Luckily for me, the streams didn't show my face unless I wanted to be seen, too. I would wave at my fans from my avatar's point of view in the game.

I decided to shave before hopping under the hot water. As much as the stubble would make me appear more masculine with my strong jawline, I wasn't the kind to go out all that often, and I hadn't yet found a lady who treated me with any kind of dignity. Was that what women wanted? Masculine? Eh, I didn't care for now. Didn't have the thought for it right now after the last breakup, and with how most people viewed me when they found out what I liked to do in my free time, dates didn't come much.

Much less so with my streaming schedule. Thus, the single life for me, for now.

I lathered the shaving cream over my cheeks and chin, then over my neck. Pulling the razor from my medicine cabinet, I noted once again that except for some headache meds and deodorant, it was rather empty.

I pulled the razor across my cheeks and scraped away both the cream and stubble, leaving naturally tanned skin beneath. I could thank my mother and her Hispanic heritage for that. Had to love my ma's side of the family though, man. They were *wild.* They could party.

I smiled at the thought of my grandmother chasing the grandkids at the last family reunion we had. She was so spritely.

A pang of sadness crept into my heart, as the memory triggered another of her passing.

I closed my eyes and chased the thought from my head. She wouldn't want me to mope—especially since this had been a few years ago.

I finished shaving quickly and then hopped into the shower. The warm water soon came to a much needed scalding-hot temperature that I adored. I loved a hot shower. Washing all the grossness away and melting the tension in my body.

The doorbell rang, and the display in the shower went from water settings and nozzle rotations to a view of my best friend standing at the doorway.

I smiled and pressed a button on the screen. "Hey, Mo." Mona Hart, my best friend since birth—literally because our parents had been friends since before either of us had been conceived—waved at the fisheye camera in front of her. Her hilariously distorted features squinting as if she could see me. "You know you can always just walk in, right?"

"And not ruin your normally ridiculously long shower time?" She arched a perfectly done eyebrow at me. "I think not."

"Come on in; I'm almost done." I grinned back. I dismissed the screen after unlocking the door. She could easily get in with her key code. But I wanted her to come in; otherwise, she would keep pestering me.

I finished rinsing myself, then dried off quickly. My back adjusted as I leaned down to dry my legs, and it felt magical. I walked from the bathroom into my room and threw some PJs on. Fluffy pants and a t-shirt then walked down the small hallway to my living room. This area was much more my speed.

There were large bean bags covered in thick cloth, almost like flannel in the center of the room, with a small coffee table between them. They were gray, and the least colorful things in the room. The two couches in the rear of the room were splotched with paint of all colors and then treated to stay that way, but not feel too rough.

I had a few friends with artistic talents much greater than my own who had come in and painted murals of battles and bosses from games I enjoyed. One wall was taken by a large dragon's body that led to the wall with its head facing us. The others were various others that had come from several other games.

I pressed a button on the wall, and the dragon's mouth slid down, revealing a large television.

"That is still so delightfully tacky." Mona chuckled from her customary perch on the left-most beanbag chair.

She looked like she was ready to go to bed as well. Her pajamas matched; the little shorts were light blue with little unicorns all over them. They matched the top she wore with a much larger version of the fluffy unicorn on the shirt front. The two of us were a pair at twenty-five years old.

Her toned, athletic build made the clothes a little loose, but I mean—PJs do that. Right? Her angular face reminded me of traditional elves from the old Tolkien-inspired movies. She was just missing the long ears, sadly. Her fiery red hair and emerald eyes completed her features, though the mirth in her eyes was what made me smile at her.

She saw me staring for a moment and flashed me a toothy grin. "See something you like, 'big boy'?"

I laughed out loud at that one. "You know you aren't my type, Mo."

She faked being sad, but she knew. It was what had kept us both so close over the years. The fact that we were well and truly best friends—almost siblings—was something that would never change.

"Oh, I know your type, alright." She grinned wolfishly. "Now, throw that classic in, and let's chat."

I knew better than to go against what she wanted when she was as excited about something like this as she was. I panned over to the image of a masked man and a woman who could've been a princess on it and selected 'play' before sitting down. It was a classic love story with bits of intrigue, some action, and all kinds of humor. This had been our favorite movie as kids.

"Excellent choice, Mr. Ethelbart," she teased me.

"Thank you, Miss Hart." I bowed grandly, knowing she was eating it up.

"Spill, how do you feel about MMO?" She skipped the preamble completely, and that threw me a bit.

"I mean, I'm excited?" I replied lamely. Her perfect eyebrows shot straight up. "Yeah, the system looks like nothing we've ever seen before, I get that. The inherent magic-system in the game is unrivaled. Of course, you know that means I'm going to be losing my mind trying to know all of the best things to do. The best way to play with the magic I get."

"Unrivaled is a vast understatement, Seth." She sighed. "More like *unheard of.* Who would have thought that the game would use biometrics and an algorithm to assign magic to each player? And not just a base kind of magic—*individualized,*"—she whispered that last bit for effect— "magic. Each different player with a different level of magical ability."

"You do know that they will still have to have some kind of basis for the magic system, right? Like, the elements, maybe summoning and some other crazy stuff." I almost rolled my eyes at her enthusiasm. "There has to be a base!"

"There is!" She cried with her hands in the air. "There are the basic elements, as well as some unknown ones! Listen, I know that you have to try and rule the magic-user classes, since that's your thing, but the unknown is exciting!"

"Okay, and how about the story?" I asked her. Mona's favorite thing about a lot of games was that there had to be a damned good story.

"Mephisto's Magic Online will have a fully immersive storyline that is supposed to encourage the players to think outside the box, as well as to defeat the villains of the campaign." Mona recited as if she had committed the pitch of the game to memory.

"Yeah, and that's cool and all—but who?" I insisted.

"I don't know!" She turned toward the tv, and we watched as the dread pirate climbed a rather dangerous-looking cliffside in pursuit of the lady. "It's going to be a wild ride, though, and I'm sure the story is there."

I reached out and took her hand. "That does put a damper on our relationship." I mimicked the line that Cary Elwes had just spoken on screen, and we both laughed at our ridiculousness.

It was a game, the newest, cutting edge one—but a game, nonetheless. We would figure it out like we always have.

We continued to watch the movie in amicable silence after that.

"I wonder what type of magic I'll get," Mona voiced her thoughts, breaking the silence.

"Probably fire," I teased her. "Oh! Or you could have something to do with soul-stealing!" I laughed with my eyes closed too long.

A fist landed on my shoulder, then another on my stomach. Then the tickling came. We wrestled and tortured each other until we were sore about our ribs, and our faces hurt from laughing so much.

"You know that I'm most looking forward to playing this game with you guys, right?" I looked at Mona, who still shared my beanbag with me after all that playing.

"Yeah, we know." She kissed my cheek. "You're a great friend. And a good person. I can't wait to see what kind of magic we get. And thanks again for the equipment, though I could've gotten it myself next month."

"Yeah, but then we wouldn't have been playing together—and you know that the party hunts together." My finger waggled at her in reproach. "But seriously—my money is your money, Mo. You know that I will always take care of you and Ma. How's her back doing?"

"A lot better, actually. They've got an appointment scheduled and got it pretty quickly, so she goes in Friday." She patted my arm, though she seemed a little tense about it. "She said if you don't come over soon, she's going to beat your ass. She's been dying to feed you."

That made me smile. Emma, Mona's mom, was one of the best people I knew. And she was a damned fine cook. She had been feeling a little under the weather lately, but I was happy to know the doctors would be seeing her sooner rather than later.

"You bet, I'll pop over on Sunday, how about that?" Usually, Sundays were days that I took for myself, so that I could recuperate after being so vocal and streaming all week. That didn't mean I didn't want to see my other family.

"She will be ecstatic." Mona smiled at me.

"Of course, she will; she likes me best." I ducked the fist that she sent my way half-heartedly. "You ready to get some sleep?"

"After beating you up all night? Yeah, c'mon." She stood and helped me to my feet with a grunt of effort. I was taller than her by about a foot, but she was strong. The grunt was more for show than anything. "You've gained some weight."

"Why, thank you." I grinned. I had been trying to overcome this sickly-looking body of mine with a strict diet of good food and lifting. Lots of lifting. I flexed my biceps, and they just barely peeked out from the sleeves of the shirt. "Nice, right?"

"With that kind of gun show—who needs an army?" Mona poked one, and it deflated as I lost the flexion of it. "Time for bed, mister man."

"Yeah, yeah, mom," I grumbled and stifled a yawn. We meandered back down the hallway into my room once more. This room was painted dark; it was meant to be my blackout room. Where I come to unwind and relax. Escape.

I pulled a rollout bed out from beneath mine and plopped onto it, the heavy blanket fending the chill off the room. Both Mona and I loved sleeping in the cold, so I tried to keep it somewhat cool in my room. Especially on nights that she came over. Could she have had her own room? Sure. But we had enjoyed sleeping together since we were kids, no reason to change things now.

Sharing a bed hadn't been an issue at all years and years ago. As adults, the first time one of us had rolled over and accidentally grabbed the other; the rollout bed had become a necessity.

"We get to do some magic tomorrow, man." Mona sighed. "It's going to happen. Good night, Seth."

"Night, Mona." I closed my eyes and drifted to sleep shortly after her snoring reached my ears.

CHAPTER TWO

Mona left later in the morning after breakfast to take care of her mom, I warned her about the set up at 2 p.m., where they would come and set up the grossly expensive system that needed installation.

Mona and her mother lived together, kind of. She took the guest house out back and converted it into a studio apartment so she could take care of her mom. Poor lady hadn't really been the same since Mona's father left them a few years back with no word. No note. Nothing.

The weirdest part had been that he had been working on some kind of project—he'd been a game designer. He had been the reason Mona and I had gotten into gaming in the first place. Then, poof, he was gone in the wind with nothing to anyone.

It had hit Mona kind of hard too, but by then, she was an adult and had been able to sort of muddle through the loss. Her strength and force of character had been something that kept her mother sane some days. Though Emma was very protective of her little girl—and me; she mothered anyone and everyone.

Honestly, it wouldn't surprise me if she fed the workers coming to set up Mona's dive system today. I'd be more surprised if she didn't.

Wasn't hard to see where Mona got it at all. Though, to Mona, a good offense was her way of being protective. She preferred the proactive approach to defending her friends, and I had seen many a boss in Blood and Gore fall because they had come at us. Were they supposed to die? Absolutely.

Were they supposed to die as horribly as Mona made them? I shuddered at the thought.

I put away the rollout and stretched before I went on my morning jog to the gym. I didn't have to do anything today except be here to let the dive installation crew in, and that was just going to be in the game room, so no worries on space. Despite the fact that my house wasn't a vast indicator of the wealth I had, there was room available. I preferred a smaller home compared to the other properties on my street. It was simple. I liked that.

Granted, my snooty neighbors probably hated me since my home was the most colorful on the block. A lovely shade of red, whereas the others were a dull shade of black, white, gray, or some awful combination of the three.

I pulled on some light blue shorts that fell just below my knees, a black and green tee, and a bright yellow jacket. It wasn't dark out right that second, but the jacket would help work up a sweat as well as warm my muscles.

It was a fifteen-minute jog from my place to the gym. I hated running. With a passion. However, it weirdly helped ease my mind, and it was the healthier option to driving. And it's not like I'm in terrible shape either—I'm a fairly athletic guy despite the fact that I was still pretty thin. I liked to lift, and I don't mind eating healthy either. I just... God—hated running.

I left my house, and the door locked automatically behind me. The windows shuttered themselves, and my back door would be locked as well. After throwing some earbuds in and jamming to the music I had on my phone, I bounced a couple times on my toes to let my body know what hell was to come and set off down the row of homes toward the end of the street.

I waved to a couple of the neighbors who were outside. One, I could never remember his name, waved back. His dark beard and bald head separated him from the others, but he still had that generic look about him. Oh well. Super nice guy, though.

After a few minutes at a light jog, I shifted myself into gear. As the beat and tempo of my music turned and lifted, so too did my spirits. I was able to really *feel* the blood pumping in my body, now. I hated it. Once I got to the gym, I scanned my card at the door, then thumb printed in.

"Hey, mister Seth!" The young man at the desk greeted me kindly. He wore a purple polo tucked into some gray shorts. His Hispanic features were handsome, his closely cropped hair slicked at the top in the latest style.

"What's up, Antonio?" I bumped my fist against his with a smile. I loved it when Tony worked. The kid was a blast, and he liked my work.

"I caught the end of the stream yesterday," he responded excitedly. "That was a pretty nasty water spell you tossed at that raid boss. What was it called?!"

"Sylph's Spout, you get it as a class quest reward for the final tier as a water and ice mage," I explained.

Tony was a super fan who loved B&G as much as he loved reading comic books. Kid was old school, and I loved it.

"Oh man, I can't wait to try it out!" He looked like he was ready to log in and play right then. "I'm about six levels away from the current cap, and I'm having trouble on the class quest for level fifty-four. Any advice? You know how hard it can be to find this info, B&G has a whole team out there to stop people from uploading quest info."

I thought for a moment, knowing that it was true. The fifties had been a mad dash for me, so it was a little difficult to remember, though.

"That the one with the fetch quest that leads to a dragon?" He nodded. "Okay, cool, so take the left corridor inside the tunnels to the dragon's lair. It'll say you're going the wrong way, but it's the most direct route. Once you get to the end of that corridor, climb to the top of the wall there, then start chucking spells down at the dragon from above. You'll be just inside the quest circle, so you'll be able to get all the good loot and complete the quest. The NPCs in the quest will go in and distract it while you drop damage on it."

"Mister Seth, that's GENIUS!" He smacked the counter in front of me, excitedly.

"You can thank Sondra; she was the one who told me about that sweet spot after a friend went through the quest before me." I smiled. I'd had to beg her for the advice myself.

He shook his head. "You guys are awesome. Well, I won't keep you from your workout, Mister Seth. Let me know if you need anything!"

"You got it, Antonio." I smiled at him again as I walked toward the free weights to begin my lifting for the day.

It was back day today, so I would be lifting for a bit.

I lifted to my heart's content, taking a moment to scroll through my social media feeds between sets. I saw a few posts about the fight yesterday, and a few more about our switching to MMO, heh—that was almost too easy a name, to be honest.

Some people were upset to see us go, but Bane didn't have any plans to throw out any more content for quite some time, and it was time for us to try something new.

Plus, we were all excited to try this game. I had to admit, I was more than a little curious to see what kind of innate magic we all were going to get. I tried to search online for any news about it, but since tonight was the launch for the first wave of players, there was nothing but wild speculation. And hype bombing.

Trolls carpet-bombing peoples' hopes about the game and being general assholes. One such person was actively berating anyone who speculated about any type of magic calling them newbs and scrubs—what a jerk.

I shook my head and pocketed the device before continuing my workout.

After a couple hours, I was ready to jog home. Once I arrived, I was able to shower and grab a bite before the doorbell rang.

I opened the door to a gentleman in a suit; he regarded a clipboard. "Mr. Seth Ethelbart?" He asked with a slight German accent.

I grinned back. "Guilty."

He had short blonde hair that was almost the color of spun gold, chiseled facial features that had been freshly shaved completely smooth—a cultured set of golden eyebrows and a large, athletic build. The suit itself was obviously made and tailored specifically for him; it contoured to his body the way a suit usually did to important people.

"Excellent!" He held his hand out for me to shake, firm grip on that guy. "I'm Wilhelm—yes, like the infamous scream heard on most classic movies where someone is thrown from great height—Micahvisch, and I am a representative from the Mana, Myth, and Legend Studios. I'm here to ensure that your system is properly set up, attuned, and ready for your enjoyment."

"Wow, man. That's some introduction!" I laughed as I blinked at him. He smiled genuinely at me, mirth in his eyes.

He leaned forward, and the sparkle in his storm-gray eyes turned mischievous. "I've been working on it all morning in the mirror. The first bit, though. The second bit I've been dealing with my whole life."

It took me longer than I would have liked to realize that he had purposely switched the two sections of his speech. But when I did, I laughed and had to offer him a fist bump. He seemed... intrigued by it and gently rapped his knuckles against mine.

"Now." He clapped his hands and rubbed them together. "Where can I have my crew bring their equipment?"

"Oh, for sure—follow me." I led them through the entry to the hall that led to my room and turned into the first door on the left. "This is the room I cleared out per the instructions. I hope it's of suitable size?"

"It is. The standard is fifteen, by thirteen feet and will be all we need, this is much more room to work with." Wilhelm crossed the room and eyed the power ports in the walls. "The rewiring won't take long; our electrician is a master at his craft. Where, if I might ask, is the fuse box? This is a fairly modern home, so I doubt he will have much to do, but he will need to ensure the generator and solar power cells are adequately attached and powering the system."

"Fuse box is actually inside this closet behind a false wall panel. There is a matching panel outside on the opposite side of the wall." I explained as he took several notes on a notepad he produced from a pocket. His pen scrawled quickly, the golden object moving as if by magic.

"I see, and there is access to the rear of the home where we can install the generator?" When I nodded, he scrawled some more information down.

"What's with the generator and solar panels?" I asked curiously.

"Well, the solar panels are to store and power the machine so that the extra wattage doesn't overtax the home's grid, or that of the city." When I looked at him, his eyes never left his paper and scribbling. "The generator will have a few small wind turbines designed to capture the *barest* of winds to further charge and power the system and the generator. The generator itself is designed to function on next to no energy for days in the event the power goes out. So, theoretically speaking on my part—our scientists and techs were very insistent this was the truth—the generator should be able to power the system and all functions of those inside for twenty-four hours a day, seven days a week, for more than a month and a half."

My eyes shot open so wide it was a miracle they didn't flop right out.

"Indeed, it does seem a little far fetched, yes?" He eyed me quizzically. "Are you quite alright, Mr. Ethelbart?"

I blinked and almost had to pick my jaw off the floor, but I nodded.

"Excellent." Wilhelm smiled softly. "Installation will begin with the power sources and generator. From there, my crew will bring in the system, after which I will attune the features and provide further information to you on how to work everything. I calculate our installation time, and tutorial will take approximately two hours, forty-five minutes and thirty-seven seconds."

I nodded dumbly, and Wilhelm chuckled to himself before stepping next to me. "I tease. It will all take roughly three hours, and my men will be in and out of the front for a while. If you would like to watch, please be my guest—but the servicing of the system is top secret, so I will eventually have to kick you out of this room for a bit while I acclimate the system to its new surroundings. Is this amenable?"

"Very, Wilhelm. Thank you for your humor and candor." I suddenly needed a drink of water. "I'll be in the kitchen if you need me."

"Very well." He walked toward the door clapping his hands twice. "And so—It begins!"

For the first hour, I heard the crew taking equipment into the back yard; the sound of drills, hammers, and other various tools and men at work filled the air. Footsteps on the roof and more drilling. Sawing from inside the room as the electrician checked the wiring that was needed and added in the necessary lines for the system.

Normally, this would result in the neighbors calling the cops—but I had done my due diligence and gotten the proper permits and sent letters to all my neighbors, letting them know what was going on.

I had done the same for the other party members as well. As they began bringing the equipment from a large moving truck inside, I went out back to see the result of their work.

The panels took up a large section of the roof, and there were a few on the ground as well, but they were lifted a good twelve feet on sturdy poles. There was a large blocky device beneath the panels on the poles, and I assumed this was the generator itself. It was matte black, with a panel that was damned near indecipherable to me, but the power was at half already.

"It comes to you half charged as a safety measure," Wilhelm startled me as he spoke behind me. "Just in case there is a surge from the fuse box, or the power does go out for some reason while you are playing."

"Oh, that's incredibly thoughtful," I observed with my eyebrows raised slightly.

I looked around my empty backyard to find several large, but thin turbines attached to propellers. Each of them faced a different direction. As I was watching the wind turbine directly south of me, a stiff breeze began to blow just across it, but it wouldn't have been the perfect direction to catch the wind right to generate any kind of power.

Or at least I hadn't thought it would have. The turbine twisted slightly so that the propeller faced directly into the wind and began spinning wildly.

"Engineering has come a long way in the last decade or so. Better sensors, and with them, the ability to minutely adjust a wind turbine." Wilhelm explained easily. "They can deviate about thirty degrees or so from their original position to make use of even the slightest wind in the area, and you have at least a dozen of them. Your generator will be filled within the next day or two—dependent on the weather, of course."

"Right." I nodded; still a little shaken from the amount of change that had happened so swiftly.

"I will now see to the perfect construction of the system, please excuse me."

***

After another hour of listening to hushed conversation, then one command of "Leave me to my work," the door opened.

The workers fled the room—well, they walked quickly— and left Wilhelm behind with the door shut.

Another thirty-minute wait after that, and he came out of the room, his suit and tie still perfectly in place, though he did seem a little more tired-looking to me. It was difficult to tell with that chipper smile plastered to his face.

"It is completed, come—time for your tutorial, Mr. Ethelbart." Wilhelm motioned for me to walk forward into the room, and I had to admit—as excited as I was—I was also nervous as hell.

I steeled myself and walked into the room, expecting some hulking behemoth of a machine taking up the majority of the room.

Instead, I was greeted by what looked like a tube. It stood at eight feet tall and was three feet wide, a clear outer cover facing me. The exterior was a sleek silver color that reminded me of quicksilver. The interior was a lush mixture of deep to light purples, blues, and reds that seemed to pulse on their own. There was a handle in the front that Wilhelm pointed to immediately.

"Obviously, the entrance to the system." He grinned as I blinked a few times then refocused on him. "I assure you—you will be able to play as soon as the game is ready. Until then—attend me. Yes?"

"You got it, boss." I offered him a slight salute that he took in stride with a little bow of his head.

"As I was saying." He motioned to the handle. "This is the handle, keyed to your *exact* biometrics—please touch it now. It will be very warm at first. Do not let go."

I gave him a stare for a second but did as I was told. I grabbed the handle, and even if I had tried to let go—I couldn't. My hand seemed to fuse with the clear material instantly, and a growl of pain escaped my throat. Then it cooled quickly, and I could let go.

As soon as I cupped my hand, Wilhelm was beside me instantly with a gel that he swiftly spread over my palm with an expertly gloved hand. Once he was finished, my hand suitably numbed, he took the glove off and tossed it into a baggie then pocketed it.

"Evidence." He smiled again, and I couldn't tell if that had been a joke or not.

Not wanting to seem rude, I chuckled a little.

"Now, I understand that you prefer to stream your sessions. Unfortunately, the in-game tutorial will not be something that is streamable; however, once you are finished with that section, there will be a command in your status screen that will allow you to stream to your adoring viewers."

He opened a laptop that was on a small box outside the machine on the left. "All diagnostics are sent directly to our engineers and personnel at all times of play—so if anything happens to you or around you while you are in the game, we will know. With that in mind, we will send medical or local law enforcement to you posthaste. Your safety and experience with us while playing are of the *utmost importance* to us at Mana, Myth, and Legend Studios. There is little else for you to know other than a few small details, but if something should happen that the game or system are tampered with, we will have tech support here right away, so you need not worry."

I nodded and motioned for him to continue, as everything he said—while weird—seemed to be centered on a perfectionist drive to have people enjoy themselves. And their work.

"Thank you." He bowed slightly again. "When you enter the system, you will need to be nude. Good gods, man—not now—have some decorum."—I grinned as I lowered my shirt.—"Anyway, you will need to be nude. Also, there is a fluid that will cleanse you and help you to fully integrate with Mephisto's Magic Online. Think of it as amniotic fluid, and you, but a babe to this new world filled with delight, adventure, and magic."

I golf clapped for him lightly, his smile returning slightly. "While you are in-game, there is a slight time dilation. Every hour you spend in-game—passes three times as fast inside. So, plan your time and gaming accordingly with appointments and whatnot. There are alarms that you can set to remind yourself, but you are an adult with the ability to care for yourself and know your priorities."

"Okay, so—about the game," I started, my mind reeling with how many questions I had on my mind.

Wilhelm held up a single finger to silence me. "I am but a peon to the designers, Mr. Ethelbart, and your questions will soon be answered. What I have been instructed to tell our lovely customers, is that the character you receive is the only one you will receive, until you beat the game. Then, you can try something different. So, there will be no quitting and starting from the first step for *anyone.* The game's operating intelligence meshes so well with the system you are in, that the given ability is as true to you as breathing or gravity. It is law."

That last bit had been said in an almost blatantly ominous tone. I was digging that.

"Okay, that's fair." I had to admit that was odd, but I suppose it kept the system from fragmenting or going overboard with the abilities and innate types of magic it gave to the players. "So, when can I play?"

Wilhelm looked at his watch and smiled. "In three hours, the game goes live. If that will be all, Mr. Ethelbart, my team, and I have one more customer to see to today."

"Is that really all there was to attune it?"

He looked back at me and grinned. "Your biometrics were partially obtained by your handprint, and the rest will take place before the game begins. I trust our machine will work its course."

I nodded and walked Wilhelm to the door and saw that the team he spoke of was already in their various modes of transport. Mode of transport? That was right!

"Sorry, Wilhelm—one last thing." The man turned to regard me. "What is the system called?"

The man smiled and turned to face me. "Focus testing amongst the employees, designers, and engineers led to a completely unanimous—albeit theatric name—for the device."

He said nothing else and turned to walk away.

"Which is?" I asked exasperatedly to his back.

Wilhelm called over his shoulder as he opened the door to his blacked-out car "Portal."

CHAPTER THREE

The wait to get into the "Portal" was truly unreal. I'd begun to see a trend in the most searched words on my favorite browser being "Mephistopheles" and "portal," though that last one had a lot of mentions about demons offering mortals passage to faraway lands and power for their souls.

Religious nuts—am I right?

After reading all that, and deciding to stop freaking myself out, I grabbed a small stand from my room and pulled it into the room with the portal. I would set my phone and whatnot on it while I was playing. I spent the last hour, just mentally prepping myself to go into the game and start the next leg of my virtual journey.

My friends were chattering in our group text conversation, jokingly accusing each other of having the worst kinds of inherent magic for the game.

Seth will probably have gravity magic—he has his head in the clouds too often! – Allen

Right, and clearly, yours will be water because you never shower, LOL. – Mona

Oh, as if you will be any better, fire girl. – Sondra

Ha-ha, chill you guys. The launch is about to happen in a few minutes! I tapped the device in my hands furiously as I typed.

The Portal says to enter, - Sondra

See you on the other side! ;) – Mona

I looked up, and the inside of the machine before me had begun to pulse with a dull light. I quickly dropped the mesh shorts I had been wearing and stepped into the Portal with my back toward the soft cushions. The clear panel door closed slowly before me as if it were a coffin lid in those old vampire movies my mom had made Mona and I watch as kids.

I couldn't help the thrill of fear that pulsed through my veins. I went through some breathing exercises I used for when I was running, and it seemed to ease my mental state a little. Until a warm liquid began to filter into the bottom of the chamber, and I had to fight myself to relax, barely winning.

After a minute, the liquid was up to my chest and pulsing with my heartbeat. It was somehow relaxing. When it was above my head, my breath just barely holding, I heard a robotic voice.

Breathe.

The hell did it just say?

Breathe, or you will lose consciousness the improper way.

They were monitoring my vitals, right? They had to know that this was going on. If they knew, then the machine did too. It must know what is going on. I forced myself to exhale, then breathed in deeply.

The liquid was thick and viscous in my mouth, then into my lungs. Everything in my mind told me that this was wrong and that I needed to get the hell out of here. But my body was relaxed. Warm, even. I floated in this tube of metal. This mechanical womb, as the installation guy had called it, had cocooned me into safety.

Download and coding will complete in ten seconds... nine... eight...

My adrenaline spiked again as the gray screen began to show slight dots to it.

five...

More color came to the fore, and I lost track of myself.

three... two... one.

Welcome, player, to Mephisto's Magic Online.

I heard the words, but I also saw them in a large, clearly legible script that flashed gold and red before my eyes. As if my eyes were open. They were open, weren't they? As I looked around, the world became less a space devoid of light and grayer in tone.

I felt a firmness beneath the feet that I couldn't see. I had no body, at least not that I could see, and there was no other tactile sensation other than the pressure against the bottom of my consciousness.

"Welcome!" Boomed a boisterous voice from the right of me. I looked over, and there stood a tall, thin man in the gaudiest outfit I had ever seen.

His long, pointed ears struck out from the sides of his bald head, and his black handle-bar mustache gleamed inky against his pale skin. Black eyes watched me as a ghostly breeze tickled the orange frilly shirt with too much lace for anyone, and bright blue pants that clashed wondrously.

It was a disaster, and I loved it.

"Oh, this dreadful bodiless business is utterly uncalled for, please—choose a race and gender." He motioned toward me, and a status screen appeared before me. It was solid white with black writing along it. "You will be able to customize more inside my realm soon enough. Choose your body first."

I looked back toward the screen and touched it, somehow. I felt pressure where normally a finger might be. Weird. As soon as I touched the race options, my attention was drawn to a screen that stood before me.

There was a human there, at first. One that looked just like me. But I didn't want that. Too many games these days had the player stuck with the race we already were. It was annoying.

Why be human in a game where you can *literally* throw fireballs and hurl lightning?

I pressed no on that, and the screen went to the next option. This one was a mixture of human and elf—half-elf. Common in a lot of the older table-top games, but not my flavor. Still too close to human, so no on that.

After that was the true elf, they had the telltale ears, lean builds, and angled features. I didn't say no right away. This was a personal favorite of mine for a lot of reasons—the elves of some of the classic movies and games I had played being the inspiration for me wanting to be a magic-user in all these games. Well, that, and they usually had the better magic stats.

The next was an orc. I toggled the male and female switches. Both were attractive for their own reasons. The male orcs were burly, muscular, and looked like they would hold up well in a fight. The females were athletic and looked like they would survive a decent brawl as well. As awesome as they looked, I doubted that they would make very good innate casters.

Then we had trolls, very much the thin, tall cousins of the orcs. They were ugly creatures. But they were a popular race in some games. They were usually counted among the bad guys, though.

There were gnomes, yuck. Halflings, no thanks. And dwarves—while cool—not my style. Bird people who didn't really have hands—nope. A fox-man kind of people, though cute, not really my thing either. Rabbit folk, nah.

There was one race that seemed interesting outside of the elves, called the Kin. They were creatures that looked reminiscent of demons. Their features were angular like the elves, they had the pointed ears, but they shot out from the side of the heads a little way. They also had horns like a demon might. Why weren't they called demons?

"Because demons are a true race and an enemy that you will be facing below." I heard the voice coming from behind me and over where my shoulder would be. His face was serious. "All of the races that you will see here are allied against the forces trying to claim this world. There are still tensions, but they have a larger enemy to confront. Though, with the addition of the immortal wanderers, times may yet change again."

I frowned or would've if I'd had a mouth and checked to see if there were other races. There were mixtures. Minotaurs, which was amazing. Centaurs and other creatures of significant sentience that were a part of the Wild Faction among the races.

I debated between the elves and the Kin for a couple moments. They both had their perks, although I didn't see them—I'm sure they did. In the end, I went with the new guy.

I selected Kin as my race and went about adjusting the physical characteristics. The figure before me untouched was a five-foot-tall male, with a lithe build and short hair. His horns reminded me of a Minotaur's the way they jutted from the sides of his head. Oh, no.

I adjusted the slider for height to the max it will go. Not as tall as I was at two inches more than six feet, but it would do. The build I wanted was a little more muscular than my toned and thin limbs. So, I slid the slider over a little farther above average, then a little more. Until the muscles looked just right, it was like looking at an Olympic swimmer. They were powerfully built, but still slim with broad shoulders and a narrow waistline. My ideal body.

The skin color went from pitch black to milky white. I put it at a normal, tanned skin tone for myself, as that was what I typically looked like. A basic white guy with a year-round tan, though it was more than a little disappointing they didn't have more skin tone options. The hair was short and cut stylishly with various lengths, and I colored it silver, with green, red, purple, and blue highlights. Had to have *something* to liven it up a little.

The facial features I left alone; they were handsome in their own right. The angular cheeks that were just this side of sunken in. The chiseled jawline that would make a movie star jealous. Thick lips with just a *hint* of fang artfully exposed and well-done eyebrows. The eyes I changed to a vibrant hue of yellow.

The horns had a slider that allowed you to change the positioning on the head, size, curvature, and color. The large horns did seem cool to me, but I toned down the size and positioned them so that they laid almost flat against my forehead and curved up over the top of my head and hair. These I was happy to leave black as they looked badass.

All the avatar wore was a ratty, rag-like shirt, a loincloth, and no shoes.

"Excellent choice, wanderer." The figure clapped. My perspective shifted, and rather than him being behind me; he was in front of me now. "How do you feel?"

I took a mental stock of myself. Other than being aware I now had a body, I felt fantastic!

"I feel great." I recognized my voice. Good, a recognizable voice would help my viewers recognize me.

"Excellent, what then, will be your name?" He asked once more. As the white screen popped into view once more, he held a hand with too-large fingers in front of it. "Do not attempt to make the name you give yourself something I will find... less than amusing. So far, I find your tastes endearing—do not prove me wrong."

I typed in the name I had used before, Kyvir Mageblood.

"Kyvir Mageblood." He stood his full height in front of me, then bowed so low that his head almost touched the floor. It seemed borderline creepy he could move that way, but he still made the movement look graceful. "I am, as you might have guessed—Mephisto. Welcome to my world. Here, there are gods, goddesses, creatures of myth, and lore. And even more important to your kind—magic."

I kept my face as neutral as I could, but a smile crept over my lips. I felt a small nick on my bottom lip, and the long canine there proved to be sharper than it looked. That was cool, something I would need to get used to. The sharpened nails as well. I flexed my hands and looked down at the physical form I had chosen to represent me in this game—realm.

"I have seen only one so excited as they bled themselves." Mephisto chuckled. "You are to be reborn as an immortal wanderer, child. Keep the demon hordes at bay—or defeat them if you can—fight the myths and legends and know that I and the deities of this realm watch over you."

I bowed my head to the god of the world and spoke solemnly, glad my friends wouldn't be here to listen in.

"I will do my utmost to rid this world of the demons and monsters who claim it with the gift you bestow upon me. I will master the powers you give me as swiftly as I can, as will my friends. The magic does not scare me, nor the quest. Mageblood is my moniker made to help all remember—there's always some kind of magic out there for everyone. In all of us. About all of us."

They would definitely have been cackling and droning on and on about my attempt at playing a role in such a grandiose manner. That last bit was how I usually ended my streams, and my friends *despised* it.

Mephisto held a hand to his lips and pulled it away to reveal a smile of almost-manic glee. "Oh, you will be an entertaining one. And I have just the power you seek—he with the blood of mages."

I had enough time to look at him oddly as he tousled my hair, then tapped me on my solar plexus before I was cast out of the gray room and into a sea of stars below me. Mephisto's tall form waved at me, and I felt a rush of cold, then turned slowly midair and plummeted through the skies.

The constellations around me were unlike anything I had ever seen. There were two moons in the sky, their silvery colors seeming to feed between the two of them—though the smaller one seemed to have a more bluish cast to it—both giving off pale light over the ground below. The reflection from the surface of the water below was beautiful and terrifying. Because if I hit the water going this fast—I would die.

As the ocean loomed ever closer, I tried to reason with the fact that it was inevitable. So, I took in what I could. I noted a short way ahead of my position, there was a city. It was surrounded by a thickly wooded forest of trees. At least it had reminded me of one with all the lights and everything.

The water was beginning to close with my rapid descent from the heavens, and I thrust my arms out in a vain attempt to protect myself. A foot from the water, my path of travel physically *shifted,* and I was rocketing toward the tree line in the direction of the city that I had seen.

I watched in stunned horror and fascination as trees zoomed by me, almost so close that I could reach out and touch them—but I didn't dare. Because while whatever it was moving me may keep me moving, it probably wouldn't stop the trees from ripping me to shreds. I pulled my arms and hands closer to my body to keep myself compact.

The wall itself was larger than my house by more than half, made completely of stone and guarded by men with bows, javelins, and an assortment of weapons they carried in case of a melee fight.

It was an interesting thing to see, but I thought that the doors I happened to be speeding toward were drawing dangerously close.

"Oooooooh fuuuuuuuuuuuuuuu—!" I shouted. As I was about to become a gamer-cake on the large door to the wall, my forward momentum was arrested immediately.

"Hahaha!" One of the guards on the bulwark laughed heartily. "Never gets ol' does it, Miff?"

"Na, no, it don't, Sammy." The other guffawed. They both wore matching leather armor with some kind of crest carved and emblazoned on the chest piece. Miff, the younger of the two, sported a bow while Sammy held two javelins. One in each hand.

My cheeks heated a little as my body turned in the air and touched down onto the soft ground lightly around twenty feet from the door. The grass and dirt beneath me tickled slightly against my bare skin. It was like having stepped outside for the first time. A warm, sea-scented breeze wafted before me, and I closed my eyes, enjoying the tactile sensations thrilling through me and made me smile.

"This is unreal," I breathed softly.

"Come 'ere, wanderer," A gruff voice called to me from the direction of the door.

I looked over toward the large doors and there was a smaller one on the inside, close to the wall on the left door. A small man—dwarf—beckoned me toward him.

"Get ye inside, so we can get yer trainin' underway." He growled. "Don' wanna be outside in the beginnin' area at night. All kind o' unpleasantness about when the sun goes down."

That was a fairly common trope in a lot of VR games out lately. There was even a mechanic in Blood and Gore that made it so that experience was doubled at night in some areas because the monsters and instance dungeons were so much harder there.

"Okay," I said, and walked toward the door.

As soon as I took a step, I heard a crunch in the tree line to my right. I looked that way, stunned, and a hulking form separated itself from the shadows. Glowing red eyes intent on me. The beast step forward.

"*RUN LAD!*" The dwarf shouted, fear on his face.

All hell broke loose. Archers on the wall began firing arrows and throwing javelins at the creature, but it nimbly sprinted between them. I froze, all the experience I had in any VR game I'd ever played fled my body. I heard a crash to my left; then my world tilted backward.

Agony filled my existence as the creature slammed me onto the ground with a massive clawed hand and growled deeply.

"Welcome to hell, wanderer." The lupine jaws of the creature filled my vision. A flash of more pain. Then nothing.

Deep crimson letters faded into view in front of my eyes.

You have died. Welcome, wanderer.

Chapter Four

I sat up a few seconds later, in the same spot I had landed on the ground twenty feet from the doorway. The stars above me were the same I had flown through earlier.

"Yup, looks like I lost that bet, Sammy." The guard called Miff said, with a grunt to the other. "I owes a drink to you and your da."

Rather than stay on the ground, I got up, immediately taking note that my clothes were fine, and I felt no blood on me. I beat feet to the door and knocked three times.

The door swung open, and the dwarf grabbed a fistful of my clothes to haul me inside. His gold-blond hair and beard were both heavily braided. The sides of his head were clean-shaven and tattooed with thick black lines. He wore leather armor that looked practical and well-maintained.

"Yer the first he's got, and he ain't gone far." The man spat on the ground. "Why did ye freeze, lad? Yer of a muscled sort—that distance were nothin' for ye!"

"I've never seen anything like that before, and it spoke to me!" I began to shake for a moment, then gathered my wits. "I panicked. I froze. What the hell was that thing?"

"A dark wolf." The dwarf waved it away. "Probably an alpha if it spoke to ye. Be creatures who typically cannot come through the barrier protectin' the trainin' grounds, but at night they're stronger 'n craftier. So, *they* can get in. Any more than one or two, and they attract too much attention and begin to be hunted by guard and huntsman."

"Sounds like that alpha was banking on making an enemy." I growled.

"Heh!" The dwarf smacked his knee. "Yer a funny wanderer. It'll be some time afore yer ready to hunt an alpha like him. Let's get ye trained up afore then, aye?"

I clapped my hands and rubbed them together in expectation. "Alright!" I looked at the dwarf. "What's first?"

"Well, first we need to confirm what yer magical gift is." He motioned for me to slow down with a grin. "Open yer status screen, then look at the section that says, 'gift' for me."

"Status," I whispered into the air.

The whiteboard that I had seen when I was with Mephisto popped up, showing multiple tabs on it. The stats tab was greyed out, which was odd, but the gift one was what I was after.

I touched it, then watched as it opened and showed me what my gift is.

Mageblood – 50% resistance to magical damage.

"Wha—" I shook my head in confusion. "That's not right. How is this right?"

"Well, the Gods are hardly ever wrong, lad," the dwarf replied gruffly. "What's yer gift then?"

"It's my namesake, but it gives me a fifty percent resistance to magical damage." Honestly, I felt highly cheated. "Has this happened before?"

"How am I s'pose to know, lad?" He harrumphed grumpily. "I know at least two hunnert folk what would give anything to have somethin' like that. Besides, gifts never stay the same—they evolve an' grow with the wanderer. What ye have now may be the beginning stages of somethin' else."

That went a little way toward easing the tension in my gut. Though I still wondered what my fans might think of the huge change. Would they blame me? Think I'm fake?

I had always been the grand mage type before, glass cannon with a badass spell for almost any occasion, and now I was getting eaten alive by rodents.

"Lad?" I blinked at the smaller man before leaning under me to look me in the eyes as I thought. "Ye there?"

"Okay, so, where are we?" I snapped out of my doubting, and then thought to add, "And what's your name?"

"I'm Felix, wanderer." The dwarf puffed out his chest and squared his shoulders. "And I'll be trainin' ye in the art of not gettin' yerself killed. *Again.*"

"Ha-ha." Though I was acting like a sullen child and knew it, he was kind of funny. "Nice to meet you, Felix. I'm Kyvir Mageblood. Pleasure."

I offered my hand to the dwarf who looked at it strangely before taking it in his own gingerly. After seeing it was no trick of any sort, he took a firmer grasp and shook my hand firmly.

"Let's go train ye then." Felix turned and walked away.

"Is there a way for me to find my friends?" I called as I followed along.

He looked over his shoulder as we plodded through an open thoroughfare through another gate on the inside of the wall. Then waved a hand for me to continue following.

I held my myriad of questions until we reached Felix's destination. The goal, it seemed, was a large circular area with six training dummies evenly spaced from each other and black colored rats held in by a fence. When I say rats, I mean *rats*. As large as a small dog. Typical gaming fair, but I was here in the area with them. They seemed docile enough. Scurrying from hay pile to hay pile.

"Now, about yer friends," Felix started. "I'm assumin' these friends are other wanderers?"—I nodded excitedly—"They will be in their own individual training areas. There were one or two who came through here earlier on, but they were able to leave rather quickly. Until ye leave here, though—yer mine."

"You got it, boss," I responded with a smile. The sooner I could leave, the better. "Just tell me what I have to do."

"A real down-to-business man. I like ye, lad." Felix's eyebrows raised appreciatively. "If ye had a firin' magic, like fire, water or somethin'—I'd have ye shoot the dummies first from here. Then work on hittin' the rats as they scurry about. But, ye don't. So, tell me then, Kyvir. Do ye prefer blunt or a bladed weapon?"

"Uh, I'm n-not sure," I stammered a bit after that.

Sure, I had used weapons in past games. Staves, wands, and other magical items, but never like this. I'd swung a bat when I was younger.

"Well, never too late to learn, lad." Felix smiled wistfully for a moment. "'Member the first time I held me axe. Felt *right.* Ye'll find a weapon for ye. Stand here and think o' ways to fight those there rats until I come back."

The man walked away swiftly toward a low, squat building more than a hundred yards away. He kicked in the door to the building and roared into the room. A raucous roar sounded in return and the door shut.

I was worried for a moment, but when I didn't hear the sound of an outright brawl, I turned my attention back to the training at hand.

Unless these were some kind of plague rats with magic, they were just normal—huge—rats. Animals. That meant my gift was next to worthless.

I would need to be sure to keep them away from the hay piles so that there was less of a risk that multiple rats would rush me. There were some small stones and pebbles that I could possibly throw? Another bang drew my attention away.

Felix shambled out of the room with another laughing and smiling dwarven man following him. The dwarf looked me over appraisingly.

"Master Kyvir, I take it?" His brusk tone, but amicable demeanor were all business at that moment. His graying beard worked in thought, and his beady eyes looked me over more thoroughly than they had at a distance. "Gimme yer paws, lad. Let me look at yer main tools."

I chuckled at him calling my hands 'paws,' but held them out for him anyway. He grasped my right hand, checking the palm and fingers individually. Then did the same with my left hand. He nodded and walked behind me. When I went to turn with him, Felix touched my shoulder and shook his head.

"Raise yer arms out to the side," the other dwarf ordered. I obeyed, and he said, "Down. Now forward. Over yer head. In front. Just yer right. Left now. Bend yer knees."

He walked back around in front of me before continuing, "Raise yer right arm, make a fist and pull the fist like ye'd swing a blade. Make it crisp, lad."

I did as he instructed, and he began to call directions for me to swing my "blade." It was an interesting thing to do, but I liked it—it was different.

After I finished and I was a little sweaty, which was definitely new to me in a game, the dwarf put his hands into his beard. He ran his fingers through the graying hair and tugged at it for a moment.

"Sword, spear, axe, shield, and possibly even the glaive," he said finally. "Anything else would take too much time to teach him to handle proper."

Felix whistled low. "Thank ye, Master Filk. Do ye have anythin' the lad can use ta make his way through trainin'?"

Filk thought for a moment. "Aye. Gimme a mo', laddie."

Filk hobbled back toward the same door Felix had gone into, kicked it open, and roared loudly. Another raucous reply greeted him, and the door slammed shut. If he hadn't told me to stay behind, I'd have run over to see if he was alright.

"Okay, one—who was that?" I looked at Felix. "Two, what the hell is in that building?"

"That was Master Armorer Filk, man has forgotten more about the art o' fightin' and equippin' soldiers 'n fighters than you would likely ever learn. And that is his domain—the armory. The lads in there maintain the weapons and equipment."

"What's with the screaming when you come in?" My brows crinkled in confusion.

"It's a precaution." Felix grinned. "Anyone goin' into his realm is to announce hisself, or the lads get to play. And by play—I mean kill ye. So, if ye ever mean to enter his armory, ye best be loud about it."

"Noted, thank you, Felix." The dwarf nodded in return, and I asked my next burning question. "So, those motions he was having me go through?"

"He was checking how yer body would move if ye held a weapon." Felix pulled out his axe. "He was lookin' for deformity in the muscles' motion through a position, or specific movement. Each movement would serve a function with a weapon in hand."

"That's amazing," my eyes widened, my voice hushed in awe as I took a second glance at my hands then toward the place the older dwarf had walked into.

"I told ye he were good, lad," Felix responded coolly.

"And ye better grease tha' leather proper, lad—or I'll tan *yer* hide and show ye how, eh?" Filk shouted at someone in the room as he left it. Then he turned and hobbled over to us once more.

As he came to us, a grin appeared on his aged face. "What good lads we have here, Felix! Smart, and quick as whips, they be."

"Weren't you just threatening them?" I tried to keep my nose out of things normally, but this was too interesting not to ask.

"Oh, aye." He nodded sagely. "Apprentices get complacent an' make mistakes if ye don't yell or shout a little every now an' then."

Hard to argue with logic like that. I shrugged and waited to hear what was next.

Filk reached in front of himself, and his arm disappeared for a second before reappearing. He began handing weapons to Felix, who just held his arms out like a rack. There was a sword, a spear, an axe, shield, and the last one resembled a spear but had an axe-like head to it.

"Ye look confused—the last one there be a glaive. Or a type o' one. It's for beginners." Filk explained. "Let's ye get a feel for the proper use o' the weapon before ye go daft an' start to using the double-headed kind an' hurt yerself."

"Oh, thank you." I reached for it, but he rapped my knuckles with a stick he must've pulled from his inventory.

"Ye get the sword an' shield for now. Clear the rats from the trainin' grounds in twenty minutes, an' ye can pick any *one* other weapon as a backup weapon. I will let ye know, they are poorly made. So, there are much better weapons that ye will find out there once ye leave."

"Why would you give out a poorly made item?" I tried to keep the disgust and confusion from my tone, first out of respect, and second out of fear. If he took them back, I'd be shit out of luck.

"Poor quality be cheap to make and practice with." He waved to the item dismissively. "Ye use that and don't get yerself killed? Ye'll likely be a' right to use proper weapons, but tha' be like throwin' away coin—and I do nae waste coin, lad."

A notification bounced into view obscuring everything from view.

QUEST RECEIVED – Kill all the rats in the training grounds before the end of 20 minutes. Reward: Double experience and one back up weapon from Master Filk. Failure: No added experience, weapons must be bought.

"Seems straight forward." I picked up the shield in my left hand and the sword in my right. There were nicks and dents in the shield, and the sword was top-heavy and leaned to one side, the crossguard was wobbly at the top of the hilt. "Man, you weren't kidding about poorly made weapons."

"It's a weapon, lad." Felix shrugged and let Filk take the rest from him. "Havin' somethin' sharp on yer side is never bad."

"Are they not supposed to have any stats?" I stared at the sword and shield intently, but nothing happened. "Where are *my* stats?"

Filk shook his head. "Weapons of poor quality and lower have no stats. They deal minimum damage for the weapon ye use, which is typically one. After poor, which is common—ye begin seeing stats. As for yers? Ye gotta *earn* 'em."

His guffawing as he said that last bit made me roll my eyes, *What harebrained game makes you earn your stats like this?*

I nodded, then walked toward where the entrance to the training grounds was. The gate was simple, it latched on this side with a bar and string over the top. I stepped into the training area and found that there was a musty scent vaguely familiar to our class pet rat's little cage. It had been years since I had smelled something similar, but it was so gross I guess I never forgot it. It came from the closest hay pile. But, thinking back on my earlier decision to use some of the stones and pebbles I saw on the ground, I had the beginnings of a plan.

I transferred the hilt of the sword to my left hand, where the shield was. It wasn't really all that heavy of a shield. It was wooden, about the size of a pizza box, and stained brown with two leather straps to secure it to the wielder's arm. And the sword wasn't that heavy, either.

I knelt, grabbed a stone, and threw it into the hay pile as hard as I could.

1 dmg to Rat.

"Oh, that's so cool." I smiled as I looked for another stone. I heard a shriek and saw that I now had company.

Lvl 1 Rat – Hostile

"Shit!" Its HP bar was only knocked down by one-fourth, and it was careening toward me. While it was cool as all get out that I had done a point of damage to it with a small rock, it was shitty that the thing went hostile straight out the gate.

Or hay.

I tried to get my sword into my right hand and tripped over another rock that I hadn't seen. I rolled onto my back and glanced down in time to see the little beastie clambering up my leg. I grunted, and instead of relinquishing the sword into my right hand, I gripped it with both and stabbed down into the rat's open mouth.

CRITICAL STRIKE

4 dmg to Rat.

Lvl 1 rat died.

10 EXP.

Awesome. I heard a rustling off to my right across the training ground and saw another two of them poke their heads out from another two piles of hay.

"May wanna stand up, lad," Felix called. I looked over, and he sat perched on the fencing with two more men. The two guards from the top of the gate! Miff and Sammy. I'd almost bet they wagered another round on this.

I scrambled to my feet as quickly as I could without tripping again. This time I was prepared with the sword in the proper hand. I had it held low. No point holding it high and getting tired.

"Good form, lad!" Felix called. "Hold yer shield afore ye as they charge. Then, as they crash against ye—jab 'em good."

I took the advice and waited. They approached cautiously, slowly setting one paw before the other as they scanned me for openings.

I set my feet a little wider apart, shuffling my right foot back a little to get a solid base, pulled my elbows in tight to my body, and waited. They didn't seem to want to approach me, but the corpse of the rat next to me was still there. So—I kicked it.

They screeched at me, both of them, and charged forward. I took a steadying breath as they closed in and smacked one away with my shield.

"Bad move," Sammy said, then grunted. "Now, he's left an opening."

I didn't get time to react to that as the other rat swept into the gap between my shield and me. It was able to bite me before I sliced it with the sword. It was a shallow cut, but the rodent let go and backed up.

1 dmg taken

2 dmg to rat

"Might wanna watch his back, right, Sammy?" Miff observed loudly.

1 dmg taken.

The other rat bit my left leg and I smacked it with the edge of the shield as the sharp sensation of teeth dug in. Pain wasn't unheard of in a lot of games like this, something about it helped with realism and the escapism of it. Made it feel like real life. That didn't mean I wanted to be a chew toy to a group of rodents and that hobbling around from being made one would be okay. It wasn't enough damage to make me limp or anything, but it did sting.

1 dmg to rat.

I growled and sidled out from between them. This was going poorly. I didn't even have a health bar yet, damn it. Did I even have stats?

"Solid idea, lad." Felix grunted with a chuckle. "Now, take the fight to 'em."

I rolled my eyes but listened. Being on the defensive would be a bad idea. But, one thing I learned from PvP combat, especially in a one on two situation, was to keep one enemy between you and the stronger enemy. Whittle them down and kite, run around if needed.

The cut rat went between the mostly whole one and me, then I walked in a circle around them. It would try to leap at me, I'd pull the shield up and deflect it. Then I would stab and deal a point of damage because it wasn't smart enough to see it coming. Two stabs, and it was dead.

Lvl 1 rat died.

10 EXP.

"Properly done!" Miff cheered, though I ignored him and his clapping.

The other rat looked like it was ready to bolt. An idea occurred, and I feigned an injury dropping to a knee and my shield hanging limply to my side. The rat rushed forward, obviously thinking of an easy victory. As it leapt up toward my face, I sliced up with the blade like I would if I were going to uppercut someone in the face. I felt some resistance and looked down in time to watch the rat's head fall into the crook of my arm.

CRITICAL STRIKE
4 dmg to rat.
Lvl 1 rat died.
10 EXP.

"Oh, that's gross." I grunted loudly as I let the head drop and stood before looking around me. At least six more sets of eyes peered out at me from varying locations. "Time to get to work."

It took ten minutes to kill all six of them by whittling them down the same way, but I did it. I was starting to get a little tired. Sure, about ten pounds of wood wasn't much, but after twelve minutes of constantly lugging it around—your arm started to burn a bit. The sword weighed a little less, but it was poorly crafted, and the balance didn't feel right.

After the last of them fell, I huffed a bit in pride and turned to Felix and the others with plenty of time left on my counter. "Well, that's it then!"

"Did ye get yer quest notification?" Felix raised an eyebrow knowingly.

I looked around, and sure enough, I hadn't. "What the hell, man?"

"Don't ask the trainer, boy—ask that big rat behind you." Sammy pointed, and I whirled in time to see a slightly larger rat with a white mark in the middle of his forehead resembling a crown. He was dark-colored like the others had been, but this one had foam coming from the corners of its mouth.

Lvl 2 Rat King – Enraged

"Oh, boy," I said, then growled as I set my feet. "Well, then—come and avenge your people, Your Majesty."

The rat screeched at me, and a tremor of fear roiled through me.

Fear spell resisted.

Oh, that little—I grunted in my head, but it was too late to really finish the thought. It was on me and it was all I could do to hold it at bay with my shield. I brought my sword up and tried to slash at it, but the creature shoved against my shield and backed away.

I had just enough time to glance at the front of the shield and saw deep scores in it from the Rat King's clawed forepaws. I checked the timer—seven minutes left and ticking lower fast. Time to get risky.

"Remember, boy—you have more weapons than a shield and sword!" Sammy shouted.

I came forward, my movements methodical and measured from a little practice. Steady and controlled, my focus was completely on the Rat King. It paced a little to my left, away from the blade in my right hand.

"Come on, then!" I shouted at it angrily.

It squeaked at me deeply then trotted forward. I underestimated its speed because at the last second before I blocked it was gnawing on my leg.

2 dmg taken.

1 poison dmg taken, poison resisted.

"*Ahhhg!*" I gritted my teeth and grabbed the back of its neck in my shield hand, and started trying to crush the rat's skull with the pommel of the sword in my hand.

1 dmg to Rat King.

1 dmg to Rat King.

1 dmg to Rat King.

After three solid hits, it was able to squirm out of my grip but stumbled a little. I used its momentary weakness to smack it with my shield as hard as I could with the edge as if I were punching it. I misaimed and cracked it in the throat.

CRITICAL STRIKE

3 dmg to Rat King.

Rat King suffers from Suffocating Debuff.

The creature coughed and wheezed as it shook its head back and forth. I huffed after the exertion. But my advantage was now. I needed to kill this thing.

I brought my sword into both hands and stood to the rear of the Rat King as it choked. I brought the sword down in a stabbing motion like I had seen some knights do in older movies. My foe lurched forward out of the way, and the blade stuck into the ground, then snapped in half as my balance shifted forward too quickly for me to recover.

A new weight hit me, the rat trying to bring me down to get to my throat. I shoved it back with my shield as I fell and tried to roll on my shoulder, but tumbled to my knees instead. The Rat King took his own advantageous position as he climbed onto the shield protecting my chest, and I fell backward with his weight on me. We struggled for what felt like forever, my chest and throat safe, but the bottom of my stomach was exposed, and that's what he went for with his back legs. Kicking and digging his claws into my abdomen while trying to bite my neck. He got my left shoulder, a pulse of nausea hit me, and I knew the next message was going to suck.

2 dmg taken.

1 poison dmg. You are poisoned.

Damage per second halved.

I roared and brought what little blade was left on the sword in my hand to bear on the side of the Rat King.

1 dmg dealt.

1 dmg taken.

1 dmg dealt.

1 dmg taken.

1 poison dmg taken.

My limbs grew numb. My grip on the shield already waned quickly, and the Rat King's eyes sparkled as he stopped kicking and tried for my throat, even as he continued to wheeze and cough.

In a last-ditch effort—I kicked my hips up into the air, tossing the Rat King from me. My feet touched the ground, and I mimicked the motion once more to roll my feet up over my head and then onto him tiredly as drool and spittle dripped from my lips. My vision blurred slightly, but that just sharpened the outrage I felt.

I would *not* die twice in one night. Hell no. Not me. Not Mageblood. I had no magic. I had no weapons. I had no fighting abilities. I didn't even have a *level*. But I *would* have this.

"*Raaaaaaaargh!*" The hatred pumping through my heart fueled me just enough to stab down into the chest twice, then I grabbed what looked like an ear to stabilize myself. As the last of my strength drained from me, I used my body weight to drive the broken weapon up to the hilt into the beastie.

Then darkness.

CHAPTER FIVE

"Right unfair, that was Sammy, and you know it." I heard Miff's voice as if through a dense helmet.

I strobed my eyes a little bit, the light that filtered in bright and painful.

"Rest yerself, lad—ye did it. Ye can check yer status an' notifications in a bit. The poison is gone, but yer still recoverin'," Felix's voice drifted to me from my left.

"Whatur they argu-ng 'bout?" I mumbled. My speech was slurred, and suddenly the room spun as if I'd been drinking.

"That'll be the antidote I give'd ye." Felix chuckled, and I could hear the pride in his voice. "Ol' family recipe."

"It was spirits," Sammy's gruff voice rang out loudly near where Miff's voice had been.

"Like I said—ol' family recipe." Felix huffed.

"Water." I groaned. My hands groped at the air like a dying man in the desert would grope for a mirage.

I felt a leather thing press into my hand, Miff's younger voice was softer now, "It's open already. I'll help you sit up to drink it. But we go slow. Felix's booze can be very powerful."

"Thank ye, lad." Felix sounded proud once more.

Sammy snorted, and two sets of large hands grabbed onto either side of my body. They helped me sit up, the room spun dangerously, but I just brought the leather container to my lips. The water spilled a little from the corners of my mouth, but the cool liquid went a long way toward helping me feel better.

I stopped drinking and narrowed my eyes at the room around me. I could see Felix and the two guards.

"Did I do it?" I asked groggily.

"Aye, only one I seen do it like ye did, ta boot!" Felix chuckled.

Miff grumbled, "And now I owe Sammy and his da another round."

I blinked at the young guard, vexed that my lack of dying seemed to be what the bet had been about.

"I'm sorry I didn't die so you could have a free drink, Miff." I barked, harsher than I meant to.

He waved it away. "Not my night is all—and Sammy cheated"—the younger looked at the elder accusingly—"by giving you blatant advice."

"Didn't you do the same?"

He shook his head. "I was makin' *observations* that could just so happen to be overheard."

Felix was smiling at the young guard. "I'll buy ye a drink lad, fret not."

I shook my head, then ran my left hand shakily through my hair. My hand slid over the semi-rough texture of my horns, and it brought me back to the present.

I saw the notification from the finished quest.

QUEST COMPLETED – You killed all the rats in the training grounds before the end of 20 minutes. Finished in 17:32. Reward: Double experience and one back up weapon from Master Filk.

I checked, having killed nine rats and the rat king.

Total experience earned: 230 (9 rats at 10 EXP, and rat king at 25 EXP x 2)

Level Up!

Congratulations wanderer! You have managed to acquire not only your first level, but the second as well. You are now ready to move on!

Do you wish to move on? Yes? / No?

I had the option to select an answer, but I held off.

"Hey, Felix?" The dwarf turned toward me with a questioning look on his face. "How do I level up here? It doesn't seem to give me the option. Also, what happened to all the experience I earned in the fight? I should've earned enough to get most of the way to the next level."

"The EXP ye earned was held until you either finished or failed the quest, so what ye earned is that. Ye weren't cheated. Open yer status screen, then select Stats. From there, ye have the option to apply yer new stat point to whatever ye wish." He explained, slowly motioning into the air before him as if pressing screens. "Ye get ten points to apply at first level, and one per level after, so make 'em count. At level three, ye unlock yer abilities table, and from there, that's how ye grow yer magic."

"Thank you." I nodded, and he thumped my arm.

I did as he explained and looked at my stats.

Kyvir Mageblood, Level 2, Race: Kin
HP: 80
Strength: 6
Skill: 6
Heart: 5
Knowledge: 5
Serenity: 5
Presence: 5
Unspent Stat Points: 11
EXP to next Lvl: 230 / 300

Felix and the others must have seen me hesitate because Sammy spoke up, "Tap the attribute you want to learn about or all of 'em and you can learn what they do. If you have questions, let us know."

I smiled at them and tapped them all in succession from top to bottom.

Strength – The amount of power you can exert upon the world with your physical body. Adds 5 HP and 5 pounds of weight that can be lifted and carried per point. This attribute can affect certain spells in different ways, as well as damage output with weapons, and what kinds of weapons and armor can be worn. (One point added as a racial bonus)

Skill – Your ability to properly handle and manipulate objects and your body in a manner that will benefit you. This attribute is used to ensure that spells and certain weapons can be properly cast and handled. (One point added as a racial bonus)

Heart – Who you are and how hearty you are. This attribute will affect your will and endurance, as well as your health and regeneration. Adds 10 HP per point in this stat. Without the right level in this attribute, some spells may affect you in different ways.

Knowledge – The facts necessary to control and bend the aether to your will and put it to proper use. This attribute directly affects the amount of power behind certain kinds of spells, spell damage, and range.

Serenity – The will to calm your mind and the universe around you, understanding deeper truths and how best to approach the world and its aether. This attribute affects your ability to recover your aether and how you can assist others.

Presence – How the world perceives you, your aesthetic, and your actions can affect many things, some being your ability to move among people and creatures. Some spells and situations can be directly influenced by this attribute.

Okay, so that was a huge start. But I didn't have any spells. I was stuck with resistance. Unless…

"And points don't just disappear if you don't use them after a while?"

Miff looked to the other two before shaking his head. "No, but you'll be severely limiting yourself in a fight if you aren't decisive enough about it."

That was fair. "Thanks, you guys, and one more thing—gifts do grow, right? Or evolve and change? I know you said it once before, but I'm just confirming. Do you know anything else on the matter?"

"Some of 'em, aye." Felix scratched the side of his head. "But if legend serves, 'cause until recent that's what the lot o' ye were, there's a tree o' skills and spells that unlocks at level three. And the first true evolution of a skill or type o' magic takes place at either fifth or tenth level. Can't remember, though someone said somethin' 'bout this bein' the basics and told me to piss off, so I haven't really gone o'er it with anybody else."

So, there was a chance that I could acquire magic or spells soon. That would mean that if I spent the bare bones, and saved some points, I could use those extra points to my advantage. Cool. First order of business was to get my health up above one hundred because more health never hurt anyone.

I sank two points into Heart, bumping it to seven. Then one apiece to Strength and Skill. Those would help me to defend myself until I could get to my friends at the very least.

"Okay, I've spent what I'm going to." I looked over to Felix as I swung my legs over the side of the bed. I felt better. More robust, if not a little stronger as well. "Is it all right if we go see Master Filk for my quest reward?"

Felix grinned and smacked Miff with the back of his hand. "Got respect, this one. Like 'im, I do. Come on then, lad. Let's go make our presence known!"

With a mischievous glint in his eye, the dwarf waddled out of the room we were in and motioned that I follow.

"See ya, fellas." I waved to the two smiling guards as I walked outside. They waved back, and we were on our way.

We were on the opposite side of the training ring from the armory now. There was no one about, but I did see the rat corpses still in the area. As I watched, they began to dissolve and slowly sink into the earth.

"Felix? How long does it take something like a corpse to disappear?" I watched as two more did the same thing.

"About half an hour." He stopped and quirked his head to the side. "We, normal folk, don't. So, remember that afore ye start ta murderin' indiscriminate like."

I felt like that one was a joke, so I snapped my fingers and grumbled, "Aw, man."

The dwarf snorted, and chuckled and we walked once more toward the armory.

Once we arrived at the door, Felix froze and stepped aside, motioning to the door. "Yer turn to do the honors, lad."

"You're sure?" I raised an eyebrow. He nodded and pounded his chest and jerked a thumb toward the door.

I took a deep breath and settled myself before I push-kicked the door open as hard as I could, landing just inside the well-lit room. I loosed a loud bellow, flecks of spittle flying from my mouth into the face of a burly dwarf that made me think of old action heroes. He was that jacked for one reason and one reason only—to kill.

He blinked at me in surprise, then loosed a cry of his own as the other dwarves and humans inside took up the raucous call.

Once the shouting died down, I saw several of those inside begin to laugh deeply.

"Shouted righ' in yer gob, Yildur!" One dwarf teased as he went over a belt with a cloth and some grease.

Felix stepped in and bellowed one burst and all of us returned the call.

"Ye taught him proper, I see Felix, laddie!" I heard Filk, barely. The older dwarf careened out from the back of the place with a smile tweaking the sides of his beard. "'Twas a good shout, lad. Good indeed. Heard ye killed tha' Rat King quick-like too! Good lad, good work."

"I broke the sword, though, Master Filk," I corrected, slightly embarrassed.

Filk rounded on his apprentices. "See that respect, ye sorry lot?" The older dwarf spat. "Not even mine an' he calls me master! Manners!"

The others just smiled at their master and shook their heads as he turned back to me. "Aye, an' what a fine job ye did using it to the very end. Broken, snapped it was, an' ye gored that beastie anyhow!"

Filk's strong hand whipped out and slapped me on the shoulder twice. "Feeling stronger there, lad! Come to choose yer weapon then, did ye?"

"Yes, sir." I nodded.

The dwarf's eyes widened, and he looked around him until he picked up a small wrench and threw it at the dwarf oiling the belt. The would-be victim deftly dodged the improvised projectile and merely looked up.

"Go fetch the good weapons! Common only, lad—and bring 'em here!" He touched my arm and hand once more. "Sword, spear, glaive, and axe—hand-axe not battle."

The dwarf set his work down and hustled into a room behind him.

Now that I had a good look at the place, this seemed to be the fitting and maintenance portion of the armory. There were benches with tools and tapes for fittings, clothes for polishing and oiling, and barrels that likely held supplies for their craft. Small hammers and other tools lay on other surfaces while we waited.

"How did ye like the sword and shield lad?" Filk asked brightly.

I realized that I didn't have either and my face flushed a bit. Felix produced the shield that had been given to me and handed it to Filk.

"Used it well by the gashes here." He held it up and looked it over with a discerning eye. "Used it to punch one o 'em with then?"—I held up two fingers, and his eyes widened and he whistled appreciatively. —"Two? Aye? Clever, lad. And the sword?"

"It was good, and if it would have been balanced properly, I'd have likely been better off," I answered as honestly as I could. I wouldn't gain anything if false pride stood in my way. "I have a lot to learn still, but I'm willing to put in the work with better materials."

Filk tittered with laughter. "Oh, he be a good one, Felix, he do." The armorer tossed the shield to the burly dwarf, Yildur, and ordered, "Repair it."

The apprentice set to work without question with his tools and materials in easy reach.

"Since I like ye so much, I'll let ye keep the shield, get ye a new sword of similar quality, and then ye can have a common weapon." Filk nodded. "How's 'at?"

"It sounds very generous, thank you," I opened my inventory, I had what looked like ten silver coins. "Are you sure I can't pay you for some of it?"

"That ye offer makes me want it all the more, lad." A glint shone in his eyes. "Don't insult me generous spirit with yer coin. Aye?"

I nodded once and dismissed my inventory all together. The first dwarf appeared, his arms full of weapons of all sizes and shapes that he laid on the bench next to us. Different kinds of swords, spears, hand-axes, and glaives of various styles.

"These be all common quality an' therefore will have stats and the like." Filk lifted each one up and offered it to me. I held the sword he gave me and looked it over, a little window popping up from it to show me the stats. It wasn't a heavy weapon, but the difference in balance was noticeable immediately.

Basic sword
Quality: Common
Base dmg: 2-5 dmg
Durability: 10
Worth: 5 silver.

The other weapons were much the same, except the damage ranges varied. The glaive did the most at three to five damage a hit. But it was also a two-handed weapon. It would be good for use in a lot of situations where range was needed, but it wouldn't be ideal in close quarters without some serious training. But if I was going to be smart about this, I could take it and sell it, then use that money to buy a better-quality weapon, or two if it sold better. Then, potentially, I could have two common weapons and be better off.

In the end, I picked the glaive, and Filk gave me another poor-quality sword to use as well as the shield.

"Thank you so much, this will help me a lot in the coming days." I held out a hand to shake Filk's, and he grabbed me by the wrist.

"Be strong out there, an' don't ever become complacent." He smiled and then looked to his apprentices. "Complacency will kill the lot o' ye, but this one has hope!"

The men in the room just stood up and grinned at me, clearly used to their master's antics. I waved goodbye to them all, and as Felix opened the door, they all shouted in unison.

Felix and I roared back and walked outside. We walked a few feet away from the armory, and Felix nodded to me. "Ye ever make yer way out here again, be sure to look for me an' the lads. Tell us yer tales over a pint. Aye?"

He held his hand out for me to shake, and I took it and shook it firmly.

"You bet, Felix. Thanks for teaching me."

"Pleasure. Now, go save the world."

I opened the blinking notification in the lower left-hand side of my heads-up display and clicked yes to leave.

CHAPTER SIX

Welcome to Iradellum, wanderer.

The message greeted me after I blinked and suddenly, I stood in the square of this gigantic city. The colors were exciting as the sun peeked over the structures in the east, bathing the area in deep purples and oranges with hints of red and gold light, just behind some large buildings. The sound of running water behind me made me turn around.

The fountain was massive, quadruple tiered, but the interesting part of it was that there were creatures and beings playing in it. Sprites with blue skin and shimmering wings skated and glided across the floor of the lower portions with huge fish that resembled koi chasing them as they giggled and squealed in delight.

Cat-like creatures with long tails, fins on their ribs, and whiskered faces basked in the light of the growing dawn. Their purrs sounded a little stuffy to me, like a stub-nosed fat cat, but they seemed fine. I was a bit of an animal person, and they did look cute, their aquamarine-colored skin reflecting the refracted light from the water beautifully, so I wanted to touch them.

"Probably not a good idea wanderer," A soft, melodic voice reached my ears from the top level.

I looked up to the top-most bowl of the fountain, a large statue of a mermaid holding a pot of water on her head with water flowing out of it, down her body and into the fountain below. I thought for a moment that it had been the statue that had spoken to me, but a head of roughly the same shape peeked out over the bowl before completely coming out of the water to lean over it with a friendly smile.

"They really only care to be touched by creatures with an affinity for water magic, so unless you have a water spell somewhere in you, they may get upset with you."

"Well, thanks for that." I looked longingly at the animals before loosing a defeated sigh. I had no idea what to do now.

"Looking for what to do next?" The mermaid asked cheerfully.

I blinked up at her a few times before responding carefully, "Ye...s?"

"This is Wave Square, if you follow the rising sun to the other side of the city, you'll find the basic quest board. There, you'll be able to take jobs to get you experience until you're strong enough to join the adventurer's guild." She pointed to our right, east, and then settled back down. "It's a bit of a hike, so don't get too worried if you don't find it quickly. Folk in Iradellum are usually pretty friendly, so you'll be okay asking for directions."

"Thank you, I'm Kyvir, what's your name?" I waved at her and stepped closer.

"I'm Trickle, and this is my home. So, if you ever need someone to chat with, I'll be here!"

I looked from her to the area around her, and I was surprised to see a massive river of water that fed straight into the bottom of the fountain and stopped. On the other side of the fountain, water fell out of the side of it and into a single deep-looking well that had small bits of rising water coming up the sides into rivulets along the ground covered in a glass-like substance as it moved off out of sight in all directions.

"Hey, Trickle, where does the water go?" I bent over the side of the well but saw nothing.

"Water from the ocean is diverted here to me, I cleanse the salt from it, and purify it so that the people of the city have water to drink." She smiled down at me again, a little wider this time. "No one has cared enough to ask me that. Especially not the wanderers. Thank you, Kyvir, and good luck!"

She ducked back behind the lip of the bowl, and a gout of water splashed out toward me. That was so cool.

—Where are you?— A character called Monami Sunfur whispered to me through the chatbox. It was weird because I could see it, and hear it too. A small pulse at my left ear.

I responded, tapping the question and chose to respond in a whisper. A pop-up explanation flashed in front of my eyes.

Whispers – select a name that you know, and simply whisper your message to them. They will receive it in seconds.

That's super cool. And convenient. I wondered what the party chat feature would be like. Would there be one? Likely.

—I'm in the Wave Square, on my way to the quest board in the eastern outskirts of the city. You? Are the others here?—

—I'm already there. See you ASAP!— she responded quickly, and I took off at a speed walk.

I was careful not to hit anyone as I walked. Sometimes waiting for people to move or offering a hello. There were weapon vendors and the like everywhere, but people seemed to tense up when I approached, and skitter to the side.

I saw one guy, this hulking orcish fellow, mow down an entire group of passersby in his hurry to get somewhere. And he was dressed similarly to me. A wanderer.

I heard a muttered curse and stopped to help one of the people on the ground up.

"Bloody monsters, the lot of them," the person grumbled, then realized who I was and just hurried away.

Okay. I moved on.

The city was beautiful. The stonemasons who built it had done a fantastic job since their work seemed brand new. I didn't see much in the way of impoverished folks, but that didn't mean it wasn't possible they lived or congregated elsewhere.

I walked in a straight line for about twenty minutes at a brisk pace, taking in the sights and sounds of my surroundings and still wasn't there. Finally, after almost an hour total of walking the streets and asking directions, I found a large gathering of wanderers on the eastern side of the city.

—Mona, I'm here, where are you?— I whispered to Mona.

I watched as a figure in wanderer clothes separated herself from the crowd. I recognized the poof of hair immediately, the proportions were a little off and the body was different, but that was Mona all right. She had kept her green eyes under all that now-tan hair.

"Hey, Seth," she greeted me warmly as she crossed the distance easily.

She was a lion woman, her curved figure more pronounced. Her fur was a light tan, her facial features a perfect mix of lioness and human. Her hair wasn't a mane per se, but more like a curly mass that hung artfully to the left side of her head. Her sparkling green eyes seemed a bit distressed.

"We've got some issues," she spoke in a low tone. "We need to find the others and get somewhere quiet where we can discuss."

"Okay." I joined her in looking for our friends.

We walked casually through the wanderers, whispering harshly, "Al! Sondra!"

I bumped into a large slab of flesh. The hulking green-skinned person turned around, their rippling muscles trembling as they did and looked down at me.

"Hi, sorry—was looking for a friend," I muttered and tried to get away.

"You wouldn't recognize me, would you, Seth?" I looked up at the person—woman—and realized it was Sondra grinning down at me.

"You're huge!" I struggled and mouthed other words that made no sense, but she just laughed, a massive hand clapping onto my shoulder in a friendly gesture.

"Thanks!" She grinned, her tusks flashing slightly.

Sondra was an orc, but not just any kind of orc. She was *buff* as hell. Her muscles bulged in ways that would put a female bodybuilder to shame, and she seemed so natural that way. Her skin had a myriad of markings all over it that looked like war paint, and I didn't dare touch those without permission as they were *everywhere.* Her storm-gray eyes shone with mirth, and her buzz-cut styled swath of purple hair made me love her style dearly.

Sondra was our tank. Veteran gamer and lovely person, her tyrannical personality was reserved for our enemies and them alone. We were the only ones who got to see her goofy, fun side.

"Love the hair, Sondra." I reached up, and she had to lean down a little from her nearly eight-foot height so that I could run my fingers through without pulling her hair.

"I knew you would." She stood back up and looked around. "You found Al yet? I've been looking for all of you, but he's not using his usual name, then again, neither are we since those seem to be frowned upon 'by the gods.' You are, though 'Kyvir.'"

"Creature of habit sometimes." I flashed a grin that split my lip once more.

"Oh, would you *please* just step aside?" I heard a familiar English accent growling in exasperation.

Sondra grinned savagely. "Found him." She waded through people easily and eventually came back, hauling a lanky elf who appeared thoroughly bemused by his current situation.

"I could have made it out on my own, you know," the elf said, then harrumphed.

He was about the same height as my avatar, slim built with sharply pointed ears, his skin was a deep black-brown almost the color of warm umber, and his hair was a shocking white by contrast that was coifed perfectly atop his head in a shorter style. His glimmering blue eyes observed his surroundings quickly before settling on me.

This was Allen, our healer who swore up and down that healing was a game within a game, and that was the only role he cared to play. And he was amazing at it.

"Seth." He nodded once.

"Al." I tried to look demure, but I ended up grinning like a little kid on Christmas. "How awesome has this game been so far?!"

"Very, but there are... complications," Al muttered as he looked around before finding what he had hoped to see. "That alleyway, let's go."

We turned and headed that way, I whispered to Mona to let her know what was going on, and she found us easily enough.

"We have a problem," Mona started, her arms crossed.

"Indeed," Al echoed. "First of all, I would like to be the first to say, this has been absolutely mind-blowing, and I am truly in love with this world so far."

"It is pretty awesome." Sondra smiled and nodded. "But the issues being... annoying? Not good."

"Let me guess, each of you got a gift from so far out of left field; it felt like a different league was playing?" I asked. The others looked confused, so I blurted, "I have no magic. I'm resistant to it by fifty percent, but that's it so far."

"It seems our personalities and biometric readings have decided against us, I will begin." Al huffed. "My gift is for fire magic. I'm level two and have one spell so far. It's like a Fire Dart, wait, that's the name itself."

So, our healer was a DPS now. Cool. Cool, cool.

Mona cleared her throat. "My magic is Presence-based, and it's called Allure." Her face was beet red. She didn't embarrass easily. So, this was going to be hard.

"I have a healing totem." Sondra cut to the chase. We stared at her, and she just blinked in return.

"So, all of us are basically the opposite of what we would normally choose." I reasoned. "And we're stuck with these gifts until we can figure out how to grow them, or change them, hoping that they evolve. So, these are likely basic, but there could be more down the road, right?"

"Seth's right." Sondra shook out her arms and stretched. "All we can do is move forward. We have a few days until we start streaming. I say we get our heads wrapped around our new roles, and we can put a spin on it. Worst comes to worst; people get to make fun of us for not knowing our new roles."

"Okay, that's doable, though more than a little irritating." Mona sighed.

"How does Allure work?" I watched her cheeks flush slightly, her whiskers flicking slightly in what looked like annoyance.

"It attracts attention and can distract a subject of my choosing," she explained. "It'll be difficult to get used to that kind of attention, but I guess it would be a gateway to our secondary DPS role. And it looks like our resident mage is going to be our acting tank."

"Fun times, that." I snorted. "We need a quest."

"I'll share the one I was able to get before that mob crowded the board. Turns out that the eastern side of the city is considered the newb zone. Everything outside the city into the plains is meant to be lower level and easier for us to handle."

Party invite from Albarth Remell, do you accept?

I selected yes, and then another notification popped up.

QUEST SHARED – Gather pelts from wild sheep in the plains. Amount 15. Reward: 30 EXP, and access to starter clothes.

"Great thinking, Al, by the way, we should really stick to in-game names for now. Call me Kyvir." I eyed the crowd that was beginning to disperse a little.

Sondra flashed a grin. "Sundar Strongtusk."

"Albarth Remell." Al held himself a little prouder having said the name.

"Monami, and don't worry guys—we can do this." With a look of determination, she turned and walked away. Her tail flicked behind her. I didn't know if she was controlling it or not, but that was such a cool additive to the game that just set it even further apart from anything before it.

As we walked, Sundar decided to give me a crash course on tanking.

"Take the hits, get the hate—keep it—and you should be fine. I'll keep you healed up." She patted my shoulder. "You got weapons?"

"Sword, shield, and glaive, yourself?" I watched her reach her arm into the nothingness that was her inventory and pull out a sizable club made of wood that could have been a tree limb pulled straight off the trunk.

"You know I'm more of an intimate fighter." She winked suggestively, and I coughed. Sondra had this effect on me. She might be the eldest of us by a few years, and the most experienced, but by god, she was the *worst*. Her changing her name didn't mean her lewd teasing would change.

"How about you two?" I asked. Albarth simply shook his head and waggled his fingers. Monami reached into her inventory and pulled a common quality dagger out and flashed it.

Different kinds of wanderers had taken a tried and true form of gaming to heart by going out into the fields populated by dozens of sheep in close proximity to each other where they could try their new powers and fight it out. Good idea for some, I saw several throwing all kinds of interesting magics. Small fireballs, water hardened into ice, piercing the wooly sides of sheep. Some other people used weapons like clubs, maces, and other things to minimal effect, but it was still good to see. The area grew steadily more crowded, and the flashes of magic I kept getting glimmers of made my head throb fiercely and my eyes close as a reaction.

We walked well past where the other groups might wander into our hunting grounds, where the wild sheep dotted the plains a little more sparsely. There was nothing as far as the eye could see, except what maybe looked like green clouds off in the distance to the southeast of us a little. Opposite that, these plains that seemed to go on forever. The sun had risen into morning light by now, and the sheep seemed only slightly perturbed by our presence.

"How do we want to do this?" I eyed the sheep, knowing damn well they had no intention of being easy prey.

"Standard pulling tactics," Albarth explained. "Since you're no longer the caster here, and I doubt these things will take a hostile status, we will have to lure them. Monami, that's where your ability will come in handy. You will pull it close enough to distract it while the rest of us get into position to take it down. Got it?"

Al's plans were usually pretty spot on. As the healer, he was able to watch us more effectively than we could and help us pool our talents where they were needed. We all nodded and set to work.

Monami slowly made her way forward toward the closest sheep and began to exude a slightly pinkish aura.

"You guys see that?" The sheep turned and trotted toward her as if she were a long-lost owner and friend.

"How easily she lured that thing? Yeah. That was perfectly done. Now get ready." Sundar snorted, getting her club ready.

I sighed and drew my shitty sword and equipped my shield just to be safe. I would be tanking—didn't mean I needed to be dumb about it.

Lvl 2 Sheep – Friendly

Once she was in the center of us, the pink glow dying from around her, Monami rushed forward with us as we fell on the level two sheep.

1 dmg dealt

8 dmg dealt

4 dmg dealt

4 EXP

The eight had come from a flaming dart hitting the poor creature in the eye, it bleated miserably after that.

It fell when our orcish healer brained it as hard as she could with her club.

It felt like a betrayal that the creature had been friendly when we killed it, but that was the nature of some things. The lowered experience was expected too, though four for a level two enemy was a little rough on leveling progression. Granted, a four-man party was siphoning the experience that might otherwise be easily obtained solo, but we preferred it this way.

We did the same thing for another, having earned one sheep pelt from the first sheep, and earned another when this sheep fell. As we went to pull a third of them, another creature sprinted into existence in the area.

Lvl 3 Ram – Hostile

"I'm on it, don't worry about using Allure," I shouted and put myself between the others and the ram with my shield raised.

I slapped my shield with my sword, trying to bring his attention to me. It seemed to work a little as it lowered its head and charged forward. I took a steadying breath and felt a solid presence at my back. It was Sundar. Her body molded against mine, and she helped me settle into the position better.

"Tense just that arm and shift your weight forward. The sword will come out, and around the second it hits, and you can try to gore him. We've got your back." Her presence was gone, after that I refocused my mind.

A second later, the ram crashed into my shield, shattering it easily.

13 dmg taken.

Stunned – 3. Prone.

The ram was busy trying to stomp me out like a four-legged river dancer from hell, and I couldn't move at all. The Stunned effect was going to really suck.

2 dmg taken.

2 dmg taken.

Stunned – 2. Prone.

A burst of red and pink flashed above my face, and the ram *chuffed* loudly just before Sundar clubbed the beast in the ribs and knocked it off of me. She took a kick that I didn't see a damage notification for, but her health bar looked a little depleted from it.

Stunned – 1. Prone.

The stun wore off and I vaulted myself up onto my feet like I had been in one of those old-fashioned fighter movies. Time to get some revenge.

The ram was busy trying to make out what to do with Monami when I decided what to do. The splintered shield was still on my left arm, and a jagged piece stuck out just over my fist.

While the ram snorted and pawed at the ground in front of my friends, I bolted forward and tried to lodge the jagged edge of the shield into its left eye. My aim was off by a hair, and the ram smacked my left hand away with a horn. I used the momentum of the blow to shift and swipe at its body with my sword, scoring a decent cut on the chest as it passed by.

1 dmg dealt.

"Mo!" I got her attention and tossed the sword to her feet.

The ram took that opportunity to charge at me once more, but rather than take the blow, I waited and dodged to the right of it. A dart of flame smacked it in the face, its HP bar lowered by a quarter.

I reached into my inventory to retrieve the glaive that Filk had given me. It felt decently balanced, if not a little heavier with the small axe at the end of it. It reminded me of a hatchet's head with a spike at the tip.

I took a calming breath and settled my weight into a wide stance that Sundar had showed me briefly with the shaft of the weapon in both hands.

As the ram turned for another pass, I sidestepped wide, and whipped the axe portion into its rib cage.

6 dmg dealt.

Sundar sprinted at the ram where it stopped as its eyes panned to me and tackled it with her shoulder like a linebacker. She grabbed one horn and planted her feet in the ground, desperately trying to slow him down.

I lowered my glaive so that the pike faced forward at the last second and the ram crashed into it chest first.

CRITICAL STRIKE

11 dmg dealt.

Bleed dmg added 1 per second.

Suddenly Monami was there with the sword in her right hand and her dagger in her left slashing and stabbing as much as she could.

8 EXP.

"That was *insane!*" I hooted. The others smiled and sat down, seeming a little more drained from the brief encounter. I tried to check and see if I was going to recover naturally, but it seemed slow at best, which was odd for a game like this.

I glanced over my notifications and looked at that last bit of damage. I wasn't told specifically about it, but I felt like my Strength or Skill were taken into mind with damage calculations, so I did more damage than the weapon was capable of doing as a base. I sat with the others and wondered at that while waiting to see if my health would regen.

Sundar made a series of grunts and motions with her hands and a small wooden totem with an orc face, and a plus symbol on its forehead popped into the center of us. The entire time, a blue aura had exuded from her skin. Weird.

Healed +1

Healed +1

Healed +1

I stopped paying attention to the notifications and sighed in relief. "How long does this last, Sundar?"

"About a minute or so, but it heals 1 HP per second, so it'll get us up. I'm wondering what other things I'll get." She leaned back and looked to be enjoying the warmth of the sun playing along her green skin. I noted the mark where she had been kicked on her hip, the dirtied area with a hoof print there. Her health raised as mine did, and I relaxed a bit.

"When we're up to full, let's finish the rest of these sheep off. We'll have to watch out for the rams, but it should be all right if we can limit their movement, right?" The sun was really nice today, and the light was doing wonders for the area around us. The lush fields and plains moving along with the breeze. It was magnificent.

"Let's get this over with, so we can get some new clothes." Albarth stood and brushed himself and his wanderer rags off. "These are dreadful."

"Agreed," Monami said. "We need gear. These weapons are okay for now, but it's time we got better gear."

Speaking of, I checked my glaive, and the durability had decreased by one. Considering the use I'd gotten from it, I could see the necessity of repairs after our time here was finished.

We collected ourselves and started the process again. The good news was that each sheep we killed netted us another pelt each. Also, a new ram spawned after every two sheep were killed. It took a little more than an hour, but we had a system down, and it was safer. Though having to wait for respawns for the sheep and chasing off other players was annoying. They had started to come our way, but Sundar cut an intimidating figure, and after the first one tried and almost got socked for it, the others kept away.

On the initial pass, or in this case charge, Sundar would gain control of the head, then the rest of us went at the beast as hard as we could. It wasn't hard since I took the majority of the damage, but she healed us where we needed it. Another cool part was that a couple of them dropped ram pelts, and it looked like they were a little better quality than that of the sheep. We put those into our inventories. We killed an even sixteen sheep and eight rams. A good haul. Sixty-four experience from the sheep, and then sixty-four from the rams, so an even one hundred and twenty-eight total.

Boom. Level three, just like that.

"You guys want to level out here in the wild or wait until we're back in the city?" Monami looked longingly at the notification but glanced at us.

"Better to be safe where we may be able to find answers to any questions we may have." Sundar sighed knowingly. We were an impatient bunch. Fighting the urge to at least peek at it was so hard, and I would have rather taken a shot to the groin by a ram than wait too much longer. I could tell the others were itching for it, too, but we had better discipline than that.

With that, we began to evaluate our tiny amount of gear. Their weapons were okay, the sword I gave Monami breaking at the hilt this time in a ram's throat.

My weapon though was battered and on its last legs at 3 durability. I had miscalculated a slash and struck a ram on the head and cracked the shaft.

It still worked, but I could feel the shift in the weapon that wasn't pleasant and threw off the balance.

I put the weapon into my inventory, and we were on our way back to the city under the noon-day sun. The clouds above us passing lazily by covering the sun in spots here and there, lending an even more pronounced thought about the amount of work and attention to detail the designers had put into this game.

More than once, I had wondered if my withholding points for the sake of later use had made me subpar as a tank, and I contemplated spending them but held off. If only just barely.

"Any specific kinds of builds you guys had in mind?" Monami asked lightly enough that I could barely hear her. We were passing through some groups now, and she likely didn't want to have anyone listening in.

"I think we should probably discuss that either when we aren't in-game, or when we actually take a look at the skill trees," I advised as we entered the gates to the city. They were lightly guarded, the armored city guards a mismatched couple with likely what weapons the armory would provide and whatever armor they could afford.

"Skill trees?" Albarth grabbed my shoulder and turned me so that I could look at him. "Where did you learn this? Have you been peeking? And why the secrecy?"

I snorted me? Peek? Nah. "I had a conversation with Felix, the guy who trained me about it. He mentioned it, though he wasn't entirely certain how it worked." I glanced around at the plains around us with all of the other noobs running around in easy earshot and lowered my voice. "As for discussing it secretively, well, it just seems weird that we let other people around here know our builds. What if someone wants to bogart our quests or tries to start PKing us? Plus, what if some of our subscribers are here? Do we want to ruin the surprise?"

"Is that what took you so long?" Sundar raised an eyebrow. My explanation of the need for privacy seemingly ignored.

"Look, you all had things to help you fight those rats and whatnot, actual magic. I had to get up close and personal. That's not like me, and you know that. It took me a while, and I barely survived." I was a little angry, but these guys knew me better than anyone.

"Newb." Monami shoved me, and we started walking again. "I will admit, I hadn't really spoken to any of the NPCs when we came here other than what was needed."

"You? The story queen?" Albarth looked aghast with his mouth open and a hand to his chest in shock.

"I wanted to hurry and get to you guys." She pouted a little, her feline features lending a little added emotion to the look somehow.

"Lot of good that did any of us." Sundar chuckled. "Where we need to turn that quest in again, Al?"

He took a look at his screen and mumbled, "The Woolen Womb?"

"What an odd name." Monami laughed. "Lead the way, then."

"Is there a map?" I thought about it, and a round mini-map populated the upper right-hand corner of my vision. "Never mind. Interesting that it takes a conscious thought to bring that up. I love it."

"The green question mark icon is where we need to go to turn the quest in," Albarth explained, and I saw it on the edge of our mini-map straight ahead. "I also find it enlightening that two of the better players I've ever worked with can be so stupid."

Both Sundar and I teased him for a moment with jabs and rib pokes, but his grin and air of superiority stayed firmly in place as we exited the plains. We walked for a few minutes longer in silence after that, taking in the sights and sounds of the bustling city and commerce around us. Dwarves, halflings, animal creatures, elves, and just wild creatures. I didn't see any Kin, though, but they might not come here for whatever reason.

We eventually squeezed through the crowds and citizens into the shop called the Woolen Womb. The clothing inside was an assortment of wool and wool-adjacent materials. What they were? No clue, but they were there. And woah. There was some serious lack of color in the place. I'd have to see if there was a place to get dye.

"Welcome, welcome!" A burly figure greeted us from behind a spindle. His foot pumped without thought as his beefy fingers deftly worked the fiber through. "How can I help you today?"

My eyes adjusted to the lack of bright light and heavy shadow quickly, and I noted that the figure was an ogre. Massively built, taller even than Sundar and looked to weigh easily seven hundred pounds. His thick brow was slightly covered by a large gray bandana the same shade of his skin, and a brown leather apron adorned his chest. His meaty leg, surprisingly light as it pumped the wheel for the spindle, was covered by woolen breeches that reminded me of rough-spun sweatpants.

"We came to see about turning in your requested materials, the fifteen wild sheep pelts?" Albarth spoke for us. "As you can see, our clothing leaves *much* to be desired."

"Heh!" The ogre's deep timbre reached our ears, his smile was pleasant despite the broken, chipped, and yellowed teeth in his mouth. "I'd say. Sounds like you've got a good sense of fashion there, sir. I can already tell that you and I will get along mighty well. I'll take those pelts from you, thank you. And we can see about getting each of you some clothes, eh?"

"You're right about that," Albarth spoke. "While we have your attention, could you perhaps tell us where to find someone who could sell us better equipment? And maybe repair what we already have?"

"Well, the repairs could be done at the smithy up the road, speak to young Alvor, tell him Codgy sent you, he'll help you out as best as he can." He took the pelts that Sundar offered him with a nod of appreciation. "I'll also let you know for free, that if you were to do him a favor, and bring him some materials like you have for me, he might be more inclined to help the lot of you more. That or create something new for you."

"Bring us better materials, and we can provide you with better gear, clothing, and equipment. Know, also, that some folk don't entirely trust that the wanderers will do as they should and will make you work for every inch you get with them, and then some. So be prepared."

That was kind advice. "Thank you, Codgy, was it?" The ogre looked at me, his smile never leaving his face.

"Name's actually Codilgoren, but the young smith's apprentice calls me Codgy, partly because he thinks me old, partly because I lecture him a lot. Codger like, I suppose. You can all call me Codgy, as well." Sundar laughed, the sound eventually making her snort. "Find that amusing, do you?"

"Infinitely." She beamed at him. "I'm the eldest of the four of us, and they make sure I never live it down. Glad to finally find another soul in a similar situation."

The ogre clapped her on the shoulder lightly. "I like you too, though you hardly look 'old' enough to warrant that treatment." He set the wool in his arms on the counter and turned back to us. "I have some clothing available for purchase at present. What can I offer you? If you have materials, I can also work for trade or offer advice for a small fee."

"Well, how about some starting clothes, just some plain ones to get us out of these rags, and we can go from there?" Monami took over.

We purchased a set of starting clothes for five copper pieces, a copper piece being a tenth of a silver. Ten silver to a gold and so on. Five copper for a starting set of clothes wasn't bad, but we had also bargained three of the ram pelts as leverage to get him to lower the price. We dressed there just by selecting and equipping the clothes. A figure of my body popped into view in my status screen with the equipment tag highlighted when I did so. It looked like the clothes didn't prohibit me from putting armor over top of them. Awesome.

"Do you happen to have any dyes?" I asked, hopefully.

The ogre looked a little bashful for a moment. "Well, uh, no. No, I don't. I am not one for colors, actually." He saw my confusion and held out a hand as if to forestall judgment. "Ah, I—my kind—don't see a lot of colors too well. I can tell grays, and blacks, whites, and some other shades, but greens and reds and such evade me. So, I stick to colors I know. My apologies."

"No!" I blurted, panic surging through me at having possibly insulted him. "There's not a thing wrong with that! I just like a lot more color for no reason other than I like pretty things"—I blinked and realized I had probably offended him by saying his clothes weren't pretty enough, my hands went clammy as I watched the large man regard me stonily, my heart pounding—"Not that your clothes don't look good! Uh... uh... They look great! Super comfortable, by the way, did I say that? How comfortable? I'm going to shut up, Mona, help!"

Codgy eyed me worriedly before Monami took pity on us both and spoke up, "What he means to say, is that he doesn't feel like himself if he isn't expressing his love of loud, bright colors. And he wants everyone to stare at him and see the wonderful work you've done with something as simple and elegant as your starter clothing. Does that make sense, Codgy?"

He blinked. "No, but I appreciate you explaining it to me. Thank you." He turned back to me, a genuine smile in place. "And thank you, as well. I don't have any, but some of the armorers or other clothiers may sell some in the market near where you'll be going to see Alvor. It may be a bit expensive, though. Forgive me, I don't buy it, so I'm not too aware."

"That's perfectly fine!" I assured him with a nod, hands out to wave away the thought. "You've been very helpful, thank you."

"Come back again, and I'll take better care of you. My clothing does wonders!" He called as we left the area.

I had no doubts that it would, and it would be majestically colored. I loved that idea.

"Before we go and get the new gear, we need to decide on our builds, so we don't waste time, money, or points." Sundar pulled us into an alleyway and spoke as she opened her own status screen. "Talk us through each step and process, okay? No one make any concrete decisions without talking it out."

The rest of us gave her motions of agreement. The level up had been nice and all. I got another point to use for the level, which was great, but that skill tree was beautiful.

Opening it up, it had my ability at the top, Mageblood, with its fifty percent resistance to magic.

The level beneath it had two skills that were open for viewing, and the three after that were heavily blurred with nothing else visible at all. The one on the left-hand side, **Blood Thief**, and on the right, **Aether Sever**. There was also a stat increase that came with each.

Blood Thief – When you cover yourself in the blood of your foes, you have a chance (15%) of borrowing their magic (for one use) and using it to your own means.

+1 Skill and Knowledge.

Aether Sever – When you attack and injure your foe, you have a chance (15%) of cutting off the aether from the spell, injuring them with the backlash.

+1 Skill and Serenity.

Woah! So, if I took the one on the left, I'd be able to borrow magic from the things I fought. That was a start toward being able to be a mage! I'd take it, but first, to see what the others had going on for them. Though I wondered what the interest in increasing Knowledge would be like for actual magic, if I ever got it since all the abilities in our group seemed to be cool-down based.

Sundar smiled. "For me, it's Berzerker, lets me use rage to attack and defend—halves damage—but my mental stats are halved too, or the other that allows me to summon animal spirits to buff a single ally. Honestly, since I seem to be the healer—I think I should go with the spirits. It will allow me to be able to buff you all, that and the added stat boosts are nice..."

"Thanks for being a team player, Sundar," Albarth spoke softly, genuinely to her. "It's hard not to be the party's healer, but if it would be anyone, I'd like for it to be the most experienced of us."

"Aww, you know just what to say to make a lady blush." The giant orc woman teased him as she bent to look into his eyes.

"And you've ruined an otherwise wonderful gesture of trust and friendship with your lascivious ways." The elf sighed. "My two options are evolutions to my Flame Dart, the first is Bombardier, that makes the spell explode on impact and affect anything within five feet, and the other is Elegant Flame, which is a weapon buff that covers my weapon in flames for an added five percent damage bonus. I can still cast the spell as a projectile, I think, for the second. I take it all of us received some kind of stat boost attached to the ability?"

We nodded, then looked to Monami, who looked to be deeply embarrassed.

"Well?" Albarth prodded. "How about yours, kitty cat?"

"Call me that again, tree-boy and I will claw your eyes out." She growled as he just smiled, this being a typical interaction of theirs.

She really was embarrassed.

"Mine are to be used in conjunction with Allure," Monami explained, the fur of her cheeks tinting red slightly. "My options are Dance and Sing. Both are designed to make Allure more distracting."

Oh god. That was why. Mona loved to sing, but she was *terrible* at it. I would know because I let myself into her place at her mother's while she had been singing in the shower. When she had realized I was there, the thrashing she had given me had almost seen me to a hospital.

"They'd be distracted all right," I muttered before a rough, clawed grip fit snuggly around my left arm.

Mona dragged me closer to her so that I looked her directly in the eyes, her fiery red hair covering her face as she growled low. "Say another damned word, Seth—I dare you."

"I'm good." I smiled at her.

Albarth chuckled. "Elegant Flame. I think I make more of a skill type build then and focus on mobility and intellect so I can DPS that way. Any objections?"

The rest of us shook our heads. Being light on his feet would be well within Al's wheelhouse after years of running around, avoiding being hit as a healer before this.

"I'm going to take Dance." Monami growled, her hand still around my arm. "I can incorporate that into a fighting style, I think. So, I'll be a Presence and Skill build. It goes without saying that we still bring our health up where we can, but I saw that there are skill paths that let us take more stat points too. if you focus on your choice you can make them out."

"And you, Kyvir?" Albarth raised a brow at me.

"I have Aether Sever, it gives me a chance to cut a caster's connection to Aether to prevent a spell and injuring them if I hit them. Then I have Blood Thief that allows me a chance to steal someone's magic if I hurt them." I tried to swallow the lump in my throat, gulping nervously. "I think I'll be going with Blood Thief. What about you guys?"

"That's fair, the second one sounds like a mage killer's silencing ability." Sundar grunted, tapping her screen. "We know what I'll do—the spirits do seem cool. And I think Ky should take Blood Thief so that he can cast a little bit, as well."

"Seconded." Albarth slightly raised his hand.

Monami let go of my arm, her eyes finding mine. "If it was a reliable ability with a higher chance of proccing, I'd say sever, but it isn't." Her reasoning stated, she raised her hand as Al had.

"That's settled, then." I tried to hide the relief I felt at their decision.

If they had suggested the other tree, I would have done it so that I could fulfill my role as tank. But now I would be able to use other spells on top of my own abilities. And the possibilities with that seemed limitless with all the spells and abilities out there.

"I'll focus on Skill, Strength, and Heart, then." I looked over my actual stats and prepared to spend the rest of the points I had but stopped. "I'll add a point to Knowledge every now and again if I can, too."

"I'll focus on Strength, Serenity, and Heart so that I can help off-tank if needed, but I'm stronger by nature, it seems. Don't forget, strength adds five HP per point as well. So, there's merit there too," Sundar advised as she spent her own points.

"I would advise against that if you can, it might help you stay alive, but we may need you to actually focus on healing. We can play it by ear." Al looked at me briefly. "You should also put a couple points into knowledge if you'll be stealing spells, Ky. If you'll have them, they need to hit hard, and that's what that stat is meant to help with." Albarth was spending his own points as well.

I selected Blood Thief, and little fireworks jumped into my vision, making me gasp and laugh. The others glanced my way, their faces confused, but I just told them, "Pick your skill, and you'll see."

After a second, they were laughing too. What an absurd, delightful world this was. Amazing.

CHAPTER SEVEN

I looked over my stats and saw that I had eight points to use to adequately bump up my stats. With Blood Thief, I got an extra point to both Skill and Knowledge, which would be helpful, as it put them to eight, and six respectively. Thinking about it, I would need to improve my Skill and Heart some more. Plus, my Strength. Okay. Three each in Heart and Skill, and the final two in strength.

> *Kyvir Mageblood, Level 3, Race: Kin, HP: 145*
> *Strength: 9*
> *Skill: 11*
> *Heart: 10*
> *Knowledge: 6*
> *Serenity: 5*
> *Presence: 5*
> *Unspent Stat Points: 0*
> *EXP to next Lvl: 358 / 400*

"I like this rolling EXP thing," Mona observed to the rest of us with a grin. "I also like the little boosts in experience based on active participation in the fight. Like when I get a point more than all of you because I shanked the absolute guts out of that ram?"

I rolled my eyes at her, and Sundar snorted as Al laughed at her. She seemed to be relaxing a bit.

"It's likely the easiest way to get people to level ten. There are plenty of ways games offer that; remember that one game—oh, what was it..." Sundar blinked and held her hands in front of her as if it were right there.

"Storm Factor?" Albarth asked.

The large woman clapped her hands. "Yes! Thank you. They had rolling experience until level ten, then it went to a pay system. You get all the experience for the level, and the rest goes away. Unless you have enough to hit the next level on top of that."

"Could you imagine being most of the way to the next level, and it just *all disappeared?*" Albarth looked disgusted. "Complete game killer, if you ask me."

"Enough of all that." Monami growled, a look of consternation on her face as she bit her lip. "Let's not jinx it. What're your stats all looking like? Here, look at mine."

Monami Sunfur, Level 3, Race: Helinx, HP: 105
Strength: 7
Skill: 11
Heart: 7
Knowledge: 5
Serenity: 6
Presence: 10
Unspent Stat Points: 0
EXP to next Lvl: 360 / 400

"Looking good!" Sundar raised her eyebrows and nodded approvingly. "Here you all are."

Sundar Strongtusk, Level 3, Race: Orc, HP: 160
Strength: 10
Skill: 5
Heart: 11
Knowledge: 5
Serenity: 8
Presence: 5
Unspent Stat Points: 0
EXP to next Lvl: 350 / 400

"One hundred and sixty health!" Albarth looked at me with a sly grin. "She has you topped again. Some tank you'll be."

I rolled my eyes as he shared his stats with us.

Albarth Remell, Level 3, Race: Wood Nymph, HP: 75
Strength: 5
Skill: 13
Heart: 5
Knowledge: 9
Serenity: 9
Presence: 5
Unspent Stat Points: 0
EXP to next Lvl: 346 / 400

"Wood Nymph? Really?" Sundar guffawed.

"It came with a wonderful addition to the Skill stat and come now if you start calling me 'nympho' I *will* set you on fire." He looked dangerously close to doing so as he spoke, but Sundar just waved it away as she tried to breathe.

"Okay. So, it seems that the current goal is to get better gear and see about getting to ten where the true game content lies. Right?" I asked, checking the in-game clock against the out-of-game one. It was later afternoon now, but it was around midnight in our world.

"Yeah—sounds good to me." Monami stretched, more catlike than I would have imagined, but it did seem like something was off. "Call it a night, hit it hard tomorrow? Sundar, you gotta work?"

"Took the weekend off. Wouldn't miss this for the world." Her grin flashed her tusks, and her eyes sparkled joyously.

"Then we should reconvene tomorrow morning for you lot, and night for me." Albarth yawned before he nodded once and logged off. His avatar faded from view slowly and then was gone.

"See you two in the morning, I'll have the coffee poured by eight, in by nine?" Sundar looked hopeful. I'd seen her this excited once, and that had been a very *productive* weekend.

"Sounds great." I nodded and went through the process of logging out while she faded when Monami stopped me.

"We need to talk. I'll be over as soon as I can." Then she was gone.

That was weird. I pressed the log-out button, and the world faded around me.

You have opted to log-out, thank you for playing Mephisto's Magic Online.

Preparing for liquid evacuation in 3... 2... 1.

This may feel odd.

A suction around my nose and mouth sealed so tightly that I felt as if my soul were being sucked from my body. I opened my eyes to see the lid of the Portal closed over me and the house dark around it. I had forgotten to turn the light on. I opened the clear pane with a slight touch and tumbled out of the pod, gasping for air.

"You're okay, Seth. You're fine!" I muttered to myself once I had control of my breathing. I stood up and went to quickly shower. I knew it wouldn't take Mona long to get here, and I wanted to at least get this stuff off of me before she came.

After I was out, I heard the door open. "Seth!" Mona's familiar voice called.

"Coming out of the shower now, Mo!" I was in the middle of toweling myself dry when she came in, tears streaming down her eyes.

"What's wrong?" I forgot instantly that I'm almost completely in the buff.

"As we were meeting and talking about our classes, I got a message. It was from what could have been a throwaway account—you know like the ones that sell in-game currencies for real money?" Her voice was strained, and she sounded like she was bordering on panic.

"Yeah, what about it?"

"It said, 'Don't trust it, all is not as it seems. Grow strong quickly. D.'" Her panic seemed to subside a little when I pulled her into my arms, my towel draped over my hips as best as I could manage.

"Well, I will admit, that is weird." I blinked as I caught a whiff of something. Something floral, and it smelled fantastic. So alluring. "What's that smell?"

She looked up at me, her green, gem-like eyes partially hidden by her red hair, and it was so hard to think of anything else at that moment. Weird.

"What are you talking about?" she asked. "What smell?"

"It smells floral." I blinked, and the sensation was gone, but for an instant in the mirror, I could see the outline of pink around her. I rubbed my eyes, and it was gone.

Like the one that had been in the game. Huh. That was odd too. Maybe it was just a figment of my imagination after having spent a few hours in-game. Yeah, that was it.

"Sorry, but do you know anyone named 'D,' Mona?" I asked as I let her go, gripping my towel a little tighter.

"Not really." She wiped her eyes and stepped out into the hall so I could finish drying off. "At least not anyone who works for that game company."

"Well, then let's pay it no mind. Could just be one of the game devs messing with you." Developers in past games had been known for being insanely crazy about their games.

There had even been tell about one guy who tried to get people killed if they found bugs in his games. A rumor—but still kinda crazy.

I put on the same mesh shorts I had worn earlier and stepped out into the hall next to where Mona sat. "Come on. Let's get a bite and then go to bed. You can stay here tonight. Matter of fact, I insist. What do you wanna eat?"

"Can we go to our favorite joint?" She gave me her best, pitiful puppy dog eyes.

I sighed; it was a fifteen-minute drive just to get there, but it was twenty-four hours, so it was doable. And I was a sucker for her sad face. Always had been since we were kids.

"You driving, or am I?" I asked.

"You buy, I'll fly?" She asked, hopefully. When I nodded, she seemed to cheer up instantly.

I changed into a pair of boxers, sweats, and a bright red t-shirt that said "I like to game" on the front. I nabbed my wallet on the way out of the house and walked out to Mona's car. It was a conservative model, a twenty-thirty-something with great mileage, and it was painted a metallic blue that I loved.

Mona's driving was as stellar as always, and I only thought we were going to die when she toyed with her playlist. Finally, after the third honking car, I bellowed, "I will handle the music—you drive!"

She pouted, but I put on a song that we both liked and we sang along terribly with each other. She knew the car was a safe space for her to sing, and I loved the sing-a-longs we had.

Once we pulled into the parking lot of the dingy little dive, we parked and walked inside. The neighborhood around here had gotten a little better lately, but the owner of this restaurant would tolerate no violence in his place. No sir. I'd seen him go medieval on someone for pulling a knife in a *less than friendly* situation between two groups of people. That had been terrifying.

"Mona! Seth!" The gentleman behind the counter walked out to give us a hug. We had been coming here for years, and he felt like family. He was older, in his fifties, grayish-black hair on top of his head with a wisp of a goatee on his face. His deep brown eyes sparkled in the light of the room as he looked us over. His white skin sagging with age didn't mean he dressed any less dapper than he normally did. His purple dress jacket was starched and ironed over his black dress shirt, a matching purple tie, and his black slacks.

"How's it going, Bill?" I asked, genuinely curious. It had been months since I'd been able to drop in. I was trying to eat better and all.

"Not too bad, little Katie's off to college!" Mona gasped and smacked his arm excitedly, his friendly Brooklyn accent made me think of those old mobster movies. "Hey, watch it, kiddo, that's my burger flippin' arm!"

"What's she going to school for? Where at? How is she doing?" Mona grilled him, grossly ignoring his answers.

"Mona!" I barked at last. "Let the man speak, jeez."

She looked a little cowed, but Bill just smiled. "She's goin' to school for Synthetic Kinesiology and Advanced Robotic Synapse Sciences. She's at the community college, for now, working on her general education courses, but she's doin' fine so far as I can tell."

"That's a lofty study." I whistled, looking pointedly over at Mona, whose smile was plastered on her face. "She apply for any scholarships or grants? I know of a couple she would likely qualify for."

"She found a scholarship with the school, but she might try for one next year," he explained, and I smiled. So, I would be able to help her then, after all. Between my family's investments, academics were something my parents really loved and had multiple grants and scholarship foundations set up to help kids like Katie.

"If she needs any advice or help, send her my way!" Mona took his hand and made him agree with a nod before she would let go.

"I'll send you some links while we eat, Bill, pass them on to Katie with our love, okay?" He smiled and nodded my way.

"Two of the usual and hmm..." he looked Mona over critically before adding, "and a chocolate milkshake, large, no cherry with extra whip for the sad young lady."

"How does he *do* that?" she whispered as Bill returned to his work.

"He's been doing it since before we were a twinkle in our fathers' eyes?" I raised an eyebrow. "He's literally been telling us that for years."

"Yeah, yeah." She waved it away as she moved into the interior of the dining area. It reminded me of something out of a sixty's diner movie with all the reds and whites. Very retro, but all the bells and whistles of the modern age were well in place. Televisions played in each of the booths with the news, late night TV, or some kind of heinous new movie playing. Give me the classics, thanks.

"What happened with you in the training area?" I asked as we waited for the food to come out.

"Nothing really. I went in, lured them out with my ability, and while they were distracted, got critical strikes until they were dead. Pretty much the same thing for the Rat King. How about you?"

I went into more detail as I described the fight to her. How much different it had been than her own. It was a little messed up that I had to deal with the severe disparity in our abilities, but that was okay. Maybe I would end up seeing returns sooner rather than later? Who knew?

But what really caught my eye was the news. "Turn that up, would you?"

Mona reached over and tapped the volume button as the last scene that had flashed across the screen ended, the anchor's voice growing steadily louder so we could hear her say "...next story comes concerning a man in Ohio, who reported a robber of some kind entering his home who had glowing red eyes and seemed to have been, 'cloaked in darkness.' The relevance of this we are uncertain of, but there was a hospital fire in the area only a mile away where security camera footage depicted a figure moving through the area with some sort of hidden flame thrower."

The b-roll showed exactly that, cutting to people screaming and calling out for help before going to black.

"The number of victims before authorities were able to stop the man had reached just under thirty, with more injured. The subject has been apprehended and is currently in custody for questioning and public safety." The anchor shuffled her papers and cleared her throat. "We've been told that, at this time, the department refused any and all questions until the investigation has concluded. Up next on Channel Seven news: is your water the cleanest? When we ret..."

Mona turned the volume down until it wasn't as loud anymore. "Well. What a nut job."

"Yeah, who attacks and burns a hospital?" I couldn't help the weight of anger and sorrow I felt for the victims and those re-hospitalized because of that monster. "That cloaked in shadow and red eyes part seems a bit of a stretch for bad video quality, though. If that was true people would be screaming that it's even more of a sign of the 'end of days' and other such crap."

"So, I take it you saw all that religious speak online as well?" I nodded, and Mona smiled. "Yeah. That made me laugh, too. It's just a game. All it affects is the mind and only in-game. It's not the end of the world."

The doorbell rang, and a younger guy in a hoodie swaggered in and approached the counter where Bill waited patiently.

"You getting a bad feeling from this guy?" I muttered to Mona. She nodded back, her eyes on the counter.

"Hey Chuckles, how you been?" Bill greeted the kid the same as he had us, but his left hand dropped to his waist.

"Not bad Bill, you still holding out on the hope this place is going to weather the times?" Hoodie's voice sounded off somehow. More sinister. "How about you let me take over and keep this place safe for you, eh? I'm cheap for now, but uh, something tells me that I'll be a hot commodity soon enough. You don't wanna get burned, do you?"

As I watched, a red trickle of something leaked from him, just the barest hint before it was gone.

I didn't dare say anything, not right now. Not with the double-barrel shotgun aimed directly at the kid's head.

"Listen, kid, I got a lot of young punks who think that ol' Billy needs new blood to keep the ruffians out and his money safe." He settled his finger squarely on the trigger of the weapon. "Haven't needed anybody since you were a twinkle in your daddy's eyes, kid. Not startin' now. You leave me and mine to me, and you can leave with yours on your shoulders. Sound good?"

The kid slowly raised his hands. "You'll regret this."

Bill shook his head while the kid backed away slowly. "Like your dad regrets not pullin' out, kid? Scram."

Hoodie turned and walked out of the restaurant as Bill lowered the shotgun. He didn't put it down completely, just lowered it as he glowered after the figure moving off into the night.

He turned his gaze to us and nodded once before returning to what he was doing. Mona and I just sat there in stunned silence. Do I tell her about the aura I had seen? Would she believe me? It was so weird.

Bill brought us our orders, setting a tray in front of us both. "This one's on me, you two"—he wagged a finger in my face before I could protest—"I don't like for my customers to see that kind of behavior outta me. Isn't business-like, and I left it all behind years ago. The normal stooges don't come by until later in the mornin', so I wasn't expectin' to have to deal with this crap until later. Come see me before you leave, I'm walkin' you to your car."

The way he spoke brooked no argument, and we both nodded to him quietly. "You two are good kids. Why can't everybody be like you two and little Katie, huh?"

Bill ruffled my mop of hair and winked at Mona before going back to the front of the place to help with the kitchen.

We tucked into the food in front of us despite the events that had transpired. We were hungry and in dire need of something familiar to help us cope with the news and the change. Personally, the fact that I saw these things even outside the game was highly unsettling, and if it hadn't been for the fact that she had gotten that weird message, I'd have told her.

And poor Mona. I glanced up in time to see her dip a pair of golden-brown fries into her milkshake before popping them into her mouth with a groan of joy.

I picked up my burger, perfectly cooked with crisp lettuce, cool tomato, bacon, pickles, mayo, ketchup, and mustard on a pretzel bun that had been toasted to perfection. I had to swallow the drool in my mouth as I opened my jaws as far as I could to get as much of the greasy goodness in my body as I could. Oh. Oh yeah, that's it.

Turkey burgers had *nothing* on this.

We ate in near silence for almost a full twenty minutes before Mona belched loudly and waggled her eyebrows at me. Bill clapped and pointed at her. "Good end to the night, right there! That's how we know it's good food."

Mona held her hands up in victory as the guys in the back poked their heads out and joined in the clapping. I snatched her milkshake while she was distracted and took a long pull on it. She went for my head with her fist, but I ducked out of the way with a laugh, and she shook her fist at me.

"You keep nabbing her shake like that, and she'll do worse to you than I ever could, Seth." Bill beamed at us. "You both ready?"

She and I nodded and brought the plates back up before the busboy could get to the table. I passed him the stuff, and he held up a folded bill in confusion. I winked at him, and he grinned. Twenty bucks, not to do much? I'm sure anyone would be happy about that.

True to his word, Bill grabbed his shotgun and marched us outside to Mona's car, before we left, he tapped the roof. "You both be careful out there, I got my guys comin' in tellin' me about some freaks out there doin' weird things in the last few hours. And both of you mind them games you play, okay? I know you like 'em, but there's more to life out there."

Mona leaned up and gave the older man a peck on the cheek. "Give our best to Molly and Katie, will you?"

He nodded, and I tapped my phone. "I sent you some of those links, have Katie look into it and if she needs any guidance or help, give her my number."

Bill raised an eyebrow threateningly. "You tryin' to hit on my granddaughter, boy?"

I guffawed, and he winked before backing away with a wave. After that, we were on our way back to my place.

"That's exciting about Katie," I observed to Mona as she eyed the road.

"It is!" She gushed. "I can't believe she's going to school for what I did. I'd probably be able to get her a recommendation letter if she wanted."

"That would likely work out well." I nodded and added, "You ever think about getting back into game design?"

She sighed, likely knowing this question was coming. "Seth, you know I love what I do."

She wasn't lying. "But it's not your first love. And I know how much you wanted to create things like your d—"

"Don't," she whispered softly. "Just don't."

I nodded and quieted myself. She had been amazing when we were kids. She would sit with her dad for hours and help him create these fantastic places, realms, and creatures so fantastic that all I could do is fake understanding because what she would describe was too wild to believe.

We rode in silence for a bit, then it seemed to be too much for her, and she turned the radio on. A childhood favorite song played as a single tear ran down her cheek.

My heart broke for her all over again, and when we pulled into my driveway, I had to break the silence, "I'm here for you, Mo."

She nodded once, then we headed inside to get ready for bed. She needed a shower, and I didn't blame her at all. It took her a little while, and I waited in the living room, reading a book on events that had taken place early in the century. Bad things, but they were the past for a reason. Things were better now, though, and that was all that mattered.

We had been able to forestall any sort of worsening global warming by sending a series of satellites into space that created a barrier between the worsening conditions in our atmosphere and us. I wasn't any kind of expert, but I thought it was to help recondition some of the ozone layer and to help filter some of the carbon dioxide emissions.

As I read over the book, I realized why I had put it down, and closed it. It was a lot of crap I didn't understand, even though we had managed to stave off any further natural disasters, it had really only been a Band-Aid on an already gaping hole.

The shower stopped, and a couple minutes later, Mona came out wearing a pair of my fuzzy PJs and a t-shirt I had outgrown some time ago but kept in case she needed something to wear. I smiled at her as she motioned toward my room, got up, and turned the lights out in the living room.

I walked just behind her as she stepped into my room, and when I went to get the roll-out bed from under my bed, she stopped me.

"You know, what you said in the car was pretty out of nowhere, and with everything going on..." she took a steadying breath, her eyes closed tightly. "I don't want to sleep alone tonight."

"It wasn't out of nowhere, Mo, it was out of concern." She opened her eyes in a pleading manner, the same slight pink aura flickering around her again with the same floral scent that was just so enticing. "But if it's just for tonight, I suppose. You really don't smell that?"

She shook her head as she smiled and climbed onto the bed; it was a queen, so there was room for both of us. The sheets and bedspread were nice, smooth, and cool, but retained heat well. Once she was comfortable and facing the wall I climbed in after her, and laid down, my back to her like we would when we were kids.

"Seth?" She spoke softly, her voice a little tired.

"Yeah, Mo?"

She was quiet a second, then spoke again, "I love you; you know that?"

I chuckled. "What's not to love?"

She was quiet again, then the bed shook a bit, and her face came over my shoulder. "You can be such an ass, you know that?"

I blinked at her innocently "But, Mona, that's part of my charm."

She laughed and smacked my arm and laid down pressed against my back.

What was I seeing? There's no way the game was following me out into life, right? And why would I just let her walk all over me like that? Well, she was my best friend, and we used to sleep like this all the time. As comforting as it was, my heart still raced oddly. What was going on with me? Also, we had known each other since before we could walk, this wasn't that big of a deal!

I tried to relax but couldn't until her breathing steadied, and she started to snore. Then, the arm around my stomach didn't seem quite so off putting or confining. It was just Mona. I did my best to ignore the orbiting questions on my mind and set my alarm for eight, then nodded off.

CHAPTER EIGHT

"Come on, Seth." Mona pounced on my chest a second before the blaring robotic good mornings blasted from the alarm to my left. She threw back the curtains, and I groaned noisily.

I had slept all right, but waking up just before the alarm was just *torture*. When had she gotten out of bed? I blinked some of the sleep out of my gaze, her chipper grin irking me slightly. I must have slept through that because I was so used to it as a kid that my body must have reached a more settled state than normal. Or maybe I was sick?

"I made breakfast," Mona began but didn't even finish the sentence before I bumped her off my lap and unceremoniously onto the bed next to me and pressed her out of the way. "Hey!"

"If you burned my kitchen down, I swear to you, Mona!" I growled before my feet even hit the floor, worried that finishing the sentence would take too much time. I could hear her footfalls behind mine and her loud complaints following me out of the room and found my kitchen and dining area almost unscathed.

Other than the plates on the counter where I liked to eat, it was almost normal.

I turned to her with a suspicious look on my face, my eyes narrowed at her clearly disgruntled face. "I've been practicing with mom, and she's been showing me things."

"Emma showed you all this?" I raised an eyebrow and jerked my thumb at the toast, scrambled eggs with a little ketchup on top the way I usually had it. There was some coffee with cream and sugar off to the side, and then some cut strawberries on a plate to round it off.

"I figured since it was like old times last night when we had been kids, I'd make you breakfast like I used to, and we could try to plan out today's gaming session." She shrugged and sat down first with me joining her.

"Mo, you tried to cook eggs and almost burnt a hole in the skillet." She rolled her eyes and crossed her arms in front of her, so I continued, "You literally threw a brand new, still-burning toaster into the trash compactor by the sink. You almost burnt down the house, Mo!"

"Can we just forget that happened?" She threw her hands up into the air and shouted before sitting and patting the stool next to her. "That was twenty twenty-five, and I was stressing out about graduating with honors so that I could get into the college I wanted with a scholarship!"

I eyed her before I took my fork up as if it were a sword and poked the eggs gently, uncertainly, as they seemed to have a light and fluffy consistency. I cut some away, without the ketchup to try it out of respect, and slipped the morsel into my mouth.

It was decent, and that was saying something. Mona had tried cooking before, and I had thought she was never going to be able to learn the art of it. Emma was a fantastic cook, so her teaching Mona had been a blessing that almost made me change my mind.

We ate a few bites, then discussion on the day took way with her beginning, "I think before we look for any sort of weapons and armor we can buy, we should consult the quest board, but also look for quests from the craftsmen and citizenry."

I nodded, then asked what had been bothering me since the day before, "Did they seem real to you?"

"Well it's only one of the largest titles to come out and the most advanced that we've seen to date, of course, the AI is going to be able to make the integration for players seem that much more realistic." Mona rolled her eyes and popped a strawberry into her mouth. "Don't you remember that one NPC who was in that game... oh, what was it called? The one with the single-player story that you loved, but the character's love interest seemed so real to you that you swore she was your girlfriend and that you'd get married?"

My cheeks were molten as I growled at her and said, "I was twelve!"

"Exactly!" She flicked my forehead and rolled her eyes as if she were talking to a crazy person. Maybe she was. "There are probably multiple AI chains working simultaneously to give the best experience they can. I mean, it's not their fault you, and other people, have difficulty telling game from life. Jeez."

"Yeah, but how many artificial intelligence systems do you think it takes to make the sights and sounds *that* realistic, Mona?" I bit into the almost-too-crunchy toast and added more butter to the piece. "How many other AI do you know of that will have some random non-player character admit to being colorblind—in a world where magic is prevalent, no less!"

She wagged a finger. "That was a truly nice touch there."

"All I'm saying is that based on what I heard, and what Codgy told us, the people in that city think we're brutes and monsters." She frowned at me over her piece of toast with my favorite triple-berry jam generously slathered on, biting it while I spoke. "If we can get them to trust us, we may unlock quest chains."

"Okay, so we approach the people in the city differently." She saw I was about to interrupt and stopped me with a glance. "And we go out of our way to be kind and helpful—I know."

She knew me too well. I glanced over at the oven clock, it read 08:06 in large, red-block numerals. "If you're planning to log in with us, you should head home in a couple minutes. Speaking of, I wonder how logging in will work."

"I live, like, a three-minute drive away from here, Seth." She rolled her eyes again. "And it'll probably be okay, we're in the city, right? Though us popping up randomly may startle a person or two."

"I know that, but Ma does have a tendency to ask questions about our nights together." I sipped the coffee, the earthy bouquet of it refreshing as the caffeine soothed my soul.

Emma and my folks always used to brazenly ask when Mona and I were going to tie the knot. Weird thing to ask an awkward thirteen-year-old couple of kids whose hormones had begun to rage and make things weird. My folks had slowly learned that I was their stubborn child and that I would know who I wanted to be with when I knew. Emma? Emma still held out hope, and that was only because her husband and she had known each other since grade school, too.

Which was why it had been such a blow when he had run off.

As I watched Mona move through the softly filtered morning light in the kitchen windows, her flaming red hair flowing behind her as she swayed to a song that only she could hear and felt like this was enough. I loved her. In my own way, and that was enough—right?

She turned her gaze on me, the soft amber glow of the light in the window, making her green eyes glow a moment just right. She smiled, and for the barest second, I could swear I saw the pink aura once more, and my hand seemed fumbled for my fork, knocking my mug of coffee over.

"Careful, Seth!" She called, and I snapped out of whatever had distracted me from my surroundings. She rushed forward with a hand towel as I blinked at her, realization dawning on me and making me blush even as the more-than warm liquid soiled my PJ bottoms.

She went to towel me off, and I howled. "Nope! I got it." I stood, more of my wasted coffee dribbling onto the floor and snatched the towel from her grasp and covered myself. "I'll go change, you wanna grab the worst of that? Be right back."

I sprinted back to my room and threw the soiled clothing into the hamper and changed into some boxers and put a pair of sweatpants on.

What the bloody he—why is this happening? I was panicking. I knew I was panicking. But this was the third time I had seen that aura about her and that guy last night? Something weird was going on, but I couldn't quite put my finger on it.

I took a few steadying breaths before I marched back out to find Mona bent down to clean up the coffee with some paper towels, and I had to look anywhere else.

"You okay?" She glanced back and looked at me oddly, then sighed. "I knew it."

"What?" I was close to hyperventilating.

"You just want me to leave so you can hop in early, is that it?" She gave me a knowing look and the perfect alibi.

I did my best to look pathetically coy as I said, "Me? Noooo... why would I wanna do that with one of the best games ever?"

She snorted, then openly laughed, her light voice sounded like music, and I wanted to bang my head on a wall. *What the hell is going on with me?!*

"Okay, I'll take the hint, and we can hop on before the others do and try to run a little groundwork, okay?" She stood and threw the trash into the bin before waving to the plates. "I grabbed the coffee, and cooked so..."

"I'll clean up. No worries." I waved her out of the kitchen, and she skipped past me toward the bedroom with a laugh that made me grin stupidly. It took all I had not to turn and watch her like all the guys in school had. I took another breath, cleaning up and putting the dishes into the dishwasher swiftly with a practiced hand.

I wiped down the counter, then the stove, and turned to find Mona watching me with a soft smile. "What?"

Her dimples flashed as she spoke, "Just thinking about what a good live-in husband you'll make someday."

"Hey—I'm the trophy husband type." I snorted indignantly; my discomfort almost forgotten as I crossed the distance between us. "I may not be able to do a whole lot without my state-of-the-art kitchen, but I know these instruments, and I play them well. Plus, with my personality and sense of style, anyone would be lucky to have me."

She adopted an indulgent uh-huh look and muttered, "Yes, you will, you blessed little thing. All these brand-new appliances do have you a little spoiled, where would you be without them?"

Her index finger bopped my nose, and I growled at her before sweeping her into a hug with a chuckle, she stiffened a bit, but relaxed and hugged me back. "Probably have to marry some rich lady to take care of me, so I don't ruin anything or die of starvation? Drive safe, and I'll see you on the other side."

She wrapped her arms around me and gave me a gentle kiss on the cheek, making my whole body freeze instantly. She stared at me a moment longer before she nodded and headed out of the house, the door locking behind her.

I sighed, more aware of where her lips had been than I had ever been in my life but decided that it was time to try and put it behind me. It was a fluke. It had to be.

Better to get some gaming done.

***

Welcome back, wanderer.

The portal greeted me as I sat naked inside, and the launch sequence of the game went through the same process. It hadn't been as scary as it had the night before, and that was good.

I blinked and opened my eyes to the same alley where we had logged out the day before, my hands found my horns and I smiled, that was nice. I looked down at my tanned skin and sharp nails. It would take getting used to, but this body, even the second time using it, felt like my own body.

I left the alley, glad that I hadn't spawned on top of some poor person walking through, or scaring someone else, and wandered into Codgy's shop. It was nearing midday, and it looked like he was still doing what he had been doing when last we had met. I could have waited for Mona, but the thought just made me feel all awkward, and I had to do something as just me to get back to myself. As I should be.

"Hey there, Codgy!" I called as I walked into the shop.

He looked up at me and squinted. "Mr. Kyvir, good day. How are you today?"

I motioned to the clothes I wore thanks to him. "Feeling much more presentable, my friend. I wanted to ask for some clarification and some forgiveness if I could."

He smiled, some of his crooked teeth flashing in his ogre mouth. "Clarification? Certainly. Forgiveness? There's nothing to forgive, Mr. Kyvir. You had a request I couldn't fill, so I was at fault, knowingly or not."

"Thank you again for that, and I really did mean no disrespect." He smiled and waved the thought away. "The clarification was for where to go, I know you had said to look for Alvor, but I was wondering if you could point us in the direction of the place?"

"Well, you walk outside here." Codgy stood up and walked me outside, then pointed north, a side street about fifteen-feet away where some folks walked together chatting. "Follow that road there, and you'll hear the forges, that leads to the Fire Square."

"Are there other squares?" It was hard to hide my curiosity. "I know about the Wave Square already. I met the mermaid there too, her name's Trickle."

A look of respect passed over the weaver's face. "You met one of the guardians?"

"Well yeah, she seemed really nice." I frowned, craning my neck to look up at him.

"They don't make their presence known to many people." He rubbed his chin, then shrugged. "You wanderers are a special lot, after all. Yes, there are four squares, one for each of the prime elements. There's fire, water, earth, and wind that we have here in the city. Then within those four sections are corresponding types of magics that break down and fall within them. Metal for earth, light for fire, lightning for wind—so on and so forth. There really are different kinds of magic out there, sometimes the magic a person can use manifests in two of the larger elements with one form. But, regardless, those who work the forges deal and craft in the Fire Square."

I lifted two coppers out of my coin inventory, and he shook his head. "You'll pay for this information a different way, if you're amenable?" I nodded at him quietly, and he continued. "I take great pride in my work, but you brought up a valid point with your request yesterday, and I feel I should make a change. I don't have an eye for colors, mind, but it seems that you do. If you will find a dye maker for me, I would broker a deal with them to supply me with different base colors to sell here with my wares."

I thought for a moment, *only base colors? There were so many different shades to be had, I was sure of it... why... ah-ha!*

"You mean to send the customers with specific color requests to the dye maker directly so that they can profit from the endorsement of your sales." I smiled at him, thinking I had cracked it.

"Well, no." His cheeks reddened slightly. "I had thought that they would be the cheapest and most easily made. However, if that is the deal you wish to propose, then by all means, please."

Optional Quest Received – Codgy would like you to broker a deal with a dye maker for reasonably priced dyes to sell at his establishment. The more favorable the deal is for him, the better the reward. Failure: Codgy won't sell dyes, and prices may be a bit steeper for you and your party.

Do you accept? Yes / No?

"We, my friends and I, would be happy to help you out, Codgy!" I reached out and clasped his hulking hand with mine as I accepted the quest.

"Excellent." He grinned down and patted my shoulder. "If you don't mind, I have a bit more work to do before I take my lunch. As soon as you're done, let me know."

I nodded and left him to his work before I started on my way toward the Fire Square. The quest to find a dye vendor or maker for him hadn't given me an area, so I figured I could ask around or explore later, but first? Time to get gear and weapons taken care of.

The buildings along the way took on a subtle orange hue to the materials that was fascinating, then I heard hammering. I followed the sound as if I were blindfolded, difficult with all the sights around me, but I managed and finally found one of the forges.

Forges in a lot of games these days were more the "hear and don't see type," and by that, I meant that you heard the sound of hammering but never actually saw someone doing it. Right now? I saw four men gathered around a large anvil working a single piece.

One man held the item with two sets of long tongs while two of the others hammered the metal into shape. The last, an older, grizzled man, supervised the hammering, pointing energetically to certain spots on the metal for the others to hammer.

"Heat!" The senior smith bellowed, and the man holding the tongs stood and rushed the item to the forge. It was a long brazier with a hood over the top that collected the smoke and fumes and took it up through the roof so that the open area around the forge stayed clear.

"Once more in 7 seconds!" The man barked as the others rolled shoulders, stretched their backs, and sweat drenched their faces. "Alvor, at the ready... now!"

The man with the tongs, Alvor, grasped the weapon and pulled it out with one smooth motion the cherry-red metal with the other set of tongs. He set it onto the anvil, and the others began to beat the metal once more. This time the master, because he had to be the master to be in charge of this whole thing, ordered the weapon to be twisted, turned, and pulled as the strikes landed where they would.

When the weapon seemed to have been beaten enough, the master barked, "Heat!"

The apprentice smith shoved the metal into the flames once more, the metal slowly changing color again. The master smith eyed the process. "Ready now, Alvor... Quench!"

Alvor took the weapon over to a long trough and dunked it into the reddish-brown liquid, a small flame bursting from where it touched, making me gasp.

He turned toward me, his face easy on the eyes, and bright blue eyes friendly as he smiled. "Hello friend, how can I help you?"

"Hey, Codgy sent me and my friends your way for some equipment." I blinked, and he grinned wider.

"The ol' weaving ogre sent you to see me?" He seemed disbelieving but took another gander at my clothes then nodded. "Well, since you're wearing his weave, I reckon he likely did. My name's Alvor, but you likely knew that, what can I do for you, friend?"

I held my hand out, and he grasped it gently. "I'm Kyvir, and I was wondering if you knew of a simple, cheap way to fix some gear, and how we might be able to acquire some more?"

"I know several ways, sir, but ain't one of 'em easy." He scratched his head and peered back at his master. "Master Ori! Did you still need me to go and fetch that ore for you from the West Mine?"

The older man lumbered over; his muscled bulk plainly visible now that he didn't have three other large men in front of him. His body was a solid slab of muscle, though a little worn with age. His long, hook-shaped nose lowered as he eyed me, then shook his head. "Not the type for smithin' sorry."

I blinked, then Alvor held a hand out. "No Master Ori, I didn't think so either, but did we still need that delivery from the mines?"

The older man blinked. "We do, do you think yourself ready to go and collect it?"

"No, sir, but if I had someone with me when I go, maybe they scratch our back, we scratch theirs?" Alvor suggested, then to sweeten the deal. "Seems like ol' Codgy has taken enough of a shine as to send them to the best smith in the city."

"Flattery like that don't work here, boy." Master Ori growled as he pointed a finger in his apprentice's face, then smiled. "But we pay back our favors."

He looked over at me and held out a hand. "Master smith Ori Loriander, and if you'll help my apprentice here with this delivery run, I'll be more than happy to assist you where we can. Now, he's only just started out, but he's quick with his wit and picks things up swift-like. If you need repairs, he will do them for a pittance over what the other smiths here would charge, and this is because he needs the training. After this task is done, mind you."

I nodded, clearly, he was a discerning man, but I had to offer a rebuttal, "I would happily offer my party's aid; however, our weapons are of low quality and flagging durability. If I were to agree to assist you now and come back with my party, could we perhaps take on repairs to our gear first, then take the task on?"

Ori thumped Alvor on the shoulder. "This is haggling and fine haggling at that. Notice how he offers you assistance in trade, but mentions not paying for the repairs? If I were to leave this to you, how would you counteroffer?"

"I wouldn't." Alvor shrugged, and Ori patiently waited for an explanation. "If I were to need to go on my own, I would be risking my life, whereas if I were to go with one of the other, stronger smiths, it would eat into our productivity. If a repair can be done swiftly in return for aid in a matter as important as this, then my time learning the craft by doing so is both well spent and secures us a guard. Likely an exclusive business partner, as well."

"Excellent." Master Ori nodded, then looked back to the other smiths who nodded knowingly. "Offer the man this quest then and see how you can repair his weapon. You have my blessing, and—" Ori eyed me for a second, reached under the counter they stood behind and pulled out a rusted pickaxe. "Fix this for him too. Looks strong enough to swing a pick, and if they can bring us materials from time to time, I'll sell it to him cheaply."

I grinned at the older man who winked at me, then nodded, and shuffled back off to talk to another smith.

"Well, sound like a good deal to you, Kyvir?" Alvor held his hands out and a notification popped up in front of me.

Optional Quest Received – Assist Alvor in collecting the material delivery from the West Mine. Your duties would be to protect him and ensure that he and the delivery return safely to the city. Reward: Improved standing with Ori's Forge, cheaper goods, and minimal cost repairs for weapons.

Do you accept? Yes / No?

I accepted his offer, then held my hand out to him to shake on it. "Why the need of the guard?"

"The creatures out there on past the western portion of the city are a little more combative than the sheep and rams that you might be used to, and I'm just a simple smith. They'll kill me sure as I stand here if I'm alone." He shrugged and looked back to his master. "They're all strong enough to fight, but I'm not quite there yet."

Seemed simple enough, escort missions were typically annoying and tedious, but they could pay off well. This was one of those times, I reckoned.

"Let's see this weapon, and I'll see if I can repair it." He tapped the counter with a smile, and I pulled out my glaive.

"A glaive user?" His eyes widened a little. "It's a good weapon; seems here that the majority of your durability took the largest hit to the haft. Luckily, we have just the thing."

He reached under the counter and pulled a large sack that looked like a grain sack from most games and reached inside. He took out a little bit of the powder from inside, sprinkled it over the haft, then held it together. I watched with unabashed fascination as the splintered section of wood melded back together as if it were new once the light green powder hit it.

"Repair powder does wonders." Alvor picked the weapon up and checked the balance and looked over the metal portion. "I'll file these kinks out of the edge here, then hone it, and that should be it."

He took the weapon to a stone shaped like a wheel and pumping his feet on a set of pedals that started it spinning. He held the blade to it with a practiced hand, then sparks flew, and he swayed it back and forth.

—I'm online, where are you?— Mona's whispered message made me jump.

I opened my mini-map, enlarging it, and checked to see if some of the functions of other games in the past worked here. I found the arrow for where I was standing and tapped it with my finger. A small drop-down menu opened up.

Log location – bookmark this location for further use.

Share location – share this location with a friend, or with a party member.

Bar location – set a block on this location for your party.

Why would anyone want to bar a location? I shared my location with Mona since we were still in our party and then toggled through a few more things, chief among them being my friends' list. I immediately sent a friend request to Mona, and she accepted it. Interesting that our party hadn't disbanded. Another nice facet to the game.

I tried to converse with Alvor, but he seemed engrossed in his work, so asking about the powder was a no go for the time being.

I waited ten minutes or so while she walked towards my location, and Alvor worked on sharpening my glaive. It took her about five minutes to find me in the square, so I had to call out to her, but when she arrived, she smiled and waved happily. It was all I could do not to try and hide my face at everything I had been feeling earlier and how I had reacted to her.

"So, Al and Sundar will be here soon." She glanced over in time to see Alvor walk over with my glaive. "Oh, we found someone to repair our weapons?"

"For a price," I amended as I shared the quest with her.

"That's understandable." She frowned, then looked to Alvor. "What level are the creatures near the West Mines?"

Alvor seemed to think it over for a moment, then shrugged. "I think in the neighborhood of five to six? The forest leading up to it is fairly calm, so it won't be too much of a problem."

"So, at worst, we're going to be out of our depth by a hundred percent—we've handled worse odds in the past." Mona grinned sardonically, but Alvor seemed to take a shine to her for it.

"Miss, what kind of weapon do you use?" Mona held out her dagger to him, and he looked it over. "Well, if you're to be that outmatched, may as well have it repaired and maybe an additional one?"

I found the offer... vexing, but free gear was free gear, and Mona seemed to be interested as she batted her eyes dazzlingly, and her pink aura flarer to life.

As the apprentice smith wandered away happily, I stepped closer to her. "Did you just use Allure on him?"

She leaned closer, the scent of her fur the same flowery and musky scent I'd caught at my place, somehow, as she blinked over at me. My heart pounded briefly as she explained, "I wanted to see if there was a non-combat use for it. It seems like there is."

"That's evil, and I love it." I couldn't not appreciate any edge we could gain, even if it made me a little uncomfortable for some weird reason.

I was going to have to get over this.

—*We're here!*— Sundar whispered violently into our ears, I could almost see Albarth sighing as she did so.

I taught Mona how to send our location, and she had the same question I did about barring a place, but neither of us had a clue why anyone would want to do that.

The others made it to us swiftly, Sundar clearing the crowds out of the way as she moved, even though she was friendly about it.

"We would have been here faster, but Sundar the Affectionate had to help an old lady across the street." Albarth rolled his eyes.

I snorted, and Mona just shook her head. "That's not nice, Al."

"He's not trying to blame me for anything guys." Sundar's eyebrows knit together. "I genuinely did stop to help a little old lady across the street. But it was worth it because she gave me these!"

The giant healer held out a plate full of cookies with chocolate chips in them. "They replenish health and some of our Aether?"

"Aether?" Mona raised an eyebrow. "All of our skills seem to be either toggle or cooldown—except for Kyvir's—when does Aether come into play?"

"Well, I'm assuming that Aether is this game's term for mana, so likely when our skills evolve, or we get strong enough." I shrugged. I had thought about it, but since I didn't have any natural magic, we would have to see how things worked here.

"Aether is the magic that your body naturally stores, but is also all around us," Alvor's voice made me turn around. He held out a dagger of similar shape and design as Mona's, then her actual weapon. "Here you are, the edges needed honing."

"Thank you so much, Alvor." Mona sheathed them at her hips slowly, a matching sheathe appearing for her to equip it with. "You were saying about Aether?"

Alvor blinked and lifted his eyes from her hands at her waist and grunted, clearing his throat. "Yes, Aether is the magic all around us. From what my father told me when I was a boy, Wanderers have the ability to manipulate it almost instinctively; but there comes a point in their progression where their natural gifts and the use of Aether will both diverge and intersect. At the divergence, they learn to use a secondary type of magic that forces them to use their Aetherpool—the place where Aether is stored inside all of us."

So, we had cooldown abilities and abilities that would cost us something equivalent to mana, but we didn't know how long it would be before that type of growth would occur, and it was highly likely that we would have to get to an appropriate level to do so.

"What else can you tell us of this world, friend?" Albarth smiled in an amicable manner and stepped closer. "Are there ways to master things for wanderers?"

"You mean such as weapons?" Alvor's eyebrows shot up in surprise. "Well, sure, if you can find a trainer to teach you the necessary skills with the weapons you want to use, you could begin the journey to mastery."

"And I suppose that allows us to do more damage? Or fight more efficiently?" Sundar bent down so that she could look Alvor directly in the eyes.

"Well, yeah, and it will also allow you to use weapons above uncommon tier." When we just stared at him he sighed knowingly. "I'll tell you this and then we need to go. Trash, poor, common, uncommon, rare, legendary, and mythic are the item tiers of our world. As their tier name states, as it goes higher, the harder it is to either find or make. Stats like Stregnth and Skill might help you use certain weapons, sure, but mastery is what will give you the ability to move up to the highest tiers of weapons. Now, is there anything we need before we go?"

We shook our heads, and he held out the now cleared and clean pickaxe for me to take. "If there's nothing else, follow me."

He grabbed a pack and slung it over his back and marched out from behind the counter, not even calling back to the other smiths that he was leaving. But hey—he knew his people.

We traveled through the city with the various people, places, and things to see. The great brazier of fire in the center of the Fire Square being one such attraction that glowed and shimmered with light of all different spectrums around what looked to be a large salamander statue. It didn't move, but there were smaller versions of it that crawled, clambered, and skittered all over it. Through the flames and out of them excitedly as we passed.

"Ah!" Albarth cried out, and the rest of us turned to find a salamander had fallen onto his head, the little red-scaled rapscallion clambered about on Al's hair as he tossed his head back and forth.

"Stop!" Alvor barked, making us freeze as we were about to rush forward to assist. "It's not going to harm him, this is amazing!"

"Well, it sure as bloody *hell* isn't on your head, is it mate?" Al said, and snarled angrily as he reached for it.

"It's a sign of favor among those who use fire magic!" Alvor rushed forward to stop Albarth from doing anything. "These creatures don't do this—ever. And legend has it that if one of the guardian's kin touches you, your growth will be exceptional... you're a blessed man, sir."

"I'm Albarth, and I don't really care for lizards." The wood nymph grumped, but looking up at the tiny creature, it seemed content. "What do I do to get it off my head?"

"Well, be gentle and try to coax it off," Sundar offered helpfully. "If an animal likes you, it's not their fault that you are scared, they just show affection how they do."

The insight surprised me, but then again, the older woman was more in tune with a great deal of things than any of us were aware of.

"All right then, you little beast, come down here onto my hand, this instant." Albarth adopted an imperious tone and held up his palm, but the salamander refused to move.

"Offer the back of your hand, animals are smarter than we give them credit for." Sundar turned her own hand palm down and showed Al how it was done. "He can likely tell how upset you are and is worried you will try to hurt him. Try to be soothing. Take a deep breath before you talk to him again, okay?"

Albarth looked like he was about to tell her just where to stick that deep breath before she growled at him, "*Now.*"

He rolled his eyes at her and did as he was bid, offering the back of his hand to the salamander. "Come now, little friend, let us take you home."

It took a couple heartbeats before the little creature stepped out on the back of his hand, but it did. The skin of its body was covered by small scales that seemed to shift and ruffle like feathers as it regarded Albarth from mere inches away from his face. It made what sounded like a small, modified crackling sound, the scales along its body glowing blue, then orange as it did so.

"Well, now that I can get a look at you, you aren't such a bad looker, are ya?" Albarth whispered to the creature. "But I'll see you home, mate, don't fret."

He held the salamander up to the brazier, and all it did was cling tighter to him. "Looks like he wants to come along," I called over to the confused man. "Either way, we're burning daylight. Let's move."

Albarth shrugged and offered his shoulder to the little creature who scurried onto it happily before we took off west again. It took us nearly an hour and a half to traverse the city, and that was with a talented guide who helped us avoid the more crowded sections of the city's thoroughfares to move more swiftly.

Eventually, the gate for the western section of the city came into view, the armed guards glancing at us and smiling grimly. Likely inwardly celebrating our impending doom.

We ignored them and walked by without issue into a lushly forested area. The blue sky filtered through the canopy of the large fir trees, their leaves giving off a needled scent that I had always associated with them. It made me sneeze. I wasn't allergic, but the scent just did that occasionally.

"How far out are the mines?" Sundar asked, pulling out her large club as we entered the forest.

"About another hour and a half or so on foot," Alvor explained, looking at the ground for a moment, then nodding and standing tall. "We'll likely have a cart full of supplies for the trip home, so it won't take too much longer on the way back as it does to get there, I hope."

"That's good, because the way I reckon, being out here after dark is a bad idea," she muttered, and we pressed on.

I rubbed my chest and confirmed it with a grunt of affirmation, remembering my first death.

The forest was alive, our presence seemingly barely registering for some of the wildlife in the area. Moving along our chosen path was relatively easy due to the well-traveled earth, shrubbery and other bits of wood life seemed to have been cleared away considerably as well.

According to Alvor, the only predatory animals in the area were wolves, and they steered well clear of the city, we would only need to worry about them near the mountains and even then, only nearer to dusk.

Travel went swiftly from there on, the trees eventually growing more and more sparse as the looming mountain in the distance came more easily into view. The shaded areas of the stone and rock face looked more and more ominous as we approached.

"There it is, the Demon-faced Mountain," Alvor's voice was a whisper as he spoke.

"Hardly looks demonic to me," I observed aloud, the apprentice smith glanced at me, before shrugging. "Any legends about it?"

"That it was formed from the face of a fallen demon lord who had almost stripped the world of its Aether until the Mages figured out a way to stop him." Mona's eyes were rolling in pleasure as Alvor told the story, but he didn't seem to notice her. "Legend doesn't say how it happened, but he fell, and his bones became that of the earth and soil, the blood in his veins becoming the ore that we mine. The items we're going to pick up now are the ore samples and the materials we need to support the war effort."

"War effort?" Albarth asked as he tickled the salamander on his shoulder. "I thought that the adventurer's guild was fighting demons, and you're telling us there's a war?"

"That *is* the war," Alvor pointed toward the mountain. "They aren't just legends, they're in this world, fighting to corrupt it and wrest control of it from us. They feed on the Aether, most of them being slightly resistant to magic and the stronger ones using it themselves."

"So then the front lines are the adventurers and the armies of several different nations standing against the demons." A sort of amber glow from up ahead flickered, and I decided to take out my glaive, just to be cautious. "Can the beasts in this forest use magic?"

Alvor seemed confused as a large bird burst from the underbrush, then he screamed, "Demon Thresh!"

Lvl 5 Demon Thresh – Hostile

The large bird looked like an eagle in coloration and size, except for the eyes that burned a crimson so deep it could've been fire.

It took a few hopping strides toward Alvor who backpedaled and fell before I rushed forward with my glaive set out and up like a spear, the tip on the top of it ready to pierce the bird's flesh.

It dodged my attack and smacked me with a wing.

5 dmg taken

The smack had been enough to turn me so that it could peck at my shoulder before a burst of flame washed over it.

7 dmg taken

10 dmg to Demon Thresh

"I'm going to use allure, get ready." Mona began to glow with her pink aura that signaled her use of her ability and then she began to sway, and the aura moved into the area around her like a wash of color.

"Go for the wings!" Albarth snarled as he waded into the fight with a stick in his hands, held like a sword.

I shifted the trajectory of my attack to go for the wings as the beast followed Mona's movements in a daze. She wove closer and closer until finally we struck at the same time she did.

27 dmg combo to Demon Thresh.

Demon Thresh suffers Broken Bone Debuff.

The bird screeched in agony and went to try and snatch Mona up in its beak when Sundar's massive club thumped against its head once, twice, then a stick covered in flames whipped into the beast's eye.

10 dmg to Demon Thresher

9 dmg to Demon Thresher

CRITICAL STRIKE

23 dmg to Demon Thresh

Lvl 5 Demon Thresh died
54 EXP

"Nicely done, but where there is one Demon Thresh, there are others, we must move." Alvor nodded enthusiastically and waved us forward.

"Seemed almost too easy, if you ask me." Sundar growled, casting her eyes about cautiously. "But hey, enough experience to get me to four with that quest I turned in for us." I froze and glanced at the others whose levels had gone up. I sighed in relief, my face slackening a bit. "Looks like you guys all leveled too. Is that right? Could it be for some kind of bonus due to level difference?"

"I agree, and I wouldn't know, but good job, though, with the fire and braining that thing to death," I cast my eyes toward the sky as I spoke, but it seemed we were okay for now. "I'm on lead, we're going forward in diamond formation, and I want our biggest in the rear. We can level and heal up when we're clear and safe. You all good with that?"

"Diamond what?" Alvor whispered as we all moved to stand around him.

"It's an audible we use to describe the type of grouping we think is best," Albarth explained from his left, where he stood less than three feet away. "Our damage dealers, myself, and Monami guard the sides, while the tank takes the fore and the brutish healer the aft."

"You sweet talker." Sundar grinned from her place at the rear of the formation. "All set."

"Moving," I stated, and we all began forward with Alvor in the center. The others would keep an eye on our surroundings while keeping our charge safe.

With constant whispered communication, we kept a good pace going forward and didn't run into any trouble, not until we got to the mouth of the mine, that is.

"What is that thing?" I hissed as I watched something that sat and licked itself clean of drying blood.

I focused my gaze and received a message with a prompt in scrawling writing.

(Nothing escapes your sight, magical or otherwise)

I blinked, and the message changed into a system message.

Skill unlocked: Evil Eyes (Greenhorn) – Your hidden skill has been realized enough to come to the fore. When you gaze at a creature and focus, you can see data concerning themselves and their magical aura. There are some who can hide their information, or tinker with what may be seen—be wary.

Skills can be obtained and grow at rates of their own, with use and practice, you can cultivate others of all kinds. Some skills will allow you the ability to grow into certain jobs. Be on the lookout.

Oh wow, so that's why I can see what I do? But why is it affecting the real world too? And what had been with that first message? And what does it mean about jobs? I guess there was a bevy of questions still to ask.

Lvl 7 Hell Cat - Docile

I motioned to the people behind me, making a circle slowly with one finger, then motioned back toward the bushes along the path we had come down.

We moved slowly and cautiously; I was grateful we had found cover when I felt something wasn't right.

Once we arrived, the others bombarded me with questions in hushed tones. "Would you all just be patient?!" I whispered harshly.

"No?" Mona blinked, and I had to fight the urge to push her off her feet where we crouched.

"Hell Cat, level seven, and it's licking blood from its body, so it has to have killed recently," I whispered hurriedly, recalling other information as I spoke. "There's a shelf above it with the entry to the mines behind it. No corpses, but there was blood on the grass and earth, and I'm not sure what's what."

"Well, the miners may be safe in a passage or something," Alvor reasoned, his eyes on the ground with his hands clenched tightly. "I'm not sure. This kind of beast doesn't normally come down from the mountain unless something drives it. Something larger, or more dangerous."

"You think we should head back and see about getting some help?" Mona glanced my way, but I was trying to paint the scene in my head again to find an advantage. The thing was three levels higher than us, but there were four of us here. Five if we counted our charge, but that numerical advantage wouldn't mean much if it got a hold of one of us. We would need to use the environment and teamwork to our advantage.

"I'm going to go scout again, as quietly as I can manage." I glanced around at the low-hanging tree branches and whatnot surrounding us. "I want you all to look around for a good place to set up a trap and let's see if we can take it."

I crouched and stalked forward as slowly as I could back to where I had seen the beast cleaning itself. It hadn't moved.

I scoured the side of the mountain nearest the entrance, the rough shrubbery in the immediate area malnourished to the point of being little more than scrub brush. No point trying to hide behind it.

The wall behind it and above the mine's entrance was scrubbed clean as well so that there would be no hope of a cave-in to stop any exit. Smart on their part, but that would leave us little to nothing that could actively help us in crushing or injuring it. The most we could hope for was to try and trick it into a manageable space, then kill it slowly using guerilla tactics.

That and likely a healthy dose of Sundar's club, but we would do what we can.

I slowly made my way back to the others and saw that they hadn't been idle in my time away.

Mona currently had a small, growing pile of sharpened sticks several inches long next to her leg beside the bush, and Sundar looked to be carving holes into a larger branch.

Alvor helped Albarth carve what looked like wooden spears out of some larger branches, and they flinched as I crept into the area.

"We have a plan, unless you saw something that could be useful out there?" Mona looked at me quizzically, and when I shook my head no, she continued, "Then this is the way we have to go, because I know you don't plan on turning down free experience. Speaking of, let's all level up and see if the added stats will help."

For this level, I didn't get an ability, but I got some stat increases and three choices for the path. One was a boost of 5% to my **Mageblood** ability, and a +1 to my Heart stat. The second was a +2 to Strength, and the last was the same +2 to Strength, but another point to Skill.

Why would anyone ever just choose a plus two when they could have more?

I chose the boost to **Mageblood** and the added Heart point, then spent the one stat point for leveling on strength, putting it up to an even ten. That boosted my overall hit points up to one hundred and sixty. Nice.

—I chose a path that boosted Presence and Skill by two, then added one point to Heart, you all?— Mona sent the first whisper, I responded with my own choices.

—I trust Alvor, but we should really wait to actually share our stat sheets until we're safe, good call Monami.— Albarth seemed to be contemplating something then smiled. *—Two Heart, one Skill and free point to Knowledge.—*

—Two Serenity, one Strength, and one point to Heart.— Sundar finished it off.

I watched as the others finished their preparations, but I wasn't sure how we would pull it off, or who would be going to get the beastie. Then again, I had a sneaking feeling it would be me.

"I'm squishy, but I can rain down hellfire." Al pointed to a spot a good fifteen-feet off the ground. "With any luck, it won't realize I'm there because the three of you will be distracting it on ground level."

"The thing of it is going to be to lure it to this tree here where I can wallop it with our spike branch," Sundar explained as she motioned to the newly fashioned trap. "The key to that succeeding is going to be for Mona to distract it as soon as it comes into sight. You're going to need to duck, and fast because we only get one shot at this."

Mona put a hand on my shoulder, sending tingles down my arm. "You gonna be okay?"

"I hate running," I growled softly to myself, "but if it's for a good cause, I'll run my butt off."

She nodded, and I looked for something to throw to get the Hell Cat's attention, not finding anything, I looked to the group. "Anyone got a rock or something I can throw at this thing to piss it off enough to chase me? Not these small ones, something that will really get its attention."

Everyone shrugged, Albarth looked at the salamander on his shoulder for a heartbeat too long, and the thing squeaked at him in protest. "I'm teasing, little friend, of course I'd never let you be thrown."

"I have a small thing of ore with me, it's got some sentimental value." Alvor pulled the object out of his pocket and stared at it for a moment before offering it up. "But if it gets us inside to get the materials and to check on any miners who may have survived—use it."

I took the ore, about half the size of a baseball and worn round at the edges from constant manipulation and fondling.

"It was a gift from my dad when I was a boy, told me that ore was the good stuff, but he wanted to see one of his kids do something with it rather than just collecting it for others." A lump formed in my throat when he spoke, the realization dropping onto me like a lead weight, the man's sad eyes, and defeated countenance reaffirming my thoughts.

"Your family may be in there." He nodded mechanically, and a wave of purpose settled over me. I punched him in the shoulder, and he looked up, startled. "We're taking the fight to him, and we can't have you moping about when there's still hope. I want you to take one of those spears Al has and protect yourself, okay? Get into a tree if you can, but just stay safe. Let's do this!"

A steely look of new resolve washed over him as he nodded and walked over to Albarth. He took the offered spear and hid behind the tree Al had begun to slowly clamber up.

I looked at the others, their positions taken, and nods of assent sending me on my portion of the trap.

I stalked forward until the entrance was in sight. The Hell Cat lay in the entry, the shadows growing around it, but somehow still in the sunlight lazily lounging.

I palmed the ore from Alvor, the love of it, the hopes and dreams his father had for his boy when he had given this metal to him.

I took a slow, steady breath and let it out as I shifted my left foot forward. The side of my body facing the Hell Cat, my weight flowing back to my right leg and my left leg lifted high. My right hand with the ore in it, hidden in my left hand like a pitcher on the mound. I brought my right arm back, refocusing all my effort on the Hell Cat, and prayed silently for it to hit it, then *launched* it as hard as I could.

The lump of ore whistled through the air and smacked the Hell Cat on the rump.

3 dmg to Hell Cat

Hell Cat – Enraged

The beast looked about as it stood from its nap and scowled at the ore. It sniffed at the ground near it, and a red aura permeated its nose, and a trail seemed to flicker into life leading straight to me.

I stayed where I was and giddily waved a hello at the beast before I turned tail and booked it back to my friends. A yowl of rage followed me and a thunderous clattering of small stones and loose gravel as it gave chase.

I moved for all I was worth, wishing I had incorporated sprinting into my runs and resolved to do so when I got out of this game, but for now, I would focus on running.

I heard snuffling and huffing behind me, coming on the trap location, and sent a whisper ahead.

—Here we come!—

I plowed through some bushes, the thorns snagging against my legs and arms.

2 dmg taken

The trap was set, and I saw Mona there, moving and swaying her body, a little further, and her face filled with panic. "Down!"

I threw myself forward and low as she flared with pink energy brighter than I had seen before. A whiffing sound rushed passed my head and a *CRACK* before a bestial screech of anguish sounded over me.

27 sneak attack dmg to Hell Cat

I felt a sharp grasp at my midsection, then it flipped me onto my back, heavy paws battered me angrily.

Bleeding Debuff added to Hell Cat

5 bleed dmg to Hell Cat

14 dmg taken

14 dmg taken

22 dmg taken

"Now!" Sundar bellowed, and I heard a cracking shatter, and she cursed. "I had just gotten used to the weight of it, too. Break my weapon, will you?!"

9 dmg to Hell Cat

3 dmg to Hell Cat

It snarled, and used my weight to lift and slam me onto the ground, breaking the branch it hung from.

19 dmg taken

Stunned – 3. Prone.

Damn stuns, I grunted mentally.

A flash of flaming red streaked from the air above and pierced the large cat attempting to beat away my friends.

8 dmg to Hell Cat

Fire Resistance – Dmg halved to 4

"It's resistant to fire!" Mona called just before I felt hands on my legs.

Stunned – 2. Prone.

She grunted, breathing heavily from trying to drag me out of the line of fire. The Hell Cat turned and kicked her away, opening the wounds in its body a little wider.

Bleeding debuff worsened, dmg increased.
Stunned – 1. Prone.

The stunning debuff wore off, and I dug my clawed fingers up into the cat, likely only doing minimal damage.

2 dmg to Hell Cat

Flames wreathed the cat's claws as it tried to gut me some more, the intense heat of the flames burning me.

22 dmg taken
Fire magic resisted – 11 dmg taken rounded up
10 dmg taken
9 bleed dmg to Hell Cat

"Get this thing off me!" I howled, and I heard a grunt and great green arms grasped around its neck as it raised a paw to stomp my throat.

"You owe me a new weapon!" Sundar's frothing features came over the cat's shoulder as she threw herself over backward in an agile arc while the cat was distracted and off-balance.

The Hell Cat flailed wildly as it twisted and landed almost like Sundar had done a suplex on it. Monami limped over and stabbed both of her daggers into the cat's lower back.

Sneak Attack x 2 dmg
CRITICAL STRIKE
26 dmg to Hell Cat
Severed Spine Debuff added

I took my glaive out of my inventory and began to hack down into the injured creature. Its life bar ebbing from half to nothing as Al and Mona joined me in raining down blows as we could. Sundar had let go of it, and the creature slapped Mona as she tried to stab it, a sickening crunch and she fell backward. Sundar was there immediately to start choking the beast again and getting clawed up less and less as the damage notifications piled up.

Her legs were a mess by the time it died, but it was worth it. "Couldn't let the little shit get away from me and kill Ky, could I?"

Lvl 7 Hell Cat died

75 EXP

You have taken part in killing a known man-eater! You have earned a new title: Beast Slayer

You are among the first to receive this title at such a low level. To find out the benefits of titles that you earn, open your title tab in the status screen.

Soothing energy bumped against me, much like the other day and I looked down to find Sundar's totem between her feet. She flicked blood onto it, and a shadowy figure stepped into the radius of her spell.

It was a perfect, spectral copy of the Hell Cat, and it sat over top of the totem before disappearing. The totem itself, a small wooden mask with a plus on the head, having another appear overtop it in the shape of the hell cat's screaming face.

The glowing, soothing blue of Sundar's energy that surrounded the totem expanded to more than twenty-five feet.

"You got a totem?" I asked her quietly, startling her as our health replenished steadily.

"Yeah, you saw that too?" She blinked up at me.

"Yeah, I can see magical energy." I flicked my status screen up and shared Evil Eyes with them.

"How long have you had this?" Monami asked with wonder.

"I've had a hidden version of it that allowed me to see wisps of magical aura since the beginning," I filled them in on the things I had noticed, hesitating then deciding to add, "I've even been seeing them IRL."

They looked confused until I flicked my gaze to Alvor as he looked over the corpse of the Hell Cat.

"Well that's good." Mona held her right arm close to her body, and her health didn't seem to be fully recovering. When she caught my gaze, she motioned to it. "Broken bones don't set with magic."

"But they will with help, come here." Sundar stood up, her wounded and shredded legs healed but still bloodied.

Monami came over to her timidly, her lion features pinched with pain and fear. Sundar grabbed a spear from Albarth gently and snapped it in two easily. She held the shaft out before her and spoke softly, but firmly.

"Bite down on this and look away from me." Mona bit down on it, and I offered my hand to her. She took it with her good one and closed her eyes. "You're going to feel a sharp pain on 'go,' okay? Three, two, *go!*"

The clawed hand in my own squeezed tightly, and her whimper of pain made me groan. Poor thing. Sundar had yanked so that the bone that had been jutting out of the skin sank back beneath it. It worked, though, because Monami's HP bar began filling up from where it had been.

"Wherever did you learn to do that, Sundar?" Albarth asked quietly with a look of profound respect on his face.

"I teach a women's advanced self-defense class." The orc woman grinned as she eyed the area. "It's all in there. But yeah, sometimes we get a little too *enthusiastic* about defending ourselves and break some things. Setting the bone helps, though it should only be done by professionals. I've seen more broken bones as an instructor than I ever did while I was serving."

I had known she had been in the army before she had started gaming with her friends on the weekends, but I didn't know she was an instructor. The totem ran out, and I was woefully below half health, and the others seemed to be a little better than me.

"So, what, you picked up tanking because you liked to get that aggression out?" Mona flexed the fingers of the formerly broken arm as she asked her question.

"Mainly because I like to protect people." The haunted look in her eyes made me look askance of the others to leave off it. The sun wasn't getting any higher in the sky, and we had some investigating to do yet.

"We have a pelt, four teeth, and two claws from this thing, as well as some sort of monster core?" Albarth held up a small gem that looked like it could have been an agate the size of a large pencil eraser.

"Inventory it, and we can look into it later," Sundar ordered as she resummoned her totem.

"A core?" Alvor looked at the item with wonder in his eyes. "Those aren't common. We use 'em to make special weapons and the like. Higher tier weapons require them. They fetch a decent price, too."

We waited until we were full up on health, saving the cookies for later, then we packed up to head out.

We made it to the mine entrance unmolested; the blood was dry, the door about ten feet back hung inward toward the darkness from a single hinge at the bottom. Claw marks inches deep scored the white door while the metallic caging on the sides looking scorched and burnt.

"Eyes on a swivel," I whispered to the others as we took our diamond formation once more around Alvor.

A dim light glowed from the center of us, drawing my attention to Alvor, who had lit a torch, then pressed it to a small groove along the upper right-hand wall, then the left. Small bits of flames lit along the path, fanning out around us and illuminating the area.

"Dude, what if something is here?!" I whispered at him as I pulled him back into the diamond shape we made, eyeing Albarth reproachfully.

"There's nothing to see but blood. We have to check on the miners."

We'd entered a small chamber with three paths and one alcove that looked to be covered by a wooden shack with a small window. The majority of the blood was there, but the door was closed.

"I get that your family might have been involved here, but you are our responsibility. Let us make the unwise decisions." I eyed the shadows and thankfully saw nothing moving toward us. "Miners in the West Mine!" I called to see if anyone was still there.

I listened hard, as hard as I could, with no sound. I looked at the others and motioned from them, to Alvor. Then from me to the door, they nodded, and I moved forward as they converged on Alvor to keep him safe.

I knocked on the door lightly, then listened intently. "Is it the demon?" One voice whispered quietly.

"Is the cat back?" Another soft whisper wheezed.

"Hey!" I shouted and knocked on the door. "I might be Kin, but I'm no demon, and we have Alvor out here with us. We killed the Hell Cat."

A set of deeply glowing eyes popped up into the window. "If Alvor is with you, ask him what his brother's middle name is!"

I blinked back at Alvor; whose shoulders shook as tears flowed from his eyes. The question had not been relayed softly, and all he did was shake his head and shout, "You don't have one, you little moron!"

A cacophony of unlocking metal clinks and a chair's wooden legs scraping against stone made me suddenly realize that standing in front of that door was foolish, so I backed out of the way.

Three men bolted out of the door, followed by a limping dog that looked like some kind of collie who whimpered and cowered in the strange company.

After the men had gathered themselves, all of them bearing a strong resemblance to our guide, they began to discuss what had happened.

"Well, this man looked like a Kin, but he had a tail about as long as hisself!" The youngest whispered frantically as he explained what happened, "Well, he came in here out of shaft three and dragged ol' Frem out here and just butchered 'im like a sheep at the chops!"

The elder man shook his head and took off the knitted cap and held it in front of his chest. "'Bout the same time, that Hell Cat came in and started eatin' what were left of the man, still breathin' and beggin'. Right nasty."

"I can imagine it was a traumatic experience for all of you." Monami tried her best to smile. "If you'll get the materials we need, we can be out of here, and you can all come back with us, how does that sound?"

"Well, we would, but he took off with it," the other man explained. "Took it and headed further west toward the demon wastes."

"You lot have a tone with this whole 'demon' thing, don't you?" Albarth rolled his eyes but otherwise seemed to relax.

"The demon wastes are lands ravaged by *actual* demons," Alvor explained patiently. "It's the front lines of many of the adventurer's guild and army's quests. They keep them at bay and assist the communities in the area as well."

"That makes sense, thank you." I offered a kind smile. "It may not be what we were sent here to get, but these people have seen some things, and aren't safe out here. Let's get them back to the city, shall we?"

They looked to Alvor then back to us before the youngest bolted into the shack once more. The sound of banging and things shifting reached us and Alvor paced toward the open door when he came back out.

"What've you got there, Dill?" Alvor asked.

"A new ore that we found in the mountain, shafts three, one, nine." He held out the dark material. "We busted into a huge vein of the stuff, but we ain't sure what it was. This ought to be enough to test, right?"

Alvor examined it in the dim light. "Not enough for me, but for the master? Or one of the other smiths? It could be."

The apprentice smith looked to us and stepped forward. "It isn't part of the quest as agreed upon, and I can't change it, but it may still be enough to allow us to pass it."

"That's okay." Mona held a hand up to hush Albarth. "We would love to get you all back to the city."

"If you do so, safely, I will honor the previous quest and more," Alvor swore solemnly. "Even if I have to come out of pocket for it."

I'd heard enough, we could be pragmatic later, for now, we had to get these folks and that ore back to the city.

"Diamond formation around them, and we go," I ordered, and the others moved. The eldest went into the shack and came out with three well-kept pickaxes in hand. I'd wanted to see if I could get some ore myself, but the sun wasn't getting higher.

"We'll do our part folks, don't mind us." The elder miner winked, and we moved on out of there with the group.

We paused at the entrance, where the eldest miner stopped and bent down to pick up something on the ground. He held it out to Alvor and smiled gently. "I still remember the day I gave you this, and here it lays on the ground, worn and weathered."

"I used that to get the Hell Cat away!" I blurted quietly. The man regarded me kindly, then turned back to his son.

"Something so precious and loved, can hold many things, but with time and pressure—strength of resolve—one can make diamond." He turned the object over and passed it to a stunned Alvor. "I can still feel the pride I felt in my heart the day you left with that chunk of 'ore' all those years ago. The metal itself was a ruse, but the diamond inside would grow with care. And it has."

He patted his son on the shoulder and made a motion that we should continue forward. So, we did.

I heard a sniffle from my right and saw Mona wiping away tears indignantly before I turned and focused on our path.

The fading light seemed to be doing so more swiftly than before, to the point where we had to sprint in order to make it into the gates by dusk when they closed for the night.

Panting for a moment, the guards seemed happy enough that we had returned and even more impressed when they heard what had happened.

Though the younger-looking of the two, an elven man, tall and lithely built, seemed more deeply concerned. "A demon and a Hell Cat? Stand by here, please."

He went to the small hut by the gate and tugged on a rope inside. No sound came from anywhere, but the older-looking human guard seemed apprehensive.

"What's going on?" Sundar asked the guard who had stayed with us.

"Pulley system in there," the guard said, then grunted, pointing with his chin. "Magicked to ring to two places, the Sergeant at Arms office and the Constabulary."

"So, what's with the grim countenance, mate?" Albarth put a friendly arm around the rough-looking man's leather-clad shoulder, only to be shrugged off.

"Because, both of 'em ain't nobody to be summoned lightly." His eyes flitted from face to face. "Ain't takin' this light, but they mean business when summoned."

The guard who stepped out of the hut and we waited all of two more minutes before a thunderous crash sounded in the distance, and the surly guard paled. "It was his night?"

The elven guard calmly nodded once. "Aye."

People shouted, and voices raised as this hulking, muscle-bound figure careened into the area with a sword almost as long as my body. He had to be nine-feet tall, and that didn't include the bull horns that jutted from the sides of his head decorated with gold and silver bands and chains that dangled down an inch or so then looped through the horn itself.

The bovine features on the face seemed very soft as the Minotaur looked about the area, catching sight of us with deep brown eyes and his nostrils flaring.

He stomped forward on cloven hooves and readied his sword, his deep voice reverberating in my chest, "So you lot are why I've been called here? Raphael! Beezil! Report!"

Both guards snapped smartly to attention, the elven man saluting with military precision and bearing as he spoke, "Good evening sergeant, west gate reports that the gate is in manageable order and that no—"

A gout of steam burst from the sergeant's nostrils, and he clawed at the ground with his left leg. "Skip to why I was called, Beezil!"

"Aye, sergeant!" He kept his composure as he continued, "The West Mine has been attacked by a demon, and a Hell Cat, the folk here have proof. I thought that this was worthy of your being directly summoned and informed!"

He regarded us carefully, then picked out Alvor among us. "You."

He pointed to the ground in front of him, and Alvor strode forward to stand there with his head tilted farther back so that he could look the minotaur in the face.

"Tell the tale and leave nothing out," The sergeant ordered. And that's what happened. Alvor spoke of our findings and even gave the account that had been given to him quietly on the way there and while at the mine.

Once he finished, the Minotaur seemed much less ready to kill someone, but looked to be thinking deeply, then he smiled. A great baring of teeth, one of them capped in a silvery type of metal, laughing as he palmed Alvor's head and shoulder in his right hand.

"Thought you looked familiar." Alvor smiled back as the sergeant spoke, patting his weapon lovingly. "You work for one of the best weapon smiths in the city, and you were likely who dropped off Blooddrinker when she was finished. I thank you for your time, and your tale of events."

He brushed past the smith's apprentice, accidentally knocking him over. The Minotaur looked down, thoroughly cowed. "My apologies, I'm so clumsy outside of a fight. Please, allow me to help. There we go." He turned to the miners and said, "are any of you injured?"

They shook their heads, and he nodded his. "Excellent, Beezil, see that these men are taken to their families, and I will see that they are compensated for their losses and troubles. Raphael! The gate is mine, go and call the men in the barracks. They are to be ready for duties outside the city in half an hour, full battle rattle, with a battle priest to accompany."

Both men snapped smartly to attention, saluted, and their sergeant barked, "Dismissed!"

Both Beezil and Raphael shot into motion from where they were, collecting the miners and ushering them away as the Minotaur turned his attention our way.

"My apologies for any disrespect you might feel," he began, stepping closer to the gate and waving us closer to him. "Reports of a demon anywhere in the region this far beyond the front lines is greatly troubling, Hell Cats less so, but a man-eater must be put down. For that, you have my gratitude. If you would show me the pelt?"

Albarth pulled it out and handed it to the other man who looked it over knowingly. "Hell Cat, likely in her prime from the pelt. She have a monster core?"—Albarth handed that over as well—"That confirms it, she was a man killer all right. That monster core will fetch a nice price in the market and is a valued component in some crafting types, too, but I'm sure Alvor said as much to you already. Don't lose it."

"Well, my name's Sundar Strongtusk." Our orc healer suddenly introduced herself, pressing through us to get to him holding her hand out. "And these are my friends Kyvir Mageblood, Monami Sunfur, and Albarth Remell. You are?"

"Enchanted," he whispered softly before shaking himself out of it. "Uh, yes, I am sergeant Gage Toomgarak, current Sergeant at Arms for the day and warrior in his Majesty's army."

"It's nice to meet another non-commissioned officer." Sundar smiled as he grasped her hand, both of their arms shaking and muscles bulging as they did so. "So, what can *we* do for you, sergeant?"

He seemed confused, and more than a little disappointed at having to relinquish her hand, but he responded, "Your group has done more than what was asked already, and I do suppose a reward is in order. I did not give you the original quest. However, for proof of killing a known man-eater? That I can reward. Tell you what, you all seem ill-equipped. Making weapons is hard and expensive. I will give two of you weapons from the armory, and cash compensation to the other two."

"Do you have any weapon trainers among your guard?" Monami asked thoughtfully. Gage blinked at her but said nothing. "I only ask because some of us don't know how to use some of our weapons to great effect. We have thoughts of joining in the crusade against the demons, and we thought any training we could get would be beneficial in the long run."

"A group of wanderers who wish to learn weapons?" His brown eyes widened in disbelief as he chuckled. "Next, you'll be telling me that you want to learn how to craft!"

"That would be nice if it would help us." I frowned in thought. What kind of crafting was available to us?

Now his jaw dropped. "Wanderers who want to learn to fight and make things without magic?" He scratched at the coarse hair on his head in amazement. "Now I've seen everything. Well, I'm a greatsword, sword, and shield master, so anyone I teach will receive a training bonus from my being their teacher."

He frowned. "I do know of a couple of others that are masters as well in various forms of combat. If you'll take the weapons off the table, I can introduce you and see if they would be interested in taking you on."

"Deal." Sundar reached out and took his hand in hers and grinned. "I'd appreciate seeing how you handle your weapon."

I could swear Gage blushed as the rest of us rolled our eyes and groaned.

"Whenever you are ready, come to my home, I will mark it on your map." He touched Sundar's shoulder, and she gasped slightly. "Now, you can find me, and I will be able to teach you the sword."

"I will do just that." She grinned as he took his post in front of the gate and turned to stand with his sword planted lightly in the ground. "Stay safe."

"I am the one others need worry about staying safe *from.*" He raised his chin proudly, and the chains rustled against his horns. "But the sentiment is not lost on me."

We left him with a grin and went back toward the Fire Quarter and found the smithy cooled and the smiths gone. Alvor stood there, waiting for us with a look of concern on his face.

"What," I called out, "you think he was going to kill us or something?"

Alvor rushed over and clapped as he reached us. "No, I had wondered if you would show up and worried I might wait here all night missing the festivities."

"Festivities?" Monami looked uncertain.

"You brought me and my family back safe, killed a Hell Cat, and we discovered the mine had a new type of ore." He grinned boyishly at us. "That means drinking with the smiths with all of you as the guests of honor!"

CHAPTER NINE

Alvor coaxed us to a dingy-looking building that seemed like it was ready to fall down from where we stood.

"That's the place?" Albarth quested dryly, disbelief and disdain plain in his face.

"Yup!" Alvor placed his hands on his hips and looked about before saying, "but believe me when I say, this is just a front. Come on."

We stepped up to the door, and he turned to face us. "This place is a haven to those who create, away from prying eyes and gripping hands. You are the only non-crafters to be allowed among us, please abstain from any business while here unless approached first. Okay?"

We all nodded, and he tapped each of us, a notification populating in front of my vision.

Request to join the Crafting Guild of Iradellum (temporarily) – Do you accept?
Yes? / No?

I accepted, then looked up at Alvor. "You take security very seriously."

He nodded, then opened the door before us, and in we went to a brightly lit interior room. A coat room, with a concierge who seemed befuddled that we had nothing for him to take, led into a large room. Two stories with the inner-most portion of the room open, the top floor wooden planks with buttresses that helped relieve the weight from columns that pressed up from beneath. There were stairs to the top floor on each side of the entryway with a large bar on the far side of the room.

The smiths stood at the bar facing toward us, mugs in hand, the great master smith Ori grinning a toothy grin. "To our heroes and new friends!"

They slammed their mugs on the counter of the bar, a voice from above called, "You'll not buy a drink tonight!"

Before I could look up, a pair of arms wrapped around me and swung me toward the bar with a chuckle. I looked back to see Codgy grinning at me with a foot-tall cask fashioned into a large mug in his meaty hands.

"I dare say the red blood of a Hell Cat could be used as a dye, eh?" He joked and shoved his *mug* into my hands. "Have a draft young hero, and tonight we shall discuss no more business than what has uplifted the community this day."

"We lost a miner and brother, but several other lives were spared thanks to your quick thought and action." Ori raised his mug, Codgy took pity on me and passed me a more manageable drink to raise with a knowing snort. "To our heroes and new friends. May their blades never break!"

"Their clothes never tear!" Codgy added with a boisterous call.

And a young woman raised her own glass. "And their colors never fade."

She was bewitching but, the glass tilted up signaling the toast had been completed, and I needed to drink.

You have imbibed a strong alcoholic beverage. Your senses are slightly dulled, your intelligence will drop with further intoxication.

That was nice! The alcohol was bitter, devilishly so, but the aftertaste was nutty and sweet.

"It's a good one, I'll let you know that now." Codgy tipped his mug to his gullet and took great pulls on the liquid inside, following my gaze. He sighed as he tilted his drink back to resting in his fist. "That'll be the dye maker, Ophira, the witch. She's the one I reckoned you would see about my deal. Approach with caution, and do not speak business unless she starts it."

I nodded once before walking over to her. The first thing I noticed were the colors, so eclectic and clashing that it almost called to me. Her hair was a rainbow of dark hues all the way up to the brightest white with every kind of color she could fit in her long ponytail. Even her eyebrows were different colors, one green and the other hot pink against her alabaster skin.

Under those were striking blue eyes that seemed to pierce my soul as she watched my gait toward her falter.

"Hello, hero." she smiled and lifted her cup to her lips. Her teeth were perfectly white with long canines glimmering in the light of the bar. She clapped a single hand on the bar, then pointed to my cup with raised brows.

A rough, practiced hand reached out and steadied my mug, imparting more booze, then flitting away. But her, she was all I could think about. Her and the colors.

"You're beautiful," I whispered against my better judgment, her eyes widened slightly.

"Thank you, but I do not believe you have had quite so much to drink as would be required to state something so brazen to an unknown lady." The corner of her purple-stained lips quirked. "Unless you make a habit of approaching women so recklessly?"

I blushed furiously. "Not at all! I was talking about all of the colors, they're magnificent."

She pouted a little, her lips pulling down in an artful frown. "So you don't think I'm beautiful?"

I opened my mouth, shut it, opened it again, and failed to think of anything to say.

"I'm teasing you, you poor thing." Her chuckle made me smile. "I can see that you lack a certain, *something*, and it is rare that someone other than children think my colorful appearance attractive. I am Ophira, and you are?"

"I am Kyvir." I motioned to my own multi-colored hair. "Yes. Normally, I would be as delightfully colorful as you are, but I haven't been able to find the right... environment to make that come about. I know we aren't to discuss business here, and I won't, but may I know where to find you in the future?"

"I like that you respect our rules, but flirt with the line all the same." A mischievous sparkle crept into her gaze. She lifted her arm and touched my shoulder the same as Gage had sending a thrill down my spine that made me gasp. It wasn't pleasure or pain—just sudden knowledge.

I *knew* where to find her business, and if I didn't think it rude to present company, I would confirm it on my map.

"And a wanderer who doesn't just open his status screens once he receives something from a normal person?" Interest slid over her features as she tilted her head to the right. "Interesting indeed. Come find me tomorrow; we can discuss business then. Until then, drink your fill and be merry, hero. You did this city a fine service."

She upended her glass, downing the amber contents with a gulp and sauntered past me, gracing my cheek with a soft brush of lips that made me feel on fire.

I turned to see the others staring at me, Mona with an odd look on her face, Al sighing theatrically and Sundar grinning broadly.

Mona carefully kept her distance, easily facilitated by Ori fawning over her with guffawing pride while she explained what had happened over and over. He made her promise to come to the forge so that she could swing a hammer for him. I didn't know if that was an invitation to try crafting, but if it was, that would be great.

The other smiths tried to arm wrestle Sundar, who laughed loudly as she won some and lost others, getting sloshed as it happened.

It was well into the morning by game time, but only around noon our time. But surprisingly, I didn't feel hungry at all. Not physically. Though the bar manager—his stated title, not mine—kept passing me pretzels that tasted delicious with this cheese dip that reminded queso mixed with a hint of mustard for a little tang. It wasn't anything like what my tias made when the family got together, but it was something.

By the end of the night, I had the **Sloshed Debuff** and had to be carried to a nearby inn that the smiths were all too happy to pay for.

It felt like I was really drunk and tired, but I knew I could go on. As soon as I was on the bed, a prompt came up.

Would you like to get some rest on this bed until daybreak in 4 hours, 34 minutes, and 23 seconds?

Yes? / No?

I hit yes and knew nothing for a little while, then a blaring alarm made my eyes open as I smacked my head to try and stop it.

"It's a doozy," a soft voice stated from across the small room.

I was on the bed, taking up the majority of it, enough room for the bed, a wash basin, and a chair in the corner by the closed door. In said chair, sat Albarth.

"Hey." He waved as I sat up on my elbows and addressed him. "What's up?"

"Last night was fun, but we can't let it go to our heads." Albarth frowned and put a hand under his chin, staring out the window. There wasn't much light, so he blended in well. "Not to mention, Monami's plight."

"I thought she was acting weirdly, what's going on?"

He graced me with a thoughtful glance before his chest heaved with the weight of his sigh. "You truly are clueless."

"What?" I blinked, grimacing at the newest Debuffs I had.

Hungover – Sounds and lights are more intense than usual. Food and water will help to curb this.

No time limit? I groaned inwardly. *Better get the ingredients to get rid of it fast.*

"She's so in love with you, and yet you've never once acknowledged it." Al pressed quietly. "Seeing you with someone else last night hurt her, Ky."

I blinked, sorting through the emotions going through my head. I knew she treated me differently than other men. We had both dated other people and never really seemed to find anyone who lasted very long, but me? Come on.

"And how would you know that?" I challenged him as I sat further up onto the bed. "We've been best friends our whole lives, I see her almost every day. She's like a sister to me."

"And being on the inside of those attentions would blind anyone." He insisted angrily, smacking his hands together, making me wince at the noise. "She adores you. You're the one who she tries to find in whomever she chooses someone as a prospective date, and they *always* fall short. They never come close."

"Again, how do you know?" I rubbed my eyes with the heels of my hands tiredly.

"Because I've lived in her shoes," he whispered quietly and sat back. "We hadn't known each other since conception like the two of you have, but we had known each other for some time.

"We were so close that what I felt, that love, was as much a part of me as it was to breathe. But I always shied away from asking her hand because I didn't want our relationship to change. Then, one day as if out of the blue, a man came along and swept her off her feet in a whirlwind of romance and passion."

His normally posh, prim British voice turned bitter. "He left her when he found someone else he fancied more when it was no longer *new* with her. Her first true love gone, leaving her jilted, and broken. She hid away from the world, and nothing I did, nothing anyone did, could heal her wounded heart."

His lip trembled softly. "Until she decided to let go."

I reached out and put my hand on his, his eyes thick with unshed tears met mine as I said, "That's why you heal in-game. It's why you retreat here."

He nodded once, whipped his hand across his eyes haphazardly, and stood suddenly. "I would save one of my dearest friends that same fate—this same bitterness. If not both of you."

"It's a game, Al," I tried to reason with him, but he held up a hand. "She's not *real*."

"It doesn't *feel* that way, does it?" He touched the pine door frame gingerly. "Her lips were purple fire, as colored as her attire, but when I watched and saw her face, all I saw—desire. Mona loves you, my boy. And no matter the dalliance, virtual or otherwise, it hurts her every time."

He made to leave, but stopped, glancing over his shoulder. "If it helps, I've seen you taking note of her in the last day. I don't know what has changed, but if there is yet an ember of hope for the two of you not to follow in my frozen footsteps, I would see the flames fanned. This conversation never happened."

Then he was gone.

I stood and contemplated what he had said, then decided it was in my best interest to put it aside, for now, and try to do what I could. I could talk to her at home, maybe. The thought sent wild thrills up my spine, and I shook myself out to get my head back.

I washed my face, my avatar feeling refreshed, then did the rest of my body too. I took my time and eventually wandered out into the common room. A server waved me to a table, explaining that the smiths had even bought breakfast for us and that I was the last one to wake up.

Breakfast was decent, and the water was divine. Once I had it all down, my hangover debuff had a countdown timer added to it of half an hour. That wasn't terrible. I would definitely be going to visit Ophira before I went to see about any weapons training, that could prove disastrous and humiliating.

I opened up the chat settings, seeing there was an option for party chat, it was basically the equivalent of a whisper, it was just that the whole party would get it.

—P/ Hey guys, I'm going to go do a quest for Codgy; I'll share it with you now. What's everyone else doing?—

I took a moment to share the quest with the others, then it took a couple of minutes before anyone responded, but Sundar did first.

—P/ Party chat? This game is unreal. Thanks for the optional quest! I'm working on mastering Gage's sword... techniques. So, if anyone needs me, I'll mark my location and send it to you all. He has some masters lined up for us, so try to be here before it gets too late. Ciao!—

—P/ God, you horn dog, do you ever get the urge to not enlighten us to your lecherous ways? I'm with the smiths discussing terms with Monami and seeing if that delivery yesterday counts. We will be together for a while, so let us know if you need anything.—

Albarth being with her was no surprise. I could only hope that he wasn't trying to do damage control with her for my supposed stupidity.

I did care about her and seeing her in the light that I had been lately was nice, but at the same time—terrifying. I couldn't tell if she was subconsciously using an ability from the game, like me with Evil Eyes, and with that uncertainty, was what I felt real, or her using her Allure.

Until I knew for sure, I couldn't think about trying anything with her. It wouldn't be fair to either of us. And the last thing I wanted to do was hurt her feelings.

Trusting that she was going to be okay, I went off to find Ophira's place.

It was south of the inn that I had spent the night in, which was conveniently just outside the Fire Square by a block or two. The city had begun to wake with the sun, and soon I had to fight the tide of citizens on their way to work. It wasn't hard; many of them seemed a little startled by my presence and acted as if they somehow instinctually knew I wasn't one of them.

After fifteen minutes of solid walking through all of that, I arrived at the bright green mark on my map shaped like a home with "Ophira" above it.

The home was everything I had hoped for, loud colors that clashed like her outfit and several weird and oddly shaped windows with dyes and powders sparkling in the sunlight. It was beautiful. Chaotic. Amazing.

And to top it all off, the name of her business was To Dye For. How was this anything less than divine providence? I sighed contentedly and tried the door, just as Ophira opened it. She wore a patchwork dress with swatches of different materials and colors that hugged her sleek form perfectly.

"I had wondered if you would take your time or not." She smiled and waved me inside, leaving the door open behind her.

"What can I say?" I shook my head and took in the sights of her business, breathily adding, "I was dye-ing to see what you had to offer."

"Oh." Her eyes closed as she chuckled at my poor attempt at a joke. "I am already growing fond of you."

"Good, because if this place is even a *fraction* of what you have to offer, you'll be seeing a lot of me." I slowly made my way from a section of bottles near the door that seemed color-coded, not by any sort of system other than shades of red in one area, then orange and the other colors all the way to matte colors that were amazing.

"Well then, my new regular, allow me to be the one to share one of the secrets of my shop with you, and only you." She closed the door behind her, locked it, then took my hand and led me to the center of the room. When I looked at her curiously, she pointed up to the top-most window in the room, where a single beam of light slid lazily toward a mirror. "This is my favorite part of the day."

As soon as the light met the mirror, a single beam split into thousands that hit the colored bottles and powders washing the walls and the air itself with different blends and shades of colors. Vibrant purples battled vicious reds, and pale blues serenaded radiant sunshine as the yellows blended with oranges and whites like fire.

"How do you ever leave this wonder?" I asked her, unable to tear my eyes away. "How is the rest of the world not gray after this display of spectrum and vibrancy?"

"Because there is a life to all color, and I will see it to where it belongs." She took my hand and tugged at me, I looked down, and she looked up at me, breathless in her excitement. "It belongs everywhere, and that is my mission. To bring color like that to the rest of the world."

This was something I could stand behind, and was the perfect segue into what had spurred this visit in the first place. "Let me help you."

She smiled. "You just promised to become a customer, that is already a good start, Kyvir."

"No, I mean, I want to *really* help you." She seemed a bit perplexed as she went to open the door once more. "Let me help you get some more business to this place and spread your work and wares far and wide."

She froze. "You have my attention."

"Codgy, the weaver who made these clothes, is colorblind," I began inelegantly. "But my asking for some dyes sparked an interest in him. He's asked me to see if I can find someone I trust to give him a fair price on good dyes that he can sell at his shop. If the sales go well for simple, base colors, he's willing to promise to send them straight to you for better product and different shades. Even if they don't sell right away, it's likely to help because he can still send people to you."

"And what do you get out of this?" She turned and faced me contemplatively.

"My friends and I won't have to pay steeper prices if I fail." I shrugged, then motioned to the room around us. "But most of all, I get to be as colorful as I feel I should be. And I can share that same sight you showed me to the world in my own way. Hell, if I could learn to make dyes like these, I would love nothing more."

She blinked at me. "You wish to take up a profession?"

"Is a profession different from a job?" I raised an eyebrow. "Forgive my ignorance, please."

"A profession is like what I do as a dye maker, I create." She motioned to the colors around us to land her point. "A job is something that a wanderer unlocks with a combination of their natural skills and some that they may be fortunate enough to acquire. Say, for instance, you had decent skill with tracking, ranged weapons, and survival tactics, you could develop a Forrester type job."

"I see, that makes sense." I frowned deeply. "Is it that unheard of for a wanderer to want to take up a profession?"

"My knowledge is based on myth and lore, but I suppose a wanderer can do whatever they like." She shrugged but saw the confusion on my face. "Until recently, wanderers were a type of story that mothers would tell their children about as a bedtime tale. These beings who could die and come back, who would lead a fight against the demons before they took our planet and lives for their own twisted wants and desires."

There was the story that Mona would adore. I'd have to see if she knew that later.

"No one believed it when the wanderers were prophesied to return, but sure enough, people began to fall from the sky as ignorant to our ways as newborn babes." She scratched her head in thought. "Then one of the guards saw one fall in combat outside the gates, moments later she walked back out the same gate and went back to fighting the same creature she had fallen to before. The wanderers had returned, and now the rest of us are playing catch up and learning all of these things about all of you."

"We're a lot to take in." She nodded at my statement but said nothing more. "And as I'm sure a lot of you know, there are some of us who can be real... asses. I'm sorry, my answer is yes, I would love to learn what you do. I would happily train with you if I could."

"I would happily take you on." She smiled sweetly. "On two conditions."

I raised my eyebrows as she thought, then smiled. "One, take me to this Codgy you speak of so that we can finalize a deal, and two if you find any rare ingredients for making dyes, you bring them to me. Is that a good deal?"

"Hell, yes, it is!" I blurted and went to shake her hand.

"This is a wanderer thing?" She looked at my hand as if I was being odd, and I almost took it back before she grasped it with both of hers. "I'm only kidding."

Open Quest received - Ophira has agreed to make you her apprentice (training to be decided) provided you take her to Codgy and bring her any rare materials you might find that could be used to make dyes. This quest has one portion that is ongoing. Good luck!

"You really have to stop doing that." I rolled my eyes, and she stepped behind the counter for a moment, then came back with a colorful sign that said, "Be back whenever."

"Let's go and see this Codgy." She grinned at me, then we were off.

Using my map, I was able to find my way to Codgy's place easily enough. When we walked in, he was dealing with a couple of other wanderers, the larger brute of an orc who had shoved his way through the citizens on my first day in-game like a jerk. He had another guy with him, a troll with gray-green hair slicked back over his head, and both still wore their starter clothes.

"How about you give us seventy percent off the price, and we let you off with just a warning?" The gangly troll asked. "Since we were so nice as to bring you the pelts that *you* were too lazy to go get yourself?"

"I told you what my price was, the quest was filled already, and I don't need them." Codgy growled, his foot still pumping lightly as his hands moved deftly along his spinning. "If you don't like it, leave."

"Make us." The orc growled, red energy flaring to life around him, cloying the air and snaking toward Codgy.

"Hey, Codgy!" I greeted in a chipper tone as I stepped closer. The aura died down immediately before touching Codgy, and he looked relieved to see me.

"He's busy, runt, scram." The troll waved a hand without even looking at me, but the orc did.

"Yeah, scram, or get pancaked." The voice sounded familiar, and the aura looked that way too, but I couldn't quite place them.

"Fighting isn't allowed in the city outside sanctioned duels, or in the training grounds." Ophira crossed her arms.

The troll turned around, his long, crooked nose jutting out, sharpened teeth gnashing in disgust, and his black eyes eyeing us both seemed unperturbed.

"I said, scram." A sickly green aura that looked like the visual identity of the scent of rotten eggs washed over me.

Fear spell resisted

I crossed my arms in front of me and tapped my foot, before spreading my arms. "I'm not going anywhere while my friend is being threatened. So, you can either get out, or we can go to the training grounds where your magic won't work on me anyway."

"We can take you right here, right now." The orc growled as he took a menacing step forward, but a meaty hand wrapped around the back of his neck, and Codgy stood up. He touched the troll on the shoulder with a grimace, then smiled menacingly.

"The two of you are banned from my establishment," Codgy's voice took on a steely edge, and the two men flew across the room and out the door. I had to dodge to the side to miss getting hit.

They landed with a crash that I heard from the inside and went to go see what was going on, but before I could step out, a small hand grabbed my wrist.

"They sealed their fate," Ophira warned, looking me dead in the eyes. "They will likely grow violent, and with them trying to threaten crafters, they'll be receiving a city-wide ban momentarily as soon as—there it is."

"They've been banned by every crafter in the city." Codgy clapped me on the shoulder with one of his huge hands. "Can't even enter their establishments, and any of the merchant squares will have guards who recognize their names."

"How can that be possible?" I asked in wonder.

"We can see their names once they enter our shops, that way our dealings are fair, and the second they use harmful magic or abilities, they're subject to the Trade Accords and violating them has severe consequences, as you now see." Ophira smiled, her sharp canines catching more of the light before they began to scream and shout about not being able to come in.

"They'll leave soon." Codgy grinned and went back to his wheel, then stopped and turned about. "Ophira, my apologies for not addressing you and welcoming you into my shop sooner. I take it that Kyvir has brought you here so that we might reach an agreement on business?"

"He has and seeing the way you handled yourself with those two, I fear for any who genuinely upsets you." She smiled at the ogre and it reached her eyes. "I heard that you would like basic dyes for simple clothes, I take it at a steep discount for yourself?"

He nodded once before adding, "Any and all who seem even remotely interested in other colors or kinds of dyes, I will immediately send them your way, where I assume you will work your magic and ensnare them as you seem to have done with Kyvir."

I snorted, and he patted me on the shoulder. "Thanks, you big lug."

"I find this agreeable, I will sell you dye at fifty percent of the cost, so long as each sale of any of my dyes receives marketing and I receive a share of the profits, say, twenty percent?" Ophira offered with a small smile.

"How much is fifty percent?" Codgy narrowed his eyes.

"My basic stock will dye one item per vial, and each vial would normally sell for a silver." She held up a hand, her lips moved, and she smiled wider. "If you buy them at five copper, and sell them at eight, I will take only a copper of the sale. A sign of good faith."

"So, selling two vials, I recoup the cost for almost three vials that I buy from you." Codgy drummed his finger along his shoulder, he'd crossed his arms during her figuring. "This is amenable to me. And if it does well enough, I may buy more of your stock. We can renegotiate at any time and should they not sell, I will sell them back to you at cost."

"At cost, it is, Codgy." They shook hands, and when they did that, two things happened at once. One was that the optional quest was completed, which was awesome, but the reward didn't just automatically come to me. The second was that a long sheet of paper with ink and quill blinked into existence on the nearest surface to them.

"What in the seven hells is that?!" I cursed, opting for a little more flavor than I might normally just because it had truly startled me.

"This is a minor accord," Ophira explained with a look of patient amusement on her face. "It is a contract of the business terms that we just set under the Trade Accords—a magical contract that all crafters and merchants sign to do business within the city limits. I hope you paid attention to that deal just now, as it will serve as your introduction to the accords and how they can be made."

"So, I'll have to sign that too?" My right eyebrow raised as I tried to glimpse the contract for myself, but Codgy's massive mitt engulfed my face.

"To glance at a contract, you're not part of before it is signed is a slight most won't ignore, my friend," His kindly rebuff made me step back. "Good man."

They took turns signing, then the contract *poofed* away as it had shown up in the first place.

"Where are you supposed to be able to read it if you don't have access to it?" I blinked, racking my brain for places you might go in real life to do so. "City hall?"

"And the guildhall, yes." Ophira seemed impressed that I had known something like that. "When would you like to begin your training?"

"You've taken a wanderer as an apprentice?" Codgy tilted his head at her in confusion. "They aren't meant to stay in one place for long."

"His passion and mine are twins, so I will see him become a dye maker." Ophira smiled, then raised her brows. "So, when can I expect you?"

"Soon." I smiled at her, holding my hands out before her. "I'm serious about this, but time works differently from where I'm from."

"You mean when you disappear?" Codgy blinked, touching his chin in thought. "I've had people do this in my shop. Made me think they were a ghost for a little while. Luckily, they do not appear in my shop, but outside when they come back. Keeps me from being robbed, I think."

"That is disconcerting, but yes, when you come to me, I will teach you." She smiled once more, her mischievous grin signaling an incoming ribbing. "So long as it isn't too late. I am not at your beck and call."

She turned to Codgy. "I will bring some product for you within the hour, and thank you for your patronage." She turned to me, "Until we meet again, my apprentice."

I grinned at her as she swayed away, outside of the shop as Codgy chuckled, then said, "You seem to have made a friend of the witch. For your reward, here you go."

He tapped my shoulder, and I saw that he imparted 35 EXP giving me enough to level up to five! I opted to wait on going through my notifications until he was done with me.

"And you'll be taken care of as far as prices are concerned, not to mention, anything you bring me for materials; I'll do what I can to make good clothing for you."

"Thanks, Codgy, I really appreciate you taking a chance on us." I held my hand out, and he clasped it in his own, making me feel like a child. After that, I walked outside and opened my status screen to check and see what my tree had in store for me, but instead of any sort of increase, I saw affinity. I tapped it for an explanation.

Affinity – Each and every person in this world has an affinity to a specific element. Some can have more, but rare is it for someone to have none.

Beneath that, it showed that my affinity was for ice. So... I could use Ice magic?!

I had one point that I could spend on my stats, so I decided to add it to Knowledge in hopes of it being useful.

I looked over my stats, pleased with what I saw.

Kyvir Mageblood, Level 5, Race: Kin
HP: 160
Strength: 10
Skill: 11
Heart: 11
Knowledge: 7
Serenity: 5
Presence: 5
Unspent Stat Points: 0
EXP to next Lvl: 522 / 600

Was there any quantifiable amount of Aether that I had? I didn't see anything on my HUD like a blue bar or number of spells. Maybe I had to actually learn a spell first? How could I go about doing that? So many questions.

–p/*Did all of you just get an affinity?*– Mona's whisper interrupted me getting my own party message sent out.

–p/*Ice, for me. You guys?*–

–p/*Animal and sealing, a weird combination, but I'm interested to see how it will work.*– Sundar replied a little breathlessly.

Albarth's reply left me more than a little jealous. – p/*Mine are for wind and space. Mona seems to have an incredible affinity for metal according to Ori, he just offered to make her an apprentice.*–

—p/How do we even begin casting spells?— I posed to the others.

—p/Ori says that we have to go to the square that has something to do with our affinity, and the guardian there will unlock it? It's weird because both myself and Sundar will have to go somewhere very specific for ours.— Albarth explained, his voice turning sour at the end of his statement.

—p/Let's get that done, then I'll be on my way to see Gage for training. Meet there as soon as possible?— I was already moving toward the Water Square as I sent that.

—p/Sounds good.— Mona whispered back, and the others remained quiet, likely trying to figure out where they had to go.

It took a while to work my way through the city and the crowd, but once I arrived in the square, I stared up at the majestic mermaid and called out, "Hello, Trickle!"

Her head poked out of the water at the top-most portion of the fountain, where she seemed to reside, "Kyvir, hello!" She waved down at me, excitedly. "What are you doing here?"

"Well, it turns out that I have an affinity for ice magic, and I was wondering if you could unlock it for me?" I tried to give her my winningest smile.

"For you?!" Her eyebrows shot up just before she disappeared behind the edge of the bowl. Then a splash of water arced through the sky, and a shadow moved across the sun before the beads of water filled the air with a rainbow, and a splash soaked me to the bone in chilly water.

I spluttered wordlessly, trying to shake the water off of my skin and drenched clothes as Trickle giggled hysterically.

"I thought you would have an affinity for my magic if you appeared here, but some don't." Her tail flashed below the water as I stepped closer. She patted the edge of the fountain in a familiar motion that had me sitting next to her as she lounged. The water played along her skin in beads that fled from her shoulders, down her chest to her waist where her tail began. The scales there started bright green and slowly faded to black and yellow near the tail. "Enjoying the view?"

I lifted my gaze to find her mere inches from my face, making me flinch in surprise. "Uh, yeah. I love the colors on your tail, and it's nice to see you again, especially without craning my neck to see your face in shadows."

"Ah, a sweet talker, eh?" She held a hand up to her mouth almost bashfully, batting her eyes at me.

"Nah." I waved it away. "Honest and naïve, maybe? That'd be more my speed."

"I believe you." Her grin flashed at me as she relaxed, but she did nothing to increase the distance between us. "So, you have an affinity for ice magic, and you need me to unlock it? Well, that will require a trade."

"I see, well, what can I give you?" She seemed to think on my question for a moment then looked into the water around her.

"In order to unlock the Aether within you, a sacrifice of something important to you is necessary." She reached into the water near her tail and fished out a golden coin. "For some people, it's money. For others, a weapon, or a favorite item. But for you, I can tell that the only thing you truly desire is magic."

I froze, my heart racing wildly. Would I not be able to pay the price she set forth? Would I lose my affinity? Would I never be able to cast a spell in this amazing world?

"But not for the reasons that some other wanderers seem to have." She lifted her cool hand and pressed it against the side of my face as she stared into my eyes, her focus going beyond me. "You seek it for the wonder that it creates. The joy of being able to do something so spectacular, even the most minor and mundane things. You seek to find the magic in you and bring it out of others. I cannot take that from you."

My heart sank a little further. "I understand if you can't help me, my only regret is wasting your time, though I am happy that I was able to see you again."

I made to stand, feeling dejected and colder than even the water that forced my clothes to cling to my body. Her hand wrapped around my wrist and pulled me down, so I looked back into her face once more.

"I am the guardian here, and I decide the price, and for this service of unlocking your Aether, I choose to take something almost as precious to you as magic is." Her eyes widened, the depths suddenly golden, eyes enticing, and swallowing my sight as her thin lips met mine. I tasted salt, and something sweet, almost like saltwater toffee, then the sensation was gone.

"Wha—?" I tried to speak but found that it was a little difficult to put a coherent thought together as it felt like a dam burst inside me.

Aether pool unlocked.

I blinked, and an icy looking bar segmented into seven appeared beneath my health bar.

"I took your first kiss in this world, and with it, something precious that you can now never give to anyone else." Trickle's cheeks seemed a little flushed as she spoke.

"Well, it wasn't bad as far as kisses go." I narrowed my eyes at her, then glanced around to ensure that... why did I care if Mona saw or not? It wasn't like either of us was going to act on what we felt.

I had to admit, I still thought Al was full of it, but for now, that could wait.

"So, what do I do? How does magic work here?" I looked at Trickle as she watched me with fascination.

"Well, you summon the Aether with your will, and think of what you want it to do." She shrugged, motioning with her hand as water geysered two feet from us for a moment, and she stopped it by lowering her hand. "The more complex the thought, or spell, the more Aether consumed. At higher levels, your ability to manipulate Aether may change, and experience definitely plays into things."

Something simple, I could do simple. There were several ice spells at low levels in some of the games I've played, so I thought of one that had served me extremely well. I focused on trapping the cold in my palm and pressed it forward with the Aether in my body. It worked!

A wintry blast of freezing wind gushed from my hand, and in my surprise, I stopped it short, a single segment of my Aether pool gone.

"That was very well done, though I imagine you could come up with something more creative." Trickle observed aloud.

"So, you're really only limited by your imagination?"

She nodded but held up a finger. "And the amount of Aether you have. Depending on how serene your mind is, your Aether may not recharge as fast as some others, and should you try to cast spells without the necessary Aether, you will pay a steep price."

"Thank you for your warning." I smiled at her and then looked toward the crowd who watched us speaking together. "And for your help. If you ever need me, please get a hold of me, okay?"

She winked. "I might." Then she was gone in another gout of water, and I was drenched once more.

I snorted at her display and stood, resigning myself to a cool body and decided to try and find my way to Gage's place.

Only to realize I had no clue where it was.

—Hey Sundar, you wanna share Gage's house with us? The location, that is?— I whispered to her.

The location-sharing notification popped up before me, and I opened my map. His house was a few blocks away, awesome!

I sloshed my way over to the corresponding location on my map and wondered whether I was in the right place or not. It was a fenced in home, a little over fifteen feet tall, with large windows and a broad door. Blinking, I wondered if this was really it because it looked to be the size of a larger studio apartment.

The door opened, and Gage's great horned head poked out. "Hello, Kyvir, friend and party mate of Sundar. I welcome you to my humble home. Please, come inside out of the street. Do tell, how did you become so wet?"

"I had a meeting with Trickle to see about getting my ability to work with Aether unlocked." I glanced down to where I dripped on the street. "I really wouldn't like to drag water all through your house."

I glanced up at the overcast sky. It didn't have that distinct scent of moisture and ozone that usually preceded thunderstorms. But this was a whole new world they had programmed and who knew if they would think to add something like that.

"Thank you for your thoughtfulness, Kyvir, but I insist," the muscle-bound Minotaur pressed and stepped outside to motion me inside once more.

I acquiesced to his request, droplets of water plopping onto his stone floor. The inside of the home was lavish, but a little more military, as would be expected. Weapons hung on hooks and displays on the walls, but there looked to be large windows to the outside of the fenced-in portion of the home.

A cloth draped around my shoulders as Gage stomped by me, humming a genial tune to himself. Off in the corner, he approached a desk that seemed much taller than the average. A little under chest height where he worked on something I couldn't quite see.

"What is it you're doing?" I asked as I took the cloth and realized it was a towel I could use to dry myself.

"Since Sundar has opted to go and search for her magical awakening, I have decided to tinker with this. One of my subordinates likes to play music on an instrument that was hilariously poorly made." I found myself frowning at him, but he picked up an object, looked it over, then grunted to himself as he put it down with a sigh. "I respect the man, and his desire to improve himself as a civilian. His desire to master something outside of combat is exemplary, and I would see him rewarded for his efforts."

I could appreciate that. Actually, it was far kinder than I had thought the sergeant capable of.

I looked around the home some more, the simple things and weapons seeming more of a collection than instruments he would use. But he took his time working, then he snorted in what I thought could be a happy manner.

"Ah, I think I've done it." His long ears twitched as he threw his head up with a grin and held his work up. He frowned, then motioned me close. "I lack the... dexterous appendages necessary to play the notes of this particular instrument. If you would please, play some?"

He handed me a metallic item that looked like a sweet potato, ten holes punched and filed into the top of it at the location where the player's hands were to go—four along the long side and then the other side of it near the mouthpiece. There were two smaller holes just above each line of the holes, then three on the bottom. It was beautifully crafted.

"Sergeant, this is amazing." He motioned for me to play it, ignoring my compliment completely.

I tried to blow into it, my hands in what I thought was the right spots, fingers moving over the holes as I did, and the sound was horrible. The Minotaur flinched as if I had tried to hit him. He held his hand out and looked it over.

"It's a perfect match, but he played better, and here is hoping that he plays better with this than the other one he'd had." He placed it into a pouch at his hip and smiled at me. "Thank you, Kyvir, for your patience. Please, in my home, you may call me Gage. Come, let us go and see my men."

I nodded at him as he led us out into the back yard through another doorway. The yard was beautiful. The left-hand corner of it was a large garden with tomato plants, peppers, peas, and all other manners of vegetables.

"Who's the green thumb?" I asked before I realized what I was doing.

Gage's ears flicked back and forth, a look of humility settling over him. "I have no green thumb. But I find solace in tending plants."

"He's a right bundle of surprises, ain't he, our sergeant?" A gruff feminine voice called out from the opposite side of the garden where a stone pathway lay between.

She seemed to be sunbathing, her golden skin touched by the sun a little too often, in a cropped top that rustled as she moved. It was white against her skin, her perfect smile flashing as she pushed her long blonde hair behind a pointed ear. She wore a pair of trousers in a shade of olive, and lifted her bare feet into the air, launching herself into a crouch like a warrior from my dad's kung fu movie collection.

"You know better than to call me such when we aren't on duty." Gage growled affectionately. "Kyvir, this is Thea Oberon, a corporal in my command who has mastered the axe, sword, bo staff and has a good idea of some other weapons, too. The others over there talking to each other, are brothers. Ünbin, Cälaos, come over and meet my friend."

The men looked like boys to me, late teens at the oldest. Lithe bodied, dark-skinned Kin with horns that raised out of the sides of their heads like a ram's. Their hair was green, and their eyes had different shades. Ünbin had red eyes, while his brother Cälaos sported silver eyes.

"Ünbin don't like to talk much," Cälaos advised. "But he's a master of the bow, sling, and atlatl. Me? I prefer the blades. Daggers, rapier, short and long sword, and been dabbling with the spear of late, too. Master of the four others, though."

"How in the world can you be masters of that many weapons when you are not even adults?" I cried, wondering if the weapon system was broken in this game or not.

The boys chuckled to themselves, then Thea spoke, "You might be outwardly Kin, but you know little of your ilk. These boys are, what was it again, two or three hundred years old?"

Ünbin raised his pinky, ring, and middle fingers as he masked his laughing mouth from me.

"Kin age and physically mature real slow, and become adults around our twentieth year alive," Cälaos explained kindly. "I shouldn't have expected a wanderer to know, but then again, we hadn't been expecting another one. What's the meaning of this, Gage?"

The Minotaur raised his head as he spoke, "This one and three others have done us a great service by killing a Hell Cat and saving miners in the West Mine after a demon left the mine. They escorted them back to us and warned us. That's where the other squads are right now."

"At level five?" Ünbin surprised us by asking.

A heavy hand fell onto my shoulder and glanced up to see Gage grinning, "Level four."

Their eyes widened, and Thea whistled low before nodding. "Mighty deed, that. So, you brought us here to try and teach him something of the weapons?"

Gage nodded, and I stepped forward. "If you'll be so kind? I've been told by master armorer Filk that I would do well with the sword, spear, axe, shield and possibly even the glaive."

"Glaive?" Thea snorted. "That twirly thing? Well, no one here can use it, but I can get you close with the bow staff. Won't count toward mastery of the weapon, but it'll give you basic knowledge. Maybe help a bit if you aren't too daft."

"I'd be happy to teach you something myself." Gage smacked my shoulder and sent me stumbling to the right, but Ünbin steadied me.

"How long can it take?" I asked, worried about time.

"To master?" Cälaos raised his eyebrows at the question. "Months, years, decades—it'll depend on you. How much you put into it. How you use the training. If you use it at all."

"So, you're all masters because you train hard and use those weapons in battle?" I asked uncertainly, but they nodded, and I smiled. It was time to learn something new.

"Well, then bo staff and maybe the sword?" I smiled at my two potential masters. "I think I'll give these a shot so that I can protect my friends a little better."

Ünbin seemed disappointed, his face falling as he plodded back to the side of the fence, but I made a placating gesture with my hands. "My friends will likely want to learn something from you if you'll be patient with them."

He nodded and waved his brother to the side of the training area we entered. I felt a crack against my back and stumbled.

4 dmg taken.

You have entered into a training circle. All damage quartered while training. All weapon and martial combat experience doubled.

This experience will not count toward personal levels.

I blinked and dismissed the notification, turning to find Thea standing with a bo staff in each hand and a grin on her face.

"What do you know of fighting with a weapon like this?" She tossed me the seven-foot-long wooden pole in her left hand.

"Nothing," I answered, honestly.

"Good." Gage grunted as he pulled a sturdily built stool over to sit on. "She won't have any bad habits to break."

"I'll give you a couple of moments to grow accustomed to the weight and feel of it in your hands," Thea cocked her hip out and leaned against her own staff as she waited patiently for me to do as she had said.

I lifted the thick wooden staff, roughly one and a half inches thick, round, and a little more than seven feet long meant it had a decent weight to it. The wood had some give, supple but hard. As I moved it through the air, it would bow and snap back. Bend and crack at the air.

"Why doesn't it have any stats, is it below common quality?" I asked Thea from where I moved the staff about to get a feel for it.

"It's a training weapon," She explained as she took up her own weapon. "In the training circle, weapons take on a training status. Their use is the same, but durability isn't drained, and they can only be broken from improper use. Helps us maintain training for longer periods."

I nodded; it did seem straightforward. Suddenly a whooshing sound and pain in my leg and hip brought me from my thoughts with a hiss. It smarted.

4 dmg taken.

"May want to disable the damage notifications for this." Gage chuckled. "They can be distracting, and she won't kill you."

"Damage notifications, off." I barked while attempting to dodge the next blow, hoping that would work.

Damage notifications have been switched to *off.* To turn them back on—

I blinked the notification away as I flipped heels over head from a leg sweep by the laughing, vicious corporal.

I landed in a winded heap on the ground, moving my own weapon up just in time to catch hers.

"Finally!" She brayed with laughter, and the others clapped.

I mounted a miserable defense after that, managing to stand and block one of four strikes here and there. The important thing was that I was *actually* learning from this.

I could tell by her swings and jabs that this weapon wasn't meant to be as flashy as the old films and TV shows had made it out to be, twirling and spinning about in a windmill. It was painful and precise.

The whole body moved with this weapon, the arms guiding while the placement of the feet lent balance, and the hips gave the swings power.

After ten minutes of her beating me senseless, she stopped and barked, "Rest!"

I collapsed immediately onto the ground, panting and began to wonder why I didn't have any water with me.

"Here." Gage grunted, and something soft, but heavy slapped against my arm. "Drink that."

I wheezed my gratitude to him and lifted the leather bladder to my lips. Cool water cleansed me of my aches, a little of it going a long way. I stoppered it and stood, taking it back to him. "Thank you. I need to get one of those."

"Good idea." Gage smiled as he set it by his feet.

"Next, I will teach you basic forms and motions for the bo staff." She set hers down and motioned for me to take a stance with it out before my chest.

"No, like this." She took my dominant right hand and tapped it, making me put it beneath the staff, and my left hand on top. "Stabilizes it for you and makes it easier to move about."

For the next hour, she slowly taught me to move my body with the weapon as an extension of each other. Movement, placement, and proper body mechanics made each motion flow to the next she would show me.

After the fourth or so movement, she stepped back and began to bark orders at me. We went from one motion to the next as fluidly as I could manage, which wasn't that fluid at all, and she would bark corrections.

After my third time through, she grabbed her own staff and used it to correct my form. Violently.

She rapped my knuckles, my knees, my shins, and I even took a whack to my backside when she thought it would surprise me. I was bruised, beaten, and finally, sick of it.

"If I beat you anymore, you're likely to be as dark as the twins, aye?" Thea joked, seeing some kind of flaw in my form and swung her staff like a bat at my knee.

I growled and snapped my bo staff down before hers in a horizontal block that forced hers down, a modified use of the first motion that she had taught me. Not bending too far with my back and overextending.

Her weapon whipped around her hand and came down in an over-head chop that I sidestepped and shoved away with the tip of my weapon, parrying, and coming around for my own attack. The second and third motions.

She corrected and pulled back, leaping back two feet, and struck like her staff was a spear aimed straight at my core. I tried to correct as she drove the weapon through, it hit my staff, my left hand a little further up than my right.

Her momentum carried what would have been a severely painful strike to my stomach, just below my armpit and behind.

I was about to try and attack her when she was suddenly there, back pressed against the front of me with her face next to my own.

"You've got fire," she said, then grunted, and her butt pressed into my hip as my feet left the ground and swung over my head.

I landed in a pile on my shoulders and back, the wind knocked from my body as she stared down at me with a knowing grin on her face. "I like it when they've got fire."

I blushed and groaned as my breath finally returned. My head throbbed angrily, and I just laid there.

Weapon Mastery: Bo Staff
Level: 1 (Initiate)

"Got to initiate," I grumbled.

"Not the slowest I've ever beaten a weapon into." Thea's grin stayed plastered on her face. "But not the fastest, either. Good."

She set her weapon down and offered me a hand. She'd just stomped me in the worst way possible, and I was shaken to my core after having been so thoroughly beaten.

But to be completely forthright? It had been so much fun.

I reached out and grasped her hand, let her help me to stand on my feet. She was a lot closer to me than before, and she whispered, "Prettiest one I've given my attention to in a long time. I look forward to seeing how deep that fire burns."

She tapped my shoulder, and a chill ran down my spine as her own home came to my map.

"If you ever feel like sparring one on one, I have a training circle in my own yard as well." She winked a deep-blue eye at me, and I blushed furiously back at her. That only seemed to encourage her.

What is it with older women and being so straightforward? I harrumphed.

"She's being serious, Kyvir," I heard Ünbin speaking from my left where he stood watching me blush. "She has one. I'd suggest going for the help."

My cheeks burned even more fiercely as I shook my head and muttered, "I thought you didn't like talking?"

"He doesn't." Cälaos seemed curious too. Ünbin just shrugged and stepped to his brother's side. "What's got into you?"

Ünbin just shrugged once more as I limped out of the circle, hissing at the pain in all of my joints.

"You look thoroughly whooped," Mona's voice drifted toward me, and I looked over to see her following Gage into the back yard.

"I missed him getting thrashed again?" The Minotaur raised an eyebrow and shook his head. "Blast."

"I thought we were friends!" I mocked a tone of betrayal at both of them.

Gage held his hand to his chest. "I am glad you think of yourself as such, Kyvir. I would like for all of my friends to be prepared for combat, and if bruises and wounded pride are all you suffer, then I would see them supplied *most* thoroughly."

Monami snorted and patted his elbow. "I like you more and more, big guy."

Gage introduced all of the others, and Mona decided that she liked the idea of learning daggers but said she had plans for another set of weapons she could possibly use.

"What's that?" Thea asked with a note of heavy curiosity in her tone.

"I was thinking of using metal rings called chakrams," she replied. I had to admit, I hadn't thought of that. Sure, some of the characters in older fighting games used them, but how? I wasn't sure. But she seemed to have a plan.

"Metal rings?" Cälaos walked over and asked excitedly. "Are they bladed?"

"*Mhm*, they sure are. I'm not sure if I want to have them mostly bladed, or if I want them fully bladed with a handle in the center to hold them." Mona seemed to puzzle over it for a minute before shrugging. "I'll have to do more research, then see if I can master it on my own unless you know anyone who uses weapons like it?"

"I know no one like that." He looked to Thea who shook her head.

"Minh Lei." Ünbin grunted, forcing his brother to look back at him. He held his hands out like he was holding some kind of fan and fluttered his hands and eyes together while swaying.

"The soldier who uses fans to fight?" Gage frowned. "I could call upon her, but she may not teach you."

"If you could do that, I would truly appreciate your time and hers." Mona bowed her head.

"I will do this thing then." Gage left us and turned back toward his home, but I heard footsteps from the other side of me.

Cälaos has rushed over to pull Monami into the circle, excitedly. "We can start while the sergeant goes to summon her!"

He pulled out a belt with a set of daggers in it at the hips and affixed it about his waist. He opened his inventory again and pulled another matching belt from it, and tossed it onto the ground before Monami.

"Put that on and limber up!" The Kin man began to bounce on the balls of his feet restlessly as she moved.

"Don't worry, to keep things fair, he'll actually show you how to hold your weapons and a few things before beating on you the way I did Kyvir." Thea winked at Mona, both of them sharing a laugh at my expense, and I just rolled my eyes.

It took her a moment or so, but he was able to help her get things situated on her body. The hilts of the daggers dug into her hips at first, making movement odd with them sheathed. Cälaos popped over to her side and helped her adjust the straps so that they faced pommel and hilt first at an angle for her to draw easily and be able to move with.

"Thank you." She smiled at him, and he grinned back. "I think I'm ready."

"Great!" He clapped his hands happily. "And, draw!"

Mona flinched, and her hands flitted to the opposite sides of her body, trying to pull the blades crossbody.

Cälaos stepped forward and thumped both her hands with a knuckle and tutted at her. "No. The other way, blades back and out. Right hand, right blade, left to left. At ease."

She looked confused, but Thea helped by explaining, "Stand like you would normally."

Mona did as she was told, letting her hands rest naturally by her sides.

"Draw!" Cälaos barked, and Mona's hands sped into motion, grasping at the hilts of her daggers, and pulling them free. "Excellent! Now, for your stance."

They spent a few minutes going over how she should stand, her knees bent with her dominant leg back and fists forward and slightly bent like a boxer.

"Knife fighting is not only about stabbing and slashing, Monami, it is an art form." He pulled his own blades and settled into a stance that mirrored hers but seemed *much* more comfortable. As if he could live the rest of his days in that stance and never grow tired.

"Knife fighting is an art form, a dance of bladed death, constant motion defined by defense, parrying, attacking and setting up your next strike," he began to move, flowing from one motion to another, using his fists, knees, and legs to strike as much as he did with his weapons.

"So, the body is as much a part of the dance as the weapon is?" Mona asked, obvious fascination on her face as she watched the man moving.

"Yes." He stopped suddenly and faced her. "And you will learn this."

"I think I'm ready." She had a look of determination as she fell into her newfound stance and glared at her trainer.

"I like you, you cut to the chase." Cälaos grinned, sharp teeth flashing at her as he moved forward in his own stance.

An arrow whizzed between them, all eyes falling on Ünbin who had another one ready to fly as his brother shouted, "What the blazes?!"

Thea cleared her throat. "You forgot to teach her the basics, the stance is important, but you need to teach her about slicing and dicing before you get into the simulated combat."

Ünbin nodded once and let the drawn weapon slowly come to a ready position with the string released, but the arrow still ready.

"Well, thank you for the reminder." Cälaos harrumphed and began to slowly go through several cutting motions with his own weapons that he coached Monami through genially.

He was patient, but working with both hands on a weapon was odd for her, so he had her sheath one dagger, and they went about learning the absolute basics. It was interesting to see, and I felt like I was learning as well.

They switched hands and did the same as they had with her dominant hand. It was slower going with much more to correct form-wise, but Mona was working hard and asking questions so that she could understand better.

Eventually, I decided to try and see what I could make with my ice magic. Were there defined spells? Or was it only by imagination?

I took a deep breath and thought of another simplistic spell. Holding the image in my mind, I pulled from my Aether pool and cast the spell.

Ice Armor (Full) – Covers caster in frost to protect from damage. Cost: 3 Aether. Duration: 30 minutes (environment and hostile magic effects duration).

That was amazing! I looked down at my body catching sight of frosty-looking mail that slowly faded from view. It was there still—I could feel it—but I could also see that there was a small armor buff beneath my health bar. I blinked at it, and it showed me the duration and name of the spell.

Uncanny, how this was playing out.

I opened my status and saw that there was now a **Spells** tab with that spell specifically in it.

So, my earlier dalliance with magic hadn't netted me an actual spell, just a use of magic? I focused my sudden displeasure on the bright side of the situation—I could use magic. And thanks to other games I had played, I would make a competent ice mage to boot.

Just a matter of safely testing my boundaries and seeing how I can improve.

"Again!" Mona's frustrated growl brought me out of my own thoughts. She had some cuts on her arms and legs, even one on her face. Her feral snarl surprised me as she moved toward Cälaos with her weapons raised. The hair on the back of my neck prickled as I watched their brutal exchanges, Mona being beaten on and her trainer seemingly only having fun.

"He knows what he's doing," Thea offered as she stood next to me, a curious look on her face. "You clench that fist any tighter, and you'll lose it."

I blinked and unclenched my fist, the nails having dug in a little more than I would have liked, then Thea spoke again, "You're sweet on her? She family?"

I frowned and had a decision to make, opting to remain silent for a moment, then, "She's my best friend. Seeing her trounced like this is hard."

"I get that." She left it alone from there, and we went back to watching the fight.

The nimbler man eluded her clutches masterfully, opting to allow her to come to blows with him with her blades clanging off of his ineffectively.

While they danced, I tinkered with my ice magic a little more, no new spells as of yet, but it was so cool to use, and it was addicting. I tried to get a hold of the others via whisper but got nothing in return. They were still online from the party tab. Oh well.

"Fuck!" my head whipped up, and I saw Mona swinging her weapons wildly once more, her trainer dancing around her effortlessly.

She gritted her teeth as she swung toward his head, but he was no longer there. Cälaos ducked and twisted, kicking her in the stomach hard enough to send her end over end onto her face ten feet away.

She coughed and sputtered as Cälaos swaggered over to her prone form. "I appreciate your aggression, but coming at a Master too aggressively is a death sentence on the battlefield. Watch. Be patient until it is truly time to strike—*then* do not hesitate."

She held a hand aloft and put a single thumb into the air, then it flopped back down onto the ground beside her. A wash of healing energy spread about us, making me turn to find Sundar and Albarth behind us with smiles.

"About time someone tried to teach you to use your fiery head for something other than being dumb." Albarth snorted as he stepped forward toward me. "I had no idea that it would take so long to find someone to unlock my magics. Did we miss much? Sorry for ignoring your whispers, I had it turned off so I could focus."

"Only the two of us getting our butts kicked." I grinned and stood. By now, my Aether had recovered another point, making me believe that my recovery for it was close to a minute per section. "How does your guys' magic work?"

They blinked and smiled, Sundar motioning to Al first. "Go ahead."

Albarth stepped forward, then he was no longer there. I felt a tap on my left shoulder, glanced over to find the grinning wood nymph standing next to me.

"Space, I assume?" I raised an eyebrow at him, and he shook his head.

"Wind." He took a steadying breath and reached out with his right hand as if punching something, his fist disappearing, and then a resounding *thunk* on the back of my head made me yelp. "That was space."

"That's incredible!" Monami sounded grumpy, but she limped over to us and grinned. "So, you can use wind magic to augment your physical speed and then space to attack something from a distance. The applications of this are limitless."

"I'll agree, it's kind of broken." Al didn't look like there was any sort of remorse to his abilities whatsoever as he said it.

"What about you, Monami?" Sundar asked suddenly, making me flinch. "What does your magic do?"

"Well, it's metal-based, and since it is, Ori said that he wanted me to come and work in the forge with him and the other smiths." She smiled at the calls of support from Thea and Cälaos. "I start tomorrow, or rather, whenever I can."

"That's great!" Sundar smiled supportively, but it didn't seem quite so genuine now.

"You aren't sure how to use your own magic, are you?" I asked as I pulled her away from everyone else. Al and Mona moved to follow, but I waved them away with a stern look.

"I..." She looked down, her green cheeks mottling red as she glanced anywhere but at me, then she growled and shoved me away. I fell onto my rump, and she growled her frustration. "I'm a *fighter,* okay? I like magic plenty, but I don't have the imagination to take something so abstract and try to own it the way that you and the others do, okay? I'm not smart enough for that. I'm a soldier. I like guns. I like to fight and scrap and hold the methods of my strength in tangible ways. Is that so bad?"

I laughed, and that seemed to make her even angrier, her whole face reddening in rage. "The fuck is your problem, S— Kyvir?"

"Because now, of all times, our roles are reversed." The response gave her pause, but her fists were still clenched at her side as I continued. "Who was it that came to the veteran player—leader of a guild so notorious for running all the toughest content in Blood and Gore that other people were terrified to even approach her? Me. A level one newbie who knew nothing, let alone how to do any of the content. And what did she do? Pass me off to the nearest low-level scrub for hazing and half-assed help?"

She looked away, but I stood up and brushed myself off while the others watched. "Nope! She took the time to help me out because she understood what it was to truly love the game she was playing. She taught me all the secrets she could, and with her help, I flourished in a difficult game with a difficult magic system. And what did she always tell me? Come on, Sun— you know it. What did you tell me?"

She grumbled something inaudible, so I theatrically held my hand up behind my ear and raised my eyebrows. She huffed and rolled her eyes. "To never fear asking for help because the people too busy to give it suck, and the ones who love what they do will share."

I raised my arms wide and shook my head. "Do you have *any* doubt that the three of us are going to let you stumble while we flourish?"

Albarth approached slowly, his head tilted to the side as he tried to catch the big woman's downcast gaze. "My dear Sundar, I may tease you and complain about your lecherous ways, but I love all of you dearly. I would never see any of our guildmates suffer, in this world or the next. I will help you."

"Me too!" Mona said simply with her arms crossed, and furry chin raised defiantly.

"I'm a magic nerd, Sunny," I teased softly. "I will do everything in my power to assist you. And if we need to go and find out what you can do, then so be it, but you aren't alone, and you aren't a burden."

"You can seek assistance from a dryad, if needed," Gage's voice reverberated in my chest a second before I felt his giant hand alight on my shoulder. "There is one in the center of the city, though he is reclusive by nature, he comes out to speak to those with whom he has an interest. What types of magic did you say you had? Animal, and what else?"

"Sealing." Sundar raised her head, her cheeks were still red, but the rage had abated. "And sorry, buddy. I didn't mean to react so poorly."

"No man left behind," I grinned at her. "You taught me that."

"I like that saying." Gage guffawed suddenly. "It heartens me greatly that soldiers and protectors even worlds over have some of the same ideologies."

"Sealing magic is rare," Ünbin stated as he joined us. "I know a person. I'll show you."

"If you're gonna talk to everybody now, you can forget me being your mouthpiece from now on!" His brother harrumphed loudly. "Most *I've* even heard him say and to the lot of you."

"How do you know what he's thinking if he barely talks to you?" Thea asked with a look of concern on her face.

Cälaos shrugged and motioned from himself to Ünbin. "Twin thing."

"Come." Ünbin took Sundar's hand and began to tug her toward the fence in the rear by the training circle.

"Use the gate!" Gage snorted a warning to the Kin man. "I will not have my neighbors seeing someone jumping my fence again."

Ünbin turned his deadpan face to us, smiled and made to jump, but stopped and waved a hand over the fence. A gate appeared in the wood, and they used it to leave.

"Gage tells me that you are a master with the rapier?" Albarth asked the remaining brother suddenly. I turned to see him nodding vigorously before Albarth smiled. "Care for a match?"

I blinked at the man I had known for a couple years. "You know how to use a rapier?"

"I've been known to dabble in many things, Mageblood." Albarth winked at me and stepped into the training circle. "How does this work, will we be using regular swords?"

"We will use rapiers," Cälaos responded as he pulled two of the long, thin blades from his inventory. "What good is mastery if you don't carry the weapon?"

Albarth chuckled and caught the weapon by the hilt, lifting it to inspect. "Excellent craftsmanship, but no stats?"

"Training circle thing," I called out, gaining his attention. "Also, may want to turn off your damage notifications while in there, he won't kill you."

He nodded and whispered something to himself before settling into a position with the left side of his body forward, blade tip resting in the ground with little weight on it as he waited for Cälaos to be ready.

"En garde!" The Kin man barked, both weapons lifting and presenting at the ready position. Albarth had his right hand behind his back in a comfortable-looking position, his feet spread slightly wider than shoulder length apart.

The two men eyed each other for a moment, then stepped into motion. Blades clashed, whipping back and forth, the two of them exchanging blows as if almost on level ground.

"You're good at this!" Cälaos laughed, his high left arm dipping behind him as if tired. "Do you mind if I let loose a little?"

"By all means." Albarth smiled back. "It has been too long since I have crossed swords with someone."

Cälaos switched hands, his right hand catching the weapon even as it struck Albarth's own, then the speed of his attacks seemed to increase slightly, but that slight shift was enough to drive Al a step back.

The two of them continued on for a moment longer, then Albarth disengaged a second. "Forgive me, master Cälaos, but if I might have a moment to take this shirt off?"

Cälaos shrugged happily and took a drink of his own leather bladder. Albarth took his shirt off, and something caught my eye. Iridescent wings shimmered on his back as he flexed his lithely muscled body. They fluttered and moved as if of their own accord, and he shifted his hips a moment, popping his back, making him grunt softly.

"Much better, thank you." He switched from his left-handed grip to right-handed and bowed to the other man. "If you would allow me to be so bold as to 'loosen up,' I would see myself tested thoroughly here."

"Happy to have someone to spar against." Cälaos eyes narrowed minutely, and he shifted into his own stance.

The flurry of blows from one man to the other was almost dizzying. Jabs led to parries and ripostes that shook my already frayed nerves to the core. Albarth and Cälaos both began to grunt and sweat with the exertion. Their bodies in motion, muscles taut, and defining as they moved in a brutal give and take of violence that gave me a newfound respect for my friend.

"You really never figured that out?" Mona asked me in a hushed tone, the display of physical prowess still captivating her.

"Figured what out?"

"Remell?" She offered as a hint, and I shrugged. "God, you are *such* a shut-in. His real name isn't Allen, it's Alexander Remell! He's the three-time gold-medal-winning fencing champion!"

I blinked and looked at her in shock. "You can't be serious."

"Yup. Three games in a row." She turned back to watch him as he moved, blocking a particularly vicious blow meant to gore his stomach. "Started at sixteen."

"But what was that about him not going to the last games?" I racked my mind trying to figure out what had happened, what I might have read on it, but I found nothing.

"A loss in the family was what had been reported," she answered, and based off his conversation with me earlier, I think I had it figured out.

His heart had been broken by his loss, and he couldn't bring himself to go.

"Finally!" Cälaos bayed with laughter, his attacker growing more precise as he went.

A similar thrust from Cälaos, as had been seen earlier, pierced the air in front of my friend's stomach, the Kin master lunging impossibly swiftly. Albarth grunted, his hips shifting slightly to avoid the strike as his blade slapped the encroaching weapon just to the side, and his hips shifted once more as his left hand cracked the master across the jaw, sending him sprawling onto the ground.

Cälaos popped back up with a huge smile on his face. "You're a master?!"

"I would hardly call myself such—oh." Albarth paused with a frown. "I suppose the system thinks otherwise."

"Acknowledgment from the system aside, I think the only reason it took you so long to best me was that my stats are likely higher than your own. If we had been equal, you would have beaten me much sooner." I was confused as to why Cälaos was so happy about losing to someone. "But if we have time, can you teach me what you did with your blade at the end? It seemed so simple that I overlooked it, and it was my undoing."

The whole exchange confused me until I saw the multiple cuts and gashes along the man's arms and chest from Albarth's weapon, and my friend only had a few scores on himself.

"I would be delighted, my new friend." Albarth held the blade in front of his face, the hilt just below his chin in a salute. Cälaos mirrored the movement with fascination, then they both cut their salute by bringing the weapon to their respective sides.

"So, I guess we know what weapon he will be using from now on." I snorted, and Mona joined me.

"Well, of course, it's an elegant weapon—like myself."
Albarth winked at us. "But, your brother, I would love to learn
the bow, perhaps?"

"I would be happy to ask him for you!" Cälaos took his
practice weapon back and clapped the other man on the
shoulder. "Just don't tell him you beat me so soundly, okay?"

"Why ever would I do such a thing?" The look of
mischief on his face was telling, and Albarth laughed with Gage
as the Kin blushed.

CHAPTER TEN

Three of us decided to take a small break for a while, Sundar opting to push through for a bit since she was at the Kin's mercy.

Gage had explained that the person he had gone to contact was busy but would likely be available after nightfall.

When we got out of the game this time, it was around one in the afternoon, and my stomach grumbled wildly.

I set an alarm for an hour and clothed myself before going to the kitchen. The light from the fridge blinked on a heartbeat after I opened the door, *unusual*. The sandwich I had in mind after that consumed my thoughts as my stomach gurgled.

I laid my ingredients out. Wheat bread, lettuce, tomato, turkey, leftover bacon, cheese, and some condiments. I slathered a small amount of mayonnaise on the bottom piece of bread, then assembled the sandwich. Before adding the bread, I added a little hot sauce for some love to it, then dug in with gusto.

The tang and heat were amazing. Rather than listen to myself chew, I turned on the small television in the counter, it raised on a small dais until it was flush with the tile before turning on. I thumbed to the news, wondering if there was an update to the hospital thing.

I turned the volume up on a headlining news bulletin.

"—anks, Mike. We bring you this next piece from China. The People's Republic has announced that their people will be able to try—under strict monitoring—the latest launch from Mana, Myth, and Legend Studios called 'Mephisto's Magic Online.' The game boasts some of the most advanced types of gaming systems in the world, including biological and psychological input from the players that assist in choosing the 'gift' best suited to them."

As she spoke, a b-roll of Chinese leadership being led around a facility with monitors and technicians overseeing people being prepared for the game. The portal pods were blurred heavily, and I grinned, thinking about how secretive they were being.

"Here to talk about the new release and what is planned for the future is our special guest for this piece, CEO of the company, Aiden Muhng." The reporter, a fit woman with dark brown hair, turned, and the camera panned to a wider shot that showed a man sitting next to her with a smile plastered to his face.

He didn't seem worried at all, and his features seemed... bland, somehow. It was a face that would blend in if he were to step into a large crowd of people, just handsome enough to not stand out for being ugly. Sandy-brown hair and brown eyes that shone in the lights of the camera.

"Thanks for having me, Renée." His voice was forgettable too. Huh.

"Well, we understand that you acquired the studio under a former name years ago, I think it was Jamming Studios?"

He clapped and chuckled at the name. "That's right! I stepped in as CEO back when it was Jamming, and it just seemed stagnant." He shook his head almost as if guided by a cue card. "They'd had some small successes that had begun to fade, and the former leader of the company jumped ship, but I saw some potential. We revamped everything, threw out the old mottos, and rebuilt it all."

Renée affected a look of understanding. "I see, and why the name change? Were you not worried about losing some of the success you could glean from previous titles?

"At first, there were some skeptics among the staff, but the vision we had for the future seemed constrained and almost smothered under any other moniker." He smiled as the name of the company scrolled across the bottom of the screen.

"With the successful launch of your flagship game as a reborn company, how do you feel things are going, and how do you feel about the future of gaming as an industry?"

He blinked at the question. "I'm sorry, I didn't bring the specific details or numbers with me, but based on the number of logins we've seen, over just the last not-even twenty-four hours, has been incredible." His easy smile returned. "We realize that our system is rather steep in price, and we are working diligently to make it more accessible to our various friends around the world."

"Around the world?" She interrupted before he could answer the rest of her previous question.

"Yes, ma'am." He nodded. "we want everyone to play. Not because it's money in our pockets—which is nice, mind you— but because this game *is* the future. We're trying to change the world."

I snorted and shut it off. A video game? Change the world? Please. Then I paused, there were things I experienced from the game and I doubted it? I watched, a little more concerned than before, but nothing else of value was said.

"What does he think this is? Some kind of Orson Scott Card remake?" I shook my head, walking into the living room and hopped into one of the bean bag chairs to finish my meal while I researched weapon fighting styles for the game on my big screen, motioning through the various videos with an upraised hand, lazily eyeing each one for a second.

A few of them, like the glaive, seemed really difficult, especially the dual glaive that Filk had been talking about. It looked to take a lot of discipline, and I needed something sharp to deal the maximum damage.

So, what does a guy who is a guy with a disposable income do? Buys sharp toys, of course.

I bought a dual glaive, a sword, and shield of decent weight and a couple thicker daggers to practice with. I could pad them with leather so that I didn't cut anything, I just wanted to get a feel for them. I almost bought something for Mona too, but there was nothing I could find that fit something she wanted that would be safe out of game for her.

With a few more minutes before I'd jump back into Mephisto's, I watched another video of a fighter trying to defend himself with his fists and got an idea for an interesting spell.

I finished the video, and my alarm went off. It should be about dark in-game by now. If not a little before. Time to get back to it!

***

"So is Sundar in yet or not." Albarth asked as we left the training circle and cleared out of Gage's back yard.

"I think she's still with Ünbin." Monami scratched her chin and sighed. "She sent me a whisper. She's at the tree, but the dryad hasn't come out."

"Well, let's go support her!" I clapped them on the shoulder, and we headed toward the center of the city as the sun dipped below the city walls.

The center of the city reminded me of the center of a maze puzzle. The different streets and alleys acting as paths to try and get from the center to the gates. A small pool of water with green grass and stony pathways surrounded the massive tree.

The tree was awe-inspiring. Easily the tallest thing I'd seen in this world other than the mountain, but this was insane. Small decorations hung from branches and strung together shapes and sights created from the sparkling lights that flickered within them. Smatterings of golden light dotted the earth beneath it, and Sundar as well.

The large woman sat next to Ünbin on the ground facing the tree as lovers and passersby strolled the area.

"Will the dryad come, or not?" Sundar's frustration rang out in her tone as we came closer.

Ünbin shrugged.

She sighed tiredly and just sat there with her hands on her knees, looking defeated.

"Sunset." Ünbin said, then grunted. She looked up at him, but he nodded toward the tree, and I stopped the others from continuing forward.

The spells along the tree limbs flared to new life in hues of gold, green, and silver. The lights strobes at first, flickering then solidifying into a radiant halo around the tree.

"Nightfall," Ünbin whispered.

The halo expanded from around the lights of the tree until they covered the circular center of the city, meshing into a thicker band that rose into the sky, collecting other colors. Crimson, brown, sea-foam green, black, and gray. Other lights filtered in that I couldn't seem to put a color to, and once they were done, the halo fluctuated until it was far above the city.

Once it was high enough, it burst like the aurora borealis covering the world around us.

"What the *hell* was that?" Albarth breathed.

A creaking of boughs and the cracking of bark breaking made our attention fall back to the tree in the center of the city.

A large creature made of wood turned flesh climbed his way from the core of the tree, splitting it like a child climbing from a box.

He regarded the world around him, looking into the sky as if knowing something was good, he nodded and looked down at where Sundar sat in awe.

It pointed down at her, small creatures flocking to her from the world around the tree. Close but not touching.

"Why am I drawn to it?" Albarth whispered as he stepped forward.

"You're a wood nymph, it's likely to be expected, right?" Mona gasped as he moved again, grabbing his shoulder.

The creature—dryad—lifted his other hand and motioned toward us.

"Come." A lighter voice than one might expect from a creature so large, like a wind through the forest, reached me.

Our wood nymph friend moved forward as if drawn like a bee to something sweet. Once he was close enough, about twenty feet or so, the effect lessened, and his faculties came back.

"Uh, hello." He blinked at the dryad, and it nodded to him.

"Your magic, that of the animal class, is special for many reasons." He laid a great, bark-covered palm on her, a flare of green exuding from her skin at the contact, and then he turned to Albarth. "And your race is rare as well among the wanderers, though there are quite a few in this world."

"I feel...*alive*," Sundar whispered, raising her hands to her eyes as if she were seeing them for the first time as they were meant to be seen.

"Animals are most alive when surrounded by their kind, and your magic is most alive when animals are near." More of an explanation than I got for mine, but hey, the dryad wasn't

Trickle. "And you, little friend of the world, will feel most at home in the wood. Be careful in your journeys, as they will see you taken worlds away. But fret not, all will be as one in the end."

I blinked at the cryptic message. Was that a plant thing? Like, the plant life cycle? Or something else?

"But wait, I'm still not sure about my other magic!" Sundar called, and the dryad stopped, body creaking as he turned to regard her quietly. "Sealing. My other magic is sealing. I can't find any information on where to go to learn it. That crazy Kin took me to the castle gate and ran away after that."

The tree turned and prodded a finger with leaves sprouting on it at a thin circle around his tree. "This was done by the most powerful sealing mage in the city, and likely the country. His name is Armenes, and he resides in the castle on the north edge of the city."

"You're sealed here?" I found myself asking before I could resist the temptation. The dryad looked up and stepped out of the circle toward me, his great gait seeing him to me in three steps.

I took a step back, wondering if he was going to kill me.

"Mageblood?" It blinked at me and prodded me in the chest painfully.

5 dmg taken

"Quite." He dipped his head low. "Not strong enough. But yes, all of the guardians are bound to the city, as I am. We chose this life, forming a pact for protection against the demon hordes that swept our lands and homes. The encroaching darkness sweeps everywhere, and soon, nowhere, and no one will be safe from them. Grow stronger and take the fight to them. It is our only hope."

"Why the thing about my name?" I called to his back; he'd already turned to walk away.

"Because, he who creates a moniker filled with so much ire is bound to make enemies, and those who fall to him may yet add to his name."

I stood there at a lack for words. My name wasn't filled with *ire*! It was filled with wonder and the thrill of magic! And I would show everyone that.

The dryad smiled magnanimously at all of us and leaned into the tree and shifted into it like it was a bed and the bark made of blankets that lifted and laid over it like nothing had ever come out.

"That was cool and *so* creepy all at once." Monami raised an eyebrow as she looked my way. "And people have begun to take issue with your name?"

"It started at the beginning of the game—the god of the realm said that he would take interest in me solely based on my name, and my attempt to role-play didn't seem to help." I scratched my head and sighed. "All I wanted was a name that was familiar and for there to be wonder and magic about it, you know?"

"I know, dear." Sundar patted my horned head comfortingly. "But sometimes blood needs to be spilled. And *we* need to go talk to a certain mage about unlocking my other magic."

"It's the middle of the night!" Albarth tried to reason, but I thumped his chest.

"It's dusk, and if he's asleep, then we come back another time, but I need my magic if we're going to make a proper go at streaming all of this on Friday." Sundar insisted. "We've promised to get our bearings, and one of us is already operating at less than his normal capacity—sorry Ky—not to mention all of us playing different roles."

"So, first thing is magic, then gearing up." Albarth sighed, the rest of us looked at him. "You can't be serious. You all forgot about getting new gear, didn't you?"

"Well, two of us *did* score apprenticeships." I tried to smile, but his withering glance my way made me sputter uselessly.

"See if those pay off when we're getting *stabbed* in a dungeon somewhere." He sighed, thinking about what he would say next. "We may have to do a half stream at this rate; we aren't ready."

"So, we work hard and attack the problem as hard as we can," Sundar pressed. "These apprenticeships help us, and we're already learning weapons. Speaking of, how did yours go?"

Mona and I both turned to look at him, his face unreadable, so I answered for him, "Master with a rapier and would like to learn the bow or atlatl."

"I take it that he *just* figured it out?" Sundar looked knowingly at Mona, who nodded, and Albarth frowned intensely.

"Figured *what* out?" The wood nymph looked at all three of us in consternation.

"I've known possibly the longest, but I take it that you fencing for Great Britain's finest fencing team in the world three games long, has just now been ousted to the others?" Sundar motioned toward Mona and me, but Mona shook her head. "Oh. How long have you known?"

"About a year into our friendship, I finally figured it out when he was complaining about swordplay in Blood and Gore." She thought a moment, but the expert among us beat her to the issue.

"It was a cockamamie way to try and diversify a skill set for two different kinds of weapons that are used to fight in the same way—it's a damned sword, not a pig-sticker!" His chest heaved as he finished his rant, but Mona motioned for him to continue. "I said that it would put my mentors and trainers to rolling in their graves seeing sensible weapons disrespected so callously along with poor form and little imagination."

"Wow, I see why he was asked to the Olympics four times," I muttered, and he stilled.

"That fourth time was a farce." He whispered, took a deep breath, then shook his head, and walked away. "I suggest we rest and get cracking in the morning. Good night."

His back swayed out of sight toward the inn we had used the night before, and he was gone.

"What was that all about?" Mona asked softly, concern cemented on her feline features.

"He believes it was a farce because his friend beat him for his spot as the top of the team," Sundar began and stopped, frowning.

"I know." That had to have been around the time that his friend... "She didn't go."

"She didn't *make it*," Sundar corrected softly. "She had hidden away for a month or so after the breakup and then... just before the games..."

"Right." I nodded; my heart thundered.

"How is it the two of you know so much about this?" Monami questioned us both angrily, her fists clenched at her sides.

"He told me out of respect when he first joined my guild when he would have sudden angry outbursts." Sundar scratched her arm under the angry woman's gaze. "After that, he's opened up from time to time about it."

Mona continued to glare at Sundar but seemed to realize there was nothing for her to weasel out of the large woman, so her gaze slid to me.

"I only found out when we woke up, he had something to talk to me about and it came up." I offered nothing else, and she raised her eyebrows for me to continue. "It's really personal, and I'm not comfortable speaking about it right now."

She frowned; I had never hidden anything from her like this before—we were open books to each other.

"Fine." She huffed and walked away in the same direction that Albarth had.

I glanced at Sundar, her hands already in the air, "Don't look at me. That's your mess, Ky." I sighed heftily, then felt a heavy hand on my shoulder. Sundar looked down at me with a glimmer in her eyes. "Don't worry, kid. She'll come 'round."

"I take it you know about everything here, too?" I sounded tired despite the fact that I had too much energy in me right now to feel this worn down. Right?

"Know what?" She blinked, then looked from me to Mona, then thought for a moment before striking her forehead with the heel of her hand. "Well, I *knew* there was a special chemistry there that most couples seem to lack, but was Al giving you a talking to because of her?"

I nodded mutely.

"Hey, don't worry about it, if it's for you guys, it'll happen."

"That's the thing!" I threw my hands up into the air. "I don't even know if it's supposed to happen! She's like a sister to me—always has been. And with that..."

The world grew too large at that moment, spinning out of control, and panic set in.

"Hey—Hey!" Sundar grabbed my shoulder and whipped me toward her, making my head shake violently. "It isn't *just* about you, Se—Ky. There are two of you. And the *two* of you deserve to hear things out from each other. Even if it leads to nothing, you have to air it."

"Why?"

Her gaze slackened a bit, her hands fell away from my shoulders, and she looked almost defeated before she pulled her chin up and muttered, "Because cowards live in regret."

She turned on her heel and strode away, making me call out, "Where are you going? That's the wrong way!"

She glanced back, her hips swaying a little more exaggeratedly than before as she called, "Since we seem worried about waking an all-powerful mage? To grab life by the horns, kiddo. Don't wait up."

I stood there, lost to what she had said, the imagery her last statement had battered into my brain making me blush, and roll my eyes.

***

The next morning in the game, I rose early maybe half an hour before the sun and went to the forge to see about a weapon. I would likely need to learn swordplay, and a glaive would be great too. Maybe a dual-headed one. No messages through the night, so I sent one to the others about what I would be doing.

—*Gonna see about a weapon, anyone wanna come?*— I waited but no response from any of the others, so I left it alone.

Clanging lifted into the air as hammering and barked orders filtered into my ears, "Now, *feel* the weapon forming beyond the top layer of the metal and hammer it until it bends and shapes to match the layer."

I rounded the corner to find one of the other smiths working with Monami over a small, stretched ingot of a cherry-colored metal.

"Good, now put it back into the forge to heat some more." The man stood and thumped her on the shoulder with a meaty palm. "You're almost as good as I was just starting out."

"I'll be better than you ever were, Dirvish," she joked, her eyes caught me as he chuckled and walked away for a moment. "Kyvir."

The greeting was like a head nod, something given to someone you're familiar with in a hallway, or store when you don't have time to really say more.

"Hey, Mona, I wanted t—" she stopped me, her eyes hardening and a hand held aloft with her palm out as if to ward the words away.

"I'm a bit busy right now, Kyvir." She turned and shifted the metal in the flames of the forge, then turned back to me. "I've already put orders in, and with me working here and what we've done for the city, they're really willing to work with us on prices. I've put in what orders I think are good, and we're alright for now. I need some time to myself for a bit, please."

Seeing the cool look on her face made my heart sink, *What had I done that was so wrong?*

I nodded once and walked away, both of us having our first fight together, for once. At least, our first real one.

I decided some alone time would probably be beneficial and went to the low-level side of the city where we had fought the sheep, then decided against it. I was cool with Gage, maybe going to train with the army would be okay? Their training in the morning made sense, and maybe I would find them all there together. Going to Thea's just seemed like it would exacerbate things more, so I dismissed that and headed on.

I made my way toward Gage's house first, stopping one of the guards and asking where the army's barracks and training quarters might be.

"Oh, tha's easy." She yawned blearily and pointed northward with her larger-than-average arm. "Next ta the castle up yonder, go on an' git there afore they eat so they're grumpier than normal."

I blinked at her, and she snorted. "I'm teasin', yer a wanderer, any of ye what're interested in the army get treated like spun gold on account o' yer magic. They'll let ye train with 'em."

"Thank you, ma'am." I offered her my hand, and she scowled as she took it.

"Don't you be callin' me that, I work for a livin'." She winked as I scampered away from her while she chuckled at my expense.

The area to the north of the larger squares was great. Like, swankier than my neighborhood and beyond. Verandas with nice furniture, butlers and maids with nannies tutoring young men and women in various subjects. A man sang a song that made me think of an opera my mom had tried to force me to, but his voice was so amazing that I found myself stopping to listen.

I smiled and moved on my way when I heard a very different noise.

"—please, I have nothing else, please, just go and leave my family in peace!" A man pleaded in a hushed whisper off to my right, a door slightly ajar signaling something might be wrong.

I dropped down into a crouch and moved forward toward the door. The home was superb, like the rest of them, decorated in pastel pink with blue seashells and pearls painted along the sides over the wall. Windows were opened and inviting with cream-colored curtains waving in the slight breeze.

As soon as I got to the door, I caught a glimpse of the only two troublemakers I had come across so far in this world. They stood with their backs to me. That damnable pair, the orc, and troll. I hadn't learned their names, but as I leered at them from my vantage point, my Evil Eyes kicked in.

Blasik Lvl 3

Guilty GameZ Lvl 4

Huh. That was different. The orc towered over a cowering man whose family, two little boys, human, and their mother shook in fright.

I couldn't attack them because combat in the city was against the law unless it was on the training grounds or a dual outside the city.

That didn't mean that someone couldn't bring the law...

I decided to wake Sundar, hoping she had been doing what she said—for once.

—*Sundar! Bring Gage to my coordinates, now! No time to explain. Probably wanna bring some guards.*— I sent her my location with the whisper and hoped she would come.

I steeled myself and opened the door, leaning against it to affect a look of almost casual interest. "Man, graduating from being general jerks and attempted blackmailing to *actual* robbery in less than a day? Not sure whether to be impressed or concerned."

The orc turned toward me and grinned. "Ah, the pancake has returned."

"As I recall, you got kicked out before that could even happen, so I'm still me, thanks." I grinned, and a wave of nausea filtered over me, gripping my chest, clawing its way from the pit of my stomach into my throat, threatening to close my windpipe.

I fought and struggled to move, gasping for air as the fear clutched at me.

Fear debuff–paralyzed for 30 seconds
Debuff time halved.

Sonofabitch. I growled..

"Yeah, your resistance isn't all it's cracked up to be, is it bitch?" The troll, Guilty, cackled in delight as he stepped forward, large serrated tusks sticking into my face. "What, you expected that we wouldn't be able to find out about it? Well, knowledge comes from all places, and with it comes power. This *game* is going to be my stomping grounds for a while. And I have every intention of playing to my heart's content. Blasik, kill this one, then rough up the old man until he decides to give up the good stuff."

The woman protested softly, her words lost under the growl escaping my throat despite the fear clawing at my body and mind.

"Better thought, Guilty—how about we go for the ones he's protecting?" The orc lumbered toward the woman, the boys squealing in fear.

"Good idea, but the still quaking asshole first." Guilty moved out of my vision, the sound of flesh hitting flesh and a grunt of pain from the man signaling that he must have hit him.

A few seconds left, if I could hold out, I could try to help these people.

7 dmg taken

I fell onto my back after the huge fist collided with my face, my right eye filling with tears and bright flecks of light invading my vision.

"I'm gonna enjoy this." The orc growled happily as he loomed over me. His name popped up over his head tinted red, and made me mentally grin.

He was in trouble now and didn't seem to notice.

He leaned down and grabbed me by the front of my shirt, lifting me into the air with his left fist cocked back. "Ain't so brave now, without your pet bitch and the ogre asshole, huh? Getting us kicked out for a bit of business that would have gone over if you hadn't so *rudely* interrupted?"

He punctuated rudely with a punch to my gut that made me puke up bile.

6 dmg taken

1 dmg from acid

Seriously, game? Bile counts as acid damage?

"Well, I'd enjoy getting mine, but I have bigger and better things to do than to beat my irritation out of you." He tossed me onto the floor and raised his foot, just as the paralysis wore off.

I reached for the Aether within my body and snarled as I packed one bar's worth of ice around my fist, lashing out at the knee his weight was on. The limb froze, and he cried out in anger and outrage as he fell, clutching it.

10 ice dmg to Blasik

Frozen debuff given – movement slowed

"Guilty!" He groaned in warning, but I had a new toy to play with as his aura flared red, and some of it seemed to siphon toward me, my fist tinged red with his blood.

Gift Stolen

Intimidation – one target that you can see within twenty feet is affected by your sheer presence and may have difficulty attacking you.

I thought about it as Guilty the troll stepped toward me with a dagger drawn and a grim smile on his face. "Gotta do something right every now and then, eh?"

With a roar of anger, I willed the stolen gift to activate; red flared around me, and his forward momentum stopped wholly with a look of cautious observance.

"How is this possible?" He spat, the dagger still in his grasp.

"Good luck, I guess." I grinned and called to my Aether once more, spending two of the bars to create a small cube of ice and lobbed it at his foot. Instead of it landing between his legs, he kicked it, and his leg turned into a solid block of ice. He lost his balance and overcorrected, pitching forward onto the frozen leg.

It shattered loudly, like glass hitting the floor.

CRITICAL STRIKE
28 dmg to Guilty GameZ
Severed Limb Debuff given
Bleeding Debuff given
Bleeding stopped due to frozen arteries

That was interesting. He laid on the ground howling in pain as the door behind me splintered inward with Gage and Sundar entering with a cadre of guards behind them.

"What is the meaning of this disturbance!" Gage lowed dangerously with his gaze casting about the room.

"I walked in on these two robbing this family," I explained hurriedly, but the look he gave me stopped me from going further.

"Seize all of them," Gage ordered to the guards who swarmed all three of us.

"But Gage, he was trying to help!" Sundar put a hand on his bicep, but he shrugged it away.

"Friends though we may be, the law in this is clear—fighting between wanderers in the city is forbidden without the proper protocols observed." Gage hefted his arm and pointed squarely at me as manacles clasped around my wrists and legs. "His name is red, too; he is just as guilty."

"And what about me?" Guilty cried out indignantly, motioning to his leg.

"There is no blood on your hands, but there is on your blade." The troll looked down to see the man they had been robbing, smiling evilly as his hand bled.

"What's going to happen?" Sundar asked with concern on her face.

"They will be taken for trial at the castle as soon as the prince awakens for the day." Gage huffed. "I am sorry."

"Your hands are tied, I understand and so does she." I offered him a polite nod and looked to Sundar. "Right?"

"Yeah." She stepped outside as the guards lugged a struggling Guilty through the door.

They began trying to drag Blasik outside, but he struggled mightily, forcing the sergeant to step in and clobber him on the face until he passed out, and the guards could carry him away.

"Thank you for going peaceably," one of the other guards whispered to me. "The family you saved asked me to thank you."

"They're welcome." I smiled, and 'though it was forced, I meant it to be relieving. "Could one of you pass a message to them?"

CHAPTER ELEVEN

The city steadily grew more monochromatic as we traveled north, color replaced by cream-colored buildings and homes that met a tall gated wall around the castle.

It was surprisingly small for a castle, only a couple of towers built almost into the far wall of the city that peeked out over the top of the wall above the city. A large domed roof covered the building in the center, the rising sunlight flashed off it. Blue sky with silvery clouds billowed behind it like a backdrop on a new screensaver. It was breathtaking.

The matte-black gates swung open, metallic clanking as we trudged through the courtyard where soldiers gathered in a circle around some spectacle, shouting encouragement to those in the center.

"Halt!" Gage barked. He stomped over to the circle and tapped one dark-skinned man on the shoulder. He was covered in dirt, his clothes torn, and bruises all over his face. A clean-shaven chin with a slash near the ear had me concerned about infection, then I noticed more and more small cuts and gashes along his arms and legs. Whoever he was, he wasn't very good at not taking damage. Gage spoke to him quietly, and he wandered over to us with the Minotaur.

"Sundar, could you heal him real quick?" I whispered to her, keeping his cut in view. "That looks like a nasty cut on his face, and the rest looks painful too."

She shrugged, and the totem raised as he stepped into the area of effect and froze.

"It's okay, Highness, it's a healing totem," Gage grumbled.

The man sighed in relief. "Thank you. Those stung a bit." He blinked at the three prisoners and motioned with a hand. "What are these ones here for? Two of them have warrants for fighting in city bounds, and the other is missing a leg. Sergeant, explain."

Gage did his best describing the scene that he had walked in on, graciously glossing over how he had known what was happening.

"And you two were doing, what?" He stepped over to Blasik and Guilty.

"Merely collecting what we were owed for a quest, Your Grace." Guilty tried to sound sincere, but his voice held more malice than sincerity.

"Liar." The man stated simply. The troll looked like he was about to start spewing curses at the man, but the guard hauled Guilty off before they could begin. One of the guards even took special care to whack the troll in the nose for one of the insults I'd heard.

"The two of you—someone rouse the orc, please?" A guard pulled a small vile out of his trousers and unstoppered it under Blasik's wide nose.

"Fuck!" The orc came to, gagging and almost vomited on the royal questioning us. "Who the hell is this tiny shit?"

The man raised his eyebrows with a grin. "I'm the prince, of course. Who swung first?"

"I did." The orc answered, then looked to me. "Pissant."

"And this was because he had interrupted you robbing my people?"

"That was because he's small, and I hate him for other reasons." Blasik sneered.

"Ah, truth again, but avoiding a question is highly suspect, and you attacked first." The prince lifted a hand and waved the soldiers holding the orc away. He roared and fought like crazy, slapping one of the soldiers away.

Before Gage could move in front of him, the prince pounced on the man's chest. Three rapid strikes with his fists saw Blasik unconscious once again, and the soldiers dragged him off.

"Majesty—" Gage began, but the prince stopped him.

"You were the reason I took up fighting, master Toomgarak." His serene look at the Minotaur halted another attempted word from Gage. "Much to my mother and fathers' chagrin, I intend to be more than a mere figurehead to my people. Thank you. Your concern is noted, but I fear not the wanderers."

He turned his gaze back to me. "and you."

"Your Majesty." I bowed my head and took a knee before him.

"Manners, excellent." He clapped before his hands fell to my shoulders. I looked up to see him kneeling before me. "Tell me everything from your perspective from the beginning."

So, I did, it was a simple, quick tale, but I related it to him. He listened quietly and intently without interruption until the end. "So, you had been attacked by Guilty's gift of fear, and were attacked, then defended yourself and the family as the orc was down and the troll came toward you with a knife. The only reason he didn't attack you first being that you had used the gift you stole from this Blasik?"

"Yes, Majesty." He frowned at my answer but didn't speak again for a moment as he stood and paced.

"I am *sorely* tempted to see you taken out of those shackles and freed, young Kyvir." The prince glanced at Gage, his countenance and bearing unreadable. "Were it not for the stringency of our laws concerning this matter, I would see you freed and rewarded for your bravery. You protected my people from worse harm."

"Majesty?" I asked with a raised hand. The guard to my left, grasped my wrist and tutted, so I dropped the hand and continued. "I respect your laws, and no matter your decision, I will hold no ill intent toward you or your people. I like this place, and I look forward to my apprenticeship."

"Move aside!" I heard an angry Brit snarl at the guards at the gate, barging through with an enraged Monami hot on his heels.

"Forgive them for what's about to happen, your Majesty," I whispered and the man snorted, before I greeted my friends. "Hey, guys!"

"Don't you 'hey guys' us, you silly *wanker!*" Albarth hissed, taking everyone around us with a glare. "What are the charges against my friend?"

"I don't give a damn what they are, release him right *now!*" Monami's demand ended in a very lion-like roar resulting in several of the soldiers in the ring stopping their cheering and turning to see this new spectacle.

"I've got this, Gage." Sundar put a hand on the Minotaur's chest. "You two need to calm the *hell* down. Kyvir did something dumb, but brave—and in the presence of royalty, it's customary to bow or curtsy!"

The two of them frowned and Sundar motioned to the prince, who seemed annoyed.

They did their best to bow and curtsy as they would, but the prince huffed. "Please, stop. I observe no such formality in the courtyard. While I am royalty, by my garb and visage, I am no different from any other man or woman in this yard at this moment. This is not court, there is no pomp and circumstance here—only action and the right by toil and arms to better oneself."

"I am proud of this new side of you, Highness," Gage grumbled proudly, his eyes filled with the pride he felt looking at the smaller man.

"The law is simple but absolute—those who break it must pay." The prince sighed. "I will see you within the hour, young Kyvir. Gage, take him to the court yourself, and stand by for judgment."

"As you will it." Gage nodded his head and lumbered forward and grasped my shoulder gently. "I know he will not fight this, Highness, are the shackles necessary?"

"They are." The prince stopped the others with a knowing gaze. "If for nothing other than the perception of safety and control. As he said, he will respect my decisions. I tasted no lie."

I nodded, and Gage led us toward the castle itself, the looming red oak doors open at the bottom on the left with a smaller, more-manageable entryway, making me realize how large the place actually was.

The halls inside held cases of trophies of monster heads and limbs, snarling beasts that looked to prowl the land surrounding the city.

"It is a barbaric practice," Albarth sneered, his nose uplifted.

"I would neglect mentioning that to the queen, she sees it as a testimony to her strength, and battle prowess," Gage advised with a wry grin. "She is the warrior of the family, though it was she who discouraged her son from following in her footsteps."

"Why?" Mona asked, and Gage took a breath to answer her question, but Sundar shook her head and pointed down at me. "Why can't you do things normally? I asked for some time to think, and you go out and try to play *hero*?!"

"Not to mention getting himself arrested." Albarth sniffed, then grunted painfully after a meaty thud. "It's true, you ruddy she-devil."

"Shut up, Al." Sundar growled fiercely, and he yelped in return.

"I wasn't playing at anything, Monami," I replied tiredly. How had things changed so drastically? "I heard someone who needed help, and I got caught up in a technicality."

"Breaking the law, even on a technicality—*oof*." Gage grunted then sniffed. "Why must you bully me so, my dear?"

"This is their conversation, damn it!" Sundar's exasperated voice would have made me smile if I wasn't so worried about Mona. Though she did seem to be smiling at him indulgently.

"Look, this wasn't anything to do with you needing space, I heard someone who needed help and interrupted a robbery that would have likely turned into a murder if I hadn't stepped in." She turned her head away, and I grabbed her arm to pull her closer to me, whispering, "A family, Mo. Two little boys watching their father being pummeled and robbed in front of them. You think for a second that you wouldn't have stepped in?"

"I know I would have, you jerk!" She shot back, her face suddenly inches from mine, her warm breath smelling like honey and some kind of grain. "But I wouldn't have given anyone the chance to get me in trouble. And I only would have stepped in if it looked like they were about to really do some damage."

"Well, we both know how impatient I am, and they had." She was still close, so I whispered, "I'm sorry I've been a jerk lately, unknowingly as it is. I don't know what to do anymore about a lot of things, but I know I'm glad you're here with me, Mona."

She opened her mouth, closed it, opened it again then frowned. "We will talk later." A statement from her, and one that settled around my neck like a noose.

"We're here." Gage rumbled, opening a door at the end of the hall into a small chamber, with a bench and a raised floor where an uncomfortable chair ominously stood. "The courtroom. This is where many have come to face their fate, and where yours shall be decided today."

"Way to make it sound less potentially crushing, big guy," Albarth muttered from his spot on the bench.

"I do not make it a habit of lying to people I like." Gage raised his chin. "I am sworn to uphold the laws of this land."

"We understand," I stated for the others, and a tense, quiet wait kept us company until a discordant fanfare erupted in the room, and the prince bolted in.

His golden cloth trousers swished and his white and gold-trimmed jacket flared behind his white-cloth-wrapped core.

"You'll have to do better than that next time, Crenshaw!" He looked happy as he sat in his chair, cutting a drastically different sight than he had earlier. His dark hair was braided with colorful beads and metal trinkets. His skin darkened against the clothes he wore, still handsome, though cleaner than before. The outfit worked for him.

All of us stood, and I tried to bow, but Gage stopped me. The prince nodded his head once, motioning for us to sit.

An older man, balding with gray hair and almost graying features in black butler attire carrying a bugle, walked in a side door. He looked sufficiently harried as he announced, "His Majesty, Prince Klemond Alaric, acting judge of this day's trial. The accused may stand."

I fought not to roll my eyes and stood, stepping toward the chair, then stopping when the elderly man held a palm out toward me.

"The accused is guilty of having attacked another wanderer within city bounds outside of a dual and training circle." He held a scroll away from his face at arm's length, then squinted, struggling to read. The prince smirked and pressed the man's hands closer to his face. "Ah, quite right, Highness, thank you. The punishment for such a crime is banishment from the city bounds for 7 days, dependent upon the circumstances, or death by hanging from the neck at his Majesty's command."

Seven days? Was that like a ban or something? Shit, the stream would be all kinds of late if that happened.

"I also hold the right to have this death be any number of other pleasant or unpleasant things." The prince waved a hand to stop the elderly man from repeating his statement. "We've discussed this Crenshaw, my word is law, but you need not repeat it for it to be so."

The man bowed at the waist but said nothing.

"How does the accused plead?" Prince Klemond raised his voice, drawing my attention back to him. I had heard movement behind me, small gasps from my friends, and terse words bordering on treasonous plotting.

"Guilty, your Highness." My honesty made him smile, it was a good smile. The kind of smile you would see from an old friend you had met at a bar or something, I imagined.

"Highness, if we may?" I heard a reedy male voice behind me but ignored it.

"Lord Foster, you absolutely may." The prince smiled wider, wrinkles gathering around his eyes in familiar smile lines. I knew this face. How?

The same bruised and beaten man who had laid on the floor in his home stepped up next to me, his torn and dirtied clothes traded for swankier duds, a nice set of breeches and a fine blouse in pastel colors that made him seem a little darker complected than he was. Bruises covered his otherwise drawn, handsome features, strong jaw, and sharp cheekbones. Blood vessels had burst in his left eye, the one that I could see as he stepped to my right.

"This wanderer likely saved my life, and the honor of my beloved wife, your second cousin, this very morning," he stated simply before bowing deeply, though with a grimace of pain.

"You have yet to see a healer, Lord Foster?" Prince Klemond observed, though his tone held a question.

"I could not, in good faith, leave this man unrewarded for his kindness and courage." Lord Foster raised himself from his show of prostration, a little relieved. Pitter pattering footfalls echoes behind us, and the door we'd entered through burst inward.

Two tiny raised voices cried out, "Wait!"

The two boys I had seen cowering behind their mother sprinted in front of their father and I protectively, the man reaching down to grasp at his children in futility as they danced out of his reach.

"Ah, the young lordlings Foster!" The prince's face took on a serious cast, a scowling, with his eyes narrowed in their direction. "Is this how we greet nobility, now?"

They shook their heads before mimicking their father's deep bow, the youngest one bending far too far, somersaulting onto his back.

Prince Klemond roared, at first, I thought in anger, but he slapped his knee and bellowed, "Well come here then, boys!"

The two children giggled and sprinted forward to greet him with a flying hug, him picking them up, and Crenshaw muttering evilly.

"Why do you two interrupt my court, little ones?" The royal tousled their hair playfully as he sat with them standing on either side of his knees. "Lord Foster, I beg you, please sit while Crenshaw fetches the castle's healer."

"Maj—*oof*," Sundar started, then grunted, and fell silent.

"But, Highness, this is a grave matter, I can send a servant," Crenshaw complained, his face reddening slightly as if offended.

"Nonsense!" Prince Klemond barked and waved a hand. "My dear man, this is a matter of the court, and who better to fetch the finest healer in all the castle than the finest steward in the castle?"

"The damned *servants!*" The old man howled, shaking his fist at the prince.

"Crenshaw, mind the young ones," the prince tutted pointedly at the older man.

"You *are* the young one," the steward began, then growled and turned on the spot to leave the room. He bumped into a guard on his way out and snarled, "Step aside, you blundering tin can!"

Once the door slammed shut, the prince chuckled and sighed as if in relief, "Please, everyone relax. He reports to my family, and this is the second time this week, I've done this to him. He's such a stickler at times."

Gage rumbled behind me, "He means well, Highness."

"He means well but stands on too much tradition and perceived need for rigmarole that he bars true progress." The prince motioned for the boys to join their father, and they did so.

"I take it the two of you precede my lovely cousin, Tethin? What have you to say, boys?"

"He helped our father, cousin Klemond," the oldest boy, about ten years old with short-cropped brown hair affirmed. "And his bravery sparked our own!"

"Oh?" Prince Klemond leaned back in surprise.

"Yup!" The younger boy, maybe six, hopped and accidentally landed on my foot. "Sorry, sir."

I grunted, he wasn't heavy, but it had been my little toe, and it hurt. "Think nothing of it."

"Please explain, Darin and Bren, you're growing discordant again." Their father stated knowingly as the boys fidgeted.

"We've decided to take up arms and defend our country!" Darin raised a fist and put it to his heart as he clicked his heels together.

"And I'm gonna join the Kings Guard!" Bren tried to follow in his brother's smart manipulation of his body but hit himself hard enough that a small, "*oof,*" escaped.

"Well, I'll be..." Klemond raised a hand to his face to try and hide another smile. "This is a serious commitment boys, and your mother would see me flogged for even allowing you to entertain the thought without her knowledge."

"You give too much credit, beloved cousin," a strong but light voice reached my ears. I turned to see the pale woman from before, her dress matching the same pastels and fine make of her husband's attire. She seemed to float forward until she stood beside Lord Foster, curtsying gracefully.

"Tethin." Prince Klemond stood and rushed down to give her a hug, looking her over before deciding she was all right. "I would hear all of your testimonies."

They each spoke about their morning horror. Waking for breakfast only to find that their home had been invaded and was being lazily looted by two would-be thieves turned violent thugs when confronted. They had beaten Lord Foster into telling them where his personal valuables were and would have gotten to much more *valuable* items provided I hadn't stepped in.

"I see." The prince's demeanor was withdrawn, thoughtful as he considered the evidence he had been given.

It was at this time that Crenshaw returned with an older man who whisked into the room in a rather lively spirit, his huge bushy eyebrows sagging as he regarded us all.

"Lord Foster, sit on the other bench, rather lay down, son." His wizened voice was cheerful, though concerned, and as his patient did as he was bid, he set to work with a flare of golden energy around his hands.

"Thank you for coming, Heathcliffe," Prince Klemond called out, and the old man just nodded and went about his business.

He turned his attention back to me. "In light of recent events, evidence collected, and the gaining of two potentially fine men to add to our forces, I believe I have reached a verdict. Is there anyone else who would speak on behalf of the accused?"

Accused debuff received – all stats dropped to 5.

I watched in horror as all my stats dropped, and my health sank, my Aether disappearing with it all.

"I will, Highness." Gage stood where he was and spoke loudly for all gathered to hear, "Kyvir Mageblood is one of the four members here before you today who killed a man-eating Hell Cat that had taken the miners of the West Mine hostage this week. In the time I have known this group, they have proven forthright and friendly to our cause, even going so far as to protect the citizens that other Wanderers treat as ghosts until they are needed or want something."

Crenshaw frowned, leaned forward, and whispered something to the prince that made the man frown, "And this is why you had requested a stipend from the castle yesterday? As a reward for their feat?"

"It is as you say, Highness," Gage said, his voice a deep rumble.

"It is granted, with a bonus of fifty gold to Kyvir for his bravery today," though he sounded happy, there was still a look of mighty displeasure on the prince's face. "Though I cannot speak for my cousins in this matter, I would urge you to seek them out upon your return to our world."

"After he returns?!" Mona shouted, the others having to fight to restrain her. "What do you mean?"

"Our law is strict, and though I am capable of lenience, the minimum is required." He looked genuinely sad, and once again, I found myself reaching for a familiar memory trying to puzzle out why he was so familiar. "The minimum for a wanderer being... death, and restriction from returning for three tolls of the bell. I am sorry, Kyvir Mageblood."

I tried to sound cheerful, though it would put a serious damper on my being able to catch up with the others as far as gear was concerned.

My heart thundered, and I could hear the others whispering furiously behind me.

"Your manner of dispatch shall be swift," the prince stood, his voice rising over the others, and stepped toward me with his hand held toward me. I took it and shook it. "I do hope you can forgive me in this and not hold the city responsible."

"I won't, you're doing your best at a job you seem to not really care for." I smiled sadly. "I know how that can be sometimes. It's not your fault I broke the law."

"Honorable and honest." Klemond squeezed his hand gently around mine. "When you join the guild, send word to me, and I will see if we cannot reward you further for this service you unwittingly have done us, so soon after the first. And do seek out my cousin, the Lady Foster. She will likely have something for you as well. Goodbye for now, Kyvir."

He lifted a vial from his breast pocket, a dark liquid, and handed it to me.

Bane's Match – A fast-acting poison known for painless dispatch. (1 dose)

"Thank you, Prince Klemond." I looked to the others. "Get things done here for me, okay? A sword or glaive to help me fight, and then I'll be back before you know it. Counting on you all."

They looked to be resigned, though Mona had an air about her like she was ready to fight me and everyone else.

I unstoppered the poison and tipped it into my mouth. A hint of black licorice coated my tongue, and I gagged. Never could stand the stuff.

You have died.

Warning: You are close to a milestone level. After passing it, death's consequences are much harsher.

Be more careful, wanderer.

The screen inside my mind that stats seemed to play on when the game was loading flashed twice, then was replaced by the same voice that had greeted me when I'd first gotten into the portal.

You have been suspended from the game for three in-game hours, or one hour in real-time.

00:59:46

Chapter Twelve

The same clock ticked in the outside view of the portal door as had inside, so I just got out and moved into the shower real quick. Grabbed a bite to eat from the fridge and decided to scroll through some social media. The punishment had really only been a minor inconvenience, which was nice, considering it could have been seven days.

A lot of positive news at the moment. Pollen counts were low, and life on the planet seemed to be thriving.

I watched a video of fox kits playing on a trampoline as a flock of swallows flitted overhead.

A woman's voice off-screen gasped and said, "This literally *never happens!*"

I grinned and scrolled down, seeing some excitement about Mephisto's and the coming streaming we would be doing. I tried to gauge how it would go for us that all our roles seemed to have been changed, but the crowd was in a frenzy over the latest news. Apparently, the servers for Blood and Gore had gone down for emergency maintenance, so I couldn't even hop on for a minute to stream for them really fast for an update.

Some folks still seemed a little irked that we weren't playing Blood and Gore, but that was to be expected. Normally, I'd just let the stream speak for itself, but I decided to post something to the web for once.

Hey guys!

We haven't forgotten about you, and MMO is a blast! The world is so fresh and new, and the nuances of it are breathtaking. We cannot wait for you to join us, but that's all I can say since we want the stream to speak for itself.

Magically yours,

Mageblood

What would it say? Time would tell, but people would like it, or they wouldn't. I just had to hope that was enough to keep them happy.

We would be playing a game together, and that would have to be what mattered.

Scrolling past that, I saw something of interest. More attacks from shadowy figures. In the photos, they looked blurry, and a thicker halo of darkness coalesced around them in the videos, but the footage was... garbage compared to how I knew technology was.

We had cameras that could capture motion from a fly and still the wings with no motion or blur whatsoever. This looked like it had been taken on an ancient camera phone from the early twenty-first century.

It was blurry, spotty, faded in places, and then fuzzy altogether, then the figure left the frame, and things were almost crystal clear once more.

Victims appeared to consist of the ill, infirm, young, or elderly, where they gathered or populated the most densely. Hospitals. Parks.

Each time, the police couldn't find the weapon they had used to enact their hellish act of terror. Dozens wounded and dead each time.

It had gotten to the point that there looked to be a movement of former military going to guard over local hospitals and senior centers. Cops patrolling areas on higher frequency and calls for people not to go places alone and if they see anything strange to contact authorities immediately.

One anchor reported an unprecedented crop growth in Utah, while another video showed a group of teens who had planted trees weeks before in a town in Texas that had grown to more than hip height in days.

"What in the world is going on?" I grumbled to myself. The demons are supposed to be in the damned game, right?

What was the world coming to these days?

Hopefully, I never had to use those weapons I'd ordered to protect myself here in my own home.

My door swung open, banging loudly and I looked up to see Mona standing in the afternoon light, glaring daggers at me.

"What are you doing here?" I stood and walked toward her. "Why aren't you in the game, right now?!"

"Shut up!" She snarled, and I shut my mouth. "What the *hell* do you think you're doing?"

"Well, I was scrolling some social media, getting an outlook on the world around us if you must know." I showed her my phone, but she only advanced on me.

"I leave you alone for one minute, needing time to myself to think and sort through what I've been dealing with and going through, and you go and get yourself *expelled from the game?*"

"I didn't do it on purpose!" I shot back, tossing my phone onto the beanbag chair, I wanted my hands empty if we were going to be upset with each other. "You heard those people, Mona. If I hadn't stepped in—"

"People?!" She rolled her eyes and shut my door calmly. That worried me. "Those are NPCs, Seth. Non. Player. Characters. They're *AI algorithms* meant to simulate real people. They aren't real."

"No? Then what's the big deal about some non-player character kissing me on the cheek?" She frowned, and I continued. "Yes, Sondra and I knew about Alex, and we had a private conversation. We have our own secrets, Mo, and that one isn't for me to share. And you know that I'm not perfect, but I can't leave someone in need. It's not my nature. Fake or real."

"And that puts more pressure on the rest of us!" She smacked the arm of my couch. "We're all doing our best, Seth, but we need each other to do that effectively."

"And I called on who I had to call on, Sondra was in a prime place to come to my aid." I sat down on the beanbag chair, then stood back up. "I did my best. Okay? I've *been* doing my best. Is that not enough for you?"

"I know you have." She sighed heavily. She looked worn down. Tired and almost haunted. "It's a lot on all of us. It's a game. It's *just* a game. But it feels so real, and I can't help but feel like there's something so..."

She closed her eyes and frowned, using her hands to motion in the air.

"So familiar about it," I finished for her, moving closer, knowing she needed me. Tears fell from her closed eyes.

"I see so many things that my dad would have loved to make." Her breath hitched, and she sniffed. "I close my eyes, and I can hear him talking about a city made of stone so dense it was like the earth had borne it from her stony womb. Of people trading and talking in the streets. I see some of the races that we had dreamt about—Gage? He's one my father would have loved, Seth."

I drew her into a hug, holding her close and resting my chin on her head. "Look, I can't change what I did, and I can't promise I won't do something as dumb again. But it did pay off. And why on earth are you even here? Why aren't you leading the charge on getting our gear ready?"

"I took the time to get our orders in, and with the funds we got, we could afford uncommon gear, but we figured we would save money and use my discount to get good common items to fight with." She hugged me tightly around my waist, tears dotting my shirt. "The others are working on basic gear, but we can worry on that later."

She patted her eyes dry, then looked up at me, puffy cheeks and sparkling green eyes filling my sight. "Why would you bring up someone kissing you on the cheek, Seth?"

My cheeks burned and I decided that since she was here and we were being honest, I should come clean. Al had been right, Sondra too.

"Alex told me that he had thought seeing that had upset you. You did seem angry." I sighed as I sat her on the couch with myself next to her. "You know, we constantly joke with each other about relationships, but I need to know. Are we okay?"

She floundered a bit, trying to come up with words to thoughts that were racing in her mind, the same thing happening in me. My heart leaping in my ribs as she struggled to find words.

"I... yes, Seth, of course, we're okay." Her cheeks reddened. "What would make you think we aren't?"

"I never said that." I blurted almost as soon as she finished her sentence. "I meant, are we okay as we are now? Do you want... *more* from me?"

"Whose idiotic thoughts are those I need to beat out of your thick head?" She scoffed, rolling her eyes, but it was there. That hesitation she had when she was lying or trying to cover up for something.

"I'm serious, Mona." My whole body burned at that moment, and her proximity was like sitting next to an open flame. "I've been *noticing* you more lately, and part of me thinks I've finally gone off my rocker seeing auras outside the game.

Part of me wonders if this is a natural progression. Part of me wonders if this question will ruin what we have forever."

"Three parts dumb and the rest useless?" She tried to tease, but she was building a wall up, something she rarely ever did. I could see her looking at me strangely, weirder than she ever had, and it hurt.

Like she was seeing a stranger for the first time. And here I was looking at her in almost the exact same way. Did I have a right to claim I knew her better than anyone if I had thrown this at her feet, and she had kicked it aside?

"Ha-ha." I looked away, wondering why it almost hurt more that she wouldn't give me a straight answer. Now that this wormhole was open, what would come out of it other than the strange look?

I stood up, needing to be away from her for a moment, and checked my watch. Another fifteen minutes and I could get back in.

"You should head home." Even to me, my voice sounded like a croak. "By the time you get there and log in, it'll be long enough that I can join you all and we can start streaming shortly after."

"I'm sorry I yelled." Her voice was off, I turned to see her wiping her face. "It's been years since I yelled at you like that. We never fight, and you were doing your best, what the hell is going on with us?"

"Couldn't say, but hey—I'll always have your back, Mo." I heard her stand and walk toward me, but I turned back and hit her with a grin reserved almost only for her. Fake as it felt on my face, I tried.

It was better this way. No secrets. I'd come clean and I'd walk away that way, too. Besides, this just proved that we were too much like family to have any true interest in each other, right? Sure, she had dodged the question, but that was just to protect me from the rejection. It had to be. Good ol' Mona. Always thinking of me.

She looked a little lost for words, and I couldn't tell what she was thinking at that moment. "Come here and give me a hug before you go."

She took a steadying breath and came toward me; I held my arms out and blinked once as a fist connected with my abdomen.

"Ouch!" I groaned, doubling over from the sucker punch. "What the hell, Mona?"

"That was for making me worry." Her hands grabbed a handful of my hair, and she hefted my head up until she could look into my eyes. "You and I are family, Seth. And my love for you is unending—but the weird stuff in my life always comes from family, and I don't need that from you too. Okay?"

"But did you have to hit me so hard?" I whined, my stomach spasming a little painfully as I chuckled.

"I only ever hit people who annoy me." She grinned, no hesitance this time. "I love you, you big idiot. And I'll always have your back, too. Now, let's get our crap together and entertain some people while we own this game. Okay?"

"Let's." I grinned and gave her a bear hug before she left.

Time to get serious.

***

"Welcome back to our new criminal tank." Albarth clapped sarcastically as I stepped inside the courtyard.

When I respawned, Trickle had been there to splash me with water in greeting.

"Welcome back!" Her giggling followed me out of the square, and by the time I made it to the royal practice grounds that made up the courtyard, I was dry once more.

"Yeah, yeah." I rolled my eyes and fought the urge to throw a snowball at him with my magic. "How's prep going?"

"Better than well." He jerked his chin behind me, and I turned to find a freshly healed Lord Foster.

"Master Kyvir, a word?" His stern, pinched mien looked more a product of his actual features than the bruising and beating.

I stepped over to the side of the gate with him to where his family stood. "Hey, everyone. I'm glad that you all seem to be doing well."

"And it is, in no small way, thanks to you." Tethin bowed her head. "And as a show of our appreciation, we would like to offer you not just our words, but our secret as well."

I stilled. "Secret?"

"Yes." Lord Foster reached into his blouse sleeve and pulled out a small tube-like canister of vellum, it was black and inscribed with strange symbols flowing along the side.

"What is it?" I came back to myself, my hand almost touching it before I pulled my hand away.

"Something that could have made my family very wealthy," Tethin stated calmly, running her hands through her sons' hair. "It is an heirloom that secured the prophecy as more than just a prophecy. What is contained in that is Aether."

"Aether?" I waved my hands to the world around us. "From what I understand, it's all around us. How can that thing contain something abundant?"

"Not normal Aether–aspected Aether." Lord Foster thumped the container and pressed it toward me. "We knew that since the wanderers had arrived, we might be able to sell this for a steep price and live with funds bordering the royal family for a long, long time."

"Why not use it yourself?" It seemed absurd that they should offer it to a stranger.

"It is only useful to the wanderers whose bodies can adapt to a myriad of different Aether types." Tethin closed her eyes, frowning as if trying to remember something. "Each being may have some attachment to the Aether of this world, but the wanderers can adjust their new bodies to many types. If they can find them or unlock them."

So, even if your gift and magic type are chosen based on biology and certain myriad other factors that the game's AI used to divvy our power, you could still unlock other types? That was awesome.

Though, that could lead to people being rather broken. "What's the drawback?"

"His Highness's initial assumption that you were cunning was not far off from the mark, as usual." Foster's thin lips quirked into a smirk. "Your Aether pool is consumed by the magic. Think of it like having a pond, and when you only have one type of magic at your disposal, the whole of it can be used to the fullest."

He bent down, taking a dagger from his sleeve and began to illustrate his words by drawing a circle.

"Having access to more types of magic cuts the Aether by half." He slashed the circle in two making a flame on one side and a mountain on another. "Half the Aether you have can be used for one type of magic, and the other for the other. What is your current Aether pool at? Uh, how many bars do you have?"

I held up seven fingers, attempting to understand the meaning of what he explained.

"I see, so you would have three ice bars, and another three of the other type of magic." He drew out a small bar beneath it, making four slashes to separate the five bars. "The seventh and final bar is what we would refer to as the gray bar."

Before I could ask, Tethin explained, "It is a bar where the Aether mixes and can be used for either type of magic."

"So, having a gray bar isn't a bad thing?" I was hopeful for that not to be a bad thing.

"Not particularly, but it is a weaker, diluted source," Foster interrupted my thoughts of having a constant gray bar if I could manage it. "Since it isn't dedicated, the Aether pollution caused by mixing types can dilute the strength of the spell, sometimes even warping it altogether."

That put a damper on things. "But having more magic could be nice. Monami only has one type of magic, and it's metal, so maybe we could give it to her."

"No." Tethin stopped me with a hand on my chest. "We give this to you, and only you. To show the depth of what your sacrifice meant to us."

I took a deep breath, then exhaled. "As you wish."

I gratefully accepted the container and looked to Lord Foster, who mimicked opening it toward his face, then he stepped back.

I found the cap to the vellum case with my fingers, the soft material giving to my grasp as the cap twisted out of the way and almost flying out of the way as a gray vapor burst out of it.

The volume of the gaseous Aether surprised me, had it been compressed? I caught a glance of the vellum case, and it occurred to me that it had been sealed.

Whatever it was flowed around me, coming into contact with my skin, then it picked up speed as it whirled and whirled touching, then passing through me. It lifted into the blue sky, casting a slight shadow as it passed above me, then slammed into me all at once.

The force of it tossed me onto my back, my vision flickered, then solidified into a message.

Aether obtained

Aether type obtained – Summoning

Summoning?

"What type of Aether was it?" I blinked at the question from Tethin and sat up.

I looked at my Aether pool and three of the bars on the right side of it glowed deep purple.

"Summoning, is what it said, but how am I supposed to unlock that?" They looked uncertain, very much so. "Is that bad?"

"It's not bad, but we don't know anyone who can summon anything, but Armenes may know something." Tethin reached down and shoved her eldest son forward. "You remember where his office is? With how much you like to sneak in and bother him."

The boy looked slightly embarrassed, but nodded. "I can take him, momma."

"Thank you, Darin." Lord Foster tussled the boy's hair and took the youngest boy up into his arms before looking at me. "Young Kyvir, we are in your debt still, and we will see you and your friends cared for how we can. I do hope that you will call us friends from here on. Darin, as soon as you complete your task, to the back yard, boy. I will teach you and your brother the sword from this day forth. And I shall see that master Ori has work making weapons for us. He is, after all, the best smith in the city."

I nodded at them all, their smiles genuine as they turned to be on their way, Darin took my hand and tugged. "Follow me, Mister Kyvir!"

"Call me Kyvir, Darin," I admonished him lightly with a feigned serious tone. "Let's go!"

He bolted across the yard, and I followed along easily enough. He must have been eager to begin his training with as swiftly as he dodged and whipped his body between people training still in the yard.

I followed along, but sent a whisper to the others, —*Hey guys, I'm going to speak with Armenes real fast about a type of magical reward I just got. Be right with you.*—

Nothing came back from them for a moment, then Sundar replied, —*I was there earlier, be nice!*—

I rolled my eyes and sped on behind Darin. The training soldiers grunted at him, one of them almost hitting him with a pike in surprise. A decently placed elbow to the wood on my part spared Darin a wound and the guard his life.

The man blustered and sputtered a quickly fading apology while we raced away.

"Keep clear of the people swinging weapons, kid!" I shouted at him and he ducked his head once before speeding toward the castle door.

"Think ye slick, lad?!" Called the eldest guard, a large man with a thick brown mustache and receding hairline. He was burly and well built. "Reckon yer off ta the mage again?"

"Yes, sir!" Darin called excitedly.

"Well, don't ye be puttin' funny things in his soup no more, aye?" He pointed a massive finger toward the boy, his armor rattling with the motion. "Ye do, an' kith o' the royals or not, I'll be tannin' yer hide."

"I'll keep him out of trouble, sir." I offered helpfully, but the guard caught both of us easily as we tried to flit through him and his partner.

"You died once for a mistake, boy, best leave it to his conscience." The guard winked at me before I could think to take offense, then whispered. "Do mind the lad, aye? Has quick hands an' a wicked mischievous streak."

I snorted then noticed that the child was already sprinting into the building as the guard pointed to him. "See?"

I grunted affirmation and took off after him. He led me to the end of the hall, passing the door to the courtroom and then we hung a right and stopped in front of a solitary brown door. It looked like the broom closet.

He opened the door to a dark room that hid a thin set of stairs leading up.

"This leads up to his study and quarters, follow it straight up and knock, his helper will open the door." He turned to go, then stopped. "Will you be okay on your own?"

"There a dragon up there?" I asked with raised eyebrows.

He smiled. "Just the old man, Kyvir. And thanks again for saving us."

"You be sure to learn well and take care of your family when you get strong enough." I held my hand out to him so that he could shake it. "And putting things in a wizard's soup is not a good way to stay alive long enough to do that."

He grinned and took off back in the direction we had come from before I climbed the stairs. I shook my head and resolved myself to the climb up toward my needed information.

I slapped a spider sliding down a web toward my shoulder.

3 dmg to spider

Spider died, no EXP

That was interesting, I snorted to myself and began my trek up the stairs, the gentle curve up only beginning to cause a dizzy tilt after a few minutes. The climb had to have been designed to disorient and keep people from fighting up it.

After what seemed like forever in that godforsaken hole, I finally came to a slight window. The view from it was upside down, and the vertigo that set my mind to reeling was unreal. The sky was down, and the land was up with birds doing loops and loops, sending my stomach into fits of pre-vomit flips. I slammed my eyes shut and focused on the fresh air coming in to attempt settling myself, then moved on upward once more.

After what felt like an even longer trek, I found myself back in the room that I had just left.

"What in the..." I turned, and the stairs were there, in the small cubby exactly as they had been.

I frowned, then snapped, "If I have to spend the rest of my day climbing *these damned stairs.*" I felt my anger flare until a light splayed across my back and flung my shadow to the wall before me.

"If you would please, lower your voice, sir." A growling tone grated from the light behind me.

I whipped around to see a younger man, then I realized he wasn't a man at all—he was a dwarf!

"Quit looking at me all moonstruck, young man," his voice had a more-cultured lilt to it that was nice, but his scowl said a lot. His beard was blond and trimmed on the sides so that the bottom was longer in a single braid down his chest. He wasn't as well-muscled as Felix or some of the other dwarves I had seen when I had first come to the game, but he was still brawny in his green robe.

"What do you want?" He said, likely for the second time with how exasperated he was. "The master and I are exceptionally busy."

"I needed to speak to your master regarding magic I need unlocked." I held my hand out to shake his, but he just stared at it.

"Another wanderer with sealing magic? That'd be two in one day, highly unusual." He tittered to himself, his fingers fidgeting with his beard.

"I don't have sealing magic; I have summoning magic." His eyes widened. "I was told that your master may know what I have to do to unlock it."

"Master!" The dwarf hollered, and a great shifting and sliding sound echoed in the room. I followed the dwarf inside in time to see a large lizard-like creature, not quite a dragon, but not fully human, either shuffling forward.

His scales sagged, and he had some kind of scaly version of a beard on his face that shook as he spoke, "What is it, Nevilin?"

"Master Armenes, this wanderer seeks knowledge." Nevilin bolted toward me and hauled me closer to the older being, his large body taking up a great amount of space. He easily dwarfed Gage, and his horns appeared to have been carved from his head.

"Another one, you say?" The great, green-scaled wizard's clawed hand lifted a pair of thick spectacles to his half snout nose before narrowing his eyes at me. "Kin? Kin do not typically have an affinity for sealing magic. Curious."

"It's for summoning, sir." Nevilin corrected helpfully, hauling a large tome from a shelf off to the left of the doorway. The room was much larger than the tower outside looked able to hold. Had to be some kind of spatial magic trick to hold more things that were popular in a lot of movies and books. Cool. Bags of holding? Even cooler.

Shelves of all sorts of varying sizes and widths covered the walls with books of varying types, titles, and colors all over. No real system that I could see was in place, but it was neat and tidy.

"Ah, yes, summoning magic is rarer even than our own, Nevilin." Armenes squinted over the tome the dwarf had brought him. "Here we are, 'let he whose body becomes the vessel for others come to the east, where she of the mountain holds sway.' That seems very straightforward."

"Forgive us, Master Armenes, we are but mortals who cannot hope to grasp the strands of time that color your life's weave." Even I was impressed by the amount of bull crap the dwarf could sling with his words, the wizard simply raised a scaled eyebrow ridge and the little man hurriedly added, "we do not seem to think it so straightforward."

"Why Nevilin, you should know of whom I speak—you grew up there."

"Belgonna's Hold?!" Nevilin gasped with a hand over his heart. Something told me that this guy was a bit dramatic. "But you couldn't possibly mean the great one, in that passage, could you?"

"Yes." he shut the tome with a soft whoosh of escaping air that ruffled my hair. "He will need to venture through the plains to visit She of the Crimson Fury. Lady of the Sulfurous Lake. Your mother."

"I have to go see your mother?" I raised an eyebrow at the dwarf.

"She is not my birth mother, she adopted me when I was abandoned." Nevilin ran his hands through his long blond hair, tucking it back behind his ears.

"Well she doesn't sound that bad, I don't know why she has all those titles." I blinked up at Armenes, he seemed content to watch and listen. "And I feel like little Darin needs a thumping for not telling me you're a dragon, *and* for putting things in your soup."

"He is half right, though I am much, *much* less of a dragon than some out there." Armenes' sharp teeth flashed in a wry smile. "I quite like the boy; he is rambunctious, and his pranks keep my mind sharp. I permit him to come into my sealed laboratory and study here so that I might see him from time to time and test his wits. As to the draconic moniker, well, that is a story for another day. Suffice it for now that I had too much greed for power at a young age and sought to overcome my mortality with an ancestral ability. Creating an abominable thing."

"I don't think that you're an abomination, Armenes." I tried to smile at him, his great green eyes narrowing at me funnily. "Intimidating? Sure. But there are so many new things in this world for my kind, and me, more than a few of us would accept you."

"That nice young orc lady gave me a kiss on the cheek." More of his teeth flashed in the brightly lit room. "Do you plan to do the same, young Kin?"

I had to laugh at his forward glance and suggestive eyebrow waggling, though my cheeks warmed at the thought of Trickle and her brazen act. "I'm not much for kisses, mermaids being the exception, but how about I resolve to come back and chat with you?"

"Another guest for a lonely old man?" He looked over to a still nervous-looking Nevilin. "Why, that would be a wonderful distraction, thank you."

"Before I go too far, is there a way to get there swiftly?" They both seemed to be confused by the question, so I asked a different way. "Would there be a way to go through a portal? Or some kind of flying creature who can take my friends and me? Including the young orc lady?"

"The young orc lady is a friend of yours?" I nodded, and he rumbled happily. "Excellent. She is welcome too. Unfortunately, travel like that requires a powerful space magic-user who has been to a place before. Unless there is one that I am unaware of here, you will have to get guild permission to travel on."

"Ah, well, thank you for your insight and formidable knowledge." I bowed at the waist to both of them. "I truly appreciate your time."

I felt a prod from a dull item on top of my head and saw Armenes' clawed forefinger retreating. "My sealing magic in the stairwell should no longer bother you. Be safe, and watch for the Lady in Crimson, while you are away. The way there is dangerous, but not overly so. She is fair, but she can also be fickle. Goodbye."

I left the master and dwarf to their own devices, the older wizard chuckling as Nevilin stuttered something at him just before the click of the lock sliding home shut me out of the room.

Getting back down the stairs was a breeze, though I felt adding stairs as well as sprints, to my workout routine was necessary if I'd be climbing as much as I was.

"Wait!" I heard a voice pant behind me. I turned to see a flushed and sweaty Nevilin rushing toward me. "Wait... please wait."

I stood there quietly as he caught his breath, then listened to him speak, "Be careful of my mother. She has a knack for collecting things—people—it matters not. Mind yourself."

"Just what is she?" I shook my head at his attempted warning. "You make her out to be some sort of monster."

"We are forbidden to tell those who do not already know anything more but please." He looked a little manic now, making me worry. "She is not what she seems to be, and she is stronger than you could ever imagine. She has a good heart, and is full of wonder and love to give, but do not cross her, or my siblings. They will devour you."

"Noted, thank you, Nevilin." I offered him my hand once more and remembered he didn't like that, so I took it back and offered him a slight nod of the head instead.

He gave me one in return then panted his way back up the stairs. No wonder he was a little less built than the other dwarves I'd seen.

Leaving the castle was easy enough, but a direction after that was a little more difficult.

—p/Where are you all?— I whispered to the others.

—p/We're all over at Gage's place with Alvor. He has our gear.— Sundar explained.

I grinned like it was Christmas all over again and made my way to his place at a light jog.

I arrived there with only one person cursing at me for him not paying attention to where he was, so I was happy about that.

I found the gate to the back fence and let myself into the back yard. Alvor stood with a large burlap bag next to his left foot and spoke to the others excitedly.

Albarth, Sundar, Gage, and Monami chuckled and listened well as they hefted their own weapons.

Monami had a modified version of the chakrams, their sharp circular edges bisected by almost-s-shaped handles. They were about ten inches in diameter, and she rolled her wrists with them easily as if getting comfortable with the weight.

Albarth had a rapier on his hip as if it were the most natural thing in the world, though he was holding a blade I wasn't familiar with. It was roughly dagger sized, but thicker at the base and almost blocky until it came to a boxed tip.

Sundar carried a long sword on her hip that looked well-crafted, and the leather sheath looked very well kept.

"Here he is," Gage rumbled as he came from his garden, clapping dirt from his hands onto his pants and transferring a green vegetable between both his hands gingerly as he did so. "Welcome back, Kyvir. You'll be pleased to know that those other two who were punished got the full sentence. They are gone for seven days."

"Thank you! You know, I didn't get to ask last time, but with the instrument and the gardening." I motioned to the garden, then the vegetable in his hand. "Why?"

His head cocked to the right as he tossed me the item, motioning for me to eat it. "Why what, my friend?"

"Why do it at all?" I took a bite of the vegetable, the skin was firm and had a bitter, earthy flavor to it, but the sweetness of the inside overtook it all. A subtle hint of heat came after that, making me groan—this was delicious. "Aside from tending delicious things like this, wouldn't your time be better spent refining fighting techniques?"

His demeanor changed from curious to accepting. "Ah. This is a question I receive all too often from people who do not understand war and battle."

He grasped me by the shoulder and ushered me into the garden. "Do you see all of the things here?"

I did. Purple vines sprouted from the ground and crawled around through a lattice of white and black, where the same kind of vegetable I'd eaten grew. Rows of plants that resembled corn stood stoutly in close formation, their loads borne by thick shoots with green leaves flaring out here and there.

Other plants that resembled tomatoes grew near strange things I couldn't even liken to plants I'd ever seen on earth.

I nodded, and he smiled. "All of these plants require patience and knowledge to groom and grow. As much knowledge as it takes to lead men into battle, if not more. I choose to be the farmer who knows how to fight, rather than a person who knows only combat and comes home with nothing to offer their people but what they know."

"Is that really a thing?" I couldn't hide my ignorance. I had never thought of enlisting or serving.

"It is," Sundar answered quietly, making me look back to see a somber look on her face. "There are kids who join the military straight out of high school and train in nothing but combat-style occupations. Their very lives are about destruction and chaos. They spend their waking hours perfecting ways to destroy their country's enemies and protect the men and women to their right and left to the point that their training is as instinctive as breathing."

Her voice took on a jaded tone, her eyes closing as she seemed to recall horrid memories. "Then those kids see combat. Their friends die, getting blown up in front of them, or shot by the enemy. They get injured, and then the army thanks them for their service and sends them home to people who don't understand them and without any truly marketable skills. They're broken, hurting, and feel useless, so there's nothing for them, and that hopelessness cultivates anger. Sometimes that anger finds a good outlet. Other times... my brothers and sisters aren't so lucky."

"Then your ranks lose even more as well," Gage confirmed softly, his horned head bobbing knowingly. "This is a thing I have seen, too. I have taken great pains to ensure my command knows to teach skills, ones like music so that our people are more than just warriors. We have poets, writers, musicians, farmers, crafters, and other talented individuals among our ranks who I am proud to have had serve with me. Does that answer your question, my friend?"

"Yes." I frowned and thought about my lot in life. Maybe I should donate to some good causes for veterans, as well? I'd talk to Sundar about that. She likely knew some. "Thank you for entertaining my ignorance with patience."

"Education starts with humility, Kyvir." Gage clapped me on the back and almost knocked me off my feet. "Admitting ignorance is a start, and to start toward something better by learning about your fellow man is indeed a noble path."

"Noble path or not, we need to get on the trail to leveling up some more." Sundar grabbed me by my shoulder and led me to Alvor.

"Hello Kyvir." he bent down and opened his pack, lifting out a short sword in a well-kept sheath the same color as Sundar's. I pulled it from its home, the heft and balance so much better than the poor quality one.

Basic short sword
Quality: Common
Base dmg: 2-5 dmg
Durability: 10
Worth: 5 silver.

I had seen a similar weapon before, but now I was worried.

"I hadn't gotten the chance to get to initiate with the sword!" I smacked my hand to my forehead, and Gage snorted.

"Nothing a bout of training cannot fix." The Minotaur grinned at me. "It adds minimal damage at lower levels, but a point or so of increased damage can add up. We will see you to rights."

I smiled back, relieved at the added thought by the master swordsman.

"Now, this one was an odd request as well, but it was more than fun to work on, and master Ori liked it so much he's decided to try making other weapons like it." Alvor grunted and hefted out a larger, odd-looking weapon.

It looked like a sword blade that started a foot and a half up the handle, came to a rounded but sharpened tip then swept back about halfway down the other side with more cutting edge. The grip had leather wrapped around it but appeared to be hollowed out near the bottom. It was a very queer attempt at a sword, seeing as the handle of it was more than a foot and a half long without the bladed portion. The whole thing was three and a half feet long.

Then he pulled out another portion that looked identical to the first.

"This is a glaive that you can separate." Alvor stepped closer to me and showed me that there was a portion of the second half that slid into the first half, twisting into place with ease. "They're twins and built to be like long swords, so if you want to take them apart and use them that way—you can."

He passed the item to me, and I had to marvel at the balance of it.

Separable Glaive
Quality: Uncommon
Base dmg: 4-9 dmg

Durability: 10

Worth: 2 gold

Woah! "That cost, is this okay?" I looked to the others. "Can we afford this?"

"With your earnings from the crown for both acts of bravery?" Gage chuckled, snorting after he finished making his nose ring flop onto his top lip. "I imagine that it would be fine."

"How much did we earn?" Monami opened her inventory as I asked and tossed me a small pouch of forty-seven gold and five silver pieces.

"That was after we paid for both of your weapons, and that's your individual earnings from the prince." Albarth tossed another small bag my way after that statement. This one held four gold. "That was from the guards as a stipend. With that, we can go get armor and things."

"And no, armor isn't going to mess too much with our magic." Mona beat me to my question, then seemed thoughtful. "Though we may want to play into our roles and skill sets as far as it's concerned."

"Sounds good to me." I heaved a sigh, they really had been pulling more than their fair share of the weight and seemed fine doing it. Time for me to step up. "Let's go get geared up and then be on our way."

"Before you leave, allow me to pass on his Highness's regards and follow an order." Gage stepped forward and look at all of us. "It may be difficult, but you all have permission to use the dungeon under the city. If you wish to go, I will show you how to get there."

"That place hasn't been used in years." Alvor hissed with fear in his gaze. "Not since the prince almost died there!"

"That is why he trusts the wanderers with the secret of its location." He nodded to us. "They are clearly braver than we, and they will return if they die. He had a quest he asked that I impart to you all."

He blinked, and a notification screen populated in front of my gaze.

QUEST RECEIVED – Prince Klemond deems you fit to fight in the crypts beneath his home. Find the cursed item at the end of the dungeon and bring it out of the crypts to nullify the curse. Reward: Negotiable, 400 EXP, and potential future dealings with the crown of Iradellum. Failure: Loss of reputation with the crown, loss of dungeon privileges.

Do you accept? Yes / No?

"That's cool and all, but I have access to only half of my magic." I shook my head. "Before we can consider that, we need it to be unlocked in Belgonna's Hold."

"Ah, then you would be even wiser to take this quest because in order to venture to the next city, you must carry a seal from the adventurer's guild," Gage explained. "In order to even join the guild, you must reach level ten. You have much to lose should you deny this quest, and I would not see that happen."

"Let us think on it?" Monami asked with a great, big smile that completely disarmed the Minotaur Sergeant.

"I suppose so. Come, young Kyvir, let us enter into the training circle, and I will show you sword forms." He looked to the others as well. "In fact, all of you could use the practice. Ünbin comes with an extra bow so that he might further instruct you in the way of archery, Albarth, please be patient."

"Of course, Gage." Al bowed his head respectfully and stepped to the side of the training circle. "I will ask, how on earth is Kyvir to carry that beast of a weapon?"

"Quick slotting." Gage walked out of the circle and drew the longsword at his hip. "Your main weapon belongs in one slot, your other weapon in the secondary slot."

He swung his sword in an overhead chop, took a deep breath, then reached his free hand behind his back and drew a greatsword that hadn't been there before. The long sword had vanished in a gray blur the second the other weapon had appeared.

"That's amazing!" Mona clapped her hands enthusiastically as she eyed him. "How do *we* do that."

"It should be in your status screen." Gage stabbed the large black sword into the ground before him like a surfer might a surfboard and stepped around it. "In the equipment section, I think?"

I hadn't needed to use it in a while, so I had almost forgotten. I selected the tab and saw two weapons tabs on the side next to the outline of my body. I put the short sword in the first slot, then the first portion of the glaive in. I tried putting the second in, but it wouldn't budge.

"Quick slotting only works with a single weapon," Gage explained, motioning to the sword on his hip and the one in the ground. "If you plan to dual-wield those, you will need to be proficient in breaking them down quickly and efficiently in order to use this skill effectively."

"Why not show 'em, boss?" Thea made her way into the back yard through Gage's house. "You up for a little one on one?"

Her grin showed she was confident in her abilities, and her wink at me as she walked by meant she was willing to show off.

"Educating the wanderers?" Gage raised an uncertain brow. "Or showing off for someone?"

"Yes?" She chuckled throatily and sauntered into the training circle. "Come on, Gage. I doubt you aren't already limbered up this morning, so let's let loose a bit!"

"You insolent little..." Gage snorted and snatched his greatsword out of the ground, digging up a patch of dirt and stomped into the circle.

Mona and Sundar guffawed loudly while Albarth and I merely glanced at each other knowingly. Sundar had been with him this morning too. She must really like him.

Thea stood ready, knees slightly bent, and her bo staff in a loose grip on the right side of the training circle. As soon as Gage stepped into the ring, he brought his long sword out of the sheathe with a metallic hiss.

"Someone wanna call it?" Thea widened her stance and brought her bo staff straight out behind her back so that it was parallel with the ground, her grip in the center of the staff.

"Delighted!" Albarth stood next to the ring, then barked, "Begin!"

Thea pounced on the Minotaur with her bo staff rocketing at his cranium, but he bounced it off his left horn. Gage thrust his sword through the swiftly closing gap between them, the light from the afternoon sun shimmering off the blade as it moved.

Thea grunted as she took the staff in both hands and shoved herself, still in the air somehow, out of the way of the blade by digging the staff into the ground.

Once his target was outside his current reach, Gage's longsword blurred, and he whipped the greatsword toward the nimble woman. She laughed as the weapon whistled over her head, having dropped onto her back to avoid the horizontal slash. While Gage tried to change the trajectory of his attack to meet her, Thea thrust the staff into his inner thigh, making the bull-man snarl angrily.

Before the larger weapon could impale her, Thea's legs twisted in the air as if she were attempting to breakdance with the weapon, the momentum of her twirling limbs assisting her in escaping the brutal attack. Her bo staff flew into Gage's face, just missing his left eye, then clattered to the ground.

"*Raaaaaargh!*" Thea growled as she brought a fairly normal-looking axe into play, the weapon slicing through the air toward Gage's greatsword and outstretched hand.

The savage attack forced the larger man to give ground or have the appendage severed, but he used the back step to draw his longsword in a backhanded grip stopping the head of the axe from coming too close. Thea choked up on the axe and shot it forward, using the flat of the head like a pool shark might a pool cue.

She tried to strike mainly at his knees, forcing her larger opponent back a step at a time, then spun about to lash out with her right foot when he tried to grab her weapon.

Gage grasped her ankle and pulled her from her feet, bodily lifting her from the ground with his left hand and leveling his blade at her throat with his right.

"Yield," He ordered menacingly.

"You know I won't, Sarge." She laughed, bringing her axe over her head—under her nearest the ground—and brought it up toward Gage's chin.

The Minotaur stepped back, bucking his head out of the way of the wild strike, only to step onto the forgotten bo staff and pitch backward. They both landed with grunts of pain and broke into a full-on bare-knuckle brawl. Punching and kicking, fighting to gain the upper hand.

"Stop." Ünbin's command, punctuated by an arrow grazing Gage's horn and Thea's cheek. Dirt caked their sweaty bodies all over, their clothes dirty and torn in places where they had fought to gain some sort of advantage.

They looked to the Kin man sourly, then at each other with scowls that melted into hysterical laughter.

"Seems we got a bit carried away." Thea snorted, it was pretty funny if I was honest.

"We do tend to lose ourselves in the midst of a good bout," Gage admitted bashfully as he stood and dusted himself off before helping Thea up. "Cleverly done with the 'discarded' weapon. I've forgotten how bad it can be to have you as an enemy."

"It was once, and I was genuinely as confused as you were to be in that alleyway." Thea's smile seemed genuine but somehow frail.

"Training." Ünbin grunted and pointed to a stand and hay target that stood near Gage's back door.

"Quite." Gage snorted and waved me into the circle. With his and Thea's help, I was able to gain initiate level with the sword after an hour and a half.

It was nearing time for us to try streaming, but I had one question, "And what does mastery of a weapon do?"

"Aside from making you more dangerous?" Thea tilted her head to the side, baring her pointed ears. "Mastery doubles the base damage of a weapon and can make critical strikes easier. It can also lower the durability cost of using a weapon you're a master of. Not to mention higher tier weapons, which you likely learned."

"That's great, but are there bonuses to being an initiate?" Sundar frowned over her notification screen.

"You'll be on your way to the next level of mastery, basic level," Gage explained, holding a hand up to count on starting with his pinky. "Initiate, basic, skilled, expert, and master."

"Is there a level higher than master?" Albarth asked.

"Grandmaster," Ünbin stated, then motioned for him to pick up his bow, before turning toward the target near the fence.

"What he likely doesn't want to tell you is that, in order to gain the grandmaster rank, you need to defeat ten other masters of that same weapon in a duel," Thea explained, taking a position close to me as we watched Albarth. "From what Gage told me, Albarth could beat the pants off of Cälaos if he were a higher level. Though masters of the rapier are rare in these parts."

She fell silent as the mute-by-choice Kin bow-master showed Albarth how to stand with a longbow at ease. He would point to his feet, aligned with the target at first, then turned so that the target faced his non-dominant side, and his feet faced parallel. Ünbin waited patiently as Albarth did the same thing but tapped his legs when the wood nymph's stance seemed a bit too wide.

Ünbin frowned just before tapping the center of Albarth's head, pointing to himself, then took a deep breath before letting it rush from his body stilling it.

He was too tense.

Hmm, maybe his twin wouldn't be needed to translate after all.

Ünbin turned his back to Albarth and took his shirt off so that the lean muscles in his back was bare and clearly visible. Albarth raised an eyebrow in surprise but said nothing. The archer raised his bow with practiced ease, an arrow nocked to the bowstring already. The arm holding the weapon was bent, but as he drew the string back, his left arm straightened with the barest hint of strain though he did it so slowly that it had to be hard.

All the while, the muscle in Ünbin's back contracted like a well-oiled machine, bunching under the strain of the large weapon.

He glanced back at Albarth, waiting until he had his pupil's attention, then took another deep breath, a slow inhale as he lined up his shot, then a slow exhale. When the air emptied from his body, that perfect lull between breaths, he released. The bound tension in the bowstring snapped the arrow forward, the projectile piercing the center red portion of the target.

I found myself clapping at the display along with Monami and Sundar.

Ünbin grunted, seeming unconcerned with the rest of us being there, but lifted his chin at Albarth as if to signal his turn.

Albarth had taken the time to sling the quiver of ten arrows over his shoulder as if he were some kind of Robin Hood character. He reached his hand over his shoulder, trying to find an arrow to grasp, but the wooden things simply evaded his grip.

"Stupid," Ünbin muttered, then lifted his own quiver from the ground and shoved it into Albarth's face. "Fools shoulder a quiver. Makes the arm tired, searching for ammunition for too long. Vulnerable. Soon dead. Lazy way is the best way. Watch."

He undid his belt a couple loops and fed it through a small slit in the leather of the quiver, then put it back loosely. Then, the strap that held fast to the bottom of the bag looped once around the inner thigh, the outside of the quiver through another small slit, then fed back up through the belt where it cinched with a strap that currently held the quiver to Albarth's shoulder.

Ünbin tightened his belt the rest of the way as Albarth mimicked his teacher's example, stopping to allow Ünbin to make small adjustments.

"It seems so odd," Albarth admitted as he walked around with the quiver attached to his leg.

"Odd because it is not what you expected?" Thea asked sagely. "Sometimes, real fighting can lull us into a false sense of security where our expectations are concerned. If it feels natural—sometimes—it's likely wrong unless you're some kind of genius. Even then, learning is hardly ever comfortable, and the right way is likely never the most endearing. Fighting is hard, brutal, and about taking the best of your skill and putting it forth. Discomfort now makes for comfort and ease in the future. Keep that in mind."

"Yes, ma'am." Albarth smiled despite the gentle rebuff, and I saw the elven woman smirk in return.

Ünbin, arms crossed over his chest, watched the exchange mutely, seemingly uncaring. When Albarth lagged in returning his attention to him, Ünbin whipped his longbow under the other man's legs and pulled his right leg out from beneath him. Albarth yelped in surprise and fell to the ground.

"Distractions can kill," Ünbin's emotionless tone caught the embarrassed man's attention at last. "Stand."

This time, Albarth drew an arrow and nocked it to a small point between two points of hard, painted resin. He motioned for Albarth to draw the string and press the bow forward at the same time, and when he failed, Ünbin went to his back and tapped his pupils back muscles for emphasis.

"Breath." Ünbin pressed again. "Always breath."

Albarth tried again, his limbs shaking a little from the strain, but he managed to draw the arrow most of the way back with a grunt of effort. Then Ünbin flicked his pinky finger, and

Albarth loosed the arrow accidentally, sending it much higher than he had been aiming. Luckily the arrow *thunked* into the wood of the fence about three inches from the top.

Ünbin motioned to his own hand, where his pinky curled into his palm, and his three other fingers held an arrow, as an example. He nodded down at the bow once more, and they went through the motions of the drawing without the arrow, though Ünbin refused to allow Albarth to dry fire the weapon, punching him in the chest angrily when he did it on accident.

"Maybe I should have tried the short bow?" He sighed during a break after a half an hour of Ünbin's cruel ministrations. "Or the atlatl, maybe?"

No sooner had the words left his mouth than an arrow pierced the ground in front of his left thigh. We all looked up to Ünbin, motioning for Albarth to stand and pick up his bow that the Kin man had forced him to leave in the training circle.

This time, Albarth attempted to fire the weapon in truth, the arrow just missing the top of the target's outer ring.

When Albarth drew the weapon, a little shaky but much more smoothly than his previous attempts, Ünbin pushed Albarth's elbow up until it was parallel with his ear.

The arrow shot forward and stabbed the target's outer ring.

"Yes!" Albarth whooped as the rest of us called out.

"What'd I miss?" Monami sprinted over, wild-eyed and curious.

"Terrible aim." Ünbin sighed, looking down. "Fire on a natural respiratory pause and focus on the tip of the arrow, leaving the target blurry. Where that tip is, the arrow will follow, but if your breathing and release are off, so is the shot. Again."

It took a few more tries for him to get the hang of it, but after his third shot came even closer to the center of the target, but never truly there.

"Stop anticipating," Sundar shouted, just before Albarth nocked another arrow.

Ünbin glanced her way, then motioned for her to step over.

"What?" Albarth looked uncertain and more than a little irritated.

"You're anticipating the shot, and since you expect it to happen, you're jerking your left hand to the side to try and avoid some of the pain of the shot." She motioned to his forearm, where welts already formed. "I can heal you, and we can get you something to protect your forearms. Pony up and own this weapon so we can *go*."

He sighed, straightened his back, and drew the bow nearly perfectly this time. As Ünbin stepped forward to correct Albarth's elbow, the nymph adjusted it himself before taking a deep breath.

After emptying his lungs, he loosed the arrow, and it soared true. Not dead center by any means, and an inch or so out of the bullseye, but he was *so close*!

"Almost a bullseye!" I hollered happily, an indignant snort sounded behind me, and a muttered apology from Sundar saw my accidental snafu quelled with the man-bull. Oops.

"And initiate level!" Albarth beamed at us proudly. "Thank you Ünbin, I appreciate your time."

He held out his hand for the longbow, and Albarth relinquished it.

"Go get a real bow." Ünbin grunted as he tossed the one he held into his inventory. "Earth Square, tell them I spoke to you about the place."

He slung his other bow over his shoulder in a practiced motion and turned to walk away, then stopped and paced back with his eyes on Albarth and Albarth alone.

He stopped a foot away and ran his eyes over the other man, then spoke quietly, "You really beat Cälaos with the rapier?"

Albarth nodded once, and Ünbin grinned like a child. "Tell them I said to ask about the special."

He turned and sprinted away, leaping high enough that he could grasp the top of the fence and vault over it.

"Use the gate!" Gage roared as he chased the smaller man along the fence with a raised sword. "Those damned twins!"

"Come on you guys, I'll take you to the Earth Square." Thea sounded like she dreaded it, but looking at her, I could see she was excited.

"We don't really have the time." Albarth sighed, then looked to us. "It's time for our audience to tune in."

"No go, guys," Monami whispered and waved us toward Gage's garden. We joined her, her grim visage foreshadowing dark tidings. "Streaming has been shut down due to someone trying to leak 'sensitive' information. Until they find the violator, they've disabled it. From the message, it happened twenty minutes ago."

"The hell is sensitive information?" Albarth growled. "It's just a game, and it's been out long enough for most players who can afford the portals to be through the tutorial portion of the game."

"I don't know, but when I tried to link up and stream you learning the bow, I got the error message, then an admin message," Mona explained. "Do you need to see the message?"

"I believe you, Mo." Sundar sighed. "I guess that leaves us open to the quest. With no one to see it, we have a chance to get stronger, then be on our way. In the good graces of the Graces, feel me?"

"Then we can join the guild and head to Belgonna's Hold," I frowned. "How can the starter city not have access to all the magics?"

"Because it's just a city," Albarth shrugged. "Maybe it's like a server choice? Who knows, but whatever it is, we need to head there. May as well gear up and get some dungeon crawling in."

"Gage." Sundar waved the Minotaur over to us and grinned, "We'll take that quest. Let us go get geared up, then we will return and go."

He smiled and offered us the quest again.

QUEST RECEIVED – Prince Klemond deems you fit to fight in the crypts beneath his home. Find the cursed item at the end of the dungeon and bring it out of the crypts to nullify the curse. Reward: Negotiable, 400 EXP and potential future dealings with the crown of Iradellum. Failure: Loss of reputation with the crown, loss of dungeon privileges.

Do you accept? Yes / No?

This time I selected yes and Thea sauntered over to us. "We going shopping?"

"We'd appreciate the guidance, yeah." Mona nodded at the other woman, though she seemed a bit angry for some reason.

It was hard to read her at the moment, and thinking about her, and her feelings just wasn't what I wanted to do. So, the pretty elven woman got to come with us.

She strutted in front of us for a few minutes, leading our group forward, when I felt a tug on my shirt.

Albarth spoke in a low tone as the girls chatted about the weapons training, "Have you spoken to her?"

"If you mean Mona," I couldn't hide the hurt in my tone despite the fact that I was okay with what had happened. "Yeah. She's not interested. I asked her if she wanted more, and she wondered who had put those thoughts in my head. Not even worthy of a straight answer."

He snorted. "That means nothing. You probably caught her by surprise, and she panicked." His knowing smile made me want to be anywhere but there. "She will come around. You just have to give her a chance and be honest."

"I was, Al. And that honesty made me feel more vulnerable than I have in a while." It was true. It'd hurt more than I'd initially thought it had and now—of all times—the emotional fallout of it was coming on.

I'd been turned down, and risked my friendship with one of the only people I had ever truly cared about because I let someone else convince me they saw their own issues in our relationship. And worse? I had let it color my own thoughts to the point that I had begun to hope for something I wasn't sure I wanted.

"Don't be that way, Ky," Albarth tried to reason with me in a soothing tone that suddenly sounded like mockery. "She'll come around."

"I don't think I care," I blurted, my heart pounding against my ribs, and grunted as I pulled away from his grip.

I found myself joining Thea, her smiling face, and blue eyes a sight for a sore heart.

"Hey there." She reached out and grabbed my hand, the contact was nice. "You alright?"

"Yeah." I tried to play off the sudden desolation gnawing at the pit of my stomach with a smile.

She pointed to her ears. "Elves have really good hearing, so I know you're lying." She didn't seem upset that I'd lied, though. "I'm not one to judge, but it seems like you kind of had your heart torn out. You don't need to pretend."

"It's less pretending and more just coming to terms that I almost lost my best friend because I was stupid."

"Love isn't stupid." She frowned and squeezed my hand.

"Less love and more people sticking their noses into our business with their own lives and baggage weighing on their 'helpful' hints." She let go of my hand, and I looked up at her now-guarded face. "Not you! Oh my god, not you. My friends, Albarth and Sundar. It wasn't their fault." I felt like an ass now. "I'm sorry. They were just trying to help, and I'm letting my worry and anger cloud my judgment. I'm not normally so... primal."

She looked relieved but didn't take my hand in hers again. "I feel a little crass for having suggested you come to my place with all of what you are going through."

"Don't." My spirit felt a little lighter for being able to talk this out with someone. "You couldn't have known, and taking you up for some training would be a good idea."

She punched my shoulder, a glint in her eyes as her nose crinkled in delight.

"We're close to the Earth Square." She waved to the others and snatched my hand up in hers. "Come on!"

We moved faster toward a group of people, and Thea simply plowed her way through the onlookers.

"Watch it!" One of the ladies shouted angrily then grunted as Mona barreled through with Sundar hot on her heels.

Dark tile floors made of granite with golden cracks and veins of other colors spread out throughout the square with a garden of several different kinds of trees and bushes surrounding the sides.

Within those gardens, several stalls stood tall, almost built from the living arboretum growing in the city like a haven. Animals of all sizes scampered about. Deer grazed on grass next to cows, rabbits munched on vegetables near the center of the square where a small mountain grew from the ground. On it sat a large bear with deep brown fur and a shock of silvery-white on his chest.

"That's the guardian for this square, Tarben," Thea explained, ensuring we kept a wide berth from the center. "He sleeps a lot, hardly cares when people come close, but is very protective."

We moved on, but I couldn't take my eyes from him. His back rose and fell as he snored like a chainsaw.

Suddenly he stopped, his eyes opening and head raising as if searching for something. Then he found it. He rose to his full height, thirteen feet of massive bulk that had to weigh a ton and tottered our way on his hind legs.

"Don't. Move." Thea's warning breath crossed my skin, goosebumps spreading down my arms at the awe-inspiring spectacle before me.

Green and purple invaded my view of the beast as Sundar advanced to meet it.

It called out, a grumbling roar, some bear noises, and then Sundar grunted and bellowed back at him.

The noise stopped, and the crowd gasped; someone dropped what they were holding a clattering sound echoed throughout the square.

"What do you want, you great big bruiser?" Sundar put her hands on her hips, listening as Tarben grunted and chuffed at the air. "Well, it's nice to meet you too, big guy. You didn't have to ruin your nap for that."

Paws appeared on either side of the large woman's shoulders, and she cried out, her hands flashing forward to shove the bear away, then wipe her face.

He trundled back to his spot and laid down but didn't close his eyes.

"Cheeky thing." Sundar continued wiping her face off, then caught our gazes. "What? He sensed me and wanted to introduce himself."

"Oh!" Monami clapped excitedly. "Her magic! Animal magic. He probably felt that and responded to it like the salamander did with Al."

"Speaking of..." I looked back toward the wood nymph. "Whatever happened to it?"

He reached into his breast pocket and pulled the little creature out of it. It squeaked angrily and scuttled back down Albarth's arm into the pocket.

"I tried to take him back, but he just won't go." He shrugged with a look of helplessness.

"So, wait, a guardian who barely wakes up, gets up just to greet you, and you have an elemental creature in your pocket?" Thea seemed confused, shocked, and completely stunned. "Who are you people?"

"Just wanderers." I smiled at her, unable to really think of an actual explanation for what was going on.

"So, where's this bowyer I'm looking for?" Albarth motioned toward the square in general, the shaded areas hidden a little from the afternoon sun. "I'm assuming it's a bowyer, right?"

"Yeah." Thea still seemed wary of us but turned toward the south end of the square. "Follow me."

We moved toward a large tree in the corner were a woman tended a piece of wood with some sandpaper. Without even looking up, she greeted us, "Welcome to the Grove. I'm Nell, how can I help you today?"

"I'm Albarth, and I had been talking to Ünbin, who suggested I ask about the special?"

The woman's head shot up, her vulpine features separating from the shadows, dark red fur covered her body, and her ears flicked back and forth excitedly. Her golden eyes narrowed at Albarth as she placed the wooden pole down with the sandpaper on it.

"You've been talking to him?" She stepped into the sunlight, her brown leather pants barely making a sound as she moved. She wore a plain brown apron over a green shirt that moved in the breeze.

"Yes?" Albarth seemed uncertain as he said it.

"I'm his wife, and he barely talks to me." She snarled angrily, her teeth bared in her muzzle. "What makes you so special?"

"I'm pretty?" Albarth tried, his usual posh accent seeming odd as he fumbled for words. And Ünbin was *married*?!

She snorted. "Good try." she walked around him, looking him over. "And he said to ask about what?"

"The special." Mona stepped in. Nell looked her over and dismissed her off hand.

"Archers only." Mona started forward, but Sundar grabbed her shoulder and shook her head as Nell muttered, "I swear the man only married me for my crafting."

She walked into the darkness and faded from view for a moment, then came back with a cloth-wrapped bundle in her arms.

"It'll be two gold for the special," Nell announced to low whistles and a glare from her. "My work is worth the price—don't wanna pay, don't waste my time."

"What does the special include?" Albarth raised his voice to get her attention, the woman's glare landing back on him. "If Ünbin suggested it, then I'll likely buy it anyway, but I'd still like to know what I'm getting."

"You'll be getting a bow and three dozen arrows." she set the bundle on the ground. "As well as a glowing recommendation to a leatherworker who will sell you an appropriate quiver and from the looks of your forearm, a bracer."

Albarth's hand automatically flew to his left forearm, but Nell just clicked her tongue. "Price of range is steep at times. You'll get used to it."

"If it's what you both suggest, my money is well spent, thank you, Nell." He stepped forward and offered her the gold with a silver for her trouble, which made her scowl fade a bit.

"Three stalls down on your right will be a gnomish man who Ünbin orders all of his quivers from, if you go there, he will get you the same kind of quiver that my husband favors." She lifted her previous work and eyed it critically, then grunted and nodded to herself. "He also sells leather armor at a fair price. North side of the square is where the metal armorers pedal their wares."

"Thank you." Albarth bowed his head politely, and she just grunted back at him inarticulately before flopping down onto her backside to work on her piece once more.

After we were safely away, farther than I might have normally waited, I asked Thea. "What was she?"

"Nell? A bowyer." She seemed confused, eyeing me as if I were dumb, then seemed to catch on. "Oh! She's a type of sylph, a kitsune. Shapeshifting fox-people. She's one of the few in the city if I recall."

"That's super interesting." Mona smiled at the woman next to me. "You're very knowledgeable Thea, how long have you lived here?"

"My whole life," Thea answered readily enough, "Born a stone's throw from Gage's place actually, though my folks left more than a century back to go to the Sylvan Forest to be with our people. I had already been trying to sort myself out when they left and got caught up with the wrong crowd. I should've died, but I met Gage before the guards raided our hideout, and he beat some sense into me. Been a part of his personal squad ever since."

"Wrong crowd?" I raised an eyebrow at her in question, but we had arrived at the gnomish leatherworker's place by now, so she mouthed *later.*

The small man oiling a leather shoulder pauldron was all too happy to sell us his wares. Each main piece of his most basic gear cost four silver pieces, and the bracers and greaves each cost two silver pieces. The pauldrons, a shoulder piece that would also protect the neck to an extent, were six silver pieces.

"Do you have anything a little more... showy for my friend here?" Sundar asked the balding leatherworker. He wrung his hands a little in thought as Mona blushed and tried to push the larger woman away. "It's just that we're trying to *accentuate* her assets to a maximum level for a fight."

He nodded, seeming to think on it for a moment with a frown, then squeaked. "I do! It's almost like a corset, with a softer leather chest to do... uh... as you say."

"How much would you be willing to part with it for my new favorite person?" Sundar leaned down over the man, casting a long shadow over him as she loomed.

"Five silver and 4 copper pieces." He counted on his hands and did some math. "For the two of you, the archer with his specifically designed quiver, the corset top, two pairs of leather pants, greaves, and bracers for each that should put the total cost at three gold, five silver, and four copper pieces. Uh, before you ask, the quiver is a gold as it is specifically crafted to Master Ünbin's needs."

"You've treated us fairly, mister...?" Monami left the question unasked so he might provide his name.

"I'm Milton Brax, miss."

"Thank you." She smiled cheerfully at him, and he blushed deeply in return. "You seem to have treated us fairly. Here is my half of that, with an extra silver for your trouble."

"Thank you miss, I do hope you like my work." The gnome pocketed the coinage and looked to Albarth, who begrudgingly forked over his funds. "And sir, I will add that this leather vest will look quite dashing with your current clothing. I wish you both protection, and should you ever need anything, come back to Brax's Hardboiled Hoard."

I was absolutely enamored by the name, and I wondered if Nell had a name for her business other than the Grove, but she was unlikely to spill that particular information, so I let the thought perish.

Armor for Sundar and I was ungodly. Price-wise, it made sense that metal armor would be a little more expensive, but that much more so? Holy crap. I was a lot flusher than my friends from the prince, so I bit the bullet and bought the armor for Sundar and me.

The elven man running the place was a talker, and if we hadn't gotten out of there as swiftly as we had, he could have talked me into another set of armor.

I bought chain shirts at eight silver for Sundar and I both, half-plate leggings with metal greaves that cost another eight silver and then four more after that. Finally, the bracers had been five silver putting the total expenses at five gold pieces. That left me with forty-six gold, five silver, and zero copper pieces. I could afford better, but there was no promise I wouldn't find better from a drop, so I left it alone for now.

The metal armor was heavier than what I was used to, but not too cumbersome to move in.

I couldn't abide the helmet as it limited my vision, the simple iron of the armor a gray color that I couldn't take overly long. I asked the others if we could stop at Ophira's place, and to sweeten the deal, I offered to buy them dyes for their gear.

As we walked through the city streets with our gear equipped, it felt like the people treated us a little differently. They moved aside a little more swiftly. Averted their gazes quickly if our eyes met in passing. It made me feel bad for being so different.

"Don't feel bad." Thea sighed when she saw the forlorn look on my face as the people around us moved aside. "They treat a lot of warriors this way. Give us a wide berth at times. Some see it as respect. Others as fear. Some enjoy both, and if you mean anything, you let it roll off you. You're here *for* the people, not the awe or respect they give you for your service."

"So, is the offer for me to come over and train with you still standing?" I glanced bashfully over at her after she spoke, and she turned my way in surprise.

"Yes, absolutely!" A little bit of a bounce found its way into her steps after that.

"Maybe after we finish this dungeon, I'll come train with you." She grinned to herself and began to whistle a spritely tune to no one in particular as we continued on. The others had fallen back a few paces, and I could tell they were speaking, but it was for them to know and me to stay out of.

CHAPTER THIRTEEN

We walked into Ophira's small shop, the colors sending a thrill of excitement through me, but also somehow calming me. The familiarity of the bright hues that I would normally choose was nice, but the thought of choosing between them all made my heart race.

"How can I help yo—Oh!" Ophira blinked at all of us before a slight smile graced her beautiful features. "Haven't even learned how to make dyes yet, and already you bring more customers than I might see in two days. Well done, Kyvir."

"I told you I wanted this." I found myself smiling despite her obvious jab at me not visiting to actually learn my craft. "We're getting ready to go on a quest, but if you have a simple thing to show me while these guys browse your wares, I'd be delighted to learn."

"Dye making is hardly simple, but I have a beginner's dye I can show you how to make." She waved for me to join her at the counter as she pulled out a bowl and a red plant that reminded me of a rose. "First, we take an item with the desired color, in this case, the red of this flower. For organic materials like this, we will try to either chop or tear it apart and put it into the bowl. Go ahead."

I lifted the flowers and carefully pulled the petals from the stems, eyeing the bottoms with a critical eye. I took the small knife that she had on the counter and sliced off the white portions at the bottom of a few of the petals, then tore them apart into small pieces before scattering them into the bowl.

"Excellent eye for detail, already I have a good feeling about you." She touched my bicep, then lifted out a vial out from beneath the counter and handed it to me. "Next, we add our tincture."

"What is it?" I held it up to eye level and glared at it, it was clear and looked like it could have been water.

"It is water, and a mixture of acid with liquified Aether." My eyes widened at her explanation. "I will not explain how to make it yet, but know that I have plenty of this tincture, and you can buy it from me until such a time as I trust you with the recipe."

"I love it!" I purred as I swirled the liquid.

"Add it to the bowl until it covers the leaves, but not any more than that; otherwise you risk muddling the color." She watched as I added the tincture until it just barely finished covering the leaves. There was a little of the tincture left that I passed back to Ophira, who took it. "Next, you can either wait or take a pestle and grind the petals until the color begins to show."

"How long might you normally wait?"

"Depending on the strength of the components you use, it could be as soon as five minutes, or as long as twelve hours." She tapped the tincture. "This is a basic tincture that only works with organic materials. Other tinctures I make can separate the color from metal, ore, stone, and even monster crystals."

"You can make dyes from monster crystals?" It was hard to hide the wonder in my voice. "How does that work?"

"Monster crystals are one of the hardest materials to use, Kyvir, and they are precious resources, I am teasing you." She rolled her eyes and giggled at my expense. I had gotten my hopes up. "I have not done it, just for the fact that I have been unable to obtain any, but if you do not wish to sell them, bring them to me, and we will see what can be done."

Optional Quest Received – Ophira has imparted a trade secret to you that she hasn't even tried yet in using monster crystals to create dyes. Bring her one to see what happens. Reward: Unknown. No failure condition.

Do you accept Yes / No?

"I'll do it if I can, I promise. I would give you the one we have, but it belongs to Albarth, and I'd like to find my own to give you." I accepted the quest, and she smiled, nodding at my reasoning, though her eyes seemed tight. I could understand why; I was keeping something so precious from her out of pride and a sense of honor, but I couldn't be budged, and I didn't think she wanted to risk it.

We waited another couple minutes until the dye set, then strained the flower petals from the liquid with an incredibly thin strainer that we poured into a small vial. "Can the color be enhanced if there is more of the base material? Like, would the red of this dye deepen if I were to add more petals?"

"No, however, the color would be more likely to take with a larger portion of the base material," before I could attempt to understand what she had said, she explained, "The more material you have at your disposal, the less time that it takes for the color to be withdrawn from it. The color stays the same, but the crafting time is lessened to an extent that is equal to the material."

I nodded and lifted the small vial of red dye that we had just created.

Basic Red Dye – Single use

"That's amazing!" I couldn't help but let the excitement of succeeding bubble from my throat in a hearty laugh. "Oh, I love this!"

"I'm glad that you do." She ushered me out from behind the counter to pick the colors I wanted, letting me have the red one I had made for being so studious.

With that, I bought all of my friend's choices of colors, even Thea, who only wanted a single vial of red dye the same hue as I had made. I gave her the one that I had made, her face unreadable as she took it with a word of thanks.

"I should go, my training circle is a mess so I should clean it before you come over." She smiled winningly at me and waved goodbye before scooting out of the door.

"Hot date later?" Sundar asked softly from my left side. Mona was off at the other side of the store with Ophira speaking about one of the colors that had caught her eye.

"We'll be training with the sword and likely the glaive." Suddenly, I felt more tired about this constant questioning than I had before.

"You're a grown man, and Al told me what happened." She thumped my shoulder softly with her knuckles. "I'm sorry, Ky. That had to be rough. You know I'm here If you need to talk about it."

"Thanks." I chose to just ignore the rest of the group and selected the colors I wanted. I chose a bright green for my chain shirt, an indigo for the pants, purple for the bracers, and I matched the pants and greaves.

The cost for the dyes had been discounted for me, running us a gold for all of it, which gave each of the others a couple dyes apiece and me all of mine. After everyone's armor was sufficiently personalized, Mona's brown leather customized to red with black accents on the straps. Albarth's armor was dyed a stone-like gray since we would be going into a crypt, ever the practical mind. Finally, Sundar dyed her metal armor orange, which looked awesome against her green skin. She looked like an orc in a traffic cone, I loved it.

We made our way to Gage's in amicable silence, and when he saw us, he rolled his eyes. "Wanderers."

He brought us to the castle grounds, and we passed through the courtyard and training grounds until we came to a large mausoleum of cream-colored stone pillars and a large, thick metal door set into the floor of it. This wasn't a normal grave building; it was like a shelter house with thick columns holding up the triangle-shaped roof.

"This is the entrance to the dungeon." He nodded to the door. "It is easy to gain access to it, all you need to do is touch the door and speak the word 'enter,' and you will be teleported inside."

"How does a place become a dungeon?" Mona asked quietly. She looked to be a little shaken, and I couldn't blame her—she'd always hated zombie movies, and here we were about to go into a crypt full of dead folks. Hardly ideal.

"A strong enough presence of monsters needs to congregate for a long period of time in order to collect tainted Aether and pollute the area, or a cursed object can be placed somewhere to summon monsters and create as it will." Gage motioned to the surrounding area. "This area is the *least* likely to have monsters in the city that would survive long enough to birth a dungeon, so we can only reason that a cursed object was placed here as the quest stated and made use of the interred inside as a source of protection."

"Damn, that's no good," Sundar muttered to herself, so when she saw us staring at her, she added, "That just means that there was someone who wanted this place cursed."

"That would be a correct assumption." Gage's horn chains jingled as he nodded his head. "We cannot guess at the perpetrator's motives, but the prince almost fell in this dungeon little more than a week past, and this problem needs taken care of."

"Why not take care of it yourself?" I asked, the Minotaur turning to regard me curiously. "I'm not saying I'm not happy to have the chance to continue being of service to the people of this city, but if it needs doing, then it should be done."

"Dungeons sap the strength of this world's people, making us weaker inside a dungeon." He eyed the thick metal keeping the entry closed. "I was there in the initial incursion as a member of the army itself, and still, my prince almost paid the ultimate price in retreating. That is why I have been relegated to working for the city guard. This is part of my punishment."

That made sense, as much as that sucked for poor Gage and the prince.

"Will we even be strong enough to do this?" Albarth eyed the metal door now as well, his hand falling to the rapier at his side.

"You wanderers gain strength swiftly in combat. This is a calculated risk on our part, but it stands to reason that you may gather experience and become powerful enough to stand against this foul curse as you go."

"Does the nightfall rule work for dungeons as well?" I found myself reliving my first night in this game and shivered at having felt what I had.

"We are uncertain, but with you being able to return from death, if you are willing to take the risk, it would be appreciated." He did seem to be generally concerned about it.

"Eh, if anything, we can just leave it, right?" I shrugged then glanced at the others who seemed to be thinking the same thing. "Let's give it a shot."

I touched the unreasonably cold metal with my hand, and I spoke the word, "Enter."

I blinked, then felt a sort of whooshing sensation as my clothes and hair fluttered around me. The clinking of my armor against my body as I stopped doing *whatever* I had to have been doing meant that I had to be done, right? Teleporting. I had teleported into the dungeon. Oh my god.

A cool draft brought a musty stench to my nostrils as I took a steadying breath. My first dungeon in a new game like this was always filled with awe. Wow. It sure looked like a crypt to me, though I only had experience with them in games. Blood and Gore's version had been more like a mass burial kind of thing. It had been highly unsettling.

Rather than the typically dirt-covered floor, dirt walls infested with spiders the size of puppies, I found the opposite. The royal crypts were near spotless except for a thin layer of dust over the perfectly built stone coffins, sarcophagi? their light-gray coloring almost blending into the stone making up the walls behind them.

"This isn't what I expected at all, but kind of is?" Sundar muttered behind me. "Not nearly as creepy as some of the other places we've crawled through in other games, eh Kyvir?"

"That's right." I pulled my sword from the sheathe at my hip and held it at the ready.

"Movement will be rough in this entry, so let's get off the pedestal here, maybe?" She suggested lightly with a hand on my back.

I turned and found that we stood on a small pedestal large enough to fit all of us, but she had been right that it would be a tight squeeze. As soon as we stepped off of it, the others appeared with similar thoughts on our current surroundings.

"Well, let's get this show on the road." I loosened the tight muscles in my shoulder, the thought of the potential fights to come causing tension to build there. I needed to be alert, but loose if this would work.

"Let's try to be stealthy about this first portion, okay?" Sundar whispered, then smiled at me in my loudly colored armor. "Or at least as stealthy as can be done."

A smirk graced my face as I turned back and crouched to move forward down the hall. The décor didn't change, but the ambiance seemed to. I could almost *feel* the taint in the air. A sulfuric scent and rotting flesh filling my nose as light around us dimmed, growing steadily darker.

I looked back to my left and whispered to Al, "Can you use your Flame Dart and light something?"

"There are torch sconces, but no torches." He whispered back just before I smacked into a shadow-covered wall, he lowered his voice further and leaned closer after my armor stopped clanking. "You okay?"

"No?" I whispered back. I was, but slapping into something solid down here in the dark was unsettling. Especially with the dead still safely held in the coffins and stone sarcophagus around us. "Maybe we leave and come back with torches?"

We made our way back to the hall that still held light and stepped onto the pedestal. "Exit."

Nothing happened after I said the word, and panic settled into my chest. "Leave, vamoose, scram, bye, let us *out!*"

"Looks like we have to keep going," Monami said.

"It's a solid wall of darkness, Mona." I motioned for her to go ahead. "I couldn't pass through it, and it's dark in there. What do you expect us to do?"

"Be more adventurous?" She raised an eyebrow in challenge. "How many dungeons have puzzle rooms, you moron? Are you sure losing the ability to make magic hasn't made you soft?"

"Hey!" I touched my chest as if struck. "I can do things with ice, you know that."

"Then cool your tits, and let's get this going!" She snarled. "We're gamers—streamers—and we don't suck. We can do this little dungeon then move on. So, if we need to light the room up, we have to do... what?"

"Find light sources." Albarth clapped a hand onto my clinking chain-linked armor. "Let's go, meat shield."

"That is *so* not my nickname," I muttered evilly and made my way back toward the darkened room. "Where do we start?"

"Opening these coffins and the tombs. There are four sconces, so four torches that need to be placed within," Albarth reasoned, his face turned up slightly. There was room enough for all four of us to move around easily if we moved away from each other. "Kyvir, you and Sundar will open one of the sarcophagi and see what is inside. Ice magic will likely not affect anything undead, so your magic may well be useless, but you can still take a hit, so make sure you're front and center."

"Yup, ready, Sunny?" The large woman nodded and took her place next to me in front of one of the stone tombs. "Let's just open it enough to see if there's a torch or something, okay?"

She nodded and motioned with a hand on the lip of the sarcophagus lid, three, two, one—*push!*

She and I strained as the stone fled from the smooth surface of the base, a strong whiff of death emanated from it, and

I almost balked, but that stopped when I heard Sundar grunt a, "Yes!"

She reached in and snatched something out of the darkness and grinned. "Got one, let's shut it, just to be safe."

"Good idea." She tossed it to Albarth, and we took the time to put the lid back as best as we possibly could.

We went through the same process two more times with no success and decided to try the coffins, but to our dismay, the wood was nailed shut.

"I still have my glaive," I offered, taking out the first glaive I had from my inventory. "Maybe we can use this like a crowbar?"

"Clever, better than burning them open," Albarth said, breathily, a sour look took over his face. "Though, I feel like this is going to be an issue when the lights come on."

"How do you mean?" Mona moved to a coffin and used the dagger that she had been given at the beginning of the game to start prying the wood apart. "We only need to do the same thing that they did with the stone ones—move enough that you can see and get in there to get the torch. Then, leave it at that."

"It could work, but as soon as light touches this area, I feel like the first of the undead mobs are going to come to life, and we're going to be in for a fight." Albarth eyed her as she worked and decided to help lift the coffin lid away while bracing it. It didn't go far, though, and Sundar had to help a bit.

"Found it!" Mona grunted as she reached into the sarcophagus and grasped at something. "It's stuck."

"Yank it!" I encouraged from behind her, and she pulled with all her might. I reached out, grasped her forearm, and pulled with her. A snapping sound echoed around us, and she pulled out the torch, but also the arm and hand that had been holding onto it. "Gross!"

She peeled it off and tossed it as far from her as she could then gave the torch to Albarth, who took it with a heavy sigh and a roll of his eyes.

After she had taken a moment to calm down, we went back to work. The next torch we found easily enough in the coffin right next to the one we had found the first. The last one we checked had it. It's always the last one.

Albarth used his Flame Dart to light the first one, then used that one to light the others. The sconces were just a little too high for us to reach, so Sundar walked from each sconce slowly with the lit torches and placed them inside. As she put the last one, a small click rang out, and the sconces themselves lowered, casting brighter light throughout the room together than they had separately.

The shadows that had blocked the door deepened, then dissipated altogether, but the warmth the torchlight gave off was hollow now. Scratching noises and light moans softly trickled from the corpses all around us in their now-cages.

"Well, I called that." Albarth looked particularly smug, then the color drained from his face as he cried out, "Bloody hell!"

The hand that held the second torch had found its way around his ankle, and he hopped about trying to shake it off.

"Mona, get that thing off him, and help us out with this door." I made my way uninhibited by the dead because our idea to leave them closed off had paid dividends. The only issue seemed to be that there was a door with a keyhole and no key.

"We may have to kill some of them," I called back to the others. "Keyhole with no key."

"Let's start with the ones in the coffins then, the wood will burn, and Albarth can set them on fire," Sundar suggested with her sword freed from its sheath. "Al?"

Albarth's weapon blazed with his gift's flaming energy as he plunged the weapon into the slit at the side of the coffin.

CRITICAL STRIKE

40 dmg to Fallen Knight

Burning Debuff Added

Lvl 6 Fallen Knight – Hostile

"Nice!" He smiled as I congratulated him, then I moved forward to start jabbing my weapon into the coffin.

7 dmg to Fallen Knight

6 dmg to Fallen Knight

CRITICAL STRIKE

16 dmg to Fallen Knight

That critical hit had gone a long way toward ending this guy, but the coffin smoldered and had caught fire already, so whether he was near half-health or not, he was coming and he'd be on fire.

I turned back and found Sundar doing the same thing as I was, and the others had moved on. Albarth dealing the ungodly damage he could while Monami watched all of our backs.

"Sundar, you want to see if you can use your healing magic to hurt them?" I called out as I stabbed the Fallen Knight in the quickly fading coffin for another eight damage. The added damage likely had to be from my increase in skill with the weapon, right? And the other stuff? Probably my Strength or Skill modifiers, whatever they were.

"Not if I don't have to, we seem to be doing okay." She grunted and lopped off the arm that pushed through the burning boards in front of her. Grasping fingers wriggled and clawed at the air as the appendage fell through the air. "That's meant to heal us."

Wood splintered and, as I had guessed, the Fallen Knight slunk through the top half of the lid that he had managed to claw his way through. His decayed and burnt flesh sloughing from the bones of his face where I had stabbed him, as well as his shoulders and chest. He was so close to being dead, well—dead again—that I decided to go for the coup de grâce by trying to cut off his head as he leaned forward.

The blade whooshed through the air and impacted the flaming coffin just before the undead being inside opened its mouth, clattering its bony jaws at me, the blade stuck into the wood.

"Come *on!*" My breath passed my clenched teeth in a snarl of frustration as I yanked on the weapon, wood creaking in protest.

Grasping hands reached out toward me, so with a couple bars of Aether, I covered my fists in ice spikes and beat on the wood and undead in a fervor. The wood splintered in a frosty clattering and cracking cacophony, and the sword loosened. The Fallen Knight just grew angrier at the one or two points of damage that the impromptu weapons did.

It grappled my left arm, fingers digging into my skin harshly, and dragged me forward. My flesh hovered ever closer to the suddenly sharper-looking teeth wobbling in its jaws.

1 dmg taken

"A little help here?" I hollered to no one in particular and made my right hand a blade, like in those old martial arts movies and lashed out, sending the pointed end into the creatures rattling jaws. No ice covered my fingers, but I did have rather sharp nails, and the ice protected the upper portion of my hand from being bitten.

CRITICAL STRIKE
4 dmg to Fallen Knight

It tried to bite down, but the ice was all it could get to at first, though it wouldn't hold overly long. Large green hands wrapped around my stuck sword changed the position slightly, and then shoved the weapon all the way through the Fallen Knight's head.

Lvl 6 Fallen Knight died
47 EXP
Lvl 6 Fallen Squire died
43 EXP
Level Up!

Sundar yanked my arm out of the deader creatures' jaws and passed me my weapon with a stern look of concern on her face. "Call for help sooner, Kyvir, we need to be sure our tank is okay. You're our damage sponge. We need you healthy so you can get beaten up. So, speak to us the way I used to, okay?"

"Yes, ma'am." I grinned at her as she rolled her eyes. "I know, you work for a living, so don't call you that. Let's worry about leveling after this fight, too."

"Exactly, let's kill the last two of these boneheads." She grasped my shoulder and shoved me toward the other coffins. "Teamwork this time. Let's do something about the bottom of that coffin and try to keep that thing from getting out."

I went to work, my frozen fists connecting lightly with the still-fine wood near the bottom up to the middle of the coffin before me. Cold spread from my hands to the wood, yet another point of my Aether gone leaving me with just the one gray left to use, and it would be weaker.

"Low on Aether," I called to the others as I would have in another game we played, signaling that I would be tapped soon so we should either hurry or find another way to do things.

"Conservation mode," Albarth said in a barking tone, his voice strained. "I'm good so far, but that could go south, soon. We need to get stabbier."

We regrouped and turned our sights on an individual and began stabbing it.

Lvl 6 Fallen Squire died

43 EXP

The last one made it completely out of the coffin as the sarcophagus lid thumped and shifted futilely. They didn't seem to be strong enough to actually shift the stone lids. Good.

"Pay attention!" Mona roared, almost leonine in her fury. "You have to be present to tank, damnit!"

"I'm on it, Mo, I'm trying to watch our backs, too!" I rolled my eyes and marched forward, the sword in my hand low. I wanted this to end—now.

I feinted left with it, and the slowly burning figure reached out toward me with expectant grubby fingers. I brought the blade up in an arc with both hands as if I were swinging a bat, aiming for the wrists. The left hand fell to the ground with a sickening splat, and the blade severed the tendon of the right hand in the lower forearm before the strike lost power. I needed to disengage or get too close.

The mouth gaped wide, and the only way to avoid it was to throw my left arm up behind the flat of my blade as if it were a thin shield. Teeth grasped my flesh and bit surprisingly hard, the pain glaring and numbing almost instantly.

12 dmg taken

Festering Debuff resisted

A whooshing sound caught my attention, and Monami twisted into view with her chakrams flashing in the firelight.

8 dmg to Fallen Squire

8 dmg to Fallen Squire

"Duck!" My body moved of its own accord while a slight whistle passed my ear, scoring my forearm and puncturing the still-attached zombie through the eye next to the nose.

30 dmg taken (3 fire dmg)
CRITICAL STRIKE
65 dmg to Fallen Squire
Lvl 6 Fallen Squire died
43 EXP

"What the hell, Al!" I grasped at my arm, the singed flesh smarting but not hurting nearly as badly as it could have. I shut my damage notifications off to keep from being dizzied by the numbers flying over my screen.

"Your reaction times are abysmal." He raised an eyebrow, his weapon still burning, but the once-bright beacon appeared to have grown a little dull since he first summoned it.

"Anyone notice a difference in how pain has been working?" The others looked confused but shrugged. "It was really bad earlier to get hurt, and now it feels bad for a moment, then the pain is gone. Is there a place to check patch notes? Gimme a second."

"We're on a bit of a mission here, Kyvir." Sundar huffed, crossing her arms under her ample chest. "Let's focus and kill these guys. Now, how does Aether come back, and do you all need to wait?"

I eyed my Aether bars and frowned. I was still sitting at just one usable bar, so I opted, "Wait, I think. No one really bothered to explain how it worked in combat. And with any new content, the first few have to try and figure it out. You remember that greater demon in B and G? How we had to fight him eight times to get the mechanics down and *still* wiped because of the tank buster?"

Sundar grinned despite our situation and nodded. "That sucked. But I get it now."

"What's your Serenity stat?" Albarth stepped over to me, and I checked it for him.

"Five, why?" He smiled, and a notification popped up in front of my vision, so I read it out loud. "Serenity – The will to calm your mind and the universe around you, understanding deeper truths and how best to approach the world and its aether. This attribute affects your ability to recover your aether and how you can assist others. For every point in this stat, the recovery time for Aether decreases by 0.1 seconds of the total time needed to recover when not in combat (current decrease of 0.5). Aether will not recover in combat without certain abilities. Seems unlocking our Aether made it change, interesting."

"So, the explanation evolved?" Monami stood with a hand on her hip. "So, what, we just sit here and time it?"

"Yeah." I grunted back at her frustration and sat down. There was a clock interface, and I watched it. Less than a quarter of the way through the rotation, I got one of my Aether bars back. After that, I watched again. This time, it took almost a whole minute for it to come back, flickering into color just before the full mark. "It takes a minute. Even with five points in it. So, I'm guessing that I have fifty-nine-and-a-half seconds out of combat to get it back."

"And the ability thing is concerning, but that's fair, I suppose." Albarth rubbed his chin. "I'll need another few moments, then. My recovery is not as good as some of our party's."

"It's still better than mine," I said, then sniffed but couldn't be too upset over his lead. The guy seemed to be made for this game. "But let's try and do this smarter. The ones in the coffins were affected by fire, and I would like to try and put the rest of these coffins to good use if we can."

"We drop burning wood on them and what, shut the lids?" Mona bit her bottom lip uncertainly.

"Yeah, that could work, but we'd better hurry; that wood won't last all that long." Sundar frowned in thought as she took the initiative and began breaking the nearest coffin while the rest of us planned a bit more in-depth.

Once she finished, we were topped off and ready to begin anew. The plan executed flawlessly on the first sarcophagus. Anything that reached out at us when we pushed the lid far enough back, Monami carved off with her chakrams, then I stabbed it in the chest to hold it down while a coffin's worth of wood went in. Sure, I would be close to them, but only for a few heartbeats until the act was done.

Then, Albarth set it alight and stabbed a critical strike into the noble zombie's head to start things off right. I pulled my blade free of the thrashing zombie, and then we shut the lid and moved on. After that, I turned my notifications back on.

The damage notifications were a bit much, nowhere near as bad as last time but still crappy, so I ignored them and focused on the task at hand because turning them off was out of the question. The next one was a little rougher, the noble zombie inside bit me, and I resisted the festering debuff again but was still hurting. Not too badly, but the added eight damage I'd taken wasn't helping either.

After we took care of that one, the other one went better. Much more smoothly than the other two. Like it hadn't really wanted to attack for some reason.

"Last one, we ready?" I asked as I rubbed the wounds on my arm. They itched a little, and as we went on, they ached numbly.

The others nodded in unison before Sundar, and I heaved the lid aside to find nothing in the sarcophagus' bottom.

"Wasn't there a zombie in there?" I asked cautiously before something that seemed off caught my eye. "There's a hole there!"

A small figure launched itself over the side of the stone grave and grasped onto my shoulder before I could react in time to defend myself from the assault. Tiny clawed hands grasped and scratched at my face, neck, and arms as I struggled to clear myself of it.

3 dmg taken

2 dmg taken

4 dmg taken

"Ah!" I snarled, whipping my head left and right as my friends tried to get my attention, but I couldn't hear them.

Finally, I got a hand on it and used my Aether in a burst, willing the magic to freeze it.

The slightly frozen figured slowed down a heartbeat, long enough for me to shove it away and step back as it fell.

Lvl 4 Sheltered Ghoul – enraged

Frozen Debuff slightly resisted

Slow Debuff added

That had cost me two bars of Aether. Crap. Sudden blue light engulfed us, and Mona went wild, the outline of a Hell Cat settling over her and roaring soundlessly. Her weapons slashed and carved into the snarling ghoul's exposed back. My face forgotten, it tried to cover its face to protect itself, but it was useless.

The others fell on it and made short work of the little thing, stabbing and slicing in all the right places.

Lvl 4 Sheltered Ghoul died

37 EXP

"No better time to experiment than now." Sundar hauled me by my shoulder to a middling ground in the center of all the sarcophagi. Warmth built around us, and I finally noticed her totem in front of me.

"That buff was something, Sundar!" Mona grinned as she looked over herself. "It raised my striking speed. No damage boost to it, but that's okay if I hit more often, right?"

Panicked moans and groans of pain muffled by stone reached my ears, and she smiled. "It does work. Maybe we should use it a little more, then?"

"Maybe." I agreed and sat down. "You gonna have to stab some more, Al?"

"If this doesn't kill them? Likely." He seemed in good spirits but also contemplative somehow. As if plotting.

4 dmg to Fallen Noble
4 dmg to Fallen Noble
4 dmg to Fallen Noble
Lvl 5 Fallen Noble died
40 EXP
4 dmg to Fallen Noble
6 dmg to Fallen Noble
Dmg multiplied due to exploited weakness
Lvl 5 Fallen Noble died
40 EXP

"That was easy enough." Mona smiled as she glanced at us. "Al? Sunny? You wanna make a go at the last one while Ky rests and recovers?"

Sundar shrugged. "Sure, that'd be fun." The woman stood and shook herself out before glancing at me. "Just chill for a second."

I held a thumb up while they went to work, then I decided to check the durability on my sword. It had lost a couple points, leaving me with eight of ten left, which I was happy about. I'd have to see about procuring some of that repair powder that the smiths had.

I had little to no doubt that if my debacle hadn't been an issue, we would have. But things happened, and the past wouldn't change.

Lvl 5 Fallen Noble died
40 EXP

"Great work, guys!" I called to them, pulling up my status screen to see about leveling up. I checked my tree, and it was still grayed out, but I was delighted to see that I had leveled up to level eight, leaving me three points to raise my skills.

"Level eight!" Monami hissed excitedly. "Is the tree still gray for you all as well?"

I nodded, and so did the others. "We may want to ask about that, but I'm putting two points into Knowledge and one into Heart."

I did so, putting both at nine and twelve, respectively, while the latter point raised my total hit points to one hundred and seventy.

Monami did her own and stated, "Two for Heart and one for Knowledge."

Albarth nodded to Monami. "Same, though it seems a waste." He seemed sad but looked at Sundar. "You're a healer; how does your Aether work? How many bars do you have?"

"I have ten Serenity, so that makes my healing a bit more potent. And even though it's only one point per second, it's still a lot since my totem lasts for sixty seconds, and my Aether only takes fifty to return." She pointed a finger at her status screen and looked to be counting. "I have five bars right now, but mine isn't like yours. If I seal something, I don't get that bar back until the seal is broken."

She sighed heavily as she tapped her screen three times. "Which is why all three are going into Knowledge."

I whistled low, but that would give her an even number of Aether bars, and that would help her a lot.

"Do you know how you want to seal things?" I asked her in a low whisper as we readied to depart deeper into the dungeon. The ghoul had snagged the key somehow, and other than rotten flesh and bone dust, nothing of value was here.

"I do, but I haven't gotten to meet any animals to make it happen yet." Sundar shrugged noncommittally, and we began toward the door.

It stood ajar as the key simply vanished five feet from it, the off-white coloration of it marred by scratches on this side of the wall. Maybe the ghoul had been attempting to get to something else? Who knew?

"Tank gets the lead." I shouldered my way by the others, a large hand smacked my rump as I did. "I said lead, not groped, Sundar."

"Could've fooled me, meat shield." She winked, and the others snorted—good-natured fun.

The door opened slowly as I pressed my shoulder against it, peering into the darkness. "Maybe we should grab torches?"

"That'd be a good idea, but we can't be sure that taking a torch out won't trigger some sort of trap." Albarth huffed, looking into the void with me. "We can try it if you're too afraid to move along?"

"None of that macho bullshit right now." Monami groaned. "Let's get going, I kind of have a little night vision anyway, and I can see that this place isn't too terrible."

She pushed me into the next room and followed me in with the others as we went further.

"Wait." Sundar stilled, listening. She released a breath and whispered, "Come to me, please?"

"Have you lost your mind?" Albarth grumbled as he settled into a low stance, and eyed our surroundings.

"No." She looked fierce for a moment, then relaxed. "Hello, little friend."

She leaned down and held her hand out for something before standing up. A rat squeaked in her palm, whiskers twitching as it scented the air.

My eyes bulged, and I instantly moved to Mona, barely clamping my hands around her mouth before she screamed bloody murder. She hated rodents, but rats and mice were particularly bad.

I took an elbow to the gut for my efforts, luckily not taking any damage, but she looked more than a little frazzled.

"Relax, he's harmless." Sundar smiled and whispered something to him before he climbed up on to her shoulder, and she put a hand over his body there. She closed her eyes in the dim light and inhaled before pressing down. A muted swell of slight gray power washed over her, and the hand came away from her left shoulder. "It worked!"

She hopped up and down excitedly before her eyes began glowing amber in the dull light. "And now I can see."

"Would you be so kind as to explain what in the world is going on?" Albarth hissed as he eyed our surroundings once more.

"I can seal things, right?" She motioned to herself. "But half of my power comes from animal magic. So, what if I were able to mix the two? Gain power from animals by sealing them in my skin?"

"Does that work?" I found myself asking as I stepped closer to look at the marking on her shoulder. It was shaped like the rat, almost perfectly, but it matched the war paint on her body. "Does it kill them?"

"No, our connection is different, sure." She patted it affectionately. "But he's as alive in there as you and I are here. This magic is *amazing*."

"Yes, it is." Mona shivered. "Can we hurry up now?"

I grinned at her proudly and muttered, "And here you thought you wouldn't be able to do it on your own. I would've never thought of that, Sunny." Mona cleared her throat, and I looked to our healer. "You ready?"

Sundar nodded, and the two of them led us through the darkened corridor we entered. It took ten minutes to walk it, slowly checking for traps or ambushes when we cleared another exit. No longer in just a tomb, but a sort of underground cavern filled with stone burial mounds. Not made of stones, but piles of them over the dead and their remains.

The place was ripe for an ambush and based on the lines and tension in the bodies around me—my friends expected the same.

There, glowing in the center of the room on a pedestal of light-colored marble, was a pulsing orb.

"I'm glad that you could make it through that little test." A disembodied, heavily modulated voice greeted us from the shadows.

"Who are you?" I called out wearily, eyeing our surroundings more thoroughly.

"A friend with little time to waste, so please stop trying to find me and listen," the voice sounded exasperated, but it could've been a ploy. "All of you need to get stronger. I've interfered more than I probably should have, but there's too much at stake to let things go as they are."

"And why should we listen to you?" Sundar challenged. "You won't even face us as you are, mister dungeon boss."

"Adorable, kid, but a boss, I am not—stop interrupting." Some sort of black energy floated from the ground and wrapped around her face. She tried to speak, but nothing came out.

"You're an admin," Albarth blurted.

"Bingo, and if you figured that out, it's only a matter of time before they do," the voice responded. "You aren't ready for what is coming. Not with one of you at half-strength and so under-leveled. So, take this cursed item to the prince and ask if he can get you access to the guild early, so you can get to the next city to unlock your full magic."

"How do you know about our quest?" Mona's tone suspicious.

The voice hesitated a second, then responded, "I put it here. The orb that is. I made this place to have this conversation with whoever came in. Thankfully, it was you and not some other Neanderthals like the prince and his goons, who failed the puzzle spectacularly. Luckily it would have taken a decent amount of social maneuvering to get here, so that would keep most out. Look, get to Belgonna's Hold and get *stronger*. Soon."

"Why are you helping us?" Mona blurted, frustration dripping from her voice. "It's just a game, why the rush? And why hide yourself?"

"Because you aren't ready, and neither is anyone else," the modulated tone cracked back. "I'm doing what I can because... because I have to. I hide because it's harder to track me like this. Just do as I say, and for the love of god, stop taking things at face value."

The voice disappeared after that, and Sundar's voice came back to her. "What a dick."

"Let's get the orb and go." Mona huffed as she stepped forward toward the glowing sphere.

"I should mention that this room is trapped, and that you just stepped on the trap." The voice came back as soon as she was close to the orb. My heart fell into my stomach as I watched for any kind of reaction. "Don't be so clueless, I rigged this. There's treasure in the piles, but what did I say about taking things at face value, Red?"

Mona and I stilled completely. That had been something that only her father had called her.

"Dad?" Mona whispered, tears springing to her eyes. "Is that you?"

No answer came as we stood there in the glowing light of the orb pulsing near us.

"Let's get that and loot this place before we go." Albarth tapped me on the shoulder, whispering, "We have this; you be with her."

Mona hyperventilated next to the pedestal, streaks of tears falling from her chin as they went. "Hey, hey—Mo. That's a common saying for people who have red hair!"

"My hair is *tan* here, Seth!" She hissed, her shoulders shaking. "That was my dad; it had to be."

"Let's take a step back here, okay? There's a chance, but how could he possibly know who we are?" I had to admit, it did sound like it, and it was very odd. "Your dad left, and though it took a little while, you were over it. Why would he come back now? It makes no sense. And that guy was probably just D."

"What if he didn't have a choice?" She wiped her tears away. "What if he was taken? What if he *was* D? D for *dad.*"

"There were no signs of a struggle in his office, Mona," I reasoned. We had looked. We'd looked everywhere for any kind of clue as to what had sparked his leaving, but to no effect. "And you know admins usually have letters or numbers assigned to them. Maybe it was a fluke."

"Pros wouldn't leave one, or what if he went willingly and they're holding him captive?" She seemed to be piecing herself back together, but it was in a very weird way. I pulled her into my arms by her shoulder and held her tight. "I have to know, Seth. I have to."

"Look, if it makes you feel better, we can bump dinner up to tomorrow, and I'll come over to help you look for something, okay? But you need to promise me that you will focus on the here and now until then."

She didn't seem to trust herself with words, so she nodded, and I let her go, and we went to work looking in some of the piles. We found some money, coppers really, bone dust that looked to be a material, some ore, and one weapon that was really just a large femur with a metallic cap on the large portion of it.

That automatically went to Sundar, and the rest we decided to divvy up once we got out of the dungeon. Mona grabbed the item on the pedestal, and we booked it back to the exit.

CHAPTER FOURTEEN

"I was worried you wouldn't be back!" Gage greeted from inside the light of a lantern. "How did things go—is that what was causing all the trouble?"

Mona tossed him the orb. "This is for Prince Klemond, please pass him our regards and let him know that his kindest greetings to the guild would be appreciated—we need to move on."

She walked away faster than the Minotaur could even respond and left us all standing under the stars aghast at her behavior.

Could I blame her? No. Not really, and even if that *had* been her father and not a severely weird coincidence in wording, what could be done? We had no way of finding him, and there was nothing to be done now, and she seemed to need the space.

I had said I would help, so I would. But I'd give her some space, too.

"Well, I will take this to the prince right away and pass on your desires." Gage shrugged and glanced at Sundar. "I'm glad all of you made it through. Once he has this, the quest will be complete, and I will be able to negotiate on your behalf for entry into the adventurer's guild. But what's the rush?"

"We have to be able to go to Belgonna's Hold to unlock the other half of my magic," I supplied, unsure of how much we should let him know. "The sooner, the better, right? All for fighting the demons and being the best we can be."

"Ah, preparation and dedication—fine traits." Gage's easy smile confirmed that he wasn't suspicious as to our reasons any longer. "I will let you all know through Sundar when I have confirmation of what will be done. Since she will likely be closest to me when I escape his Majesty's clutches."

He walked off, and the others turned to me, the light of the lantern fading and leaving us all in shadow.

"I'm going to be training tonight at Gage's place," Sundar advised, stretching a bit. "I was kind of hoping that dungeon would be a little more fun."

"Well, they did leave us a decent puzzle for a beginner dungeon, and gave us a means to cheat the system a bit since things here are so realistic," Albarth reasoned, lifting his weapon to his gaze. The metal looked slightly warped and pitted. "Magical fire didn't seem to affect it much, but the fires from the wood seemed to be bad for it. I'll go tomorrow and see about getting some of that repair powder as a quick fix."

"Good idea." I frowned, then sighed. "Mo will need some time, so I think I'm going to go do some sword training. I need to see about a shield too. If I have to tank, might as well go sword and board for some of it, and I need to be prepared."

"You aren't going to go after her?" Albarth raised an eyebrow at me in challenge. "And you should have done the 'sword and board' bit *before* the dungeon, Kyvir. We're better than that."

"If there's a part of 'Mo will need some time,' that you don't understand, Al, by all means, follow her and get a beating." I began to walk toward the exit to the grounds. "I'm not up for that right now, and gaming is about learning, too, Al. I'm all about learning."

I glanced back to see his dour face but decided that I really needed to be away right now.

I'd made a promise, and Thea was likely still up, or I hoped she would be, and I could use the training. Opening my map to find and follow the most direct route from the gate, I found I wasn't far away from the place at all. I took a left outside and followed the wall to a small home with lavish crawling ivy all over it. This place was nice, large, and a lovely shade of green with a forest scene depicted in paint on the front and the one side that I could see.

I walked a little more slowly toward the door, appreciating the artwork and paint when I heard a snort and a giggle from above me. I blinked and glanced up to see Thea seated on a balcony carved like woven branches with a book in her hands. "Hello handsome." Her warm greeting made me chuckle, her normal tone changing to that of a royal lady. "It has been some time since a gentleman suitor came calling so late at my door. Need I be worried about untoward action and impure thoughts?"

My smile deepened, shifting toward a grin as I did my best courtly bow, raising my head to reply, "Nay, my lady. My heart is as pure in intent as my actions. I only wish to join you for a time."

She laughed then, a deep belly laugh, before dropping gracefully from her perch and landing in front of me. "That's almost too bad; I think I would prefer the impure thoughts."

I had to laugh at that. "Nice to see you, too. Your offer to train still open?"

"With you?" She leaned forward, her green shift dress falling away from her chest, exposing a little of her body that made me fight to keep my eyes on hers. "Of course, it is."

Her hand grasped mine, and she tugged me along behind her to the side of her house where a small gate stood, a small whistled note, and the latch on the other side of it fell away. The gate opened as she pushed, and in we went. The garden inside wasn't like Gage's either, all flora and fauna found in a forest-like some sort of dreamscape grew around us, silhouetted against the night sky. A grove of saplings surrounding a circle of packed earth that looked to be our destination as she tugged and chuckled at my expression of wonder and amazement.

"So, what will we be practicing with tonight?" Her lips pulled away from her teeth in a grin as her nose wrinkled and eyes crinkled in delight. A strange expression for someone to take when wanting to fight.

"I could definitely use more training with the sword." I scratched the back of my neck nervously. "I'm the tank—the guy who takes all of the damage for the group—so I should start working with a shield. Plus, with Sundar learning from Gage, it would help to learn a potentially different style of swordsmanship, right?"

"Well, I'm no good with those clunky things, but Gage is, and the dwarves are usually pretty handy with them as well." Her smile turned wistful a moment, the moonlight playing across her tanned skin. "And since it seems that Belgonna's Hold is your next aim, you'll likely be able to find one there who can teach you if you don't learn from sarge. And that is correct, if you'll settle for me teaching you swordplay in his stead?"

"Of course, I will, but are there dwarves there?" I cocked my head to the side with the question. "At the hold, I mean? I haven't seen too many here except for wanderers."

She laughed and began to whistle a tune to a tree off to our right. A shape sprouted from it that she plucked as if picking fruit. The shape was a wooden sword that reminded me of practice weapons that martial artists used in movies. She did the same thing with another tree and tossed the first weapon to me.

"How do you do that?" I couldn't help the awe that crept into my voice as she brought herself to stand before me.

"My gift." Her coy grin made her eyes sparkle in the moonlight. "By the way, tonight I will be teaching you an elven form of sword fighting." She motioned to her weapon, then mine. "It involves using traditional weapons like this, and the whole body with it. But don't worry, my parents taught me well before they left."

"So, it's just you alone here?" I figured asking about herself before pressing her about her magic would be the least rude option of the two questions fighting in my mind.

"Yes." She put the point of her sword in the ground and motioned to our surroundings. "My magic is plant-based, like many of my kind from the forest, but mine is stronger. I sang all of these plants into existence as a gift to my family, but all it did was remind them of home. They left to go back because this was too good of a reminder of what had been lost."

I stood there at a loss for words. My parents traveled the world, into third world countries trying to better peoples' lives how they could with their technology and medicines. I knew all about what it was like to have the people you love far away, but I had always had Mona and her mom to help. Because they were family, too. Made me think of what Mona was going through right now. But the last time her father had come up between us, it had been a week before I had been able to safely be around her without getting a thorough tongue lashing. I trusted her to sort herself out or to reach out to me if I was needed.

We were usually so good about that.

Even before I could feel pity for her settle into my stomach, Thea was moving. Her wooden weapon striking out toward my head, I ducked just in time, feeling the wooden blade slap against my hair.

"You can feel a lot of things for me, Kyvir." Her earnest gaze met mine, determination and knowing in her eyes. "But that look in your eyes that I have seen from so many others? That is not one of them. Pity should never be one of them."

I'd always felt the same. "Me? Pity you? Please." Damn, this game felt so real.

She grinned, and our sparring began in truth. She would whack me in the shoulders and arms three times for every one strike I managed to block. After several bruises, she finally took pity on me, and we stopped.

"Sorry, I let my frustrations get the better of me, but you seem to be much better with the blade than the staff." She motioned me into the center of the ring. "Come, I'll teach you our ways."

"Is it okay for a Kin to learn an elven way of fighting?" I wouldn't lie and say I wasn't highly interested, but if she would get into trouble, I'd definitely think twice about it.

"Only because it's you." Her mischievous grin after that was surprising.

"Why me?" I asked suddenly, making her pause to look at me.

"I like heroes." She shrugged. "Meeting you was nice and all, but something about you and the way you carried yourself was endearing. And the way you fight, or try to, is attractive. I keep thinking of your potential, and it excites me."

"I...see." Suddenly, the air was hotter, and I couldn't tell if it was my face or the world itself.

Thea moved closer, her hips swaying as she stepped one long leg in front of the other toward me. Her eyes piercing in the soft light. "There are few things out there that attract me so, other than a good fight, good booze, or something to explore. But you excite me."

"So, I'm a fascination to you?"

Thea stood nearer to me now, her athletic body so close to mine that I could smell the forest along her skin and almost taste the earthy tones in the air around her. Large blue eyes stared up at me, lips parted slightly as my heart beat against my ribs.

"Is that so bad, Kyvir?" Her hands encircled my waist, not pulling, just there. "That I find you attractive? That I see what's there, and I am unafraid to reach out and show interest? You could deny me, and I would still respect you for it and what you did. I would still offer you help and training."

I had no words for what I was feeling. Sure, I could be feeling vulnerable for having been basically called an idiot for stirring feelings for my best friend. Maybe not in so many words, but the implication was there, and it had stung something fierce. Still did. I ached.

Longing for something that I never knew I even wanted—something I didn't want all at the same time. I was alone now with a longing that no longer had a goal. Thoughts of being lonely forever began to consume me, visions of me sitting around by myself until I was old and gray clawed at my mind and heart.

"I know that your heart isn't mine—and that's fine." That brought me out of my thoughts. She had heard my conversation with Albarth, me snapping at him for his meddling. "That doesn't diminish my own desires, and from what I recall, you recently had your own shoved aside for you."

I flinched, closing my eyes at that, and relinquishing my sword to the ground by my feet. I could feel my body tensing, my hands balling into fists. Why was that so damned upsetting? It was fine. It should've been fine. Why wasn't it fine?

A calloused hand caressed my cheek. "I like you for you, Kyvir, and I would learn more about you if I could."

I opened my eyes to see her standing there, chest pressed against me, and staring up at me. And I wanted this. Suddenly more than anything else in the world, I wanted to be selfish and to forget the pain flooding my soul at whatever it is that I had lost with Mona.

Innocence. I had lost the innocence that we'd had all our lives, and now I felt as though I had none on my own.

I reached down and wrapped my hand around Thea's waist and pulled her against me, insistent but gentle before leaning down and claiming her lips with mine. I tasted copper and felt a sting against my lips, realizing that my sharp incisors had pierced my lip and hers.

But she didn't seem to care, and suddenly, neither did I. The stars above us looked so real from the ground of the training circle, but I could only see them if I wasn't paying attention to the woman in that circle with me. And she did her absolute best to claim all of that attention.

***

"Now, as you go through the second form, what's it called again?" Thea's question brought me back to the present.

"The sprouting." My arm moved from the first form, the seed, with the wooden weapon in it. The blade rose in an upward strike as if a sprout had broken from the ground. "Then the budding, the flower, petal fall, and finally the fall."

The wooden blade slashed horizontally before me, I twisted and did the same again, spun a kick at an imagined enemy and ended the attack with a savage overhand slice.

Weapon Mastery: Sword

Level: 2 (Initiate)

"Oh!" Startled, I let my weapon fall to my side at rest. "I leveled up my weapon mastery with the sword."

"Excellent!" Her wooden blade cracked me on the shoulder and I grunted in pain. "Never lower your weapon!"

She came into view; we had neglected to put our clothes back on, so the way she moved in the dawn light was distracting, to say the least. But seeing the way her muscles flexed and contracted during each form and movement in our fight had gone a long way in helping me recognize the way my body should move to match hers. It helped her in being able to adjust me and see the minute details in how I would react to an attack of movement with the weapon.

That and it gave her easy access to grope me and flit away before I could retaliate. The perv that she was. To be truthful, I hadn't had so much fun in a while, and this was about as naturally occurring with her as it seemed to be in real life.

She stretched, arching her back, then shook herself out before grinning at me and stabbing her wooden blade into the ground. "We should get you ready for the day, not to mention that I have duties to attend to, as well. Would you care to bathe?"

I glanced down at the dirt, grime, and sweat that had built up on my body throughout our skirmishes, lessons, and *liaisons*, then nodded. "Yes, thank you."

She chuckled, the throaty sound making me smile as she cupped my hand in her own and tugged me toward the rear of her home. She reached into a crevice beside the door, grunted, and then the simple white door popped open and admitted us inside.

Painted murals of green plants and wild animals decorated the hall. Doors, their handles being the only way to differentiate them from the walls, dotted the walls to our right and left. She chose the one immediately to our left and swung it inward.

"Your family must really like art," I observed out loud, the painted waterfall on the far wall looked so realistic that it could have soaked us.

"This all happened after they left." She tugged me in and shut the door behind us. "This was my way of trying to cope with their absence." Her eyes glinted mischievously, and she smirked, "As well as a way to rebel and have a little revenge for ruining the austere, pale colors they adored."

"You're a talented artist, Thea," I pulled her close to me into a hug. "That waterfall looks as though it's real."

"It is." She laughed at me then, because my jaw dropped, and I instantly moved forward. "The paint used to make it was enhanced by Aether and a spell to make the painting come to life. The water is silent, because I neglected to make the fall larger, so there's no crashing sound. It drains into the city's aqueducts, and Trickle purifies it as she does water from elsewhere."

"You know Trickle?"

"She was the one who helped me magic the paint." Her grin eased a little, a curious expression coming to the fore. "Wanderers pay a price for their magic in this realm. Tell me, what was her price?"

I blushed, then did my best to just breathe through my initial embarrassment as I answered, "My, uh, first kiss here in this world."

Her laugh rang out in the room, echoing off the walls weirdly, and pulled me close. "I can't believe she beat me there. I'll have to have a word with her."

"I don't think she meant anything by it." I smiled back and joined her beneath the water, it was cool but soothing.

"You don't know her the way I do, but that's fine." She pulled out a small bar of something scented and began to lather it in her hands before running them over my body. The scent was less flowery and more refreshing than I had expected from a place covered in flowers and plants.

QUEST COMPLETED – Prince Klemond deems you fit to fight in the crypts beneath his home. Find the cursed item at the end of the dungeon and bring it out of the crypts to nullify the curse. Reward: Negotiated, 400 EXP and future dealings with the crown of Iradellum. See Gage for the results.

Level UP!

Level UP!

You have reached the milestone level of 10! From now on, your experience will no longer be rolling. Therefore, you will start from zero and work your way from 0 to 1,100 EXP!

That loss of EXP hurt, but I was still one step closer to fully unlocking my power!

"Hell, yes!" I growled, looking at my stats, now that I had reached level ten, I could see that my skill tree was back, which was nice. And I had two points to spend on my stats as well.

I checked my map and found that a green quest marker had populated over Gage's place.

"Congratulations." Thea pressed her chest against my back. "What will you do now? You meet the requirements to get into the guild, so you can take on quests there and have your fun."

"And go to Belgonna's Hold." A weight of worry slumped off my shoulders. I found I could breathe a little easier.

"Then how about one to go on?" Thea turned me and pressed me against the wall behind the waterfall. "And when you come back, I'll be here to have some more training sessions with."

I laughed then. "I would like that."

Thea has offered to become your friend.

Do you accept? Yes / No?

I selected yes without a thought, and she grinned. "That means we can send whispers to each other."

I raised my eyebrows at that, surprised that a non-player character could have that level of interaction with the system and players, but that was a really cool system.

"Now, where were we?" A low growl issued from her throat and her hands, slick with soap, were more insistent.

"Oh, boy."

***

"Have a good day!" Thea waved to me as I grinned like an idiot. "And don't forget to ask Ori for an elven sword!"

"I won't!" I called and waved back to her. The suggestion had come after I had seen the swords hanging in her armory. The elven variety of blades had beautiful curves, a thick base that thinned near the middle and thickened a little before coming to the tip like a sword version of a kukri. The backs of them came straight down to the hilt, thick to give them support to block or parry with. The way the elves treated them to keep them strong but supple was a secret that one of Ori's smiths learned from his travels before coming to settle here, which was why she had suggested him for the job. Likely why Ori had taken the man as well.

—*Where are you?*— Albarth's whisper startled me as I jogged toward Gage's place.

My quick response —*On my way to Gage's now*— appeared to be met with silence.

I rolled my eyes and upped my pace just a bit, coming to the fence and gate moments later.

"And just *where* have you been?" Mona's folded arms and evil glare seemed to be how this in-game day was going to go.

"Training, initiate two with the sword—you?" I didn't even so much as raise an eyebrow as I answered.

"With Thea?" Albarth cut in, trying to look as menacing as Mona appeared, but he was nowhere near as intimidating as she could be.

"Yup." This was for the birds. "So, Gage, how did negotiations go?"

"Well!" He produced a sealed envelope. "I have a letter of introduction from the prince for you to give to the guild administrators and from there, permission to travel abroad as required for awakening your magical abilities."

"If it went well, then why did it take so long again?" Sundar tilted her head to the left, curiously.

Gage heaved a sigh. "The prince wanted to help, but it had to appear as though he stood to gain something more, so I had to offer to teach him some things in order for it to be *more* stacked in his favor. That's where the debate began."

"I take it you'll teach him more on how to use the sword?" Sundar grinned, and Gage nodded tiredly. "He's been hounding you for days, it'll be good for him."

"I would see him sheltered a little longer, but that is my desire and not his." Gage shrugged and handed Sundar the letter. "I would suggest going to the guild soon, they open their doors to quests rather late to give people time to gather so it will likely be a madhouse there if you dawdle. Not all of them are the minimum level, mind you, but they tend to congregate there regardless."

"Thank you, Gage." I bowed at the waist a little. "If there is any way we can repay you, please let us know."

"I have grown fond of Sundar in our short time together." His hand found hers and he pulled her close. "If you would please keep her safe and grow strong enough to push the demon hordes back, I would consider my time more than repaid."

"Silly, I can't die!" Sundar kissed his cheek, and he grumbled at her ineffectually. "Besides, it's *my* job to keep these troublemakers alive."

I snorted, and she gave me a wink. "Let's take his advice and get going. Before we need to leave, there's a thing I need to see about at the armorer or with Ori."

Without waiting to see if anyone was coming, I turned on my heel and left for the gate, then strode out of it.

It took me walking for ten minutes before I felt a hand on my shoulder at a crossroads, an irritated Albarth glaring at me sighed. "We've been waiting for you to realize that you have no clue where you're going for about eight minutes, now. Any farther and we really will be late, follow me."

He took me left and led on from there, silence falling over both of us. I chose to remain quiet more out of anger than anything else. I was a grown man, and my time was my own.

"I'm sorry." I almost couldn't believe my ears, what I was hearing had to be the equivalent to how some people felt winning the lottery.

I stayed quiet, content to let him speak.

"Look, I get it, okay?" He stopped walking so fast, and I allowed myself to fall into step with him as he sighed and continued tiredly, "I never had to go through what you did—at all. My loss was different, but at least now there's no 'what if?' No regret."

"Of course, there is," I corrected him immediately. "She and I lost the innocence that our friendship had, and while I may have developed some kind of recognition that she's beautiful, smart, kind, funny and amazing—I've always known that. It was just on display in a different light, and with what happened and the way it happened, everything we've fought to maintain because of our closeness and our bond was in jeopardy. I appreciate you trying to help, hell, Sunny too, but this is no longer something either of you needs concern yourselves with."

Before he could try and say anything else, or throw himself into a hole of some sort that he couldn't climb out of, I added, "Look, it's not like it was malicious, and I know that. It's the only reason that this conversation is possible. I know you meant well and that you wanted someone to have the chance that you felt you should have had—Mona and I are not you. We aren't her. We are our own people, and I am *clearly* not a viable option for her. So, let's move on. I want to be cool with you again, Al."

He sputtered a bit, but finally cleared his throat and muttered, "Well, thank you for the second chance."

I nodded, and we continued on. It took about half an hour to get to the guild, and the outside of it was a crapshoot. Players stood around, hawking wares, items, gear, and other things they had found. Looking for a group, party invites, and other such borderline harassment-level crap took place in front of a large building made of gray brick and black mortar. It was tall and wide, a wall with guards atop it allowed them to look down over the crowd below, and the crossbows they carried seemed to be trained on someone for a second, then moving on to the next person. Not a threat, but a way to ensure that they knew their shenanigans had better not be malicious.

Open windows let out music from some kind of player inside with a lute, singing a song they had to have written themselves, the words escaping me. The door, large and deep mahogany in color, stood open.

Sundar began shoving people aside, one person cried foul and met Mona's evil glare and wound up running off. A few minutes later, we stood at the front counter where a lizard-like woman with an apron on flashed sharp teeth at us and turned her head so that she could see us a little better.

"Welcome to the Adventurer'ss Guild!" Her greeting bubbly and cheerful as her fingers clacked on the clear tablet-like object before her. She lisped and drew out her S sounds. "My name iss Ssveltarina, and I will be assisssting you today. How can I help you?"

Sundar grinned and handed her the prince's letter of introduction. "We're here to join up and move on to the next city, ma'am."

"I sssee." She gave us a placating smile as she used a talon to tear open the envelope. She read the letter, and her hands shook slightly. "You truly are."

"We aren't in the business of lying," Albarth quipped haughtily with his chin raised. "If you'll simply induct us into the guild, we will be out of your hair—er, scales."

"No offensse taken, dear." The smile returned, and Sveltarina seemed to be back in her element once more. "Have all of you finished leveling up? You cannot fully be inducted into the guild with leftover pointss and powerss."

I quickly added one of my free points to strength, then the other to Knowledge. Looking at my tree, I had only one option, and it freaked me out a little.

Aether Vampire – Consuming the blood of an opponent has a high chance (55%) of replenishing your Aether (one bar) and an increased chance to steal a gift or spell.

The weirdest part was that it looked like it was upgradeable.

Spend one free stat point to gain more power in this area. Result of upgrading – Unknown.

Well, there was that. I picked it, and my incisors tingled uncomfortably. Then they shrank slightly, thickening in my mouth, but the teeth made room for them.

"You okay, Kyvir?" Monami asked with a look of concern on her features, her brow furrowed and gaze on mine.

"We can talk about it in a bit." I sighed and looked to the others. "We good?"

They nodded, and we turned back to the administrator at the desk. "All you'll need to do iss touch thiss."

She held up the little tablet she had tapped on before and motioned for us to touch it with our whole hand. Albarth and Monami went first; their data populating on the rear of the item for Ssveltarina to observe and nod to the next. She had to turn it completely so that Sundar's huge hand would fit onto it, but her data seemed to be fine.

"My turn." I grinned and pressed my hand onto the tablet and waited.

"Thiss iss...interessting." She frowned and pulled the item closer to her for inspection. "Your data iss here, and while all of you have very unique and powerful abilitiess and affinitiess, it mentionss that your magic issn't fully unlocked."

"That's why we need the ability to roam freely, the person who can unlock it is in Belgonna's Hold." She made a sound of understanding, then put the tablet down.

"If you would all open your sstatuss sscreenss, you'll be able to ssee the tab for the Adventurer'ss Guild has been unlocked for you." Each of us followed along as she spoke, tabbing through the bevy of information. "In it, you can make a guild party, name it and everything, it'ss rather clever like that. Within it, you'll be able to show that you have the right to move freely to Belgonna'ss Hold."

"What's to stop people from moving on without guild blessing?" Mona inquired politely.

"There iss a barrier to keep wandererss from wandering too far." She seemed particularly pleased with her joke by the size of her grin. "It iss sso that thosse not in good favor with the guild cannot missrepresent usss." She frowned, then leaned forward, lowering her voice. "There are wayss of getting around it, but they can be deadly and dangerouss. I do not ssuggesst them."

"So, to move forward, we would have to have joined you?" Albarth crossed his arms with a frown.

"You would have optionsss." She shrugged and motioned to a flyer for the king's army behind the counter. "You could join the king'sss army or become a much higher level and break through the barrierss on your own. Ourss isss a much more practical and *freeing* route of ssservice."

"Well, we will take that as a good warning and do our best not to go through the barriers." Sundar grinned and held out her meaty hand. "Great to meet you, ma'am."

They clasped hands, and we headed off to do what we could to prepare for our trek east. It was midnight in the real world, so I should be pretty tired.

"Hey, Mo." I caught up to her as we cleared the crowd in front of the guild building. "You think I could send a request to Ori for a shield and an elven sword before we log off for the night? That way, he has plenty of time to work on them if it's needed?"

"And I'm supposed to just traipse over to his smithy and ask for you?" The testy edge to her voice was sharp and biting.

"No, I know that you are aware that we can send whispers to NPCs, and that's probably how you can find out if he can or not." Her eyes widened slightly. "You didn't know?"

"No." She crossed her arms in front of her chest. "How did you come to find out?"

"Thea told me." Mona rolled her eyes, and that was my breaking point. "What the hell is going on with you, Mona?"

She looked stricken, then angrier than before. "You leave me hanging after I just met someone who could have been my father—missing for years with no contact—so that you can go and 'learn' from someone you just met? Let alone an NPC."

"You seem to be forgetting that when you get like that, I know you need space, that nothing I can do will help you or be good enough." She snorted, and I growled at her. "You forget that I know you better than *anyone,* Mona. I know how you can be, how you *have* been. So instead of doing nothing and getting in your way, I went to go get help getting stronger just like that guy who *wasn't* your father told us to. If you're going to sit there and judge me for doing exactly what I needed to so I can help you figure this all out, then figure it out your damned self."

I turned and made to storm away, then stopped cold as she sighed and muttered, "I guess you don't know me as well as you thought." That cut through the anger welling up in me.

I turned and strode back to her, fury dying on my face. "I'm sorry that I can't be good enough for you, Mona. I'm sorry that I broke the one unspoken rule that we had by thinking you could be interested in someone like me as anything other than the friend I am."

"That's not what's wrong, and you know it!" She shot back, anger returning to her features, hard lines in her face making her seem harsher. "Would you just get your head out of your ass?"

"We're family, and I was stupid to listen to anyone else's input on what we had," I continued, my face now inches from her own. "It's all my fault that things are weird between us now. I don't blame anyone else; it's me. I get it. I'll go ask Ori myself. Thanks."

She made to stop me, but I ripped my hand away from her and stalked away. Her shouts to me to stop and listen to her fell on deaf ears. I muted her whispers, and those of the rest of the party too just to be safe. I knew they would mean well, but I couldn't take it right now. I was being petulant, and I knew it, but I was hurt.

I almost sprinted to Ori's smithy, giving him my order, and paying the fee outright. Ten gold seemed like a lot, but I was okay if that was the cost for both of the items. The most expensive one being the sword, since it had to be a special metal alloy that they had little of, and was difficult to make.

After that, I went to Ophira's and spent more time making other types of dye. It was simple, mind-numbing work, but it helped to soothe my aching soul.

I shouldn't have been so crappy to Mona. I'd been a real jerk, and I was acting like those guys who called a woman names for not being interested. I couldn't shake that I was feeling worse and worse.

I bought seven vials of the tincture from Ophira at a discounted rate of one silver per vial.

She hugged me after the sale, muttering, "I am not one for physical contact sometimes, but you seem to need it this moment. I am free to talk and guide you if ever you should need it."

Ophira has offered to become your friend.
Do you accept? Yes / No?

I accepted the request. "Thank you." Then turned to leave before I felt a hand on my shoulder, Ophira frowned at me and offered me a single vial of some clear liquid.

I took it and saw the description.

Heart's Bond Dye – This single-use item shows the user's emotions to the world in a colorful display. (1 use)

"I made that so that I could see how much you were truly enjoying yourself, but I would like you to give it to your friend as a token of truce if needed. It will allow you to know how she feels. Or her you." I tried to pass it back to her with a shake of my head, but Ophira pressed my hand back. "I will not train you further if you do not accept it. I can make others. And as soon as you see the colors, you will know what they signify."

"Thank you, Ophira. I'll consult you as often as I can, and I'll be back as soon as I can be for more training." She smiled and waved me out of the shop.

The sun's light faded and fell in the west, so I opted to log out then.

CHAPTER FIFTEEN

I opened my eyes to the suddenly dull, dreary real existence that was life outside of Mephisto's world.

The light was on, and there on the floor, sniffling and sobbing in her pajamas was Mo.

Great, I sighed to myself.

I opened the portal door just enough to grab the towel on the table and cover myself before stepping out. I hadn't brought that into the room—she had.

"Hey—" I opened the door, and she looked up at me, standing and coming forward until she could pull me into a hug as tight as she could.

"I'm sorry." It was the only thing I could think to say as she sobbed and hiccupped into my chest and shoulder. Her tears dripped onto my chest. "I'm sorry, Mo."

"It's not... just, you." Her chest spasmed against mine. "My fault. It's all my fault."

"Hey now," I tutted at her softly. "I am too. I've been a jerk, and I know it. You know it. I should have never done anything I did the other day. I'm so sorry."

It took a few minutes of hushed "it's all right," to get her to calm down enough for us to hold any semblance of a conversation.

"What's going on with us?" She whispered into the air, her normally wild hair seeming tanner and tamer than usual as she shook her head in disbelief. "I haven't been entirely honest with you."

I stilled, looking down at her carefully.

"Mom had cancer," she whispered, the gravity of that one statement floored me. All I could do was stare at her while my heart plummeted into my stomach like an atomic bomb.

The world started spinning, and suddenly, sitting up was a labor of sheer willpower.

"It's gone, Seth." I looked into her green eyes refilling with tears, and she whispered it again, "She made me swear not to tell you, and I only found out because I read a letter that she had left out. That's why she was teaching me because she was worried that she wouldn't have too much longer with us."

"How long?" I tried to get my mouth to move, and say more but it's all I could muster.

"A few weeks, it was in the early stages, but her sister Kara had died of it swiftly, so we thought the same." She hiccuped again. Her shoulders shook, and she looked up at me with a small, sad smile on her face. "Her appointment was to check and see how bad it was progressing, if it was and they would be able to get to it if it had slowed, but..."

"But what, Mo? Is it worse?"

"It's all gone. They confirmed it today, and I just found out. Mom's been gardening in the back yard to kind of come to terms with it, and now it's just gone as if by—" She tried to find the right words but seemed to be having serious trouble.

"Magic." I finished, things connecting in my mind. "The game is somehow changing things outside of it."

"What?!" She hissed; incredulity written all over her face. "That's crazy."

"People spitting flames all over in populated places?" I challenged her, needing to stand and move with the realization beating across my conscious mind. "Me being able to see magical auras like in the game? You being able to use Allure outside of the game? Yes, you've done it, don't you try and deny it, you do it without thinking. And now this?"

She stayed quiet, then shrugged and threw her hands up. "You're not going to give that up, are you?"

"No! And now this?" I threw my own hands out to my side. "The signs are all over and that guy telling us to get stronger faster? How does that not mean something big is coming to you?"

"It just sounds so unbelievable, Seth." Her voice had a sense of calm to it now. It did look like she had calmed down quite a bit. She wiped her eyes and averted her gaze so that I could at least put on the mesh shorts that I'd had folded on my little table.

"Crazy or not, that's what I'm going to be trying to prepare for." I scratched my head nervously as I considered what it could mean for the group. "I don't know about you guys, but I'm going to be doing everything I can to get stronger and prepare for what is to come. We need to get mom into the game and my folks, if possible."

"Can that happen?" Mona asked softly. "It took months trying to get these portals together with us, and this is happening *now*, Seth."

"I'm not sure." An idea occurred to me, and I tapped the support function on the console of the portal.

A ringing sound emanated from it, and a calm voice answered, "Mephisto's tech support, this is Kevin, how can I help you?"

"Hi Kevin, Seth here, I wanted to ask—can other people play the game from my portal?"

"Unfortunately, not, Mister Ethelbart, the portals are keyed to the owner, but ordering a twin for the portal isn't difficult. Expensive—but not impossible." The man's smooth voice didn't sound too contrite, but that was fine. "All purchases would need to be handled through our purchasing department by phone or online."

"Thank you, Kevin, I appreciate your time." It had been a little odd that he had known my name, but then again, I did call from my pod, which kept track of my medical data.

Once the call was complete and I hung up, I immediately went to the purchasing site for the game and ordered the premium package so that a second pod would be brought to Mona's home and hooked up on Monday.

"Seth, that's ridiculous, there's no way, and that's thousands of dollars—" Mona's worries were valid but finishing that thought wasn't necessary.

"My money is your money, Mo." I growled softly, a saying I told her often. "And if I'm right, we need all the power we can get, and I want Ma taken care of."

"What about your family?"

"I haven't been able to reach them on their phones when I tried." I shrugged. "May seem callous, but they are in third world countries with their travels hidden and secret even from me to keep them from being targeted by unsavory folks. I'll send them an email and see if they get it in time. I can only hope they do."

"They always were pretty secretive as well," Mona agreed, then frowned. "You said that I use my gift outside the game. How did you mean, and when was this?"

"Normally, at times when you wanted something, or when you're feeling vulnerable," I frowned, thinking about it. "Like when you had asked to share a bed the other night. When you were asking, I got befuddled and said yes because the effect was there."

"So, you didn't want to?" Her face was unreadable as she asked.

"I would have anyway, but it felt like I had no choice, and then after that, I was acutely aware of you." My cheeks warmed deeply, trying to stamp that down.

"So, you were attracted to me, but only because of that." Something in her expression fell, and I sighed.

"I've always known how special you are, Mona, I just saw it differently because of that. Don't worry, it's okay. I know it's not on purpose. And I will still come over tomorrow to help you look around your dad's office." She looked down, then stood, and turned to walk out. "Mo?"

She stopped but didn't turn around. "Yeah?"

"You okay?" I paused, stepping closer to her. "Are we okay?"

Still turned away from me. "Yeah, Seth. Of course, we're okay. I'm not mad anymore, and our friendship is more tried and truer than ever. I'll let mom know that dinner will be tomorrow, and we can have you come over a little earlier to help me get in there."

"Ma has it locked again?"

"Yep, but we both know where she keeps the key, so it's no worries on getting inside dad's office." She walked out of the room, and I followed her out.

"You don't want to stay?" I couldn't help feeling like something was still wrong.

"That was a lot to take in, and I wanna get out of here before mom starts blowing up my phone." She turned to face me, a smile in place, and her eyes closed. "I love you, Seth. You're the best friend anyone could ask for."

"I love you too, Mo." That set my mind at ease. "I'll see you in the morning in-game."

With that, she smiled and left the house.

***

I had tried to reach my folks again with nothing working, so I opted to send them that email detailing what I had found and that they needed to get home so that I could try and get them into the game as well.

I doubted that they would understand, but they had an easy time supporting me, and usually, if I worried over something, they heard me out.

I ate a light breakfast, then logged in, the countdown to come in a blur, but once I was in the game, things cleared up. As if stepping out of a fog.

Eight hours of sleep had seen me back twenty-four hours later in this world, and as the world darkened, I found myself reaching out to Thea.

—Thea? You up?—

—If you plan to come and see me, do so. I'm training with a friend currently, but she would be more than happy to train with us— She sounded out of breath but excited at the same time.

Since I had been over by Ophira's, I was a little further away than I might normally be, but with it being dusk, there weren't too many people out. I jogged to her place, a little warm-up if I was going to be fighting and training with a friend of hers and clambered my way over the fence to find Thea standing there with a hand on the latch.

"Oh, that was swift." Her smile grew as she gave me a friendly thump on the shoulder. "Kyvir, come, let's introduce you to my friend."

We walked from the side of the house to where the training circle was, and in it stood a slight woman who looked to be human but for the golden scales that traveled down her face neck and shoulders. She wore what looked like it could have been a kimono, but it was shorter slightly, showing her legs and shoulders as she moved through her own forms.

"This is the friend you spoke of, Thea?" The woman's husky voice reached us, and there was something haunting to it.

Her floral-printed short kimono, cream-colored red and green plants growing around black sparrows fluttering toward a golden dawn, settled and rested against the smooth swell of her thighs. Her gaze, as golden as the scales surrounding the bridge of her eyebrows and sweeping from her cheeks down like some kind of makeup on her ebon skin, swept to me. I could feel her scanning me as a threat.

"My name is Kyvir." I moved forward to offer her my hand, and she only smiled as my foot entered the circle.

"Prey." Her slight upturn of thin lips widened savagely, showing sharpened teeth. She grasped my hand and whipped her body around, throwing me over her shoulder into the center of the ring.

I landed with a grunt of pain that turned into a growl a heartbeat later. "What's your deal, lady?"

"This is Minh Lei, and she has a problem with men, so I figured you being here would help you both," Thea called out, "She can't kill you, but getting your weapons out would be highly suggested."

I thought about drawing my sword, but something sharp sliced the air next to my head, and I scrambled away from the scary lady wielding a weapon that looked like a glaive.

"Yes, draw your weapon, prey—show me that you are a worthy hunt." Minh's pupils, slitted black depths thinned vertically, and she paced forward.

I dodged her next stab by rolling and popping up into a low stance. Since she wanted to use a glaive, so would I. I focused on where the weapon would be if I had it equipped and grabbed for the spot on my back.

My hand met the solid handle of the glaive, and I whipped it over my shoulder, aiming the bottom blade at her shoulder.

She snarled and stabbed forward with the blunt end of her own weapon, catching me in the stomach. I had set the system notifications so that when I entered a training circle, my damage notification shut off, then turned on automatically.

I came up from being doubled over for a second too long just in time to stop her attack with the handle of my glaive. She was too good with this kind of weapon, but I was better with a sword.

Gripping the middle of the individual sections as if I was about to make a stand made her fall back a step, giving me the room I needed to disengage the lock with a flick of my wrist. I yanked my right hand away from my left and twisted, guiding the weapons apart as I bolted forward.

I kept them together just enough to give her the idea that my reach would be limited and that I was unversed in the weapon's use. It paid off.

She struck at the center of the weapon with her own, hoping it might stop my forward advance, but the weapon split, and her weapon sliced into the ground.

The sword in my right hand sliced diagonally across her chest, her backpedaling keeping it from being a deeper cut. Still, the kimono split where I had sliced, and her face became an unreadable mask, her almond-shaped eyes narrowing dangerously.

"I think now is the best time for me to actually step in." Thea tried, but Minh fixed her with a glare so pointed I thought she would start bleeding where Thea stood outside the circle.

"I like that weapon; who made it?" Minh called as she stabbed her own glaive into the ground.

"Ori and his people," I answered as I flipped the sword in my left hand so that it faced the right way up. "It's the first of its kind, I'm certain they would make you one if you ordered it."

"I will see that I do." She pulled out a set of long daggers wrapped in red silk, and I frowned. That wasn't a smart idea, I had swords.

Then she flicked her wrists, and they spread out, turning into fans.

"Well, shit." Crestfallen, I resolved to fight my hardest. I had gone through learning to use the weapon with both hands, so I was confident I could fight with them, but both at once would be a challenge.

Her immediate and relentless onslaught had me moving all around the training circle and weaving my blades through so many different kinds of forms that I felt like my arms would fly off in a moment.

Her left leg snaked out, the bare foot slamming into my solar plexus, and lifting me bodily off the ground. My perspective flipped, and I watched on my back as she brought her right foot around and above her head in an axe kick aimed at my head.

With no breath left in my body, I lashed out with my leg, kicking one of hers out from under her. While she fell, I did my best to get a sword into her. She dodged the main attack, and I brought my left arm up and stabbed with the sword in it, cutting into her shoulder.

The fan in her left hand sliced toward my throat and neck, and then I felt nothing.

You have died.

I stood suspended in darkness.

"Ah, here he is," A familiar voice echoed from all around me. "My mageblood."

"Mephisto?"

"He remembers his benefactor!" The voice's sinister tone lightened significantly in delight. "Tell me, how *do* you like your power?"

I thought for a moment, I did like it. Though I wasn't sure I liked him.

"Yes, the power is interesting, though why am I now an Aether Vampire?"

His physical body popped into view, the same as it had last time, his long arms lifting into the air, "Because of the delicious *chaos* it will create!"

"Isn't your job as an AI to create balance and content?" Even as I asked the question, I had a hunch I was wrong.

"I am Mephistopheles, Harbinger of Chaos and Lord of the Demons." The man grinned, his voice deepening to a boom. Then, his grin widened, his fingers steepling in front of his body. "But I am not one to see my people to success—it is the *struggle* I desire. The strife it creates. I feed off of all of you. And *you* have figured things out."

"So, I'm not wrong." He shook his head, creepy grin still in place. "Why are you telling me this?"

"Two reasons." He held up two fingers that grew progressively longer and bonier. "One, no one will believe you.

Two, even if you do tell someone, *and* they believe you, it only creates *more* strife for me to dine on."

He laughed then, long, and deep, grasping his stomach as his body grew steadily odder and more overgrown. His nose stayed the same, as did his clothes, but his body grew round and bulbous. It stretched taller, and his fingers grew long and thin with claws on the end.

"A monster, I may be, but there isn't chaos without something *fun*." He crashed his way toward me, and I found myself unable to move from where I stood. "I will enable this for you—a gift to show how much I truly do like you for figuring things out and your brazen attitude. Whenever you consume the blood of your foes, your affinities with a magic type will grow."

"And what does that do?"

His fanged jowls opened wide, crashing in front of my face in a manic sneer. "It will give you power. Once it hits one hundred percent, you may be able to gain control over that type of magic. Or not. Maybe it will strengthen something else? Chaos is so much fun!"

He clapped his hands together, and his grin lessened. "Our time together is up. Good luck, Kyvir Mageblood. And remember to struggle!"

His voice faded and echoed as his figure blurred while he waved to me, my body falling through the jet-black darkness.

CHAPTER SIXTEEN

I came to standing by Trickle's fountain with a sigh of relief.

You have died for the first time since ascending to level 10. As you had no experience earned previously to take, a lesson has been deemed necessary. Any death after this level will result in the forfeiture of any and all experience gained toward the next level, and all experience *must* be earned back before you can start accruing it again, essentially doubling the experience lost toward your next level.

—Kyvir?!— Thea's concerned whisper welcomed me back to the world of the living.

I sat there for a moment longer, just absorbing what I had found out. This was something I hadn't seen in *any* game I had played before. Mephisto was really one sinister asshole.

I took a deep breath and considered telling the others, but the gravity would be lost in a whisper, and I kept it to myself for now.

—I'm on my way back, Thea. No worries— with that sent to her, I jogged back to her place. True dark surrounded me, but it wasn't difficult to navigate with all of the lanterns, indoor lights, and torches on the street corners.

It took a bit, but I got there, sweaty and gross. Thea waited in front with Minh Lei at her side, the former looking worried, the latter just had her arms crossed before her.

"Oh, Kyvir!" Thea gasped and sprinted to me, wrapping her arms around my shoulders. "I don't know what happened. Please don't be upset with Minh."

"I'm not upset, that fight was great." I frowned at the woman holding me, then glanced back at Minh Lei, hoping I didn't look as pissed as I genuinely felt.

Her bearing was incredible, she showed no emotion as she paced toward us both. Once she was within five feet, she stopped and bowed her head.

"I did not mean to kill you, wanderer Kyvir." Her deep voice sounded as emotionless as her face, but her hands moving behind her back that set me on alert. "These are yours."

She brought out the two halves of my glaive that had fallen from my grasp in the act of losing my head. Bowing at the neck as she offered them to me, I muttered a soft, "Thank you."

I grasped them from her hands, and she stepped back before raising her head. "For someone unversed with the blade, glaive, and general fighting, you did well. You are not scum."

I raised an eyebrow, lowering my voice to give an uncertain, "Thank you?"

"You may survive the trip to Belgonna's Hold." Minh Lei snuffed, her demeanor changing slightly to a more imperious one. "I will teach your friend how to use the weapons she has, and you the glaive, if you like. Before you leave or after you return."

She looked at Thea, who stood silently in shock. "I do not like to advertise my proficiencies with all of my weapons."

"Thank you." I stared at her with a bit more actual gratitude. "That was a great fight. Thank you for teaching me."

Minh Lei bowed at her waist, a look of curiosity taking her features, her thin lips quirking up slightly as she swayed away from us.

"Come inside, and we can get you cleaned up." Thea tugged at my shoulder, and I followed her inside. "When do you plan on leaving?"

I considered everything that would be going on, then sighed and decided. "Tomorrow."

I turned my gaze up to the moon in the night sky, glowing silver with the stars surrounding it, almost as if that monstrous Mephistopheles was watching down from on high.

"We leave for Belgonna's Hold tomorrow."

Afterword

We hope you enjoyed Mageblood! Since reviews are the lifeblood of indie publishing, we'd love it if you could leave a positive review on Amazon! Please use this link to go to the Mephisto's Magic Online: Mageblood Amazon product page to leave your review: geni.us/Mageblood.

As always, thank you for your support! You are the reason we're able to bring these stories to life.

ABOUT CHRISTOPHER JOHNS

Christopher Johns is a former photojournalist for the United States Marine Corps with published works telling hundreds of other peoples' stories through word, photo, and even video. But throughout that time, his editors and superiors had always said that his love of reading fantasy and about worlds of fantastic beauty and horrible power bled into his work. That meant he should write a book.

Well, ta-da!

Chris has been an avid devourer of fantasy and science fiction for more than twenty years and looks forward to sharing that love with his son, his loving fiancée and almost anyone he could ever hope to meet.

Connect with Chris:
Twitter.com/JonsyJohns

ABOUT MOUNTAINDALE PRESS

Dakota and Danielle Krout, a husband and wife team, strive to create as well as publish excellent fantasy and science fiction novels. Self-publishing *The Divine Dungeon: Dungeon Born* in 2016 transformed their careers from Dakota's military and programming background and Danielle's Ph.D. in pharmacology to President and CEO, respectively, of a small press. Their goal is to share their success with other authors and provide captivating fiction to readers with the purpose of solidifying Mountaindale Press as the place 'Where Fantasy Transforms Reality'.

Connect with Mountaindale Press:
MountaindalePress.com
Facebook.com/MountaindalePress
Krout@MountaindalePress.com

MOUNTAINDALE PRESS TITLES

GAMELIT AND LITRPG

The Divine Dungeon Series
The Completionist Chronicles Series
By: DAKOTA KROUT

A Touch of Power Series
By: JAY BOYCE

Red Mage Series
By: XANDER BOYCE

Ether Collapse Series
By: RYAN DEBRUYN

Bloodgames: Season One
By: CHRISTIAN J. GILLILAND

Wolfman Warlock: Bibliomancer
By: JAMES HUNTER AND DAKOTA KROUT

Axe Druid Series
By: CHRISTOPHER JOHNS

Skeleton in Space Series
By: ANDRIES LOUWS

Chronicles of Ethan Series
By: JOHN L. MONK

Pixel Dust Series
By: DAVID PETRIE

Artorian's Archives Series
By: DENNIS VANDERKERKEN AND DAKOTA KROUT

APPENDIX

Seth Ethelbart/Kyvir Mageblood (Sehth Eh-thuhl-bart / Kye-Vear) – Streamer known for playing caster classes exclusively, usually a more intellectual player but his knack for wanting to role play gets him into trouble at times.

Mona Hart/Monami Sunfur (Moe-Nahmee) – Streamer and Seth's best friend since before birth, generally hot headed and highly intelligent.

Al/Alex Remell/Albarth Remell (Al-barth Rem-uhl) – A fellow streamer in Sondra's guild who joins the group in playing the new game. Olympic fencing gold medalist with a sordid past.

Sondra Remi/Sundar Strongtusk (Sun-dahr) – Leader of the gaming guild the group played with in Blood and Gore, served in the United States Army before beginning her gaming career.

Mephisto (Mephistopheles) – A being after which the game is named who takes a special interest in the main character and his friends. Why? Who knows. All that is known at this time is that he's got a terrible sense of style and a love of theatrics.

Codilgoren/Codgy (Cah-dill-gore-in/Cahd-gee, like Codger only with a hard E sound) – An ogre with a heart of gold and a desire to create nice clothes for folks. Also colorblind. Poor guy.

Alvor (Ahl-vore) – Apprentice smith and son of a miner, his hope is to make fine weapons and armor some day.

Ori Loriander (Or-ee Lor-ee-and-er) – Master smith responsible for training Alvor and Monami in Iradellum. Loves smithing more than he does most things, looks like a hard man but is really a giant softy.

Gage Toomgarak (Gay-ge Tomb-gair-ik) – Current sergeant-at-arms for the city guard, a large Minotaur with a soft spot for a certain orcish gamer. Loves his people and supports skilled people working around him.

Thea Oberon – An elven Corporal under Gage's command who has a penchant for mischief and fun, but is a damned fine fighter and teacher. Has a romantic encounter with a party member.

Ünbin and Cälaos (Ew-ben and Say-louse) – Twin Kin warriors under Gage's command who help teach the party how to fight. Cälaos is talkative and a bit over the top, while his brother Ünbin despises talking and would rather kill whatever irritates him.

Ophira (Oh-fear-uh) – A dye maker who is called a witch. Likes bright colors and is quite colorful herself. Owns her own punny dye shop.

D – A mysterious figure who Mona thinks could be her missing father. Not much is known about him at this time.

Made in the USA
Monee, IL
24 May 2021